THE RUSTED SCALPEL

When I open a Timothy Browne novel, I expect a compelling storyline driven by relentless suspense that will transport me to a new world where evil is exposed and hope endures. Chapter by chapter, The Rusted Scalpel exceeded my expectations again...and again...and again. My favorite book in the series so far, Dr. Nicklaus Hart is at his best--and so is Timothy Browne.

— Karen Sargent, author of *Waiting for Butterflies*,
2017 IAN Book of the Year

Fantastic...a story woven with intrigue, suspense and romance. Browne gives us full-throttle exploration into the human brain, big pharma, and the ancient rainforest of the headhunting Iban. I loved every minute of this riveting adventure.

— Don Stephens, Founder of Mercy Ships

This is the finest story in the Nicklaus Hart series of medical thrillers. Dr. Tim has the background as an orthopedic surgeon and as a medical missionary to write vivid thrillers set in the remote and forbidding ends of the earth. This taut, suspenseful medical thriller draws the reader from Montana to exotic Singapore, to India, and to the remote areas of Borneo once known as the land of the headhunters. The memorable characters drive the story from one man's struggle into the broader human battle between good and evil. Goodness and seductive evil reveal themselves slowly from the gray areas, one decision at a time, to the breath-taking conclusion.

— Joni Fisher, author of the *Compass Crimes Series*

Easily the best of the Dr. Hart thrillers! If you're familiar with IQ and EQ, I would add a third component...SQ (spiritual quotient). I literally felt myself growing significantly in all three areas while reading.

— Glenn Price, YWAM Missionary

Browne's trilogy offers a fast paced, roller coaster ride with plenty of romantic soul-searching along the way. The author has lived his novels and skillfully mixes internal and external struggles, mystical aspects of faith v. reality, international political intrigues, and current issues such as the collapse of modern medical practice under the heavy influence of the pharmaceutical industry. As a result, he offers details most novelists would miss – details that enrich the dangers and near-death encounters the characters experience and offer glimpses into the masculine mind surrendering to love.

— Julia Loren,
author of the *Shifting Shadow of Spiritual Experiences Series*

Having read Maya Hope *and* The Tree of Life, *I anticipated the arrival of* The Rusted Scalpel *with eagerness that was not disappointed. In fact, it is the best yet! Dr. Timothy Browne continues to write with skill, beauty, and depth as he takes the reader in the company of some familiar characters, like Dr. Nick and Maggie, and others into the inner workings of a major pharmaceutical company. The handsome, wealthy head of the company is multinational and multitalented, and adds intrigue and complexity. The reader journeys, not to the Middle East nor South America in* The Rusted Scalpel, *but to Singapore, Borneo, and Calcutta; jungles and cities. Again, Dr. Tim describes the peoples and places with affection and understanding that draws the reader into his perspective. And again, he includes faith and relationships expertly in realistic terms. Power and money nearly overwhelm through big Pharma, but integrity and strength of character founded in God produce a spell-binding struggle.*

— Deyon Stephens, Co-Founder of Mercy Ships

Browne's best work yet! I work as an integrative physician where we deal with both acute and chronic neuro-psychological issues. Dr. Browne's latest book delves into complex neurotransmitter chemistry in a way that is both intriguing and factual. The story line is woven through threads of deception, romance, murder, and emergency surgery. Anyone who loves medical thrillers will want to read The Rusted Scalpel.

— William J Brown, MD, Brown Integrative Wellness

Dr. Nicklaus Hart Series

Maya Hope
The Tree of Life
The Rusted Scalpel

Timothy Browne, MD

Please visit
TimothyBrowneAuthor.com
and sign up to receive updates
and information on upcoming books by Tim.

Follow Tim on Facebook
@authortimothybrowne

A MEDICAL THRILLER

the RUSTED SCALPEL

A Dr. Nicklaus Hart Novel

The Rusted Scalpel, *a medical thriller*
A Dr. Nicklaus Hart Novel, Book 3
by Timothy Browne, MD

Copyright © 2018 by Timothy Browne
All rights reserved.

First Edition © 2018

ISBN-13:   978-1-947545-09-0 (pb)   978-1-947545-11-3 (pb/BN)
            978-1-947545-10-6 (hb)   978-1-947545-13-7 (hb/BN)
            978-1-947545-08-3 (epub)

The events, peoples and incidents in this story are the sole product of the author's imagination. The story is fictitious, and any resemblance to individuals, living or dead, is purely coincidental. Historical, geographic, and political issues are based on fact.

Every effort has been made to be accurate. The author assumes no responsibility or liability for errors made in this book.

Scriptures quotations used in this book are from the HOLY BIBLE, NEW INTERNATIONAL VERSION. Copyright © 1973, 1978, 1984 International Bible Society. Used by permission of Zondervan Bible Publishers or from the NEW AMERICAN STANDARD BIBLE®, Copyright © 1960, 1962, 1963, 1968, 1971, 1972, 1973, 1975, 1977, 1995 by The Lockman Foundation. Used by permission.

Scriptures are taken from the KING JAMES VERSION (KJV): KING JAMES VERSION, public domain.

Scriptures are taken from the THE MESSAGE: THE BIBLE IN CONTEMPORARY ENGLISH (TM): Scripture taken from THE MESSAGE: THE BIBLE IN CONTEMPORARY ENGLISH, copyright©1993, 1994, 1995, 1996, 2000, 2001, 2002. Used by permission of NavPress Publishing Group.

Episcopal Church. Protestant Episcopal Church in the Confederate States of America. The Book of Common Prayer and Administration of the Sacraments and Other Rites and Ceremonies of the Church: Together with the Psalter or Psalms of David According to the Use of the Episcopal Church. New York: Seabury press, 1979.

Cover design, Book layout by Suzanne Parrott
Cover art, maps by Suzanne Parrott

Library of Congress Control Number: 2018908182

Printed and bound
in the United States of America.

To: The most courageous people on the planet…
those that suffer from depression and anxiety.

To: My parents, John and Ginny…
you taught me love and compassion

ACKNOWLEDGEMENTS

I am so grateful to my readers. Without you, I could not continue to fuel my imagination with story. My hope is that these stories touch something deep within you.

To my Beta readers, thank you for diving into the story and helping flush out areas that were not clear but mostly for your encouragement to continue to write.

To my story editor, Burney Garlick who has the hardest job of all when she receives the raw manuscript. Thank you for not just sending it back but caring for it like a grandmother would their grandchild. Loving unconditionally and gently offering advice and wisdom.

To my editor, Erin Healy who not only found spots where the story fell short but is a master craftsman of words. Thank you for helping me become a better writer.

To Suzanne Fyhrie Parrott for the amazing artwork, design and your patient guidance in publishing. As a new author, I quickly realized that writing the books was the mere beginning of the journey. It reminds me of standing at the bottom of my beloved Mission Mountains in Montana and pondering how I could possibly get to the top. It's easier to turn around...but don't, you'll miss the treasures ahead. The best way to proceed is with a guide, someone that has been there before you and can point out the hidden pathway and warn you of the dangers. Full of integrity, Suzanne is that perfect guide with the experience as both an author and publisher. She will guide you into the publishing wilderness and help you find your vista.

To my family who mean everything to me. To my boys, Timothy, Joshua and Jacob and their beautiful wives, Jamie, Sarah and Devlin. You all make the work worth it and to my wife, Julie... you have lived the adventure.

CONTENTS

"Come to me, all you who are weary and burdened, and I will give you rest. Take my yoke upon you and learn from me, for I am gentle and humble in heart, and you will find rest for your souls. For my yoke is easy and my burden is light."

—Matthew 11:28–30

"May the God of hope fill you with all joy and peace as you trust in him, so that you may overflow with hope by the power of the Holy Spirit."

—Romans 15:13

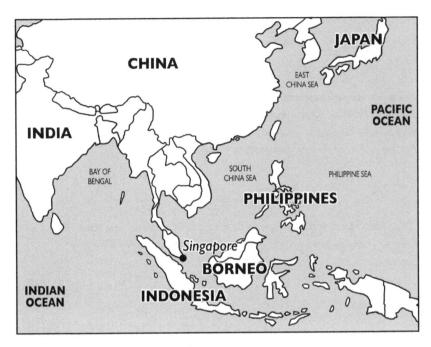

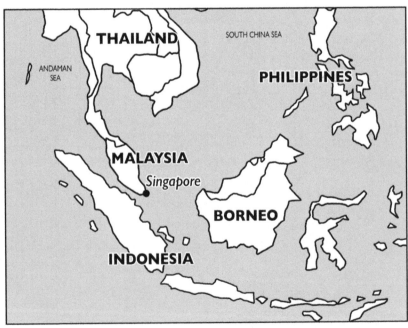

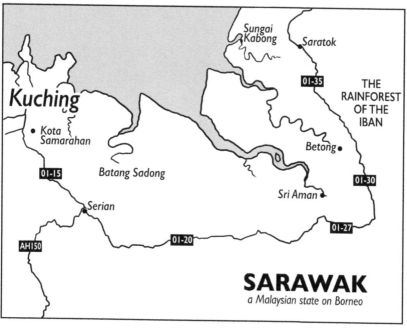

PROLOGUE

BORNEO—SOUTHEAST ASIA

Sayau had never seen a blue baby. He brought the lantern closer to the newborn to make sure his eyes weren't playing tricks on him. He pushed on the infant's leg, and it blanched white but returned to blue with the release of pressure. It looked like the parents had dipped the child into a vat of indigo.

"The *ulat's* blood is blue?" Sayau asked the frightened young mother. She did not answer and diverted her eyes to the floor of the longhouse. He meant no disrespect calling the baby *ulat*, worm. All Iban babies were termed that for the first year, and this one was only a few hours old. Sayau looked the mother up and down. She was of childbearing age and appeared well nourished and neatly kept.

"What did you or your husband do?" he asked. Pinpointing the broken custom or taboo would give Sayau clues to what caused the baby's discoloration.

The girl's father answered for her. "She is without marriage."

Sayau nodded and stared at the baby, who uttered a weak, gasping cry. A baby out of wedlock was not unusual and could explain the curse on the baby, but it gave him no further understanding.

Sayau glanced at the girl's father and then at the *dukun*, the medicine man of the longhouse. He wondered if they read his thoughts. *I wish Grandfather were here.* The beloved man died three months ago, and because Sayau's own father had died young, succession of the position of the *manang*, witch doctor, passed to him. He took pride in being the youngest witch doctor among the Iban people, but lately, the mantle was a heavy burden.

After his father's death and his mother's inability to ascend the depths of mourning, he lived with his grandparents. He accompanied his grandfather in all duties including deaths, marriages and every other aspect of life in the rainforest that involved the *manang*. Sayau had attended to dead babies, and infants born with strange deformities, but never a blue one. Grandfather would have known what to do.

"It is like the *ulat* is without breath," the medicine man said. "I have warmed the child next to the fire and sprinkled him with ginger root, but his color does not change. I burned dragon's blood over him and rubbed it behind the neck, but there is no improvement. There must be an evil spirit in this child, so our chief sent for you. Our longhouse is without a *manang*."

Sayau was a *manang mata*, the lowest level witch doctor, but his grandfather, a *manang bali*, taught him well. "Undertake one sickness at a time and always settle your *sabang*, fee, before attending to the patient." The fee was nonnegotiable, whether the sick person lived or died.

Sayau surmised an evil spirit was at the root of the infant's condition. He would call upon the gods of the hills for help. His grandfather had taught him the ancient incantations to make his plea—but which one should he summon?

Sayau closed his eyes to listen for his grandfather and the spirits, but for the last six months he had heard only silence. The night air in the longhouse was cool from the drizzle of the evening rain, but heat rose through his spine, making his head spin. Maybe it was the white man's heart medicine that made him feel so off balance. He had voted with his chief to participate in the medication trial. The money was a help to the people of his longhouse, but now he wasn't so sure he should have agreed to it.

"I am sorry, Sayau." The girl's father put his hand on Sayau's shoulder. "I can see by your expression that you cannot help this child. I should have told you this when I came to get you. As I went downriver, I heard the shrieks of the *Ketupong*, the Rufous Woodpecker. This sign from our omen bird indicates that the child cannot be cured by you." The man let go of his shoulder. "I am sorry, Sayau, for making you come all this way. I tell the truth so nothing more happens to my family."

Sayau tried not to act too pleased, because he didn't know what to do for the child and was tired of looking foolish. Instead he frowned.

"Please, Sayau…please accept my offering to you and plead to the gods for my family."

Sayau nodded and then decided to add, "I do not understand the meaning of the color of this child, but I think it would be best to take the baby far downriver to the white man's medicine lodge. They may be able to help."

He put a hand on the baby's belly, and the infant's arms and legs trembled, followed by a stream of urine arcing through the air. Maybe that was a good sign. Sayau chanted an old incantation over the child, one that his grandfather's grandfather had passed down. Since nothing in Iban history is recorded, Sayau figured it must be one from the beginning of time.

When he finished, the girl's father held out some money to him, and Sayau waved it off. He had done nothing, and he, too, had to answer to the spirits that ruled the rainforest.

* * *

Sayau took care to guide his longboat down the river in the darkness. The rainforest never frightened him, but tonight the jungle seemed darker and more ominous. A light sprinkle wet his face, and he pulled a burlap bag from under his seat and wrapped it around his bare shoulders. It smelled strongly of fish, but at least it cut the chill.

He knew this river by heart, and with only the slightest glimmer of light reflecting off the water, he let the current pull him home more than the engine pushed.

The jungle creatures had silenced their choir, and the only sounds were the water lapping at the boat's sides and the wind whipping through the thick canopy. He imagined an intense earthly battle between the spirits that inhabit the tops of the trees and the spirits from the summits of the hills.

The constant war between good and evil spirits was something that his grandfather spoke about often, frequently stopping in the midst of an ordinary moment. "Do you feel that, Sayau? Do you hear it? Pay close attention so you know how to pray," the old man would say.

Sayau shivered, feeling the strain of good against evil. These were unsettled times. A man from his longhouse had disappeared without warning. Among his people it was unheard of for a middle-aged man with a wife and four children to leave without warning. The man's wife said he had grown more and more agitated and enraged over the past few weeks, then he was gone.

Several people in the community were sick. They had a spectrum of symptoms including muscle pain, fatigue and nausea. One of the young men who traveled to civilization for a job in the offshore oil rigs suggested that it was the mosquito-borne dengue fever. But their symptoms had lasted for months and no one suffered the classic fever, so the elders concluded the cause was spiritual, and they all looked to him. Sayau had been their *manang* for only three months. He didn't have the answers, and his people were losing confidence.

Then there were the dreams. Sayau became a *manang* because of vivid dreams he had as a young boy that his grandfather deciphered for him. His grandfather would tell him: "A man becomes a *manang* in obedience to commands spoken in his dreams by the spirits. To neglect these commands brings punishment by death or madness inflicted by the enraged specters."

Sayau couldn't ignore the nightly revelations, but he wanted to shake the images that he was now having—dark, chaotic and dreadful. *If only Grandfather were here to help me interpret them.* In the dreams, the only consistency was the heightened state of danger and the running. He was always running, always being chased.

There was also the smell. It was a combination of the rotten garbage and sewage from the dirty side of the longhouse, combined with the decaying corpse of an animal from the jungle. He'd practiced daily *pirings*, offerings of food and drink, to the gods. He'd even performed *genselan* twice since the illness had descended onto his community—slaughtering a pig and sprinkling the blood on the doorposts of their homes. But the stink and the dreams remained. Ignoring them was not an option and would only bring more haunting of the spirits.

Sayau sniffed the air and thought that even now he could smell the bitter stench. *My imagination is playing tricks on me.* The evil spirits could do that, coming in and out of the physical world at will. He squeezed his eyes shut and then opened them wide, trying to absorb every fraction of light. He should be to the big bend in the river shortly, then the warm fires of the longhouse and glow from kerosene lamps would welcome him home.

He wished his grandfather would be there to meet him—to put his arm around him and comfort him, to reassure him that someday he, too, would achieve the level of *manang bali*.

The ceremony to become a *manang bali* was the one ritual Grandfather refused to talk about. Sayau was twelve when his grandfather went through the *bali*, the change, but he remembered clearly the other *manangs* that came to officiate the ceremony. With their ornate headdresses of rooster and pheasant feathers and their torsos adorned with mystical tattoos, they'd strutted in like the champion fighting cocks that Sayau loved to watch battle in the gaming rings.

This highest level was only obtained when a man changed his sex. No one except the witch doctors witnessed this rite, and it was rumored they made offerings of pigs, chickens, eggs, and *tuak*, the local rice brew, to the gods. At the end of the mysterious ritual, the chief's wife had vested Sayau's grandfather in a female garment. Then the witch doctors had introduced him to the assembly with a new name. Even to the Iban, the process was so unnatural it could only be obtained by supernatural means.

Sayau's boat bumped a floating log he hadn't seen in the black of night. He reached back, killed the small outboard motor and tilted the propeller out of the water. He was close enough to drift home.

He sat on the boat's wooden seat and leaned against the motor for warmth. The cooling engine clicked and hummed, then quieted. He tightened the burlap around his shoulders and looked to the sky, but clouds shrouded the stars, and all that he could see were varying shades of black. *Grandfather, are you here?*

For a moment, Sayau thought his grandfather was speaking in his heart, but the sound he perceived was only a low rumble from the jungle. No, it was a growl. Or was it a hiss? It was a noise he had never heard before. Was it a leopard or the Iban's great ape, the orangutan? Sayau straightened, dropped the burlap from his shoulders and grabbed for the machete at his feet.

He opened his mouth, sucking in small sips of air, and his heart pounded in his head. He saw only darkness, but his ears were on high alert.

Something was out there, and he was floating past it. He held the steel machete in front of his body to shield himself from an attack. It never came, but his memory ignited with stories his grandfather had told of the *pasun*, lizard, the demon-hunting dog of the underworld. His grandfather would try to imitate the *pasun's* snarl but would get frustrated and say, "You'll recognize it when you hear it."

That must be it. The demon dog of the *antu gerasi*, the Iban devil that hunts the souls of those who disobey the warnings revealed to them in dreams and omens. His grandfather had warned him: "Sayau, if you hear the *pasun*, the evil Huntsman is not far away, and you should quickly abandon your work and return home to burn the *lukai* tree bark."

Sayau twisted from side to side, flashing the blade through the air. The demon Huntsman was the most feared of all the spirits, said to be covered in coarse hair and possessing the strength of ten men. Even the sharp machete would be useless against him.

Sayau was glad he would be home soon to burn the *lukai* bark to protect his people. The longboat bumped along the edge of the right bank.

Yes, he was at the large bend before the longhouse. He blindly felt for the paddle at the bottom of the boat, and holding both the oar and the knife in his hands he pulled the paddle through the water and into the main current of the river. As he had done thousands of times, he would steer the bow across the water and to the bank below the village.

But as he rounded the bend and the wooden longhouse came into view, a sense of dread filled his mind. It was evening, and the vibrant community should have been alive with activity—parents corralling their children to bed and the elders sitting on the porch smoking and sipping *tuak*. Something was wrong.

Sayau let the tip of the boat slide onto the muddy bank, and he searched his home with his eyes and ears. Smoke from the cooking fires filled his nostrils, and two kerosene lanterns glowed from each end of the structure, but there was no sound and no movement.

With the stealth and agility of a cat, he climbed the length of the boat and jumped onto the shore, placing the paddle on the ground and tightening his grip on the machete. He glanced over each shoulder and then stepped toward the dirt path to the longhouse, his bare feet not making a sound. He recited the protection incantation under his breath as he crept forward.

He took two steps at a time, stopping halfway up to search his surroundings, then made his way to the top of the stairs.

At the patio, he stopped when a bamboo slat creaked under his weight, and he waited and listened. Nothing. Where were his people? They would not abandon their shelter unless they were attacked. Grandfather had told stories of tribal wars and headhunting, but that was ancient history. The Iban had lived in relative peace for a hundred years. The taste of fear coated the back of his throat.

He took three more quick steps across the patio and thought he saw movement but decided it was the flicker of the lamps. The main door to the longhouse was open, and he took small steps toward it. The final bamboo slats squeaked against their lashings.

Sweat dripped from his brow, and he reached for the wooden door. The interior of the longhouse was dark, and he stood at the threshold trying to see inside.

He may have smelled it before seeing it—the musky odor of a wild animal—but the creature hit him square in the chest. Covered in dirt and thick hair, it drove him back and farther back. Its massive shoulders lifted Sayau off the ground. Its eyes flashed with red-hot rage.

He was helpless against the Huntsman's power.

The creature drove him across the patio to the dirty side of the longhouse. Would the monster stop before propelling him into the garbage and sewage below?

The demon slowed its push, and Sayau realized that it had skewered him on a spear through his abdomen. He didn't understand why he wasn't in more pain. The monster pushed farther and farther back until his back smashed through the railing and he fell into the debris with the creature breathing its wretched breath in his face.

That smell. That awful smell. It was all Sayau was aware of.

The Huntsman roared and yanked the spear from Sayau's belly. The demon laughed and with eyes ablaze in madness, he plunged the spear into Sayau's chest.

Sayau could do nothing as the Huntsman lifted its hairy arms and roared again—nothing except surrender unto death.

CHAPTER 1

BLINDED

JANUARY

"What do you see, Mr. Hart?"

What a stupid question to ask a blind man. Nick was not going to answer it. With his ears submerged in water, he pretended not to hear. He didn't want to be here; it was a waste of time. The warm water he floated in only intensified the heat rising in his soul and the darkness into which his world had descended.

After departing Turkey, he'd spent two weeks in London undergoing surgeries on both eyes. He'd been under the watchful care of one of the world's leading eye surgeons. The surgeon and his team had been hopeful when he started to see shadows until scarring covered his corneas, and the shadows disappeared. At first, Nick had faithfully followed instructions, inserting eye drops multiple times a day, but when he saw no changes or improvements, he became less compliant. He hung his hopes on his surgeon's words: "Sometimes these things reverse themselves."

After a second and third opinion back in the States, he'd learned that a corneal transplant might be an option in a few months, but "there is no guarantee." He realized with irony that it was the same caveat he had given to many of his own patients with difficult bone deformities.

The last thing he remembered seeing was the red laser dot on the terrorist's forehead—a point in time five months ago when his life exploded. Memories of the White Snake's cold-blue eyes and steely smirk triggered his adrenals to pump adrenaline through his veins. Nick panicked, gasping for breath. He flailed his arms and kicked his feet.

"Stop, Mr. Hart," the man's voice said. "Relax. I've got you."

Large hands gripped his shoulders. Nick tried to surrender and go limp. He lolled against his supports, and his ears gurgled with water.

"Can you let go, Mr. Hart?"

"I don't think I can do this," Nick murmured. He willed against his fight-or-flight reflex. He was no longer in the cold operating room at the hands of his torturers, so he tried focusing on where he was—in a therapy pool straining to gain new perspective on his life with sightless eyes. Now that he was helpless at the mercy of this man, there was nothing to do but submit and hope it would be over soon.

"Relax, Mr. Hart," the man said. "Breathe."

Nick inhaled through his nose for a count of five, then exhaled for a count of ten. Why had he let his dad talk him into this ridiculous therapy? Yes, it was good to be back in Montana, but even that didn't completely relax him. Instead, it filled him with more sadness than his heart could bear, because he could no longer see the beloved mountains that surrounded his hometown of Whitefish, and he'd never behold the glorious peaks of nearby Glacier Park. He'd never be able to hike the trails meandering through high meadows of wildflowers and towering alps in the summer. He'd never be able to ski the fresh powder of Big Mountain in the winter.

"Mr. Hart, you're okay."

His world had shrunk to this—pool therapy.

Nick's father had started this. "People fly in from around the world to see the man," he'd told Nick. "The least you can do is give it a try while you're home."

Nick tried to divert his mind by wondering how big this pool was and what the surroundings were like. He wished he'd asked those questions before allowing himself to be led down four steps into the water and to a stranger—a man he was trusting to keep him alive in water of unknown depth.

What is his name? Wong? Chong? —something like that—Chinese I guess. Not North Korean, I hope. Nick shivered at the memory.

He was wary of the therapy, especially the loss of control, even though foam noodles were supporting his back and legs and a small raft was under his head to keep his face out of the water. But with his ears submerged, the sound was eerie. He guessed the humming was the pool pumps and the splashing, a waterfall cascading into the pool.

Worst of all, this guy called him *Mr.* Hart. Whatever happened to *Dr.* Hart? *Oh yeah, he's dead.* He was no longer Dr. Nicklaus Hart—no longer the talented trauma surgeon or the confident defender of the broken. He was no longer the sought-after nurses' catch or the proud pilot of the aqua-blue Porsche Carrera. He still owned the car, but it sat idle, gathering dust in the garage—a reflection of his own life.

"I've got you, Mr. Hart."

So here he was, Mr. Hart—poor Nick—I'm praying for you, Nick—I can't stand to see you this way, Nick. He was ultimately blind Nick.

Depression and loneliness churned the water and filled his ears. He punched the liquid, struggling for breath and light. But it was no use. His spirit was broken. When the flash grenade took his sight, it took everything. In the past, he hadn't known the real impact of a grenade when he used the word as a metaphor. Back in his practicing days, he had said a divorce was like a grenade tossed in the middle of a household, dividing a once vibrant family.

Now a grenade had exploded his life, and nothing was left. He could no longer command the head position at the operating table. His income was zero, and his savings were bleeding out. Perky nurses that had cornered him with smiles and bottles of booze no longer darkened his door. He didn't blame them. Who would want to date him in this condition?

"Breathe."

Nick sighed. He had nothing to offer the world. Hell, he couldn't even get himself to the store. He had gone from being fully alive to becoming a screeching disability—even a burden.

Of course his friends and family never, ever complained, but they had their own lives to live. And then there was Maggie. The darkness erased so many of his hopes. Heaviness filled Nick's chest, and his shoulders quaked as he began to weep. He could not hold back his grief.

"Yes, there it is," the man said. "What do you see?"

Grief turned to panic when the support under the small of his back disappeared, setting Nick adrift like an untethered boat in an ocean. Storms raged in his heart and mind and fear gripped his soul. He tasted the fear on the back of his tongue and heard ringing in his ears. He was sure his chest would explode.

He splashed frantically, trying to gauge the man's location by the sound of his voice, causing the noodle supporting his shoulders to slip away and plunging his face under water. The more he flailed, the worse it got. Without the slightest indication of where the side of the pool was or which way was up, Nick was trapped in a riptide of panic. He fought for breath, gulped a mouthful of chlorinated water and sank to the depths. The terror of drowning gripped his mind until hands clutched his waist and lifted him up so his head came out of the water.

"Stand up. Stand up, Mr. Hart."

Nick coughed and gagged. His feet touched the bottom of the pool, and his torso felt air, turning his panic to anger.

"You could have told me I was in four feet of water, you asshole!" Nick yelled. "And, by the way, it's *Dr.* Hart." He coughed again and pushed himself free of the man's grip. "I'm done here," he yelled and moved to where he imagined the side of the pool was.

Nick had taken three steps to his right when the bottom dropped out from under him. He staggered and slipped underwater, gulping another mouthful. Anger tumbled to terror, and his mind thrashed for purchase as fast as his arms and feet. He screamed but the bubbles swallowed his words.

Then an arm encircled his waist and clung tightly, dragging him out of the deep water. Nick gulped for air and shook his wet head. Still holding him, the man encouraged him to stand. Nick gingerly got to his feet until his upper body lifted out of the water.

"Nicklaus, it is okay. I have you, my friend."

Terror subsided to relief as the man guided him to the steps and placed his hands on the railing leading out of the pool.

"Can we be done? I think I'm done," Nick said pulling himself up the steps and groping for the granite pool deck.

"Yes, yes, of course. If that serves you."

Nick defiantly stood, took two steps onto the granite, and drove his shin into the side of something hard and immoveable. He fell against the object and landed hard on the deck. All his emotions—fear, grief, anger, terror—boiled to the surface. He rolled to a sitting position, rubbed his shin and cursed everything, especially his own sorry life. His eyes filled with tears.

Then he felt a warm towel wrap around his shoulders. "That was an excellent start," the man said.

Nick's tears dissolved into a chuckle and then a laugh. "That's what you call a good start, huh?"

Nick felt the man's warm breath on his face and realized they were sitting beside each other. The man smelled of incense. It was a comforting aroma, and Nick started to relax.

The man took his arm and laughed with him. It was a deep and reassuring laugh, like a Santa Claus. "Yes, a very good start, indeed."

Nick used the corner of the towel to wipe his face. "I'm sorry, I didn't mean to get so angry at you and call you that name."

"I've been called much worse," the man said and chuckled. "Here is some water." He guided a cup to Nick's hand.

Nick took a drink. It held a hint of strawberries and cleared the chlorine from his throat. "Thank you."

"Can you tell me what you saw?" the man asked.

Nick laughed. "Why do you keep asking me that? You do know I'm blind, right?"

The man replied by squeezing Nick's arm.

Nick puffed air out between his lips. *He's not going to let this go.* "I haven't thought about this for a long time, but I saw an image of a friend who drowned when I was young. I had joined the swim team here in Whitefish. It was only my third day of practice and a friend, Brian, had a seizure in the water and drowned. It was the image of the EMTs giving him mouth-to-mouth resuscitation. We all sat by stunned."

"How old were you?"

"Hmmm, I guess about nine or ten. They did chest compressions that seemed to go on forever. I remember watching Brian throw up as they did mouth-to-mouth. The EMT spit it out and continued." Nick's chest began to quake uncontrollably.

The man's grip on his arm tightened. "What happened then?"

Nick shook his head. "That's strange. I don't remember much. All I remember was getting home. I suppose my Mom picked me up. We sat at the kitchen table and said the Lord's Prayer together."

"You go back to the swim team?"

"Hell no!" Nick shouted, then apologized for the outburst. "They couldn't get me anywhere near that pool again." He took another drink of water. "So, is that why I'm screwed up?"

"Are you screwed up, Mr. Hart?"

"It's doctor. Why do you keep calling me mister? Are you trying to piss me off?"

The man laughed softly. "Are labels important to you?"

"Well, you'd understand if you knew how many years it took me to become an orthopedic surgeon. I worked my ass off for that label. And now I can't even float in a pool without panicking. So I guess I deserve to be called whatever you want." He cursed under his breath. *If the man wants to pick a fight, I'll give him a fight.*

But instead of rebutting Nick, the man just laughed. If Nick could have seen the exit, he would have stormed out. But he knew he would just embarrass himself by smashing into something else or falling into the pool.

"Okay, okay, my friend," the man said calmly. "We have a lot of work to do, you and me. Why don't we reboot? What would you like to know about me?"

The man was making it hard to argue, and Nick felt ashamed. "Yeah, sorry."

"Dr. Hart...do you mind if I call you Nicklaus?"

"I suppose not."

"Nicklaus, nothing is off limits here," the man reassured him. "This is your time, and I am here as your humble guide."

"I'm sorry...I don't even know your name."

"That's a good place to start. Everyone calls me Chang. My

full name is Kwai Chang."

Nick had to laugh. "Kwai Chang…Caine? Like the *Kung Fu* series?"

The man matched his laugh. "Well, yes, sort of, but I'm Kwai Chang Johnson."

Nick couldn't contain his laughter. "Now you're fooling with me."

When the man didn't respond, Nick turned his blind eyes to him.

"Actually, I don't know my birth name or even if I had one," Chang said. "I was adopted from China when I was eight and don't have many memories of that time. Maybe, as a joke, the orphanage gave me the *Kung Fu* name because I was coming to the States. I was adopted by the Johnson family, but I know nothing of my biological family. For all I know, I may even be from North Korea. If that's the case, it's possible my parents were killed once they crossed the border." Chang was still holding Nick's arm. "We all have our pain, Nicklaus. So many people go through life holding onto that pain and never releasing it. Feelings buried alive never go away. That's my belief."

Nick's mind flashed to the hundreds of thousands of people that he'd seen buried alive in the earthquake in Turkey. "Yes, I guess I understand."

"I want to help you find peace," Chang said. "You and I are not so different. I too was once a surgeon—a cardiothoracic surgeon in Seattle."

Nick shook his head in disbelief. "What? Why didn't someone tell me that?"

"Not many people know or care. I certainly don't. That label doesn't fit me anymore." Chang paused and laughed. "But I like thinking of myself as a different kind of heart surgeon."

"Why'd you give up medicine?"

"I had no choice. I developed severe macular degeneration in my forties. I had only practiced twelve years. You see, Dr. Hart, I know what you are going through."

Nick was stunned. "You're blind? Why didn't anyone tell me that either?"

"Because blindness is not what defines me. What defines you, Nicklaus?"

CHAPTER 2

STORM

Wright Paul grimaced at the angry, black cloud formation roiling in front of them. The storm danced with lightning, and he tightened the shoulder straps holding him in the pilot's seat of the Airbus helicopter. The shifting winds jounced the craft, and it was all he could do not to reach down between his legs, grab the control stick, and disengage the autopilot. As they flew into the thunderhead, the luxurious, well-lit Airbus cabin darkened, then strobed with lightning that flashed through the clouds like a Tesla plasma lamp. His research facility was less than a mile away, on the other side of the ferocious storm.

He glanced over his shoulder and smiled at his CEO, Leah Boxler, who always sat behind and to his right. An appropriate position for his right-hand man. Her stoic German affect never changed, but the sweat beading on her upper lip betrayed her fear. She preferred Ms. Boxler—he called her Leah. The only time he had seen her somber mood soften was last year when he gave her that tiny black-and-white Shih Tzu puppy. She'd named it Muffin, and the dog rarely left her side, except for helicopter trips. Muffin was terrified by the sound of the rotors.

Wright, however, was thankful for the throb of the blades. They were all that kept the travelers from crashing into the Batang Ai Lake as monsoon rains slapped the windshield and cyclone-force winds buffeted the aircraft. Leah ignored his smile and the reassuring nod.

His attention snapped forward as a gust of wind tossed the helicopter acutely sideways, and an alarm sounded on the dash. "Caution, caution," the mechanical female voice blared, along with a high-pitched warning signal. "Significant crosswinds over fifty miles per hour!"

"Yes, yes, of course." Wright answered the emergency warning, reached to the dash and pushed the flashing red button to silence the alarm. He looked at his copilot who was biting his lower lip. To make matters worse, the weather radar flashed all orange and red, and the wipers couldn't begin to stanch the beating rain.

These were the circumstances in which it was tempting to take control of the aircraft, but it was usually a fatal mistake. Wright had known other men who had doomed themselves and their passengers by doing that. But he was flying one of the most advanced civil helicopters built, maybe more advanced than many military copters, and he trusted the autopilot to steer them through the storm.

Wright held up his hands in surrender and laughed. "*Regarde Mère, pas de mains*...look Ma, no hands," he said in perfect French, English and then repeated in Mandarin, "*kàn mā mā, méi yǒu shǒu*", trying to coax a laugh from the copilot. The man was not amused.

"I told you we should have waited another hour to let the storm pass," Leah scolded. Her German accent grew stronger through his headset.

"I don't think the child has an extra hour," Wright said. "Besides, we'll be fine. We've seen worse," he added calmly, not knowing if either was true. "By the time we land and get the baby and her mother loaded, the worst of it will have passed, and our trip back to Singapore will be a breeze."

Wright checked the gauges; they were now only a half a mile out from the Zelutex Research Center on Borneo, something the Airbus H155 helicopter with a top speed of two hundred miles per hour would normally cover in nine seconds. But the storm and the autopilot had slowed them to five miles per hour, so they should be landing in six minutes. The reinforced roof over the heliport would open automatically, matching the speed and distance of the Airbus. The rain was not unusual for Borneo in January, in the heart of Southeast Asia. Rainstorms could be fierce this time of year. They would be safe soon. That is, if he could land the aircraft in one piece. The wind shifted the Airbus side to side, lifted it up and down, then pushed it sideways again. It was going to be like dropping a quarter into a shot glass through a jar of water and watching it flutter through the fluid.

Five minutes. The panels of sophisticated electronics glowed green in the darkness of the storm. The autopilot flew them only forty meters off the ground, and though Wright could not see it, he knew the approaching canopy of the jungle below was half that distance. Not good. The roar of the rotor blades oscillated with the wind, but if the wind dropped them twenty meters, it would not end well. He took a deep breath, restraining himself from reaching for the cyclic, the control stick and taking command of the helicopter.

As he glanced at the altimeter, a blinding flash of light and an instantaneous boom filled the cabin. It hit with such force, the lightning blinded Wright and the thunder deafened him with a loud crackle through his headset. The electromagnetic pulse from the lightning strike seized the electronics, and they blinked off, disengaging the autopilot and stopping the craft's momentum.

The helicopter and time paused like a heart going into asystole. Either the copilot or Leah gasped, and Wright reflexively grabbed for both the cyclic and the throttle. The controls were dead, and the Airbus began to drop. Wright's heart sank.

In an instant, the high-tech backup system kicked in, and somewhere deep in the electronics a pulse like that of a cardioversion jolted the chopper back to life. The electronics flashed on, along with at least five separate alarms, the most critical announced by the female mechanical voice: "Stall, stall." Even she sounded frightened. "Stall, stall."

Wright threw the throttle to full, and the two turbo engines roared over the storm, sending power to the five Spheriflex blades, gripping for traction in the air. He had no idea how close they were to the tops of the trees and didn't look at the altimeter but pulled up hard on the control stick. "Don't overcorrect," he told himself. Pulling the helicopter up at too steep of an angle would stall their momentum that much more. The blades grabbed for every molecule of air to gain lift, and Wright sucked in a breath as if that could lighten the load. Gradually, the turbines won the battle against gravity, and the Airbus rose.

Two minutes. Thankfully the radar was still working; otherwise, they would be flying blind. Lightning flashed around them. He would trust the gauges but would land it himself. He had experience; he'd set down the Airbus on his yacht in a horrific storm with both the helicopter and the ship moving. This attempt should be a piece of cake with a stationary landing pad.

One minute. There were no signs of light from the helipad. Perhaps this was not a good idea. After all, what was the life of an Iban baby worth? The jungle was cruel and held a 10 percent infant-maternal mortality rate. Was it worth the life of the chairman of a vast financial and biotech empire and his CEO? Maybe Leah was right as she was so often. "*bèn dàn,* egghead," he cursed himself in Mandarin. But every child deserves a chance, and if this was how his life would end, it was okay with him. He had already lived a fuller life than most.

The landing radar sounded and flashed green, indicating they were now over the heliport. He shot a glance at the altimeter. He had elevated the helicopter to over eighty meters off the ground. He gently pulled back on the throttle with two fingers of his left hand and guided the craft with the cyclic in his right and the two pedals at his feet, allowing the helicopter to circle left and drop slowly. He wished he had made the helipad twice as big.

Sixty meters. The wind pushed the helicopter off course, and the landing radar flashed red. He allowed the storm to blow the chopper north and he circled right to head into the wind, but overshot the target.

He closed his eyes to visualize the heliport, took a cleansing breath and relaxed his shoulders. He opened his eyes and focused on the landing radar. He imagined sitting comfortably at home playing a video game and moved the controls to steady them. The cruel wind pushed the aircraft sideways, tilting it at forty-five degrees. He massaged the foot pedals to level it.

Forty meters. The helicopter shook against the prevailing winds and the driving rain.

Thirty meters. The twenty-million-dollar machine gained the upper edge.

Twenty meters. He had the craft centered above the helipad.

At ten meters the rain and wind diminished, and he finally saw the helipad's lights glowing through the jungle's mist—a safe haven at last. The storm gods seemed to relent and release their death grip. With the skill of an experienced pilot, he aimed for the center of the large green H painted on the heliport, set the aircraft down, and immediately pushed buttons and pulled levers to shut off the engine.

"Well, that was fun," Wright said, glancing at his copilot, who made the sign of the cross over himself and looked as pale and sickly as a man on chemotherapy. "Your god was kind to us."

He didn't dare look at Leah. He didn't want to encourage her wrath.

She gave it anyway. "I told you we should have waited."

Wright leaned in and looked through the top windshield and watched the heliport roof close. "We made it, didn't we?"

"Barely," he heard her murmur before slipping off his headset. He turned his attention to the weather radar and pushed a button. In real time, he watched the storm that had formed in the Pacific Ocean, swirled its way through Indonesia, used Borneo like an anchor to pivot up the South China Sea, and would now slide past Vietnam and hit the eastern edge of China. They had hit the western edge of the storm and barely escaped with their lives. His calculations had been five minutes wrong. Miscalculations were typically not part of his methodology. He snuck a peek at Leah, whose expression hadn't changed, and her arms were tightly crossed over her chest. Her body language said it all; he should have listened to her. He should always listen to her.

He smiled, shrugged, and pointed to the radar. "See, clear sailing home. The storm is moving north."

He turned away from her scornful look. She would get over it; he paid her plenty to get over it. Wright pulled on the latch of the door, and it swung open. He was instantly met by Robert, his faithful Iban caretaker and butler, ready with a crystal glass of iced tea. He took a long, hard drink and handed the glass back to the old man. "That was a rough one."

"We are glad to have you home, Master Paul." Robert flashed a wide grin. "Dr. Amy waits for you, sir. She asks that we hurry for the baby's sake." He stepped aside, holding the silver tray with one hand and the iced-tea glass with the other, bowing slightly.

CHAPTER 3

ANGER

"What are you looking for, son?" the elder Dr. Hart asked.

Nick shot him a dirty look. "I don't know, Dad, maybe some peace in my life." He scowled. "And to figure out a way to make a living, as you are so quick to point out."

His dad quieted and steered the car west through the small ski town of Whitefish to Chang's house, set atop Whitefish Hills. They rode in silence, slush spraying the underside of his father's SUV as it started climbing the mountain road. A Chinook wind blew over the January landscape, lifting the Montana temperature from below zero to a balmy fifty degrees in a matter of hours. The warm wind rapidly melted the foot and a half of snow that had fallen last night.

Nick's dad broke the hush. "You know the story of Thunderbird who got angry?" Nick sensed his father look at him. His dad continued before he could comment. "She punished the humans who lived in her valley after a careless fire destroyed its beauty. She sent the cold Northeast Wind to scatter the people from the valley."

"Yes, Dad, you have told me that story a hundred times."

He knew his father loved retelling the story, especially when Nick struggled with anger. Nick's affirmation did nothing to stop the story once again.

"Her daughters, Crow, Magpie, and Blue Jay, went with the tribe, and when Thunderbird became lonely, she sent away the Northeast Wind and invited the Chinook Wind to bring life back to her valley. Her daughters told her, 'Mother, from now on, do not get so angry.'"

"Thanks, Dad, that is so helpful."

Silence filled the car, only to be broken by more slush hitting its underbelly.

"Dad...I'm sorry. I have no idea what to do with myself—with all this anger."

"How did your appointment go with Mr. Chang yesterday?"

"Okay, I guess...I don't know...our family hasn't exactly thrived on the touchy-feely stuff," Nick said and added, "Did you know he was a cardiothoracic surgeon?"

"I had no idea that Chang was a fellow cutter," his dad said. "And yes, I'm afraid I haven't been a great example for showing emotion."

Nick wished he could look his father in the eyes and catch an inkling of what the man was feeling. As a general surgeon, his dad worked hard all his life, providing well for his family, until he retired from medicine a few years ago. "You survived medicine way better than I could ever think of doing, Dad. You are a good father."

The car curved around a circular driveway and slowed to a stop. He thought he could hear his father sniffing away a tear. "You know, Nicklaus, I am very proud of you. Even if you had chosen a different path, I would still be proud of you."

Nick sighed. It was one of the few times those words had come from the stoic man. Like a sponge, Nick thirsted for more.

"Chang is here," his father said. "He's standing outside your door to meet you, son. Hope you have a fruitful appointment."

Nick swung the car door open, and Chang grabbed his hand to help him stand. "Welcome, my little blind friend." He bellowed his contagious laugh.

"Yeah, the blind leading the blind," Nick said.

"So true, my friend, so true."

Nick sensed Chang leaning down to greet his father. "Hello, Dr. Hart."

"Hi, Chang. I'll be back in a couple of hours."

Chang shut the car door and pulled Nick from the SUV as his father drove away.

"How did you know it was my dad?" Nick asked.

"I could smell him—he wears Old Spice. It reminds me of sitting in the surgical lounge as a med student. All the old guys wore it."

Nick thought he knew where the house was and took a step in that direction. He was anxious to get on with it. The sooner they started, the sooner this ridiculous therapy would end. But he stepped wrong and stumbled over some shrubbery. Chang caught his arm.

"Whoa there, cowboy. How long have you been blind, Nicklaus?"

"Five months, I guess, but who's counting?"

"Aren't you tired of smashing your shin or nose into things? You can see with more than your eyes. I know you are hopeful that your next surgery will bring back your sight. I am hopeful for you as well, but even if it's successful, let's take advantage of this time."

Chang slipped his arm through Nick's. "Now, close your eyes."

"Funny, Chang."

Chang laughed and said, "It is a beautiful day, don't you think? Tilt your head up to the sky and let your face turn toward the sun."

Nick did as instructed.

"You got it? Now, your appointment is for 10:00 a.m. Can you show me which way you think north is?"

Nick turned until he thought he could feel the warmth of the sun equally on both cheeks and then estimated where the sun would have risen in the east. He extended his left arm out and then his right in the opposite direction toward the west. Like a compass needle settling on its bearings, he adjusted his stance until he thought he was correct. "North would be behind me," he said and turned to point.

"Yes, that's pretty close." Chang adjusted his arm by ten degrees. "That's true north, and now you're pointing over

Whitefish Lake and the ski hill. If you hone this sense, your internal compass will serve you well. Now tell me what you smell."

Nick sniffed. "I can smell the pine trees as the sun warms them. I can smell a wood-burning fire. Is it coming from your house?" He pointed in the direction he thought it was coming from.

"Yes, good."

"I can smell you." Nick smiled. "You must have burned sandalwood while you meditated this morning…and was that before or after you had bacon for breakfast?"

Chang laughed heartily and squeezed his arm. "You may make an adequate blind man yet."

"Why's the heart surgeon eating bacon?"

"We all have to die of something, Dr. Hart. Now please come in, come in." He urged him into his home.

* * *

Even with the disastrous start yesterday, Chang convinced Nick to return to the pool and encouraged him to grope around the edge of the pool room to get his bearings. The surge of fear, like a little boy separated from his mother in an enormous department store, evaporated, and he was able to enter the pool again. He took a deep breath and eased—or at least tried—into the headrest and the foam noodles supporting his weight in warm water. He focused on relaxing a muscle in his leg and his neck tensed. He didn't realize how difficult it was to let his entire body go limp.

"That's it, Nicklaus. Let go. I've got you."

"Said the blind man," Nick said, stifling a laugh so he didn't slip off his supports. "Okay, I'm trying," he said, calming his shoulders and his face. Chang placed a larger raft under Nick's head, understanding that having his ears out of the water was less disorienting. Nick could feel Chang push on the noodles to send him in lazy circles around the water.

"Where is all this tension coming from?" Chang asked.

"What tension is that, Master Chang?" Nick said, trying to

make light of their relationship while stress surged through his body like untethered electricity.

"You know that stress accounts for over 95 percent of all diseases. That is why it is called that."

"What's that?" Nick asked.

"Dis…ease—lack of ease. The word comes from the French word *desaise*, meaning 'lack' or 'want.'"

Chang's hand came to rest on the center of Nick's chest above his heart.

"So what is it that you lack, Nicklaus?"

"Well, I can think of two things," Nick said, raising an arm and pointing to his eyes.

"Yes, yes," Chang said and pushed Nick's arm back down to rest on the noodle. "I want you to listen to what is coming from here," he said, putting his hand back on Nick's chest. "This is where the scriptures say, 'Watch over your heart with all diligence, for from it flow the springs of life.'"

Chang's hand pushed deeper into Nick's chest, almost causing him discomfort.

"You know, I often think about the hundreds of chests that I cracked open to repair people's hearts. I was like the mechanic trying to fix an engine that the owner neglected to put oil in. The damage was already done."

"Do you miss medicine?" Nick asked.

"Oh, my ego cries out occasionally to stand once again as the captain of the surgical ship. To be recognized for my skills. Power and glory are intoxicating, but I understand that now I am doing more healing than I did with my scalpel. Back then, I was treating the symptoms; now I am treating the causes. Besides, the practice of medicine has been corrupted. It has become an industry rather than a healing art. You can't have something as sacred as medicine driven by profits. It corrupts the spirit of it."

"Yeah, it seems like a lot of people are becoming rich on the backs of the sick," Nick said.

"You know, insurance companies won't pay for many holistic or even preventive approaches. My patients tell me their insurance companies turn their nose up to functional medicine— stress reduction, diet, exercise—terrible things like that. I guess they would rather pay for a $120,000 open heart surgery or a $10,000-a-day cancer treatment."

Chang touched the space above Nick's eyebrows. The tips of his fingers bore into Nick's forehead as if they had come out of a forging oven.

"Take a deep breath and relax these muscles, Nicklaus."

Nick let go, and the energy from Chang's fingers flowed down his face and jaw, through his chest, and hit him square in his solar plexus. He didn't understand what was happening, but the energy was a spark igniting the red-hot rage hiding there. Images flickered through his mind and vision, and his blood went from temperate to boiling. In an instant, he was back in the operating room where the monsters from ISIS tortured him— and blinded him.

Nick fought for air.

He thought he was sinking and flailed his arms and legs until he was off his supports and standing on the bottom of the pool.

"Yes, that's good Nicklaus," Chang said, holding him around the waist. "I think it's time to remove that boulder, don't you?"

"I'm not sure I understand, Chang."

"Anger…it has to go."

Chang guided Nick to the side of the pool and put his hands on the tile surrounding it. "I'll be right back. Don't go anywhere."

Nick put a life grip on the edge. "Yeah, thanks."

The sound of the waterfall tumbling into the pool increased, and spray from the water feature wet his face.

Chang returned to his side and held his arm. "You ready to get angry?" he shouted over the waterfall. "Here, take hold of this."

Chang placed one of the foam noodles into Nick's hand and guided him closer to the waterworks. "I want you to take that noodle and beat the crap out of the people that did this to you."

The waterfall roared in front of Nick. He began to panic when Chang let go of his arm.

"I'm right here, Nicklaus. Don't be afraid. I'm not afraid of your anger, and neither is the waterfall."

Nick took a pitiful swipe toward the sound of the roaring water, and the force of the water nearly ripped the noodle from his hands. He readjusted his hands like he was holding a samurai sword and took an aggressive swing. He shrugged and tried to give his toy sword back to Chang. *This is stupid.*

"Oh, come on, Nicklaus. These people took your vision. Isn't that what you lack? Didn't you just tell me that?"

Yes, that did make him angry. He hefted the samurai noodle and swung at the water with all his strength. And then again, even harder. Again and again. The foam slapped hard against the water. The lump in his solar plexus grew the more he beat the terrorists. He saw the smug look the White Snake had given him after she'd killed Vladimir.

"You stupid bitch!" he yelled.

"Yes, that's right, Nicklaus, tell her what you feel. Scream at her!" Chang yelled from behind him.

White-hot rage filled Nick's mind as visions of her laughing, sneering face floated in front of him. "Look what you did to me!" He swung harder and harder. His arms began to burn with lactic acid. He wanted the gun that he'd held before the rescue. "I should have put a bullet through your head!" he yelled.

"Scream louder, Nicklaus, she can't hear you."

"AAAAGH!" A primordial scream shot out of his mouth as he opened his throat to the pain lodged deep within him. He summoned the remainder of his strength for one last slice with his sword. As he swung at her face, his right foot slipped on the pool floor, and the waterfall sucked him under. In seconds, the catharsis shifted from relief to terror.

As the force of the waterfall pushed him to the bottom of the pool, pinning him to the tile, Nick found himself in the operating room at the hands of the terrorists. The wet, black hood over his face, preventing air from moving in or out of his lungs—he was suffocating. It was happening all over again. Anger gave way to fear.

Let go…concede, that's it. Fear gave way to surrender. *God, just let me die.* He had nothing to live for. Everything of value in his life had been stripped away: his profession, his value to the world. Many of his colleagues had abandoned him. *Father, what am I to hold onto?* No answer came, but surrender yielded to peace. The complete relaxation he had so desperately searched for now spread through his body and his mind.

Just as he thought he might be losing consciousness, strong arms grabbed him around the waist and pulled him to the surface.

Nick sucked in air, sputtered and coughed.

"Nicklaus, I've got you. You okay?"

"Is that what you had in mind?"

"Well, yes, except for the near-drowning part," Chang shouted over the waterfall. He laughed, guiding Nick back to the side of the pool. "Don't let go and I'll turn it off."

Nick gripped the side of the pool with both hands. The pounding waterfall turned to a small trickle, and Chang returned to his side. "You okay?"

"Yeah, I guess so. I didn't realize that rage boiled so superficially. But I'm not sure if it dislodged the boulder or grew it."

"You're right," Chang said. "This cathartic therapy's value is to identify the anger, not remove it. But now we know where to work."

"Great…I thought we were done."

"We can finish anytime you like, Nicklaus. You are the one that will decide how deep we go. But before we stop for the day, can I ask you a sensitive question?"

"Of course."

"Were you ever physically or sexually abused?"

The question shocked Nick. "Uh…gosh, I don't know…I've never thought about that…I don't think so."

"Nicklaus, when I put my hand on your heart, I can see your anger. It is more than a burning ember—it's a raging fire. It could strictly come from what happened to you in Turkey, but in my experience, that sort of anger often comes from abuse, either physically, emotionally or sexually…or all three. The sad fact about the state of the world right now is that one out of four girls and one out of six boys are sexually abused before they reach adulthood. Nicklaus, you may have been one of the lucky ones, and your anger is from something less hideous, but the anger is there, nevertheless."

"I don't know." Nick tried not to let his anger betray him.

Chang put his hand over Nick's chest and pressed. "Nicklaus, we all carry pain of some kind. If you are alive, you can't escape it. You may or may not ever know where this pain originates. You certainly have plenty of sources to account for much of it. When we first talked over the phone, you told me that you struggle with intimacy and have an unhealthy attraction to sex. It sent up red flags for me. Spend some time tonight giving it thought and prayer."

"And if it's true?"

"Whether it is true or not doesn't matter. What's important is we help you displace this anger with something else," Chang said, pushing harder on Nick's chest.

"Something else?"

"Love, of course. The Beatles were right after all." His deep laughter returned. "Nicklaus, when I was meditating this morning and praying for you, I saw you sitting alone. And the Spirit of God told me, *'There is a man without hope.'* Love is the only thing that can restore hope."

CHAPTER 4

BLUE BABY

A swirl of wind and driving rain echoed off the heliport's roof as the storm tried to take one last swipe at them. Wright cocked his head toward the ceiling, relieved to be out of the elements, but the damp armpits of his linen shirt and his intense body odor betrayed his cool demeanor. The trip from Singapore to Sarawak, Borneo, was only a little over two hours—four hundred and fifty nautical miles.

Robert held the heavy door from the heliport to the facility's breezeway, but Wright waited for Leah to come from the other side of the helicopter. She moved more slowly than usual. She limped as a result of childhood polio that shortened and deformed her right leg, but Wright guessed that the bumpy ride must have aggravated her herniated lumbar disc and made her abnormal gait more pronounced.

"You okay?" he asked and pushed his long hair back over his shoulders as she made her way to him.

"Nothing a little stroll won't fix."

"I can have Robert get the golf cart for you."

"You go ahead, and I'll make sure the copilot has the helicopter ready for our return. Besides, your little heroic rescue won't take long," she said, looking at the diamond-encrusted Rolex that he had given her six years ago as part of the enticement to work for him. "I'll wait."

Wright smiled at her. Boxler's German edge annoyed most others, but it was part of the reason he worked so hard to scalp her from the Geneva Bank. He found it refreshing and always knew where she stood. It saddened him that her brilliant mind was hindered by her failing body.

"Suit yourself. The turnaround time should be quick," he said over his shoulder and walked toward the open door.

"The baby is in the clinic, Master Paul," Robert said.

Wright squeezed the man's bony shoulder. "Thank you, Robert." Wright had often told the old Iban warrior to call him anything but Master Paul and eventually quit trying. The Zelutex Research Center had been built ten years ago on Robert's land, for which he was paid handsomely. As far as Wright knew, the only thing the money had bought for Robert was an oversized suit and a new bed for the longhouse upriver where he lived. Wright had offered to help the man invest the money, but it was probably buried in a barrel under his house.

Wright had visited Robert's house many times for dinner, and even though at home, the old man shed the butler suit for shorts and sandals, the formality remained. Robert's Iban name was Rentap. It meant "shaker of the world" as he explained proudly and often. When the missionaries came, he'd taken his Christian name.

"Thank you, Robert," Wright said as he stepped into the expansive crystalline tunnel. It was just a walkway, but it was one of his favorite structures of the complex. Perhaps it reminded him of Alice and her magic portal into Wonderland, or simply that he loved being in Borneo. Traversing the tunnel was like coming home. He looked through the arched glass panels and saw the fast-moving storm was moving on, and small patches of blue glistened in the south through the emerald-green jungle canopy.

Robert's footsteps followed quickly behind him. "How's your family, Robert?"

"Well, sir. We've missed you," Robert said. "When will you visit for dinner? My wife will fix something special for you."

Wright looked back and smiled at the man. He knew something special for dinner meant they would kill a chicken and fry the pieces like they always did. He loved traveling upriver to spend time with Robert's family. It was like stepping back in time to a much more innocent and simpler life. In the rainforest and his natural state, Robert wore only shorts or a floral wrap around his waist, a string of large pearls looped around his neck. Traditional tattoos covered his shoulders and arms. Even though the skinny old man was a foot shorter, Wright wouldn't want to get into a tussle with him because he was all muscle and as tough as the roosters they ate on his visits.

"Thank you, dear Robert. Tell your wife it will be soon. What else is new?"

"Just the baby, sir. It is so kind of you to help. We have been deathly afraid that he would die before you arrived."

"Do we know where it came from?"

"Far, far upriver," he said and motioned with a bony finger.

Robert slipped in front of him with surprising agility and opened the thick door to the research center, and Wright stepped through the tunnel into the large glass atrium that overlooked Batang Ai Lake. It was a magnificent view, taking his breath away every time. The storm was rapidly moving north, and fingers of sunlight illuminated the blue-green lake.

But he didn't have time to enjoy it because the baby didn't have the luxury of time, so he quickened his steps to the clinical lab.

Robert once again caught the door to the lab and allowed him to step into the hermetically sterile environment. Wright blinked against the bright fluorescent lights and white walls. He didn't understand how Dr. Amy could stand this lack of ambience, knowing the fierce beauty that surrounded them outside. But as the medical director, she had her choice and had designed it this way. She had little life outside these walls. Her obsession with work was good for the company.

He heard voices from one of the exam rooms and stepped inside.

"Thank God you made it," Dr. Amy Anderson said. Relief resonated through her upbeat Kiwi accent. "I wasn't sure you'd get through the storm."

"We were fine," Wright said. "Just don't ask my passengers. Our ride back to Singapore should be smooth." He looked at the blue-tinted baby on the exam table and then at the young, frightened Iban mother standing next to it and smiled at her. Dr. Amy was at the head of the table attending the newborn, holding an adult oxygen mask near its face.

"It's all that we have," she said, reading his mind. "You think he's blue now; you should have seen him before we gave oxygen, aye. They came downriver this morning. I am surprised the baby survived."

Their facility was not a hospital, but this was not the first, nor would it be the last, family to show up with a medical problem. Wright looked at Amy and realized, even in the air-conditioned room, she was sweating. It was probably the reason she was in research and not clinical medicine, but the New Zealander doctor was a valuable part of their team. He had been as thrilled to hire her as he was to hire Leah. With training in internal medicine, epidemiology and endocrinology, she was a perfect fit for Zelutex and their development of bioidentical hormones.

"The mother is asking where you will take her baby," Robert said.

"We're flying them directly to KKH in Singapore," Wright said.

"KKH?" Robert asked.

"The Kangdang Kerbau Hospital. It's one of the best children's hospitals in the world." He nodded to him to interpret for the mother.

"And they know we're coming?" Dr. Amy asked.

"Yes, I talked with their CEO, Mr. Kwek. It's one of the perks of having built their newest wing." He smiled. "I have Dr. Tang, the pediatric cardiac surgeon, waiting on us. I passed your finding on to him. You think the child has Tetralogy of Fallot?"

"Yes. I did an ultrasound, and the ventricular septal defect and the telltale thickened right ventricle were obvious."

Wright tried to picture the hole between the chambers of the heart. He knew of the congenital heart defect only because one of the late-night show hosts in the US had a child with the condition and it was all over the news. A large hole in the heart allowed the unoxygenated blood to mix with the blood that carried oxygen, resulting in a blue skin tone. The only treatment was open heart surgery. "Dr. Tang said they would have the boy's chest cracked open an hour after we arrive. I have no doubt."

Robert was already translating for the mother, who looked even more frightened. She said something to Robert and tears fell from her eyes. He responded to her and turned to Wright.

"She broke an egg two weeks ago and thought it was why her baby was born blue."

Wright looked at the mother, wrapped in a traditional sarong dress. The Iban were among the most superstitious people groups in the world, and their culture was filled with all sorts of taboos during pregnancy, including breaking eggs. A recent myth he'd heard said that the parent must not plant a banana tree or else the child will be born with a big head.

"Well, we know that's not true," Wright said and nodded to Robert to communicate the truth. Being a chief of his longhouse, Robert's voice carried weight. Speaking with compassion, he held the young mother's shoulders and answered her questions.

She appeared to be in her teens. Her olive skin and long black hair glowed with natural beauty. She was barefoot, and Wright wondered if they should try to find her some shoes. He also realized that this might be her first trip out of the jungle. What would she think of the towering skyscrapers of Singapore? Has she even seen a car before? Wright couldn't wait to see her eyes as they lifted out of the heliport and she rose above her sheltered life.

He listened to their rhythmic Iban conversation. He understood the language better than he could speak it, but he was still learning.

"*Ulat?*" he interrupted Robert. He didn't know the term, but the mother kept saying it and tilting her head toward the baby. "Is that his name?"

Robert gave him grin. "No, Master Paul. *Ulat* is what my people call their young. It means worm." He smiled again but then turned serious. "We do not name our babies until they are almost one."

He didn't have to explain why. With the high infant mortality rate, it was bad luck to name the child too early.

"Well, time is wasting," Wright said. "Let's get the little worm to the helicopter. You're coming, Doctor." It was a statement not a question.

"Yes, of course. I need to talk to you and Ms. Boxler about some of the trends I see with the new drug. I am quite concerned."

CHAPTER 5

BAPTISM

Nick and Chang stepped away from the elder Dr. Hart's SUV.

"Sure you gentlemen don't need a working set of eyes to get you there?" Nick's dad called out his window.

"We'll be fine," Chang answered. Nick thought he'd rather be in the warm pool. But the Chinook winds continued to bring their warmth, and the sun shook off any remaining winter chill to the point that Nick couldn't decide if he needed his down jacket and wool beanie.

"Are you sure about this?" Nick asked.

"Of course. A little field trip will do the heart good," Chang said and extended his folding white cane. "I hate these things, but they're a necessary evil so we don't fall into the icy river," he said with all seriousness, then gave a hearty laugh.

Nick put his arm through Chang's; he wasn't about to let that happen. The water pouring out of Glacier National Park this time of year was freezing, and they wouldn't last a minute. He sensed Chang pause to get his bearings.

"This is one of my favorite spots in the world," Chang said as they made their way down the pathway. "I think of it as one of the 'thin places' on earth."

"Thin places?" Nick asked.

"Some people believe that there are places on earth where the separation between us and the divine is…thinned out somehow. Like we can hear His voice easier. Who knows? I just like it here. It's called Running Eagle Falls, named after a Blackfeet warrior who happened to be a woman. It was unusual for a female to be honored like this, but legend has it that she spent four days here on a vision quest. Maybe even then the indigenous people thought of it as a thin place."

"Oh, I didn't know where we were going…I've been here before as a kid," Nick said. "In the summer, my Dad and I used to jump from the rocks into the deep pool at the bottom of the waterfall. It was spectacular…when my eyes worked."

"Well, today you get to see it with new eyes," Chang said and continued down the trail.

* * *

Nick had grown up in the woods. It was his happy place until today. With the icy trail, the frigid river flowing alongside them and the roar of the falls, it was not comforting. At least they were safe from hibernating grizzly bears, but other creatures resented their intrusion. A crow and squirrel scolded them from nearby trees for disturbing their wintertime solitude.

They safely maneuvered the short distance to the falls, and Chang felt for a flat rock at the edge of the trail, where he swept away any remaining snow and spread a blanket. He helped Nick sit down.

"What a beautiful day, don't you think?" Chang said, sitting next to him.

"Yeah, I guess so."

"You think more on what we talked about yesterday?"

"Look, I've racked my brain until I can't think anymore. I honestly don't know if I was abused in any way," Nick said. "Certainly not by my immediate family. I don't have many memories outside our home before first grade. I guess I ran into my share of bullies, but I don't remember something super bad happening."

"That's okay, Nicklaus. It was just a thought," Chang reassured him. "Trauma in our lives comes from different sources. Maybe a one-time event or a steady diet of being beaten down. The one thing I have learned is that no one escapes life's pain…no one."

"So what do you do about it?"

"Well, you can internalize it and let it eat your stomach or your heart…or your mind."

"Yeah, that sounds like a really productive option," Nick said.

"That's what so many people end up doing. I have also seen people spend thousands and thousands of dollars on medical appointments and still not get to the source of their sickness. Then they put their hope in other things like medications, self-help programs, supplements, and other ways to find wholeness."

"Or even pool therapy?" Nick said coyly.

"Yes…touché, my friend." Chang laughed. "Even therapy. Not that any of those things are bad. What I have seen and what I know is they all play a part. They can be helpful, but they are pieces of the jigsaw puzzle."

Nick glanced in the direction of a chirping squirrel and sighed. "Chang, I know I'm depressed. Maybe I should start an antidepressant?"

"Possibly," Chang said. "They can be life-saving, but we also know that cognitive therapy and exercise can be effective for depression as well. Good nutrition, exercise, and supplements put the body in an optimal environment. After all, our bodies are meant to heal themselves. Just look at bones. I know you bone guys think you're something special, but I've seen your work. You guys get the bones close together and let God do the rest."

"Yeah, something like that." Nick smiled and paused. "I'd sure like to hear what God has to say about this mess."

"Well, that's a thought. The scriptures describe God's voice like the sound of many waters. I think we're in a good place to hear His voice, don't you?"

Nick only shrugged.

"Nicklaus, I know you're upset. You're angry. You're afraid. I get that. But we have to find some joy in your life."

"I guess I have been unhappy for a while. Maybe even before I lost my sight."

"Yes, that's a good place to start. Do you know the difference between happiness and joy?"

"I guess I've never really thought about it."

"Happiness is rooted in circumstances. I'm happy when this happens; I'm sad when that happens. Joy is much deeper. It's one of the foundational truths, one that we must choose. Joy is not dictated by good or bad circumstances."

"I'm not sure I've experienced joy."

"Then I pray as Paul did in Romans that 'the God of hope fill you with all joy and peace in believing, so that you will abound in hope by the power of the Holy Spirit.'"

Nick listened to the falls splashing over the edge of the cliff and tumbling onto the boulders as he tried to understand.

"Nicklaus, I am sorry for what happened to you," Chang said. "But you never know where these circumstances will lead you. You must put your faith in the divine…in your destiny."

Chang paused to chuckle. "I know it's hard to imagine, but growing up, I was a world class skier," Chang continued. "My freshman year in high school, I took gold at the Junior Olympics in the Super-G. Two years later, I had my eye on the Winter Olympics but crashed qualifying for the team. When I spent three weeks in the hospital recovering, my desire to help people grew, and I decided to pursue medicine. When the problems with my eyes started, it was clear that season was ending as well. Not to diminish the pain or the challenges I've gone through, but I am so fulfilled with what I'm doing now."

Chang draped his arm over Nick's shoulders. "The thing is, circumstances won't save you from bumping up against one of the age-old questions: What do you do when your life doesn't measure up to your expectations?"

Nick did have expectations for his life, but now they were more out of reach than he could imagine. Grief inundated him like the water tumbling over the falls, and he wept.

Sorrow gushed from the depths of his soul. He let it flow. How did he get here? He had tried to be a good person. He worked hard. Yes, he made his share of mistakes, but he really tried. This was not how his life was supposed to turn out. Medical school was tough and residency even tougher, but he thought once he got his training, he was set for life. As an orthopedic surgeon, he would turn a high six-figure salary, affording him anything that his heart desired, including a beautiful wife—and who knew, children? Ski vacations, trips to Hawaii, maybe even a condo at one of those ritzy places? A nice car and home were a given. But now this. It was nothing that he had envisioned, nothing he had signed up for. Life didn't match up to what he had imagined or prayed for. *God, are you listening?*

"Everything has been taken from me," he sobbed. "Why has God allowed that?" Tears flowed over his cheeks. "Doesn't God hear me?"

He held his head in his hands and squeezed his scalp, fighting for understanding. "The church says that God is good, but look at my life. I have lost everything. I've lost my best friend, I have lost my sight, I have lost my profession…I have lost my future."

Nick was no longer able to control his own body from shaking. When he was in Guatemala and then in Turkey he thought he'd fallen to the bottom of the pit. He'd thought he couldn't stand another ounce of pain. But here he was and the pain was worse.

Chang squeezed Nick's shoulders. "That's it, my friend, let it all pour out. There is no shame here, no judgment."

Nick's shoulders quaked and his tears fell like the waterfall.

"Yes, Nicklaus. Let that pain and that grief come out."

"I don't understand, Chang. I don't understand. Maybe I was abused, and maybe I wasn't, I don't remember. But why does this battle rage inside of me?"

"Nicklaus, it's hard to know. I will be honest with you. Life is tough. Not sure anyone ever helps us to prepare for that. This I know as a certainty—no one gets through without battle scars. But, Nicklaus, I'm going to tell you one of the most important things you need to hear."

Chang paused and rested his hand on Nick's shoulder.

"Your heart is made for God's Kingdom…not for this world," Chang said, squeezing his shoulder. "Our hearts know what has been lost and we spend our whole lives searching for it."

"You mean Eden?"

"Yes, of course. Once you understand this, it will help explain so much for you. You were made for paradise, and this world is a very far cry from the garden. This will be a huge help to you, explaining your anger, your disappointment with life, your addictions…your hopelessness."

"Why would God do that to us?"

"Because God has a glorious plan—because this life we live now is only a blip on the radar of eternity. Jesus does return, and when He returns He ushers in a renewal of all things."

"You mean heaven?"

Chang laughed. "It would be good for you to read the scriptures, my dear friend, so you know how this crazy story ends. Jesus promises to make all things new again."

"You mean the earth…and you and me?" Nick asked.

"Yes…all means *all*," Chang said.

"Are you Christian?"

The question brought a surprisingly loud laugh from Chang and a slap on Nick's back.

"Why yes, of course. I am a follower of the Way…of Jesus. Did you think that because I am Chinese, I am Buddhist?" Chang laughed louder.

"Well…" Nick fought to rephrase his words. "You kinda smell like my Buddhist friends from the incense you burn when you meditate."

Nick's words sent Chang into another fit of laughter. "Yes, yes…and I left my robe at home. How unlike a good monk. Thank you for the laugh, Nicklaus, it does the body good."

"Well, I'm glad I can be so helpful." The sarcasm in his voice was palpable.

"The more I study the scriptures, Nicklaus, the more hope fills me. I believe that in the end, we don't wind up playing harps on some celestial cloud. God doesn't destroy the earth but restores our bodies to live on a restored earth—on a glorious renewed planet. An earth as it once was, as He made it in the first place. That's why I love this place. It gives us a glimpse of how the world was meant to be. How it will be again…our eternal home."

"But what about now?"

"Yes, that's an excellent question. God's promises seem to be woven into our lives, but they come in glimpses. Somehow we see only the flickering of how life is supposed to be—like a far-off glow of a warm fire as we stumble through the darkness…a faint hope we can barely name. Hope against hope. Our journey now is to be reborn into a new awareness and experience what Jesus called the Kingdom of Heaven."

"I agree with you that I have lost hope," Nick said.

"You and much of the world. Part of the problem is we don't know what to put our hope in, and the other is how we think about hope. The world has distilled hope down to wishes. I hope it doesn't rain today. I hope I get that new job. I hope the results of my MRI scan are clear. But divine hope is so much more. The biblical definition of hope is the kind that makes you sit on the edge of your seat, beside yourself, because you know what is coming your way. It is like the child waiting for Christmas because they know what good is coming."

"So what is it that we are hoping for?"

"It's back to the renewal of all things. Your life may feel grim and ugly right now, but in the end, you must put your faith into God's promises. In Romans, Saint Paul says that 'when everything was hopeless, Abraham believed anyway, deciding to live not based on what he saw he couldn't do, but by what God said He would do!' Abraham didn't give up and think there was no way his hundred-year-old body could ever father a child. Neither did Sarah's decades of infertility make him lose hope. He held onto the promise that God would make good on what he had said."

"Maybe it was easier for Abraham."

Chang snorted. "It wasn't. In fact, the same passage says that 'God made something out of Abraham when he was a nobody.' That is the definition of hope against hope—to continue to hope even though the outlook does not warrant it."

"Compared with Abraham, I'm a nobody. Even when I had my sight, I wasn't sure whether I was doing well with my life, and now…" Sorrow overtook him again, and tears fell from his useless eyes. "I don't know what I'm going to do with myself."

"Nicklaus, that is where you are so mistaken. I know God has so much more for you. But the eyes of your heart must be opened to the truth that you are His child, gushing with more beauty and power than you thought possible. Every time I am with you, I see healing coming from your hands."

"See?"

"Metaphorically, of course. But yes…see…feel…sense. Whatever you want to call it. But healing is so strong with you."

"I don't know what you are seeing or sensing, but I sure the hell can't heal anyone when I can't even see my hands." He stretched his hands in front of him and brought them to his face. "All I *see* is darkness."

"You think you healed anyone before, when your eyes worked?"

"Of course…" Nick started, then stopped. "I don't know. As you said, we bone doctors just get the pieces back as close as we can, and the body does the rest."

"So, were you doing the healing?"

Nick shook his head slowly. "I don't know. I guess when you ask like that…no."

"God is the healer. Sometimes physicians assist in the healing, and at other times it comes by divine intervention. Nicklaus, I have had visions of you. I have seen you laying your hands on people and praying for them and God touching them. You know the stories in the Bible, yes?"

"Yes, of course, but I am nowhere close to those holy men… those disciples."

This brought more laughter from Chang. "Like Peter. One minute Jesus is telling him that he is blessed, and the next minute He is saying, Peter, you knucklehead, you still don't get it. 'Get thee behind me, Satan.' The disciples were broken men like me and you. They were fishermen. But even Peter's shadow ushered in healing as it fell over people."

"Then why is God stripping everything away from me?"

Chang grabbed Nick's shoulders and turned him so they were face-to-face. "Because emptying must precede filling, my dear friend. He wants to empty you so you can be filled to overflowing."

"Filled with what?"

"With the Holy Spirit, of course. That is when our lives get interesting. Even Jesus told His disciples to wait for the baptism of the Holy Spirit. Then He said something remarkable: 'You will see even greater things than what you saw me doing.'"

"How in the world does that happen?"

"It only happens when we abide in God…when we pull close to God…only when we listen to God. That's the only way we find fulfillment, contentment, or even joy. This is the hope we must grab onto with both hands and not let go. And if you're holding onto this hope with both hands you can't be holding on to anything else."

"Maybe I'm beginning to understand," Nick said. "You mind if we head back? I'm getting pretty chilled." He felt for the rock to steady himself and edged his feet to the ground.

Chang got to his feet and helped Nick stand. He laughed warmly and took Nick's arm. "Let me pray over you as Saint Paul prayed over the Ephesians. 'I pray that out of his glorious riches he may strengthen you with power through his Spirit in your inner being, so that Christ may dwell in your heart through faith. And I pray that you, being rooted and established in love, may have power, together with all the Lord's holy people, to grasp how wide and long and high and deep is the love of Christ, and to know this love that surpasses knowledge—that you may be filled to the measure of all the fullness of God.' Amen."

"Amen," Nick repeated and felt Chang squeeze his arm.

* * *

Nick shed his jacket and hat as his dad drove them home. The trio sat in silence when Nick's phone rang. He hit the button to answer it, and the call came over the Bluetooth speaker.

"Hello," Nick answered.

"Nicklaus," Maggie said.

"Hey, Maggie…I'm with Dad and my therapist, Chang. You're on speakerphone."

"Hi, Dr. Hart."

"Hi, Maggie," Nick's dad said. Nick could hear his dad's voice soften. He knew his dad had a tender spot for her.

"Hi, Chang," Maggie said. "Nick has been telling me about you. You beat any sense into him yet?"

Chang laughed loudly. "You know him all too well."

Nick wished they were off speakerphone. Actually, he wished that they were on some remote tropical island together…alone.

"You see I have my fan club with me," Nick said. "How's it going?"

"Nicklaus, you will not believe it. I got the grant!"

"That's awesome, Maggie." Nick turned to his companions and explained, "Last year Maggie applied for a grant on behalf of the Hope Center from a foundation in Singapore." Then he turned his attention to Maggie. "Did you get the full amount?"

"No," Maggie said. "They want to give us twice the amount. My Lord, Nick. They want to give the Hope Center four million dollars." Her voice was full of emotion. "Can you believe it? It is so much more than I could have wished for. It's unbelievable."

Nick joined the cheer that rose from the SUV. "That is so great, Maggie. Way to go!"

"Well, I give all thanks to God, 'who is able to do immeasurably more than all we ask or imagine.'"

"Ephesians," Chang said with delight. "I was just praying a prayer from Ephesians over Nicklaus."

"Yes, thank you, Jesus," Maggie said. "So here's the catch. The foundation has asked that I come to Singapore to receive the money directly. They want to throw a bit of a celebration for us. They have booked two first-class tickets to Singapore and told me to invite someone special to go with me."

Nick held his breath.

"Nicklaus, I know how much you love to fly, but will you please come with me?"

Nick didn't say anything. As much as he wanted to be with Maggie, it sounded like a terrible idea. Yes, he hated to fly, but worse, he couldn't imagine traveling internationally in his condition. He was about to put her off, saying he'd think about it, when he felt Chang's hand squeeze his shoulder.

"I believe you now have two journeys," the therapist said, "your spiritual one to see yourself as the Father sees you, and your physical one with Maggie."

CHAPTER 6

CHA-CHING

Wright dipped an edge of the bluefin tuna sashimi into the mixture of soy sauce and wasabi and bit it in half. He swished it from side to side in his mouth, like he was tasting a fine wine. His Japanese chef stood stone-faced, staring straight ahead, his arms crossed over his statuesque posture. It probably annoyed the chef that Wright would dare dip such a fine piece of raw fish into the seasoning. The huge bluefin tuna cost over one million dollars, and his chef was friends with the restaurant owners who'd bought the fish. Wright imagined some late-night transaction over whiskey and cards that negotiated the transaction of such an expensive piece of the fish—three thousand dollars a pound. The piece he held in his chopsticks was worth a mere 170 dollars.

"Yes, Mr. Fujimoto. It's very nice. Thank you."

The chef let his arms fall to his sides and bowed. "*Hai,*" he said sharply as he rose. "Is there anything else, sir?"

"No, thank you, Mr. Fujimoto. This looks like a feast; don't you agree, ladies?" he said to Leah and Dr. Amy.

They both nodded, stabbing at pieces of the expensive fish with their chopsticks.

"Yes, that will be all, Mr. Fujimoto. Thank you." The chef bowed again, left the room and shut the door to the luxury penthouse office on the sixty-sixth floor of the Wright Tower in the Marina Bay Financial Center.

Wright turned to the women. "We have much to celebrate tonight, I believe." He reached for the small, ceramic sake flask and poured three cups. The rice wine was chilled to just below room temperature. He handed Leah and Dr. Amy each a cup and held his up to eye level. "Here's to the health of the young baby and the release of our new drug...Welltrex." He raised his cup and took a swallow of sake.

"Here's to Welltrex," Leah toasted and took a large drink.

"Yes, to the health of the baby," Amy added, then touched the bitter wine to her lips and set the cup down.

Wright saw that Amy had politely attempted to taste the sake even though she clearly didn't enjoy it. "Here, let me pour you some water," he said, taking the crystal water pitcher and pouring each of them a glass of ice water.

"Thank you, Wright," Amy said. "I'm not sure what the Japanese see in the stuff. It's a bit sharp for my taste, aye," she added in her Kiwi brogue. She smiled and took the glass. "Thank you again for coming to get the baby. I was at my wits' end and thought the poor little guy might not make it. I worried he was going to cark it at any moment," she said. She raised her water glass to Wright. "I'm keen he made it through surgery, aye."

Wright took another piece of the tuna and let his tongue savor the flavor before swallowing. He looked at Leah and nodded to Amy. "Tell Dr. Amy the good news."

"We received the approval letter from the FDA today."

She said it so nonchalantly that it may as well have been old news of politics and taxes.

Wright had to laugh. "You'd think that after eight years and a quarter of a billion dollars, you could manage to show a little enthusiasm."

"I thought I was," Leah shrugged. Failing to pinch another piece of sushi with her chopsticks, she put them down and grabbed a fork.

Wright smiled at her and addressed Amy. "What Leah is getting so overjoyed about is that not only did we get the FDA's approval, we received every one of the indications that we applied for."

Dr. Amy looked shocked. "All of them?"

"Yes!" Wright couldn't contain his excitement. He jumped to his feet and counted off on his fingers. "Depression, anxiety, acute and chronic pain, and treatment for addiction. Can you believe it?"

Leah imitated his gesture but after each one she added the sound of a cash register. "Cha-ching, cha-ching, cha-ching, and cha-ching."

Wright ignored her and looked at Amy. "Never in my wildest imagination did I think they would give us treatment for addiction. With the growing problems with opioids, heroin and fentanyl, think of the good we can do."

"Not to mention, the FDA just added billions of dollars in profits to Zelutex," Leah added. "Cha-ching."

"Dr. Amy, thank you for your very competent work." Wright raised his sake cup to her. "We could not have done this without you."

She blushed and looked away. Wright had not become the twenty-fourth richest man in the world with a net worth of over twenty-seven billion dollars without being able to read people. He sat and returned to his dinner, plucking a spicy tuna roll with his chopsticks. He pushed the entire piece into his mouth, all the while observing his medical director. Her long hair fell straight over her shoulders and framed her plain face, free of makeup. Her black oval glasses were too wide for her face. He wondered if Amy was having her period because of the angry red pimple on her chin. She wasn't unattractive, but her calf-length skirt and outdated shoes made her look dowdy. She appeared to ignore his gaze as she tried to bite a piece of sushi in half and spilled the contents on her lap.

"Oh geez," she said, trying to pick up the mess. She forced a smile. "I'm such a klutz. Probably why I'm a good meat-and-potatoes Kiwi."

A flash of light filled the office windows and a loud boom startled them. "Aha, the city has joined in our celebration," Wright said, jumping up again and walking to the windows overlooking the Singapore harbor. Fireworks filled the night over the Marina Bay Sands Complex. Leah and Amy joined him just as a golden burst of light followed by tentacles of red sparkles illuminated the sky. Detonation of the mortars percussed the windows and were quickly followed by exploding flowers of color. Four huge spheres of blue, red and silver filled the sky framed with waterfalls of golden sparkles. Two more erupted, sending trails of silver stars like a weeping willow.

"Beautiful," Amy said. Wright saw her smiling. He liked that it made her happy. Not surprisingly, Leah's expression had not changed, but when a brilliant flash and a loud explosion hit simultaneously, she jumped, and he laughed.

A laser show erupted from the lotus-flower-shaped ArtScience Museum and spread over the Marina Bay Sands Hotel. The hotel touted the world's longest elevated swimming pool, suspended over the skyline by three large buildings, held to the sky like an offering to the clouds. The display and the views, which he had helped create, were stunning. Heavily invested in the Marina Bay Sands complex and the world's largest casino that paid huge dividends, he believed it was worth every penny. The diversity of investment had been Leah's brainchild, and it was growing Wright's empire daily.

"Have you been to the new ArtScience Center?" Wright asked Amy.

"I have not...but would love to go." Her eyes brightened even more.

"We designed the bowl-shaped roof so that rainwater is captured and channeled down the center of the building. It cascades into the reflecting pond in the atrium and is recycled for the building's landscaping. It's very biofriendly."

"Mr. Paul's foundation built it at a cost of eight hundred million dollars," Leah said with disapproval. She always called him Mr. Paul when she wanted to make a point.

"And I think creating an educational focal point for children was worth every cent," Wright countered. "After all, that's what the Wright's Kids Foundation is all about—children." When Leah merely shrugged, he turned back to Amy. "Well, anyway, you should plan a visit when you can. It's marvelous."

He waited for her to respond, but she stared at the remains of the night display. He sensed something else was amiss. "You okay?" he asked.

"I'm sorry," she said, looking at the floor as if to collect her thoughts. "It's all very exciting." She reached for the window and instantly withdrew, realizing she'd put her sweaty handprint on the glass. She blushed and turned to Wright, "You know I'm so grateful for my career here with Zelutex, and I'm thankful for both of you. I think our new medication, Welltrex, is good as gold. It'll help millions." She paused and swallowed hard. "You pay me to be objective, aye, and I guess I'm a skeptic. Honestly, I have been waiting for the other shoe to drop. What…we have developed six drugs with Zelutex, and I worked on over twenty more before joining your team?" She crossed her arms. "And I've never seen a drug that has gone through development, animal trials and now clinical trials so smoothly."

"Yes, only eight years and a quarter of a billion dollars," Leah reminded her and rolled her eyes.

Amy shot her a nervous smile. "Not only does the medication appear to be clinically effective, the side-effect profile appears to be one of the lowest I've ever worked with." She adjusted her glasses and looked at Wright. "I guess it's even surprised me. I worry that I've buggered something, aye."

Wright laughed, stepped closer to her and took her elbow. "What is that stupid American saying, 'Better to be lucky than good'? I don't think this is luck, Doctor. Welltrex is the result of plain and simple hard work and your smarts. Look at the animal data…your data. And, you are right, the clinical data has surpassed our wildest dreams. A handful of bellyaches that are no worse than aspirin." He squeezed her elbow. "Right?"

"Yes…but—"

"But nothing, Amy. Remember you are a shareholder now. You'll have more money than you'll know what to do with." He smiled and let go of her arm, searching her eyes for affirmation. "What, Amy? I still see doubt in your eyes."

"I went upriver last week to check on patients and I…I don't know, this is going to sound like I'm packing a sad."

"Did you see something, Amy?" Wright said with more alarm than he intended.

"Well…not what you're thinking," she said, stumbling over her words. "Nothing…no cardiovascular, psychological or neurological problems. In fact, the gastrointestinal problems we saw early on seem to have resolved."

"See, nothing to worry yourself over," Wright reassured, but her face betrayed her angst. "What is it, then?"

"A few of the spiritual leaders in the villages came to me with a concern."

"A few?"

"Two…two to be exact."

"What was their concern?" Wright asked.

She sighed again. "They told me they could no longer hear from the spirit world."

Wright resisted laughing and glanced at Leah and then back at Amy. "Go on."

"Both leaders are *manang*, shamans of their respective longhouses."

"Yes, I know who the *manang* are—the witch doctors," Wright said and pictured the spiritual leaders of the longhouses he had met—adorned with brightly colored headdresses of bird feathers, woven loincloths, beaded wraps around their calves and often holding a chicken ready for sacrifice. "What do you mean, they don't hear from the spirit world?"

"I can only tell you what they said." She swallowed. "Wright, I don't mean to be defensive, but you know what the spiritual world means to the Iban. They hardly go to the bathroom without consulting the gods, aye."

Wright searched the doctor's eyes and knew she was sincere, but he could barely hold back a smile. "Must be a bad day in the witch doctor's office. We've all had bad days. I'll bet even you, Amy." He withheld his smile until he saw her finish processing her concern.

She finally smiled back at him. "I suppose you're right; it's probably nothing."

He nodded. "You are an excellent physician, Dr. Amy, always looking out for the patients. But I don't think two of the witch doctors having bad days is enough to give us concern. With the FDA approval, you can stop all the trials now. If the medication was to blame for their bad mojo, it should go away when they stop taking it."

"To maximize our profits, we need to get to market, especially with only twelve years left on our patent," Leah reminded them both. With drugs only given twenty-year patents, they had already burned up eight years in development. They had twelve years to achieve their projections of five billion a year. "We all have too much at stake to worry about the witch doctors eating a bunch of overripe bananas…don't you think?"

CHAPTER 7

HEALING

One of Nick's problems with blindness was that darkness was a constant companion, even in the middle of the day. His brain got confused and told his body to sleep when it should be awake and wake when it was time to sleep. Nick had hardly slept a wink the last few nights since returning to Memphis. He missed his parents, his mother's chicken and dumplings, the smell of pine outside his childhood bedroom window, and most surprisingly, his new friend, Kwai Chang.

Hope...the word that Chang talked so much about. He left Nick with a final thought. "Your natural hope has to be swallowed by new divine hope."

The man held a wealth of peace, and the week with Chang had opened Nick's heart. Joy resonated from the echoes of Chang's laugh and his outlook on life. He'd said that joy could coexist with all the other emotions he was feeling because it was a truth above his other states of mind. Grief, anger and sorrow and a lighter emotion like happiness could all coexist under joy. Nick had learned to allow himself to grieve his current lot in life, and when it swelled too heavy and the flame of hope grew dim, he forced the eyes of his heart back to God's truth.

Nick pondered this mystery as he attempted a short walk alone. He was headed to the small grocery store on the corner, only two blocks from his apartment complex, but it seemed like miles in the darkness, the sounds of traffic and pedestrians and a light breeze swirling about him.

Today, circumstances demanded happiness. His former coworker Ali and Ali's wife, Astî, had fought for six months to make Ibrahim an official part of their family. The adoption of the young boy from Turkey turned out to be anything but simple. Nick had hoped, after the massive earthquake and the unfortunate reality of thousands of orphans, the process would be streamlined. But governmental bureaucracy and human corruption almost prevented the adoption from happening. Maggie had been instrumental in making it work when she'd marched her five-foot frame into the Minister of Health's office in Istanbul on behalf of Ali and Astî, promising she would not leave without his stamp of approval. Maggie had threatened to strip bare naked and sit in the man's waiting room until she was heard. Nick was sure she was kidding but had to smile at the image and her tenacity.

This was the day Nick would see Ibrahim again. Ali and Astî had brought him to the US three days ago, and today they would stop by Nick's apartment for a visit. Images of the frightened young boy with the femur fracture floated across the screen of Nick's mind—his beautiful face, his large adolescent ears and front teeth that he was growing into. And his voice…that sweet, sweet voice…always polite, always inquisitive. It was no wonder that Ali had fallen in love with the boy. Ali said that when he told Astî the boy's story—how he lost his parents and sister in the earthquake—she had suggested adoption before Ali could get the words out of his mouth.

And then there were the miracles. Ibrahim had told Ali of his visions of the man in white wandering through the children's ward bringing comfort and peace. The man called Jesus told Ibrahim to lay his hands on a girl with a severe head injury and she fully recovered. Ibrahim's own leg healed in record time.

Chang's words reverberated in Nick's mind. "God's promises seem to be woven into our lives, but they come in glimpses. Somehow we see only the flickering of how life is supposed to be—like a far-off glow of a warm fire as we stumble through the darkness…a hope we can barely name."

And so it was with the miracles—hard to talk about and harder to explain. After their experience in Turkey, Maggie reminded them all that children often usher in miracles because of their unhindered faith and innocence.

The sun must have reappeared through the clouds because the afternoon rays warmed his face as he made his way down the sidewalk. He turned his chin toward the sun. If he was going to have company, he could at least offer them snacks and drinks. Besides, he wanted to visit with Ali and his family before he left for Singapore with Maggie.

Nick's heart pounded in his chest, reminding him how much he hated to fly. In two days he would spend twenty-one hours on a plane. He had always wanted to visit Singapore; it seemed like one of those exotic places like Thailand that was a must-see. Now he would finally get there but not be able to see it. At least he would be with Maggie, and she would guide him.

Nick slowly made his way down the sidewalk. He stubbornly refused to use his white cane. Someone bumped his right shoulder and spun him around. *Damn.* He'd set his internal GPS toward the market, but now his world whirled. He instinctively extended his arms and accidentally touched someone. "I'm so sorry," he murmured, but there was no response. He hoped the person was not offended. A car horn blew to his left, and he turned away to his right, running directly into someone else.

A forceful hand pushed him back. "Hey, watch it, jackass. Why don't you go have another drink?"

The man shouted more obscenities. Nick wished he was deaf as well as blind.

Nick gingerly took two steps forward. It felt like he was nearing the edge of a cliff. His heart was pounding and his lungs sucked air as if he were endangered. His fingers touched a surface. *Yes, brick.* Nick was relieved; he'd made it to the building. He slowed his breathing as Chang had taught and fixed his mind on resetting his internal compass.

* * *

Back at home, Nick sat in the recliner in the living room still trying to catch his breath. Was he getting that out of shape or was it anxiety creeping in? He was glad to be back in his sanctuary. A kind woman, probably young by the tone of her voice and her cotton-candy-scented perfume, had rescued Nick from his death grip on the brick wall. She escorted him into the store, helped him buy what he needed, and walked with him back to his apartment. He offered to tip her, but she only giggled and left without even telling him her name. He'd met his share of kind people since losing his sight.

A knock on his door startled Nick. He heard a key inserted into the lock, then the swish of the door opening. It was Buck. Nick had given his friend a key—and Buck was always welcome. After all, he had helped Nick survive both Guatemala and Turkey, and now he was helping Nick survive his blindness.

"Hey, bud, you in here?"

"Hey, Buck," Nick called from his chair.

"You mind if I turn on a light for the living?" Buck chuckled.

"Just doing my bit to slow global warming," Nick retorted. He sometimes forgot that his apartment was in the same darkness that he lived in. He heard Buck walk past him and open the drapes.

"Ali and Astî and the kids should be right behind me. I saw them parking their car." As the words left his mouth, there was another knock at the door, and Buck hooted, "Ali… Astî…come on in."

Nick could hear Ali's voice and the chatter of children. Ali and Astî had been kind to him—always inviting him to their house or taking him on errands. Ali went with him to all his doctor appointments.

"*Selamünaleyküm*, may God's peace be upon you," Ali said.

"*Aleykümselam*, peace be upon you," both Buck and Nick said back.

Nick felt Astî take hold of his hands and kiss him on each cheek. She smelled of jasmine.

"Hi, Astî," he said warmly.

"Hello, Dr. Hart."

He had given up trying to break either of them of their formality.

"This is a great day," he said.

"Yes indeed, Dr. Hart," Astî said.

Expectant silence overtook the room.

After a moment, Nick spoke, "Well? Where is that handsome boy?" He held out his hands.

He heard Ali say something in Turkish. Then he felt small hands on his knee. He reached for them and took them into his own hands.

"Selamünaleyküm," Nick said to the child.

"Peace be upon you, Dr. Hart," the tender young boy said.

His voice instantly transported Nick back to the operating room at King's Hospital. The beautiful child with the big ears lay on the operating table with a broken leg, speaking with the same sweet voice. Tears overflowed Nick's eyes.

"Hello, Ibrahim. Wow, you are speaking English now!"

"Yes, Dr. Hart, but I'm not so good."

"I think you never sounded better, Ibrahim."

Nick reached for the boy and brought him up close for a hug. He felt Ibrahim wrap his arms around his neck and squeeze tightly. He let the embrace go deep.

When they both needed a breath, he set the boy on his knees and patted his head. Ibrahim's hair had grown out, but he still had oversized ears. Nick could sense the boy staring at him and wondered if the white clouds in his own eyes scared Ibrahim.

"How was your trip back to Turkey?" Nick asked Ali.

"Wonderful, Dr. Hart," Ali replied. "We are so grateful for Ms. Maggie's help to bring Ibrahim home."

"I have something for you, Ibrahim," Nick said reaching beside his recliner and grabbing a large package that Astî had helped him wrap a few weeks earlier. He felt Ibrahim take the present.

"Go ahead, son, you may open it," Ali encouraged.

Ibrahim tore off the wrapping and squealed with delight over the limited-edition World Cup soccer ball. Then he hugged Nick around the neck.

"Thank you, Dr. Hart."

Nick sensed the boy staring at him again and figured he really was frightened by the frosted eyes. Then he felt Ibrahim touch his face and run his fingers over his brow.

Ali approached, watchful of the boy. "Son, be careful," Ali said.

"Dr. Hart," Ibrahim said, "that is not supposed to be there."

Nick didn't understand. "What is not supposed to be where?" he asked.

"Those clouds don't belong in your eyes. I saw you in…that place."

Nick could tell the boy was struggling to find the English words.

"It was beautiful. Your eyes were as clear as the water," Ibrahim said. He laid his tiny hands over Nick's eyes.

Searing pain stabbed them. Nick jerked his head back. He thought Ibrahim had accidentally poked his eyeballs because each globe burned as though it had been marked by a hot branding iron. The agonizing pain made his head spin. He covered his eyes with his hands and held his head. He thought he was going to pass out.

CHAPTER 8

GRANDMAMA

"Hello, Grandmama," Wright said and bent down, kissing the woman on the cheek. She smelled of roses as she always did, as long as he could remember. "You are looking well."

She gave a genteel laugh. "For a ninety-five-year-old woman, I suppose you're right."

"Happy birthday." He handed her a single yellow Michelangelo rose, the bud starting to open.

Her face brightened with a smile and she put the rose to her nose, inhaling the intense lemony fragrance. "It's beautiful, my dear. Bless your heart." She paused to savor the aroma of the flower. "You know these are my favorite."

"Yes, Grandmama. I grow them in my gardens in Singapore just for you." He bent and gave her another kiss on the cheek. He could give her so much more, but he learned long ago that she would give it away. She had everything she needed in her quaint little home in Calcutta. "I also got you these when I was in Paris last week."

He handed her a wooden box of *Comptoir du Cacao*, chocolates, some of the finest and tastiest in the world. "I had them put plenty of the praline truffles in for you."

"You are trying to fatten an old woman." She laughed, accepting the box and setting it on the lamp table beside her. She would probably give the box of treats to the next delivery boy, who would have no idea as he gorged himself how expensive they were. But it didn't matter.

"You are such a sweet boy, Mowgli. Now sit and keep this old woman company." She patted the seat next to her on the old velvet couch. "And have a cup of tea."

He smiled at her and sat close. How he adored her. She was the only person in his life who still called him by his childhood nickname. He loved it. Even with wrinkles and gray hair, she reminded him so much of his mother. Royalty is the same in every country: poised, dignified, and articulate—her posture and her mind as sharp as the queen's. She lifted a small bell from the table where she had set the chocolates and gently rang it.

Grandmama's one luxury in life appeared from around the door as though he had been waiting there the entire time. Wright had no idea of the age of the Indian man who had been her butler for as long as he could remember and who had seemed old back then.

"We will have tea now, Baxter."

"Yes, madam," he said, bowed and shuffled off.

"How long can you stay, dear?"

"Grandmama, I'm afraid I can only stay for tea. I have a polo match at the club this afternoon. Then I must return to Singapore tonight for work."

"Yes, of course." She smiled at him, seeming to search him with her eyes.

His time was the real gift to her, and Wright wished there were more of it to give. He sighed and looked at the worn Persian rug.

"Did you fly over this morning?" she asked.

"Yes, Grandmama. We brought the jet over. I wish you would let me take you for a ride. We can fly to wherever you have always wanted to go."

She hooted. "I can't even imagine."

Baxter carried in a tray with a tea set and a small plate of biscuits. She waited for the man to perform his duty and pour them both a cup, adding one lump of sugar and a splash of cream to each. "Baxter, can you imagine me jetting around the world?"

She laughed and brushed the air with her hand, sweeping the idea away.

"No, madam."

Baxter carefully handed them the teacups, then hobbled from the room. Sadness swept over Wright as he listened to his Grandmama sip her tea. He knew that one of these days he would have to say good-bye to her. Worst of all, it would mean that he was alone.

"Your mother would be very proud of you," she said, interrupting his thoughts. She reached to her table and pulled over one of two pictures she kept nearby—one of him when he was about twelve and the other that he loved as well. It was a framed photo of his mother on his parents' wedding day, her elegance frozen in time. Grandmama took a small hanky stuffed in her sleeve and fondly wiped the frame.

His mother was only eighteen when she married his father. In the photo, she stood bejeweled in the customary Indian wedding headdress and gown. The diamond-and-ruby necklace and headpiece matched her earrings and bracelet. A veil highlighted the jewels with red and cream colors, and her smoky eyeshadow and red lipstick made her complexion glow with beauty. He had the same picture on his desk in Singapore, and her gems stored in his safe. The more he stared at the picture, the more it seemed his mother was about to speak, as if she were going to glance at him with her enchanting hazel eyes and smile and tell him how much she loved him.

His grandmother tenderly touched the image of his mother and took his arm. "You have your mother's eyes." She reminded him of this every time he visited, as if he didn't know he had inherited his mother's eyes and her beautiful long dark hair. Grandmama put the picture back in its place and took another sip of tea.

She did not mention Wright's father, nor would he. Wright had fleeting memories of his mother and father fighting. It was a sore point. His mother would use Grandmama's words against his father when she was angry. How could an Indian princess fall in love with an Englishman? That's what Grandmama had told her, because she had arranged a marriage to a proper Indian man of royal blood. The Englishman wasn't even of British royalty.

His grandmother picked up the other photo. It was of Wright as a boy wearing a stained yellow tank top trimmed with blue piping. His skinny twelve-year-old arms glowed brown from the sun, and his oversized safari hat, tied under his chin with a black string, covered his ears. He smiled with his mother's golden eyes and held a bouquet of white daisies that he had picked from the field.

"My little Mowgli," Grandmama said and held the picture to her heart. She reached for his arm again. "How I love my little Mowgli."

* * *

Two minutes were left in the match, and Wright's team was up by one. If his opponent scored, the match would go into sudden death. The world's best polo player drove the ball forward with his mallet, ahead of Wright. José Libre of Argentina may have been the best in the world, but so was Wright's mount, Smoothie. The best and oldest Thoroughbred bloodline pumped through his powerful black-and-white horse. Wright named the horse for his exceptionally smooth gallop, but it was his heart, speed and agility that gave him the recognition as a world-class polo pony.

Wright's brain registered the cheer of the crowd over the thunder of the horses' hooves hitting the turf. Smoothie's mouth gaped open, and his nostrils flared, straining against the bit, as he chased his rival. The horse's massive chest rose and fell under Wright's saddle. Every muscle of the steed's shoulders and legs flexed in the rhythmic gallop. Wright had to do less steering and more holding on—the horse knew what to do.

The horse seemed as eager to capture the coveted Ezra Cup as Wright. After all, the Ezra trophy was the first and oldest polo prize—the World Cup of the sport of kings. Playing the match at the Calcutta Polo Club, where polo was thought to be born, made the prize that much sweeter.

Both Wright and his horse were tired, but he coaxed another ounce of power from the beast as they thundered down the field at top speed. Halfway down the three-hundred-yard field, Smoothie caught up to José Libre, known to the world as Poncho, and matched his horse's gallop stride for stride.

"You're slowing down in your old age, Poncho," Wright yelled. Out of the corner of his eye, he could see Poncho grit his teeth and bear down on the horse's neck, urging it forward.

"You might as well go share champagne with the ladies, mate, and let me score," Poncho yelled back, gaining a neck's length.

Polo started as a war game two thousand years ago, and little had changed.

The man's mallet knocked the ball forward as his left elbow stabbed at Wright's side. At thirty miles an hour, the horses bumped down the field. Wright used his stick hand to fend off the assault and edge Poncho off the ball.

"Be careful, Poncho, you wouldn't want to scar that pretty face," he yelled over the rumble of the horses and the crowd. "Your sponsor would drop you."

The pair raced for the white wooden ball—fifty yards to go to the goal. Wright miscalculated Poncho's next move. Instead of sending the ball forward, he took a false swing, passed the ball, reined his horse to a stop, swerved to his right, circled back for the ball and redirected it diagonally toward the goal.

Wright turned to his left. Smoothie seemed to sense the strategy. He slowed and then with brilliant agility, jumped sideways and galloped ahead, almost sending Wright off the saddle. He gripped the powerful beast hard with his legs.

Wright visualized the hypotenuse, the shortest distance between him, Poncho and the goal, and didn't see the accident coming. Smoothie had accelerated to full speed when it hit. In their maneuvering, the rest of the field had caught up to the men, and his own teammate's horse couldn't stop and plowed into Wright and Smoothie. The full-speed T-bone crash sent men and beasts flying and landing in a heap. Wright saw clouds floating in the blue sky and wondered why he felt no pain. Then it hit, hard.

It happened so fast, he thought for an instant one of the horses had rolled over the top of him. The sound of a breaking bone was undeniable. He slammed into the ground and found himself face down on the turf. Unable to breathe, he scanned his body for pain—it was everywhere. He forced his body to relax and finally took a breath, then another.

His breathing slowly returned enough so he could push his chest and face off the turf and inspect the carnage. The crowd and the thundering hooves were silent. His teammate's Thoroughbred was on the ground beside him, but it jumped to its feet with the rider dangling by a stirrup. The rider was able to dislodge himself and stand without injury.

"You okay, mate?"

Wright looked up at Poncho, sitting on his horse with his mallet stick over his shoulder, trying to control his frothing horse with the reins in the other hand. The agitated horse danced from side to side.

Wright started to nod but heard Smoothie struggling behind him. He turned to see his horse lying on his side, kicking and trying to stand. Smoothie let out a painful cry as he fought to roll himself up, flailing his head from side to side. Wright arm-crawled to his horse's side and wrapped his arms around the horse's neck.

"Whoa, boy, whoa," he cried.

The horse writhed, still trying to stand—his agonizing whinny echoed in the silent arena. Smoothie's massive chest bellowed, fighting for air and freedom. His nostrils flared and his eyes opened wide.

"It's okay, boy. It's okay."

At the risk of getting crushed under the horse, Wright pulled his body over Smoothie to keep him from fighting and causing more damage. The horse's broken leg dangled at an awkward angle, and Wright's heart sank.

"Oh, Smoothie, I'm sorry, my old friend. I'm so sorry."

It took only seconds for the other riders and the Polo Club's vet to join them, while the horse's excruciating cries seemed to stretch out for an eternity.

"We have to put him down, sir," the vet said.

The vet thrust a skillfully placed syringe needle into the horse's jugular, injecting a strong tranquilizer. The Thoroughbred's pounding heart rapidly spread the medication to the beast's brain, and the horse's muscles relaxed. Smoothie laid his head on the turf, panting like massive bellows stoking a forge fire.

Wright caressed the horse's neck and watched the vet draw the blue death serum into the large syringe. Smoothie cried as though he knew what was happening. The vet held the syringe up as the lethal liquid caught the sun with a flash of cobalt. Wright shook his head and searched his brain. If there were a way to save the beast he would have spared no expense.

Poncho had dismounted, and Wright could feel a hand on his shoulder. He looked at his rival with tears in his eyes and searched Poncho's face for help. But Poncho solemnly shook his head. Every rider knew the danger. Every rider pleaded for help when it happened to his horse. But they all knew the answer, even though they didn't want to hear it. A shattered leg bone is a death sentence to a horse—always had been, always would be. It wasn't that the bone couldn't be fixed, it was that the horse couldn't survive the recovery time supine and to stand, the horse needed all four pillars. Many a compassionate owner had tried saving his horse, only to sentence the animal to six weeks of torturous suffering and finally death. Putting it down immediately was the humane thing to do.

"Shhhhh," Wright said, rubbing the side of Smoothie's massive jaw. "Shhh." Anger rose in his belly. With all his research and development of innovative medicines, he was helpless. In two short decades, his company had advanced medications that people could have only dreamed about. "You will be free soon, my friend." Wright had no idea of the afterlife, but horses and dogs must go somewhere where they can run free. He pictured Smoothie in full gallop across a green field with tail and mane flowing in the wind.

He looked back at his rival, who dipped his head with understanding. He gave Smoothie another look and saw the undeniable break. He gave the approving nod to the vet.

The sharp needle slid through the thick hide. The vet aspirated to make sure he was in the major vein and then injected the blue fluid into the blood vessel. Smoothie lifted his head, wanting to fight one last time. His heart and mind were willing, his body unable. He snorted, and Wright could feel the massive body relax and let go.

Smoothie gave up the fight.

Wright dropped his head on the horse's neck and wept.

"You were a good warrior, be free, my friend, be free."

Wright looked up at the vet and nodded thanks and did the same to Poncho, who still held his shoulder. Poncho could have scored in the mayhem, but, instead, he pulled up short. Polo was a gentleman's game after all.

CHAPTER 9

THE KISS

The local eye surgeon had not been able to explain Nick's pain. Nor could he interpret why the scarring over Nick's eyes was cracking and dissolving, like ice on a frozen river after a long winter. None of the doctors understood why Nick had regained his sight. But Nick knew, and all his friends knew. Ibrahim had once again ushered in a miracle. It was impossible to explain but impossible to deny.

The Wright's Kids Foundation flew Maggie and Nick to Singapore first-class, so they shared a pod. Their seats reclined flat, and he looked at Maggie lounging next to him. The return of his sight made traveling easier, even though his vision was still a bit fuzzy. Nick and Maggie had met in San Francisco, and now they were midway over the North Pole headed for a short layover in Hong Kong. He pinched his eyes closed and then stretched them wide. The flight attendants had dimmed the lights so passengers could sleep. For a moment, Nick worried that his vision had decreased. He hit a button on the small console between them to turn on the reading light.

"You okay?" Maggie asked. "Still trying to get used to your peepers?"

"Yeah. Just got me a new pair the other day and still figuring them out," Nick said in a Texas drawl, then laughed. "But I'll tell you one thing, little lady, you're sure a sight for sore eyes."

He didn't want to admit to Maggie of his fear that his returning vision was some sort of fluke and wouldn't last.

"I'm so happy, Nicklaus—so grateful for your miracle and thankful you could come with me to Singapore."

"Yeah, my schedule was so full, it took my secretary days to rearrange it."

Maggie touched his face and ran her hand over the top of his close-shaved head. "When did you buzz your hair?"

He could tell by the tone of her voice she preferred his blond hair long. "It was a few months ago, after the last time you were in Memphis. I was feeling life was futile. I don't know, it seemed like the easiest thing to do. Don't like it, huh?"

"It's different is all. You're still very handsome," she said, giving his stubble a rub. She rested her head on the soft foam pillow and pulled the furry blanket over her. "Have you ever seen such luxury?"

"I never knew flying could be so nice," Nick said. "I could get used to it if traveling was always like this."

"I looked up the price of the tickets before we left and felt a little guilty," Maggie said. "These tickets were twelve thousand dollars…each. You know how many kids I can feed on that?"

"Well, I'm not complaining. It must be God's will."

"Huh?" Maggie gave him a puzzled look.

"Sorry. I'm being a little sacrilegious. It was something that Chang said to me before I left. He said, 'I hope you come to a place where you realize that living *your will, not His* no longer works for you, and you can say that the only way that works is *Your will, Father, not mine.*' So, I was thinking that flying first-class was His will." Nick looked at her and grimaced with an apology.

"You're impossible, Nicklaus Hart," she said and swatted at him. "Did you like working with Chang? He sounds like quite the character."

"Yeah, he's amazing—so kind. What I liked most about him is that he spent so much time pointing out what was *right* with me—not highlighting what was wrong. He said that we all have a true self—one that is made in God's image. We're meant to live in the fruit of the Spirit: love, joy, peace, patience, kindness, goodness, faithfulness, gentleness, and self-control."

"Why do you think we don't live in that true self more?" Maggie turned serious.

"Chang liked to point out that we all have filters over our vision of that true self…kind of like the scarring over my eyes… filters that block or change that vision of ourselves. They can be caused by all sorts of things that point us in the opposite direction."

"So true."

"He said that our journey in life is to remove these blinders, these filters, and rediscover who we really are."

Nick adjusted the pillow under his head.

"We explored some of those things in my own heart. I'm still trying to understand it, but he reminded me that it is a day by day, moment by moment discovery—to see and live in that true self."

"I think I want to meet this man."

"You talking about Chang or the new me?" Nick poked her playfully.

"I'm not saying."

"Speaking of meeting people, have you talked with this Mr. Wright Paul yet?" Nick asked. "What do you know about his foundation?"

"I haven't talked to him, but the people who work for him are sure nice. They said we would definitely get to meet him. Mr. Paul will hand out the check at the ceremony," Maggie said. She reached into her briefcase on the floor, pulled out a folder, and handed it to him.

The file was covered with a large graphic—a blue and aqua earth, stamped with a hand print and the text *Wright's Kids* next to it. The artist rendered *Kids* in a first-grader writing style with a red crayon.

"I searched for Wright Paul on the internet," Maggie said, "And he appears super generous and wealthy beyond belief. I guess he's made a ton of money in pharmaceuticals. Honestly, it's hard to find much information on him. Doesn't seem like one of those guys trying to make every news magazine cover or toot his own horn."

Nick opened the folder. The first document he saw was the congratulatory letter to Maggie and the Hope Center for successfully securing the four-million-dollar grant. The letter was signed by Mr. Paul himself, not rubber-stamped. *Nice touch.* He scanned through the remaining papers that listed past and present nonprofits that had received grants. Many well-known nongovernmental organizations were there. Nick nodded. "Pretty impressive."

In the back of the folder was a listing of the board of directors that included philanthropy's heaviest hitters. The last picture and bio listed was of Wright Paul himself. Nick tried to focus on the picture. His near vision was worse than his distance but Paul looked super young and casual. The top two buttons of his shirt were unbuttoned. He was tanned and fit and looked like he'd just come in from surfing. "Man, he looks young," Nick said.

"I heard he is around your age…forty-six or -seven."

"Oh, so, really young." Nick grinned. "And equally handsome."

Maggie turned away, and Nick thought he'd offended her. "You okay?"

But when Maggie turned back, she was smiling as though she had a secret.

"What are you thinking?" he asked.

She put her hand on his upper arm. Her touch was warm and inviting, and he shifted to get closer. The intimacy brought an unexpected response as her eyes filled with tears. His old psyche would tempt him to pull away or defuse the situation with humor. She seemed resistant to explain and said nothing for a while. Her silence made his stomach churn.

She wiped her tears, revealing the depth of her dark eyes, and sniffed. Nick assumed she was missing her kids from the Hope Center. Since the death of her husband, John, four years earlier, she had become the sole director of the orphanage and hospital. She was a loving mother to over two hundred orphans. She also directed medical teams rotating in and out providing care to the poor of Guatemala, a job that weighed heavily on her tiny five-foot frame.

She finally spoke. "There's something I want to talk to you about."

The way she said it, Nick thought bad news was coming.

"Maggie, what is it? You're scaring me."

Her tears fell again but she managed to say, "I suppose I am acting a little strange. It's just…" Now she was crying and smiling at the same time. "It's just that I thought I would never consider having another relationship besides John. I was okay with living the rest of my life alone. Of course there's so much to do, I didn't have time to think about it."

Nick wasn't sure what she was getting at. He raised an eyebrow, which seemed to make her cheeks flush. "Still yet," Maggie said, "I'm only forty-five. I…uh…get kind of lonely."

Nick nodded in understanding. He had both waited and wished for this moment and thought it would never happen.

"I guess this whole marriage thing is one of God's mysteries, but I am John's forever." She pulled at the wedding ring that she still wore. "Our bands said *Forever Yours*—that will never change. But I had a dream a month ago that I've thought about a lot."

Nick's brain swam with many thoughts, but he knew enough to keep silent.

"In my dream, I was back home in Montana on our family's ranch—it was so beautiful. The towering peaks of Glacier Park to the west, the open green fields expanding east. I was there, but not there…I don't know. You know how weird dreams are."

Nick nodded.

"I was watching my dad and John standing by the horse corral observing this beautiful Indian paint. The mare was chestnut with white patches on her right shoulder and face. She had a flowing black mane and tail and ran around the corral kicking and snorting. Growing up on the reservation, my dad would tell us stories about how a Blackfeet warrior caught the first horse. The elders said that horses came out of the water as a gift from the heavenly Father. They were so big and strong everyone was afraid of them. When brave warriors caught the young, they tamed them. The ancient people called them *elk dogs* because they were as large as elk but could carry a pack like a dog."

"Elk dogs. That's funny," Nick said.

"In my dream, my dad and John seemed to have a long conversation that I could not hear. Finally, I saw John nod, and Dad handed him a large knife. With the knife, John cut thick bands of rope that held the corral gate closed. When the gate swung open, the beautiful mare came charging out with her head and tail held high."

Nick wasn't sure why she was crying, but he nodded.

"The horse circled the corral seven times," she said.

"Seven?"

"Yes, it seemed like in my dream that was important. Many Christians believe seven is the number of completeness. Once the pony expended her energy, she came gracefully back and nuzzled John. John kissed the mare on the cheek and opened his hands to set it free." Maggie demonstrated by stretching her hands in front of her. Then she let the tears flow.

Nick took her hand.

"You've seen movies where the Indians paint symbols on their horses," Maggie said between sobs. "The horse in my dream had a large handprint on its right hip. We call this the pat print, because the warrior would reach down with his hand and pat the horse with praise. It meant that the horse had brought its rider back home unharmed from a dangerous mission."

"I'm not sure I love the sound of the danger part," Nick said. "We've seen too many of those situations already."

"Right?" Maggie agreed. "I'm still trying to figure that one out. But also, painted in red on the mare's side was a large heart." At this point Maggie was staring into Nick's eyes, searching. Nick stared back but didn't know what to say. Maggie finally explained. "I believe my father and John are releasing me to find love again."

Nick still didn't know what to say. He believed that for Maggie; John had died and gone to heaven where they would be reunited someday. All Nick could do was take a deep breath and exhale slowly. He had loved her for a long time, but he'd never expected her to let go of John enough to have a romantic relationship.

"I love you Nicklaus Hart." Maggie pushed herself up on one elbow, leaned toward him and gave him a warm kiss on the lips.

It was very short, but long enough for Nick's body temperature to rise. He leaned in to kiss her again, but she held her hand on his chest. "Can we take it slow?" she asked.

His mind and his mouth were saying yes. His body was not in agreement.

CHAPTER 10

SINGAPORE

"What is your business in Singapore?" The stern customs official glanced at Maggie's US passport.

"I'm here to accept a grant from the Wright's Kids Foundation." She rummaged through her briefcase for the folder. She didn't know why she was always so nervous talking to the customs agents. Maybe they were trained to intimidate, but their demeanor was cold and authoritative. She always felt like she was sneaking in or out of the country—a con on the lam, and after two days of travel, she worried she smelled like one. She opened the folder and produced the invitation letter. The agent read it carefully and regarded her without emotion before returning her folder.

"You traveling together?" he tilted his head toward Nick, who stood behind her.

"Yes, sir," she said.

Apparently satisfied, he flipped through Maggie's passport, found an open page and stamped the Singapore seal of entry without hesitation. He did the same for Nick and returned their passports. It wasn't until Maggie reached for her documents that warmth crossed his face and he smiled.

"Congratulations, Ms. Russell," he said. "Mr. Wright is very well known here. Welcome to Singapore."

* * *

"The invitation letter said we would be met by a young Chinese woman," Maggie told Nick as they exited the baggage claim into the main terminal.

"Is that her?" Nick asked when they saw a woman waving to them. Maggie recognized her from her photo in the arrival instructions.

She approached quickly holding her iPad with their names.

"Dr. Hart, Ms. Russell, welcome to Singapore. It is our honor to have you both here. My name is Lola," she said and bowed.

The small-framed woman wore a blue dress with the pin on her right collar identifying the Wright's Kids Foundation.

"You both must be exhausted and thirsty. Please have some cold water," she said, producing two bottles from a satchel that hung over her shoulder.

"Thank you so much, Lola," Maggie said, accepting a bottle. "It feels like Guatemala here, hot and humid."

"Yes, Ms. Russell. In fact, Singapore is even closer to the equator than Guatemala. In the winter the temperature drops a whole degree—from twenty-seven to twenty-six degrees centigrade." She stopped herself and pondered for a moment. "For you Americans, I guess that's two degrees, from eighty-three to eighty-one degrees Fahrenheit." She giggled at her own joke. "I think you will find Singapore quite pleasant this time of year. It gets down to seventy-five at night, so you might desire a jacket in the evening. Please, follow me." She slipped her iPad into her satchel, then took the handles of Maggie's and Nick's roller bags.

"Please, you don't need to—" Maggie began to protest.

"It is my pleasure," Lola said, pulling the bags through the terminal and allowing for no further objection.

"There has been a change in your itinerary and your accommodations. Please forgive me. I just learned of it myself an hour ago."

Maggie suspected by the tone of her voice that they might be staying in the local Motel 6 instead of the luxurious Marina Bay Sands Hotel. But she didn't care. All she needed was a bed and a hot shower before tonight's ceremony. She smiled to herself. Lola probably had never seen Guatemala standards.

"Whatever you have for us, Lola, we will be comfortable," Maggie said and glanced at Nick, who nodded even though he looked pale from the long airplane ride. "We are so appreciative of all you are doing for the Hope Center."

"Mr. Paul has made the arrangements himself. Please follow me. Dr. Hart, I know of your eye condition. Will you be able to walk a short distance?"

Maggie looked at Nick and put her arm through his. He told her how difficult it had been over the last few months when people treated him like an invalid or a child. "He'll be fine," she answered for him, then felt guilty for doing the same.

"Yes, I'm good. Lead the way," Nick said and squeezed Maggie's arm.

"Mr. Paul will be meeting us at the private terminal," Lola said, leading them toward the exit.

"Mr. Paul?" Maggie said, startled. "I thought we were meeting him at the function tonight. Like…tonight…after I wash my hair and take a nice long hot shower, tonight…and put on some makeup." She stopped dead in her tracks. The twenty-fourth richest man in the world was scheduled to endow the Hope Center with a gift that she could have only dreamed of. She was not about to meet him in her yoga pants and sweatshirt. "I must look like a mess, and I smell like I've been traveling for two days. Please," she pleaded.

"I am so sorry, Ms. Russell. I would have never done this to you. But please, Mr. Paul may be already waiting for us." She bowed again.

* * *

Maggie was mortified as the SUV pulled up to a modern glass-and-steel building at the north end of the airport. The sign read SINGAPORE EXECUTIVE TERMINAL. No amount of pleading convinced Lola to take them to their hotel and delay the meeting with Mr. Paul. Maggie quickly ran a brush through her hair and applied a coat of lipstick before exiting the vehicle.

Nick got out of the Escalade that had shuttled them between terminals and paused to collect their bags.

"Do not worry. We'll have your luggage taken care of," Lola told him.

She led Maggie and Nick into the building, where they were greeted by a blast of air conditioning.

Maggie recognized Mr. Wright Paul right away, looking exactly like his photo. He was casually attired in a pair of tan linen pants and a light blue shirt. Its top three buttons were undone, and the sleeves were rolled up his forearms. His eyes were shielded by Ray-Bans. He was chatting with one of the security guards. As Maggie and Nick approached, the guard looked their way, and Mr. Paul turned and smiled warmly.

"Dr. Hart, Ms. Russell, I am so glad you are here," he said and strolled toward them. His boyish face and long flowing hair gave him the appearance of a twentysomething, rather than his reported age of forty-seven. "I hope your flight was comfortable." He extended his hand first to Nick, then to Maggie.

His accent was interesting. Maggie had heard it in those educated in an international school where exposure to many cultures merged—part Brit, part Australian, part Asian.

Mr. Paul put his hand on Nick's shoulder. "Mate, I want to know how your eyes are doing. Ms. Russell told my people about the accident. We have rejoiced with the news that your vision is improving."

His familiarity and warmth seemed to take Nick by surprise. He glanced at Maggie, then back at Wright. "It's been a challenge. I'm still getting used to them…and to the light…but I'm grateful to be seeing again."

"I'm grateful as well. Please let me know if there is anything I can do for you while you are here. Singapore has some of the best medical care in the world. Speaking of which, please forgive me for my sunglasses." He peeled them off and revealed a black eye and an angry looking broken blood vessel in his eyeball. "I had an unfortunate accident yesterday." His chipper countenance grew somber. "The worst part, I've lost my favorite horse, Smoothie. He was a brilliant polo pony, one of the best I've ever had."

"I'm so sorry. I know how tough it is to lose an animal," Nick said.

There was such a change in the pitch of Mr. Paul's voice that Maggie wondered if the man was about to tear up. "I tell you, mate, it's like losing one of your family members."

Maggie watched the two men interact. Mr. Paul's eyes were enchanting, even with one injured. People might call them hazel, but there was so much more color to them—the inner portion was copper and the outer, emerald green. They were like fancy glass marbles dancing with life. The men were similar in height and build, although Nick had gained a few pounds during his sedentary life the last six months.

Mr. Paul turned his attention to Maggie, who flushed with embarrassment over her haggard state. "Was your flight okay?" he asked.

"Mr. Paul, thank you so much for the tickets. I would have never imagined flying first class. You honestly didn't need to be so generous....and I'm so embarrassed to meet you in my... uh...condition."

"Okay, let's get this out of the way. Please call me Wright, and I would not have it any other way than to fly you over in comfort. The awards ceremony is tonight, and I wanted you to enjoy a restful flight. It was the least I could do," he said. "I felt so bad that I could not send one of our corporate jets over to get you. Our company has a big launch of our newest drug tomorrow, so the planes are all being used to pick up some of our board members."

He looked her up and down as she squirmed in her stretchy pants. "If you'd like, there's plenty of time to stop for a yoga class." He grinned. His laughing eyes seemed happy to add to her discomfort. "Don't be embarrassed," he said sincerely. "I think you are perfectly dressed for flying for two days. As you can see, I too like dressing casually."

Maggie looked at the floor as heat rose up her neck. The man's Italian leather shoes probably cost more than anything in her closet. "Thank you for understanding."

Wright turned to Lola. "Thank you, Lola. I'll take them from here, and we'll see you at the function tonight."

"Yes, sir, Mr. Paul. Their luggage is being taken to the helicopter," she said and bowed deeply to her boss.

"Helicopter?" Nick asked and swallowed hard.

* * *

Wright, who sat in the pilot's seat, looked at Nick sitting next to him in the copilot's seat. He spoke to Nick through the headset. "Don't touch the controls," he warned. In response, Nick leaned back with his hands up in surrender, then tightly gripped his harness.

Wright looked back at Maggie, who sat in the posh leather seat behind Nick. "You set?"

"Yes, a little nervous is all. The last time I was in a helicopter was in Turkey to meet Nick after the earthquake; it wasn't quite this nice."

"This will be a very short ride across the Singapore Strait to my home. A great deal is happening this weekend, and the city will be packed. Besides the foundation dinner tonight and my company's launch party tomorrow night, Sunday happens to be the Chinese New Year. I hope you don't mind, but I thought you both would be more comfortable in my home. The city will be outlandish, but at least you will still be able to view the fireworks from my place."

Wright scanned the tarmac and pushed a red button on the control stick. "Tower, this is Singapore 4012, ready for flight," he said into his mic.

"Singapore 4012, you are cleared for liftoff from Heliport 60 right," the tower replied.

Maggie watched Wright push three buttons on the high-tech dash with his right hand and pull a lever with his left. The helicopter's engines roared, the rotors throbbed, and the entire aircraft began to lift. Wright once again scanned the area, and in seconds they were off the ground. Maggie was surprised that her anxiety lifted as well. There was something about this man that made her feel very comfortable.

CHAPTER 11

WEALTH

The helicopter ride was quick and uneventful compared to Nick's previous experiences. The throb of the chopper blades zipped his brain back to his rescue in Turkey, where the flash grenade had plunged him into darkness. Now his vision continued to improve, especially since escaping the dry air of the long transcontinental flight. His moisturizing eye drops gave him some relief from the burning that still plagued him.

He pushed the painful memories from his mind as Wright had lifted off from the Singapore Airport and veered out over the Singapore Strait. Wright explained that its waters flowed into the Pacific Ocean. The skyscrapers of downtown Singapore towered in the distance. Wright promised to show them the city tonight.

The flight lasted only fifteen minutes. It wasn't long before they circled above an island off the tip of the city.

"It looks like a shark, don't you think?" Wright asked.

At first, Nick didn't see it. But as Wright swung the aircraft around the island, Nick could see the silhouette of a shark with its gaping mouth ready to take a bite out of the sea. A peninsula jutting into the water formed a nose, and a small inlet of water created its eye. But its mouth did not glisten with large teeth; instead, it was filled with white sand and crystal-clear Caribbean-colored water.

"Raffles Island...my home," Wright said and banked the

helicopter to the right. "Sir Thomas Samford Raffles founded Colonial Singapore as a trading post of the East India Company in 1819. His daughter Ella married my great-great-grandfather, George Brooke. The island has been in the family for a while." He glanced at Nick and Maggie and smiled.

The island appeared uninhabited with no heliport in sight. They skimmed over the island's thick jungle toward the mouth of the shark and the sandy beach. Nick finally saw where Wright was aiming. The heliport was camouflaged, painted the same dark green of the foliage. Wright effortlessly piloted the craft onto the pad and shut down the engines.

"Is this okay?" Wright asked.

"Of course," Nick said, having no idea what to expect and not knowing what else to say.

They exited the air-conditioned helicopter to an ocean breeze carrying warm humidity and fragrances of the sea. Seagulls flew overhead, complaining with high-pitched cries about the intrusion.

Two young, barefooted women with skin glowing from the island sun greeted them with warm smiles. They were dressed in red and yellow sarongs with large red hibiscuses adorning their long black hair.

"Please take Dr. Hart's and Ms. Russell's things to the guest house," Wright instructed the pair.

He waved Nick and Maggie to follow him down a path through the thick trees that shielded them from the sun. Songbirds chattered in the dense canopy, and the ocean lapped at the sandy beach glistening through the trees.

"The trees are mahogany, angsana and what we call rain trees," Wright said.

Nick smiled and nodded, continuing down the pathway to a compound up ahead. He had pictured a cutting-edge glass-and-steel building for the wealthy entrepreneur. But what they approached looked more like something out of *Robinson Crusoe*.

Wright's home was an open-air, wooden structure with bamboo railings and overhanging thatched roofs. Nick felt Wright observing him, probably sensing his amazement at this simple lifestyle.

"This is beautiful," Maggie said. "It reminds me of Swiss Family Treehouse in Disneyland."

"I hoped you would like it," Wright said. "It reminds me of the surroundings where I grew up. My parents stewarded a conservatory preserve in India. But you will find this a bit more...modern and comfortable."

Wright led them up the front stairs. At the top of the stairs was a fit and shirtless young native man with a calf-length sarong wrapped around his six-pack abs. Like the girls, he was barefoot. A string of wooden beads hung over his muscular chest. Nick snuck a peek at Maggie to see if she noticed. The young man bowed as they entered the house through the open door. Contemporary artwork adorned the walls—swirls and splotches of bright colors accenting the mahogany panels.

The young man smiled at Wright and picked up a tray from an entry table. "Welcome home, sir. May I offer your guests some lemonade?"

"Hey, Christian. Thank you." Wright stepped to the side and waved toward the wooden platter that the man held with three crystal glasses of pink lemonade.

Nick deferred to Maggie, who accepted the offer. "Thank you," she said.

Nick followed her lead and took a long gulp of the sweet, ice-cold drink. "Wow, that has to be the best lemonade I've ever had."

"Yes, please have as much as you wish. You will find it is easy to get dehydrated here in the tropics. This is Christian." Wright motioned to the young man. "He will see to any needs you may have. He is Iban, from Sarawak, across the sea," he said, pointing to the east.

The young man smiled naturally. "Please let me know how I can best serve you."

"I know you both must be exhausted but let me give you a quick tour of my home," Wright said, gesturing to the main room. The space combined a comfortable living area with a museum. There were marine artifacts of all kinds on tables and in cases. A Ramsden Sextant sat in a mahogany case, highlighted on black felt and surrounded by old gold coins. *The real thing, no doubt.*

A modern kitchen tucked off the living area sat to the right. People bustled in the kitchen until they saw Wright and stopped and smiled. A man in a tall chef's hat stepped forward, wiping his hands on a white towel.

"This is Mario, our executive chef," Wright said. "He will fix you whatever your hearts' desire."

Mario smiled and said, "It will be my pleasure." He nodded to one of his underlings, who offered a plate of warm cookies to Maggie and Nick. "These are my special white-chocolate mango cookies," Mario said.

"But be forewarned," Wright spoke up. "They are like crack cocaine." He laughed.

Nick bit into a cookie and glanced at Maggie. He saw in her face what he was feeling—the ease and contentment that filled the compound.

Maggie bit into a cookie. "Oh, my gosh," she said. "You better lock those away from me."

"You have a whole plate to yourself in your room." Wright laughed as he led them to the veranda. Nick and Maggie, their mouths stuffed with cookies, marveled at the scene. It looked like something out of one of the world's best resorts, with its thatched-roof bungalows surrounding an inviting pool. The swimming pool was designed to look as though it flowed directly into the ocean. "This is my favorite room of the house," Wright said, "one I hope you'll take advantage of."

The veranda and infinity pool emptied into the blue-green waters of the bay. A semicircular white-sand beach stretched a half mile in each direction. The sea flowed with gentle waves that softly brushed the shore. A group of white egrets, chasing the waves back and forth and scrounging for sea life, were the only inhabitants on the beach.

"My island is cradled by Indonesia. Singapore is across the strait to the north, and my real home, Borneo, is across the sea."

"Borneo?" Maggie asked.

"Ah yes, Borneo. It is the third largest island in the world— only Greenland and New Guinea beat us. It is shared by three countries, Malaysia, Brunei and Indonesia. The Malaysian portion includes two states, Sarawak and Sabah. Sarawak is my real home. It is the most beautiful place in the world—home of orangutans and my favorite people group in the world, the Iban."

"It looks like the cruise ships have found your little retreat," Nick said, pointing to the large ship off the southern end of the beach.

Wright looked at him and then to the ship. He hesitated as though he wasn't sure what to say. Then he apologized, "I'm afraid that is the *Solstice*, Dr. Hart—my boat."

The craft appeared to be as long as a football field with at least three decks above water and a large heliport on the rear upper deck.

Nick tried to hide his embarrassment with a laugh. "Forgive me, Mr. Paul. I'm just a redneck from Montana. I'm not used to this."

Wright gave him a gentle slap on the back. "No worries, mate. Love to take you on a little spin on her sometime. And, *pleeease*, call me Wright. You will find my staff is prim and proper but let the three of us put away formalities."

"Okay," Nick said, and Wright continued the tour.

Following the veranda to the left, Wright led them to a set of stairs and an expansive structure sitting twenty feet off the ground. It was suspended by the massive rain trees surrounding it. "I hope you don't mind staying in the tree house," he smiled at them.

A tree house was not what Nick would have called it. It was in the trees all right, but it wasn't exactly a house. Maybe a tree mansion or tree fortress would be a better term.

The fit young shirtless man appeared from behind them.

"Christian, would you please show our guests to their rooms," Wright said, turning back to them. "If you would please excuse me, I have some business to attend to before tonight's function." He pulled a smartphone from his front pocket. "It's almost noon. I will meet you by the pool at six. We'll have a bite to eat and a drink before heading back to the city. I wish you had more time to rest, but please let us supply you with anything you need."

"Thank you so much, Mr. Paul...Wright," Maggie said. "I can't tell you how much this means to us. I do have one request. I wanted to work on my presentation for tonight. I don't suppose there's internet here?"

"What is the speed you have in Guatemala?"

"We have about five megabits, on a good day."

"You will get to experience one of the fastest internet connections on earth at five hundred…gigabits," Wright smiled. He added proudly, "We had the cable laid from Singapore last year."

The alarm on his phone sounded, and he quickly silenced it. "Now if you would please excuse me." He shook their hands. "Remember, my home is your home. Please let me know how I can make your stay more comfortable."

* * *

Nick and Maggie stood at the railing of the tree house overlooking the ocean and Singapore in the distance. Nick shook his head with disgust. "Well, I sure looked like the dumb hillbilly. Geez, Mr. Paul, the cruise ships have arrived." He ran his hands through the stubble on his head. "This is unbelievable. I had no idea that people lived like this."

"Don't be so hard on yourself, Nick. Remember, I'm from the holler as well. Even worse, I'm from the rez."

Nick couldn't get over it. "He almost speaks in a foreign language—my airplanes, my island, my yacht—definitely words you'll never hear me say." He looked at Maggie, who was smiling at him. "At least you don't keep putting your foot in your mouth. I think you should have left me at home."

"Don't be silly. I'm so glad you're here with me, Nicklaus." She pulled one of his hands off the rail and wrapped it around her waist. "We haven't talked about that kiss?" she said more like a question and left it open-ended.

Nick looked into her dark native eyes. "Thank you for bringing me, Maggie. I wish we were here all alone in this paradise and had another go at that kiss."

She tucked her head into his chest. "I can't think of anyone else I'd rather be with."

Her words surprised him. He still couldn't believe what she'd said about being open to another relationship. He knew that John was always on her mind. Probably she was just being kind. It was something they would have to work out. But right now, they were both too tired for such an emotionally charged discussion, so he responded with a joke. "Not even Mr. Richie Rich…Mr. Handsome?"

"You mean Mr. Paul?" Maggie feigned surprise. "Is he handsome? I didn't notice."

They both laughed hard.

"Well, I still smell like two days of travel, and I want to work on my presentation." She pulled back from him. "See you in a bit."

* * *

"We are spending over two million dollars on the launch party alone. Dr. Amy, are you suggesting we delay the launch? You have to tell me *now*." Wright spoke angrily into his phone. "The board and the sales team are not flying in to be entertained."

"Nor would they be," Leah added on the conference call.

"No, I'm not suggesting that," Amy's voice came over the speakerphone. "But we had two more Iban leaders tell me their experience. They came all the way down the river, for God's sake, to share with me. The people are beginning to call Welltrex '*celap*.'"

"*Celap*…cold?" Wright interpreted. "Like cold medicine? Something like Nyquil?" The muscles in his neck and shoulders tensed. Scientists and medical staff were an inconvenient necessity. They were so rigid and fussy.

"No, like in spiritually cold." Dr. Amy sounded flustered. "I'm not articulating it well."

There was a long uncomfortable pause, and Wright took a deep breath and stretched his neck from side to side. "Okay, Amy. I want you to know that I hear you. I'm not sure what to make of it, is all. What is your suggestion?"

"Mr. Paul, I don't think we should do anything different. I suppose we should proceed with the launch. I simply wanted you to know."

"Leah, what do you think?" Wright said into the speakerphone.

"You know what I think."

"Okay then, we are a go." His mood lifted, and he sighed deeply. "Amy, thank you for calling. You are stopping the clinical trial, correct? You'll stop giving the Iban the Welltrex?"

"Yes. I will send word upriver for everyone to stop taking the medication. After the launch on Saturday, when the drug goes into general distribution, we will move into FDA post-market safety monitoring," she said.

"Leah, do we have any exposure here? Do we need to notify the FDA of this?" Wright asked.

Leah scoffed loudly. "That the witch doctors can no longer hear the voices in their heads? That would make for an interesting warning label: If you are a witch doctor, you may experience less chatter in your mind." She didn't hide her disgust.

"Okay, okay," he said. "Dr. Amy, good job. We will see you tomorrow night at the launch party. I'll look forward to introducing you to Dr. Hart and Ms. Russell."

Wright waited for a series of clicks to make sure the doctor had hung up her phone. When his phone indicated that he was no longer on a conference call and all he heard was Leah's nasal breathing, he asked, "Well?"

"We may need to consider a change," she said coldly.

CHAPTER 12

MERCY

That "bite" to eat turned out to be a feast of sushi, a couple of dishes of Asian noodles and a pig roasted over an open fire. Maggie wished she hadn't eaten so much before the helicopter flight to Singapore. She'd fallen asleep working on her presentation and awakened groggy. Now, with jet lag and a full belly, her mind drifted in a dreamlike state, cruising in sunset shadows over a strange, exotic landscape. She ran her hand over the soft leather of her seat in the rear of the helicopter. This was no dream.

Maggie was still embarrassed by Wright's extravagant compliments when she arrived poolside in a tight-fitting black evening dress. She'd been surprised he hadn't changed to formal wear. He'd simply donned a royal-blue sports jacket over his casual clothes. The invitation had read: *A CELEBRATION OF LIFE* and suggested dressing in evening wear. How was she supposed to know how to dress for something like this? After Wright's glowing attention, she'd fought the urge to run back to her room and put on jeans and a silk blouse. But she resisted when she saw that Nick had put on a suit and tie.

She peered out the window as Wright slowed the helicopter and hovered over the city. "Singapore is an island itself—only two-thirds the size of New York with five and a half million people," he said.

The setting sun showered the city's downtown skyscrapers in streams of pink and lavender. Clouds bathed in flaming orange stretched from the western horizon.

"What a beautiful night." Wright sighed. "I think Singapore is on her best behavior and showing off for you. Just wait until the lights come on." As if on cue, neon lights of every color outlined the buildings and reflected off the bay waters cradled by the city.

"This is stunning," Nick said through the headset.

"Isn't it?" Wright said. "You can see why I love it here. Just wait for the Chinese New Year celebration Sunday night. The city has been celebrating all week, but Sunday night is the finale—there'll be a show like you've never seen before."

Wright pushed the helicopter cyclic to the right, and the aircraft responded quickly and swooped them back over the water. Massive cargo ships stacked with containers lined up like an LA traffic jam, awaiting their turn at the docks.

"Singapore is a global commerce, finance and transportation hub. It holds the third-highest GDP per capita and is in the top five for education in the world. I don't want to brag, but we spend one third of what the US does per capita on medicine, and our healthcare is ranked sixth in the world—the US is ranked what…around fortieth?"

"Yeah, we're ranked right up there with Cuba and Costa Rica." Nick shook his head. "And yes, the US has the most expensive healthcare in the world."

Wright piloted the helicopter back toward land, east of downtown, and pointed to a large complex. "That's Zelutex, my company."

Wright's company included two six-story buildings covered in copper-colored glass and connected in front at a large arch. The complex expanded into a garden rivaling the beauty of the Butchart Gardens in Victoria, Canada. Next door to the compound was a large parking complex.

"How many do you employ at Zelutex?" Nick asked.

"Our global team is over eight thousand. We are launching a new medication tomorrow night called Welltrex. I believe it will do well." Wright looked at Nick and then Maggie and acted as though he'd forgotten something. "Forgive me. I should have asked. Why don't you join us tomorrow night for the celebration? It's going to be a great bash."

"Sure, we'd love to," Maggie said.

"Dr. Hart, I think you will find it quite fascinating. I know that most doctors think of the pharmaceutical industry as the evil empire, but maybe you'll see us in a different light." He smiled at Nick.

"Mr. Paul…er…Wright," Maggie interrupted, "I don't know if you are watching the time, but doesn't the foundation party start at seven? It's 7:10."

Wright laughed. "Yes, you're right, of course. But you are the star of the party and celebrities should be fashionably late. They won't start without us." He turned and winked at Maggie.

Wright pulled back on the throttle with his left hand, and the high-tech aircraft leaped like a racehorse from the gate. He directed it back toward downtown, circled acutely around the skyscrapers and aimed toward a large complex of buildings across the bay. He brought it to a hover over the area. "This is the famous Marina Bay Sands Resort."

The most prominent structure was a set of three tall buildings supporting a large platform, like three strong men holding a huge plank over their heads.

"The podium on top is the SkyPark. It is the world's largest cantilevered platform and has an infinity swimming pool that runs almost its entire length. The platform can hold four thousand people."

Wright aimed the helicopter toward one side of the complex to an odd-shaped building. Its multiple appendages extended like unfolding petals. The top was lit in pink and the base in green, giving it the appearance of a lotus flower blooming on the bay.

"This is the ArtScience building, where the function is tonight. We have the whole thing to ourselves."

Sweat trickled down Maggie's back. "How many people will be attending?" She tried not to let her voice betray her anxiety.

"We sent out two thousand invitations, but we are expecting more. People in Singapore like to party, especially when it's on someone else's dime."

Nick looked back to her. "You'll do great, Mags."

She stuck her tongue out, faking she was about to be sick. She gulped hard to catch her breath as Wright set the helicopter down in a roped-off area on the landing pad surrounded by a huge crowd. As soon as they touched down, that lotus flower burst with a laser show that lit the fading evening sky.

* * *

Maggie burped the smoked salmon pâté in the back of her throat. Fortunately, it came no farther, but she wasn't sure it would stay put as she fumbled with her notes when Wright called her to the stage. Ten grants would be handed out tonight, but until she was seated at the head table next to Wright, Maggie didn't know she was the featured speaker. She had stewed about her ensemble, and despite Wright's attire, she found herself underdressed. Many of the women wore long formal dresses, and some of the men sported tuxes. The party sizzled with the glitz and glamour of a Hollywood awards ceremony, complete with paparazzi who rendered her eyes wonky with their strobe flashes.

The banquet and the surroundings were magnificent—if only she could have enjoyed it—with elaborately adorned tables bearing centerpieces of beautiful yellow roses surrounding a large bubbling fountain. The feast was served on fine bone china with more forks at each setting than she knew what to do with. Even larger bouquets of flowers and greenery framed the gathering. It was an exquisite garden party, and Maggie felt like a royal princess. To top off the sights and scents, a string quartet played Mozart, filling the space with intimate sounds.

Maggie had picked at the fresh halibut and lobster dinner but couldn't bring herself to eat anything else. As she walked to the stage she wished she'd taken a larger drink of champagne for Dutch courage. Wright said something funny about his black eye, and laughter filled the room as she climbed the stairs to the podium. She'd missed his joke as she was concentrating on not tripping. She walked across the stage and stood next to him. He introduced her with elegance that fueled her anxiety. He stepped back from the microphone, gave her a warm hug and adjusted the mic for her height.

Her head swirled, and her heart pounded in her throat, as she looked over the impressively dressed crowd. Wright had been correct; these people sure liked to party. As she gathered herself to speak, the rumble of conversation dropped only a decibel.

When Maggie cleared her throat, it resounded in the great room, creating a squeal of feedback from the sound system.

"Oops, sorry," she said nervously and chuckled, adjusting the microphone away from her mouth. She spread her notes on the podium and silently prayed. *Father, let my words honor You.*

She smiled at the crowd, let her shoulders relax, and pushed a button on the control panel of the podium to advance her PowerPoint to the first slide. A black-and-white photo of John filled the large screen behind her. He ministered to a small, naked, dark-skinned child whose belly was so distended from parasites that it looked like it could burst. John knelt in the dirt, holding the boy with one hand on his back and with the other, the bell of the stethoscope on the boy's tummy. The child looked wide-eyed at the white man. After all these years, it was still her favorite picture of John. *God, how I miss him.*

"Blessed are the merciful, as they will be shown mercy," she said, her voice cracking with emotion. She paused, unsure she could continue as she forced herself to keep from breaking down and sobbing. The slide showed the kind of scenario, the desperation, that had propelled her and John to give their lives to help sick and impoverished people. She was a little surprised when the room went completely silent. The only sound was the bubbling fountain.

The audience's attention renewed Maggie's confidence. "The pictures I'm going to show you tonight and the stories I'm going to tell may shock you…or move you. In any case, I know your hearts will never be the same. The hardships that much of humanity endures are difficult to look at, but for me and my late husband, John, they were impossible to look away from. John and I visited Guatemala as young adults, and what we saw impacted us to our very core. We experienced a swath of humanity doing without some of the most basic needs—so many things we often take for granted like shelter, food, and medical care. After John finished his training as a general surgeon, we knew we had to go to serve."

Maggie paused and redirected her attention to the child in the slide.

"We found this little boy wandering through the destruction after a hurricane devastated Honduras. The storm had destroyed most of his village, leaving little in its wake. The survivors were living in some of the worst conditions I've ever seen—no fresh water, little to eat, and shanties made of cardboard and tin or anything else that had survived the storm. Thousands were left homeless, and hundreds of orphans roamed the streets. To this day, I can hardly talk about it without crying. Many of the people died from dehydration and disease." Her voice cracked.

"But it doesn't have to be that way." Maggie went to the next slide that showed the Hope Center with its small mission hospital and orphanage. "After a few detours along the way, John and I ended up in Quetzaltenango, Guatemala, where we opened the Hope Center..."

* * *

Maggie glanced at the timepiece on the podium; she had spoken for thirty-seven minutes about their ministry, explaining how they rotated medical teams through the hospital to care for the people of Guatemala. She showed a slide of Isabella and told the child's story and how Nick had operated and corrected her severely deformed feet. Maggie showed more slides, picture upon picture of mercy, picture upon picture of hope, and pictures of the smiling children they cared for. She concluded her talk with a few images from Turkey and King's Orphanage, which had swelled to overcapacity during the earthquake six months ago. A rumble of gasps came from the crowd when they saw the devastation.

Maggie had barely scratched the surface of privations in only two small regions of the world when she realized she had exceeded her time. She was only supposed to talk for thirty minutes.

She hastily began her conclusion. "Mr. Paul and members of the board of Wright's Kids Foundation, I can't thank you enough for what you are doing for the Hope Center. I know that God will bless you greatly for your generosity. I hope that—"

"Excuse me." A woman in a long red dress near the middle of the crowd stood and interrupted Maggie. Tears streamed down her face. "I'm so sorry, dear, but before you go, I must know what happened to that child," she said, wiping her eyes with a napkin. "The one you showed in the beginning."

Maggie smiled at the woman and put her hand over her heart. "That picture was taken twenty years ago when John and I first started. We established an IV on that little boy and gave him a dose of an antiparasitic drug." She stopped and grimaced, trying to decide if she should continue. "Some things are just too much…" she added. "That little guy was so full of worms that when we gave him the medication—" The woman's eyes urged her on. "Sorry, sometimes the truth is hard…the parasites came squirming out both ends."

There was an audible moan from the crowd.

"But the medication saved his life. This simple, simple treatment saved his life."

Maggie interrupted the crowd's applause for the rest of the story. "Many of the people of that village were not so lucky." Maggie qualified. "But for that little boy, the story ended well. We nursed him back to health, and because he was orphaned, brought him to the Hope Center, where he was fed, given a bed to sleep in and an education. He also received what he needed the most…love and hope for the future." She wiped at one of her own tears. "He has grown into a fine young man. Amazingly, he now works for the office of the First Lady of Guatemala and is attending the university. He wants to become a doctor."

Maggie smiled at the woman in the red dress. "That is what mercy can do."

The crowd erupted in loud applause and a standing ovation. Wright bounded up the stairs to Maggie's side, wrapped his arm around her shoulders, and spoke into the microphone.

"I told you she was something." He kissed her forehead. "I was not planning on doing this tonight, but I don't think we can let this moment pass. I ask each one of you to search your hearts and especially your pocketbooks." The crowd laughed with him. "And prepare to give generously to this ministry."

The woman in red spoke first. "I pledge two hundred thousand dollars." She looked at her companion, whom Maggie figured was her spouse. The man shrugged and raised three fingers.

"Thank you, Mrs. Kim. Mr. Kim pledges three hundred thousand dollars," Wright said, stirring a cheer from the crowd. "That is very generous, but I'm going to squeeze harder."

The Kims looked at each other and shrugged.

"Come on, Mr. Kim. You'll spend more than that at the craps table tonight," Wright poked fun at him. The crowd roared with laughter and Mrs. Kim frowned and slapped his shoulder.

Mr. Kim rolled his head from side to side. "Okay, okay," he said and raised two fingers. "Two million dollars."

The crowd gasped.

CHAPTER 13

WELLTREX

Nick and Maggie were both exhausted after the foundation party, too tired for romance but shared a good-night hug. They retired to their respective rooms. They slept through the night and most of the next day until they were roused to return to Singapore for more celebration.

Wright was in his element, and if Nick was honest with himself, he was just plain envious. One of his college friends used to say that the man with the most toys when he dies wins. *Wright wins.* Nick's old friend could never have imagined this kind of wealth and opulence.

The launch party for the new medication was in the Zelutex building. Nick tried to wrap his mind around how much a bash like this must cost. There was enough food to feed a large army—a large army of salespeople, he guessed—and it was no potluck. Shrimp, crab, lobster, filet mignon, beef wellington, and more side dishes than he could count weighed the tables down. He never saw an empty tray as the catering staff continuously refilled everything. The desserts alone filled one side of the room and included a living chocolate fountain that poured over a shapely naked woman. The spectacle reinforced Nick's opinion that rich pharmaceutical companies gouged every patient they could and made billions in the process.

The party was centered in the expansive atrium of the Zelutex building and spilled into the garden. At the apex of the atrium was a massive glass brain that flashed with electrical impulses of red, blue and green, suggesting it was the living brain of the pharmaceutical empire. Nick had to admit the sculpture was mesmerizing and magnificent. The designer had captured the complexity of the brain with its neuronal and hormonal intricacies.

Nick rubbed his eyes and turned from the brain. The optical overload had nothing to do with his visual impairment. His vision continued to improve, and his blindness seemed more and more like a bad dream. But his other senses were not faring well. The celebration band blared '70s rock and was giving him a headache. He wished to be somewhere else, alone with Maggie, even though she was acting a bit off tonight. He wondered why. They had rejoiced together after Wright's plea had raised another four million dollars for the Hope Center, matching his foundation's grant. Eight million dollars. It was unbelievable. But despite it all, Maggie didn't seem her bubbly self. Maybe she was just overwhelmed.

Maggie sat next to him watching the people gyrate on the dance floor. She looked stunning. Maggie had told Wright that she had nothing to wear to the Zelutex party except for the black dress she had worn to the foundation dinner. After her long sleep, she had arisen to a rack full of designer dresses and shoes to match. She'd picked a violet Benny Ong silk evening gown. Nick wasn't sure if it was because she loved the dress or because Wright's wardrobe stylist had mentioned that Princess Di had loved the designer. The shoes that matched the dress were violet high heels with a bow at the toe and bejeweled on the side in the shape of a peacock feather. Nick suspected the latter swayed the decision as Maggie would often admire the shoes and smile. All he knew for sure was that with her native black hair and olive skin, she looked like a princess herself.

Maggie reached up to make sure the strand of golden pearls with a large central diamond pendant still hung around her neck, then touched her earlobes to check the matching earrings. She had resisted wearing the expensive set, especially when Wright told them it had belonged to his mother, but he had insisted.

Wright had said with an eye on Maggie, "The Chinese believe that the South Sea golden pearl imbues the wearer with wealth and prosperity. You deserve all of that." His attentiveness toward Maggie was making Nick jealous. He didn't think Wright was flirting with her, but he knew he could never accomplish what Wright had. Right now, he could hardly make his own car payment. After being away from surgery for six months, he had no idea what he was going to do or even how he was going to make a living. It was easy to compare himself to others, but he didn't even have a yardstick long enough to measure himself against Wright. It wasn't that they lived different lives—they lived on different planets, and Nick's planet didn't have any golden pearls.

Nick rubbed his buzzed head. His hair was in that awkward in-between stage, neither short nor long. Wright's hair flowed like a horse's mane, and his chiseled jaw and high cheekbones smacked of a model's mug, but it was his casual swagger that Nick couldn't stomach. The head of this financial kingdom wore a white linen shirt unbuttoned to his chest with the collar slightly but perfectly turned up. A bevy of bracelets wrapped one wrist and a strand of hardwood beads hung from his neck. Nick watched Wright work the crowd with ease, hugging guests and conversing with employees. Wright socialized with such warmth, it was no wonder he was not only respected but beloved.

Nick looked at Maggie and back at Wright and realized something. He had only met Maggie's handsome Blackfeet brothers a few times, but Wright looked like a long-lost brother with his tanned skin and dark features. Only his black eye marred his physiognomy, but Nick was astounded to see that it was either healing remarkably fast or was well concealed by makeup.

He sighed, leaned to Maggie and cupped his hand over her ear. "Sure you don't want to dance?" He had to shout to be heard over the music.

She turned to him and said into his ear, "Nick, you are sweet to ask, but I'm afraid I can hardly breathe in this dress, and besides, I'd break a leg in these shoes." She touched his cheek. He faked a pout that made her smile. "Okay, if they play a slow one."

Nick leaned back in his chair and sighed. What in the world was he going to do with himself? He wasn't sure he even wanted to go back to medicine and trauma call. Washing out an open tib/fib fracture at three o'clock in the morning no longer sounded appealing. Chang would want him to ask the Holy Spirit. "If you desire the fruit of the Spirit in your life, you must let go of all your attempts at figuring it out yourself and let the Holy Spirit, who dwells in you, take full control of your life."

Nick closed his eyes. *Father, what am I to do?* He wanted to live in the hope that Chang so easily talked about—both now and for all eternity. Just like his eyes still getting accustomed to their restored sight, his spirit tried to see past his circumstances. Chang talked about the patriarchs of faith such as Noah, Moses, and Abraham. "They were people that could look beyond the horizon." Nick loved the image, as though there was a way to gaze past the problems and hardships of life.

He listened for God's Spirit to guide him, but all he could hear was the throbbing of the bass guitar and the reveling partygoers. Suddenly a loud cheer dominated the sounds, and twenty cheerleaders, complete with pom-poms and miniskirts, came bounding up the stairs to the stage. The band struck up Kool and the Gang's "Celebration." The crowd went wild. People poured onto the dance floor as the girls shook everything they had and then some. Nick could feel the call of his lesser comforts. *Rolling Stone* magazine called it *sex, drugs, and rock and roll, baby.* He shook his head at the state of the world, which wooed him like a drug.

The ruckus rose to a crescendo and Nick didn't think he could take much more. Then Wright entered stage right, ambling past the cheerleaders to center stage, where a band member handed him a microphone. The crowd came to a hush, but the silence lasted only a moment.

The Zelutex logo flashed on the huge monitor above Wright. An animated seedling of three healthy green leaves sprouted from the logo. Beneath the flourishing logo was the company's mission statement: *Better Living Through Science.* The crowd erupted with whoops and applause.

Wright smiled expansively and let his people revel. He pointed to the logo and the crowd, put his hands together in gratitude over his heart and bowed.

"We love you, Wright," his flock shouted. Someone started to chant "Zelutex!" and the people took it up and repeated it over and over until Wright held up his hands to quell the melee.

"Is this a glorious night or what?" he yelled into the microphone, and everyone cheered.

He raised the mic above the boisterous crowd that devoured his showmanship. They screamed as if Sir Elton John was on stage. Digital fireworks erupted on the monstrous monitor above Wright as well as on other flatscreens strategically placed around the room. The fireworks melted into the marketing campaign to promote the new medication. The Welltrex logo flashed on the screen. It was similar to the Zelutex logo. An animated leaf sprouted from the Welltrex letters. Then a raindrop dissolved the sprout and the letters, replacing them with a light-blue, heart-shaped tablet that said *200mg once a day*. The words floated in a drop of water.

"Welltrex is going to change the world as we know it," Wright yelled over the roaring crowd. "Welltrex brings hope to millions of people around the world—those who are suffering from depression, anxiety, chronic and acute pain, and those needing treatment for their addictions. Those who have given up hope."

Thunderous applause erupted.

"Come on!" Wright incited the crowd, swelling the applause and letting their optimism reach a climax. Finally, he raised his hands to silence his disciples and spoke prophetically. "The ancient manuscripts tell us that those who give a cup of cold water to those in need will never lose their reward."

The word *reward* reignited the crowd.

"I'll let you in on a little secret," Wright said, as if there could be any secrets in a room of four thousand people. "Welltrex will certainly make our lives a bit easier."

He laughed, holding out his arms to embrace all four thousand guests. His eyes sparkled. He dropped the microphone from his hand and threw his head back as balloons and confetti rained from the ceiling.

The band broke into the O'Jays' "For the Love of Money," and the boisterous music crackled through the speakers.

* * *

Nick rolled his eyes. "I promise I won't tell your new benefactor what I think, but that performance was everything I hate about industrialized medicine," he said into Maggie's ear as he held her close, swaying to the Eagles' "Desperado." "It's shameful."

"Yeah, it was a bit over the top," Maggie agreed.

He pulled her closer, his hand on the small of her back. "Have I told you how beautiful you look tonight?"

"Well, not in the last five minutes," she laughed.

Her body was warm against his, and he wanted to lean down and kiss her but resisted. "You okay tonight?"

When she laid her head on his chest, he could feel her body tremble and her spirit sink. He held her and waited. He understood where her angst came from. He battled it too. When Maggie had given her presentation last night, showing pictures of her and John building their lives together, Nick had felt like an outsider, an intruder. He knew his love for John was a mere fraction of Maggie's and what she must be feeling—that somehow desiring tenderness and affection from another was a betrayal of that love.

He didn't want her to suffer any longer and decided to come clean. "Mags, I love you so much. I'm not sure I will ever love another as deeply. I can only imagine what your heart must feel—what you are going through. Just know I am here for you...willing to give you space...willing to hold you close or love you from afar."

She began to sob and let go of his hand, wrapping both hands around his waist and burying her head into his chest.

She looked up at him, her dark eyes swollen with emotion. "Nicklaus, you know me as well as anyone. Thank you. You remember that dream I told you about? I know in my heart that John wants me to love and be loved again. I'm having trouble with that. I'm not sure I'm ready to let go. Thank you for understanding and helping me through this." She stretched on her tip-toes and kissed him tenderly on the neck.

"You want to get out of here for some fresh air?" Nick asked. She nodded. He took her hand and led her off the dance floor through the tables of employees celebrating their good fortune with Jell-O shots.

Nick and Maggie exited into the garden with its cool ocean air and glorious view of a full moon rising in the east over the Singapore Strait. The moon glistened on the water brightly enough to illuminate the ships coming to the port.

"That's better." Maggie sniffed. "I didn't realize I was suffocating in the heat and commotion in there."

They had walked only a few yards into the garden solitude when they heard Wright's voice behind them. "I thought I might find you two out here."

Nick and Maggie turned to see Wright accompanied by two women—a middle-aged woman in a gray pantsuit with a severe limp in her right leg, and a younger woman with shoulder-length straight hair framing cat-eye glasses.

"Dr. Hart and Ms. Russell, I would like to introduce you to Ms. Leah Boxler and Dr. Amy Johnson. Ms. Boxler"—he indicated the older woman—"is the CEO and my right-hand person here at Zelutex, and Dr. Amy"—he nodded at the other woman—"is our medical director."

Boxler's grip was as firm as her German accent was thick. "Dr. Hart, Ms. Russell, it is a pleasure to have you in Singapore and to our company's little celebration."

Wright must have caught Nick's disapproving glance at Maggie. "Speaking of which, I hope you will forgive us for the show," Wright said. "I too, feel like I need a long, hot shower."

He said exactly what Nick was feeling.

Wright laughed. "I believe, Dr. Hart, that your scriptures tell us to be as shrewd as snakes and as innocent as doves. I'm afraid tonight we must slither like snakes. My people work hard for their money. They practically have to sell their souls to make a living, and it's all they have to live for. They've earned some R and R. Believe me, I appreciate their work, and I wanted to give them a chance to relax and pat themselves on the back for a job well done."

Nick was surprised to hear Wright's candor.

"I know you must think this is exactly what is wrong with medicine, and you would be partly correct. But the sad truth is, to get these life-changing medications into the hands of the people they can help, we must operate within the world's system. Our sales reps must sit day in and day out in physicians' offices, pandering to them, stroking their egos, and begging for two minutes of their limited time. Don't get me wrong; my employees are wonderful people. They are like you and me, trying to navigate their way through life, provide for themselves and their families and dodge the hardships in life. Making money for the company and for themselves is how they fill their lives—"

"We encourage them to make money because money buys happiness," Boxler interrupted, surprising Nick.

Wright didn't seem to notice.

"The better drugs we produce, the more they can sell," Boxler said. "The more money they make, the better their lives are. Doctors are the same, yes? The more procedures you do, the better living you make."

"It doesn't make it right," Nick said, and Maggie squeezed his arm, trying to restrain his politics. "I'm sorry" he said quickly, "I mean no disrespect, it's just that—"

"No apology needed, Nick," Wright interrupted. "You are very right. It's awful what we have to go through." He put his hand on Nick's shoulder. "I wish there were a better way. If you know one, I'm all ears."

"Yeah, you and a room full of US senators would like to know the secret." Nick laughed, lightening the mood.

They all chuckled, even Boxler, though just barely.

Wright held out his hand to the blond woman. "Dr. Amy here is from New Zealand and has led the charge on Welltrex, directing the research and development."

Nick shook her hand. Her grip was limp, but her smile was genuine and her accent pleasant.

Amy and Maggie shook hands. "Mr. Paul was telling us about your presentation last night," Amy remarked. "He said there was not a dry eye in the hall, aye. I always wanted to do mission work." She lowered her gaze. "I guess I got caught up in other things."

Maggie's sincerity came to Amy's rescue. "Well, you have an open invitation to Guatemala. We could always use your help. I have recently come into a small fortune, and we are going to expand the hospital," she chuckled, smiling gratefully at Wright.

"That is kind of you," Amy said.

"Amy, tell Dr. Hart and Ms. Russell about Welltrex," Wright said.

The woman blushed. "I'm afraid I'm not a good salesman. But the drug has performed splendidly. The mechanism of action is quite complex. In the ventral tegmental region, located in the mesencephalic section of the brain stem, lies a compact group of dopamine-secreting neurons whose axons end in the nucleus accumbens. The stimulation of these neurons in the zone produces pleasurable sensations—similar to an orgasm."

Nick rested his chin on his hand trying to remember anything from his neuroanatomy classes in med school. Maggie's face was blank.

Wright laughed loudly, making Amy blush. "Yes, I get the same look when she tells me these things. One of my favorite quotes is from Daniel Goleman of the *New York Times*: 'The essence of emotion—the rapture of happiness, the numbness of depression, the angst of anxiety—is as evanescent as a spring rainbow. It is hard enough for a poet to capture, let alone a neuroscientist.' But that is what we are all about here at Zelutex, developing novel and innovative drugs and bioidentical hormones that can help our patients overcome some of life's most difficult hurdles."

A ship's horn blasted the evening stillness, making Maggie jump and the others laugh.

"Well," Wright said, "that's a signal for me to stop talking business and science and let you enjoy this beautiful evening."

Boxler stepped closer to Nick and Maggie. She spoke as if reprimanding small children. "Before we say good night, I must add that we believe in prosperity with a purpose. We are encouraged by what the company can do to impact the lives of those in Guatemala. Mr. Paul would not tell you this, but I must. The other day, he personally flew to Borneo, picked up a dying baby, and brought him back to Singapore for life-changing surgery. The child survived thanks to all that you see here. You can do more good with money than without."

Nick crossed his arms over his chest. There was something about the statement and the woman that made his skin crawl.

"You disagree?" Boxler asked, stared into his eyes and did not flinch.

Nick looked past her and out into the bay. How did he answer that and why did he feel so conflicted? "Maybe it's not that simple," he said.

"To me it is black and white," she retorted in an even stronger German accent.

He glanced at Wright who seemed unfazed by the conversation and seemed to be truly interested in his opinion.

"Look, Mr. Paul may be one of the few that walks out that philosophy," Nick said. "I guess I see lots of wealthy people that are more interested in building their own kingdoms: bigger houses, places on the lake, more toys. It is like the benevolence is an afterthought or some way to ease their conscience of their wealth and lifestyles."

Boxler frowned at his bluntness. Wright seemed to approve of it.

Nick raised his hands in surrender. "You know as I stand here, I honestly can't say that I wouldn't do the same. Isn't it our natural tendency to seek comfort and pleasure? I'd love to have a beautiful home and a second on some ski slope of Colorado." Nick paused and smirked. "And a butler named Alfred…I'm sure that would make my life perfect."

It made all except Boxler laugh.

CHAPTER 14

___

INDIAN PRINCESS

Wright watched with delight as Nick and Maggie lifted the lids off the steamer baskets and swallowed at the sight of the Chinese dumplings. Both appeared refreshed after a relaxing day at the compound.

"Dim sum?" Nick asked. "You must have read my mind."

"Yes, there are some, and then there is dim sum," Wright said, making them laugh. "I heard you mention yesterday that you'd like to try it. I had some flown in this afternoon from a famous hole-in-the-wall in Hong Kong. I hope you don't mind."

"Mind? This is awesome," Nick said. "Thank you!" He used a pair of chopsticks to stab a dumpling and pushed the entire morsel into his mouth. "Ohmygosh," he said with a full mouth. "That's amazing. Dim some good dumplings." He laughed, pleased with his joke.

"That one is my favorite. It is *xiā jiǎo*, shrimp dumplings. But you should try this one as well," Wright pointed to another. "*Mài*, steamed dumplings with pork and prawns."

"I'm going to gain fifty pounds while I'm here if you keep feeding us like this," Maggie laughed, stabbing a pork and prawn dumpling.

"I'm so glad you're pleased. The cooks prepared the dim sum only hours ago. That's one thing about having resources—

you can have whatever you want whenever you want it. And because you are my guests, the same goes for you," Wright said. Giving the people around him wonderful surprises was one of his favorite things.

Christian poured them each a glass of fresh-squeezed lemonade. "Will you be needing anything else, sir?" the young man asked.

"No thank you, Christian, we can take it from here."

After they filled their plates with an assortment of dim sum, he invited his guests to join him in the Adirondack beach chairs facing the ocean—no shoes required on the white sand beach. His staff had arranged the chairs in the shade of two large umbrellas at the edge of the aqua-blue water, which gently broke onto the shore.

He looked at the setting sun. "It looks like we will have two shows tonight. One by the universe and the other…the year of the horse. Happy new year," he said and raised a toast with his glass. "May it be a prosperous and healthy new year for you both. I am thankful to count you as my new friends." He took a long drink.

Wright waited for his guests to select their seats before taking the empty one.

"Wright, speaking of healthy, I couldn't help notice how fast your eye has healed," Nick said.

"Yes, leave it to the good doctor's power of observation," Wright said and pushed on his eye. It was no longer sore. "I will tell you a secret; I cheated," Wright said. "In fact, I was hoping this subject would come up, as I would like your professional opinion on a new medication we will launch in six months. I imagine that you know about HCG, human chorionic gonadotropin?"

"Yes, of course. It's produced by the placenta and helps the baby grow and develop. I know there has been some experimentation with its healing properties."

Maggie spoke up, "I've heard of people using it for weight loss. I better order some now," she said, patted her thighs and laughed.

"You are both correct. Another lesser-known growth hormone is insulin-like growth factor-1—"

Nick interrupted him and explained to Maggie, "IGF-1 is essential for the formation of bone and cartilage. It's why adolescents shoot up in height at puberty." He turned back to Wright. "There is some pretty convincing research about injecting it into joints for cartilage regeneration."

"Good, yes." He looked at them both with complete seriousness. "What if I told you—and you will have to keep this zombie, a secret—what if we have found a way to stimulate the body into producing more of its own IGF-1, creating healing in every area of the body."

Nick pinched his lips together and nodded. "I'd be impressed. And it's working?"

"We are still in our clinical trials, but yes"—he pointed to his eye—"it is working well."

"But once IGF-1 increases, doesn't the body downregulate it and slow its production?" Nick asked.

Wright smiled coyly and turned to Maggie. "Your doctor friend understands the issues with hormonal replacement. Producing bioidentical hormones is the easy part, but the human body is fickle. You start to feed the body with its own hormones, and its sophisticated regulatory system will work to keep the hormones in homeostasis…balance."

"The body is amazing. God has made us fearfully and wonderfully," Maggie said.

Wright bobbed his head side to side. "Yes, for the most part, it's just sometimes the body needs a little encouragement—a little nudge in the right direction." He turned to Nick. "We have learned some techniques to fool the body. They are quite proprietary."

"You could tell me, but would have to kill me?" Nick laughed.

"Quite!" Wright agreed. "Actually, I was going to ask you and Maggie if you would consider going with me to Borneo tomorrow. I planned on taking a few days off after the launch of Welltrex, and I would love to have you both join me. I will bore you with our research facility. And then it would be my honor to show you one of the most enchanting places on the planet, the jungle of Sarawak: elephants, orangutans, the clouded leopard, and the most genteel people group on earth—the Iban."

"You mentioned that Christian was Iban. I hate sounding dumb, but I've never heard of that people group." Maggie asked.

"Yes, the Iban—the original headhunters of the jungle."

"Headhunters?" she said with alarm. "That doesn't sound very genteel."

"Well, that was then." He smiled.

"You have shown us so much hospitality, are you sure you're not tired of us?" Nick asked. "We're not scheduled to leave until Tuesday. Isn't it a bother? It sounds amazing, though."

Wright waved away Nick's concern. "Okay, it's set then. Thank you for going with me. I'm afraid in my position it's difficult to find true friends."

"That's hard for me to imagine," Maggie said.

"Great wealth brings you many things, but heart friends are hard to find. One of my wealthy acquaintances says it best: 'lonely, but never alone.'"

"Did your wealth come from Zelutex?" Nick asked.

"In part. The company has done extremely well, and I am financially diversified, but I can't take credit for it all. I inherited a great deal. But the funny thing is, growing up I thought we were poor. We lived a very simple life. I spent my youth on a large animal preserve in the jungles of India. It wasn't until I was sent away to an international school in England that I learned we owned the hundred-thousand-acre preserve."

"You went to school in England?" Maggie asked.

"Yes, then Harvard Business School." He turned solemn. "When I was away at school, my parents were killed in a plane crash. I inherited a vast fortune." Wright's constant companion of loneliness swelled in his chest.

"I'm so sorry," Maggie said.

"Yes, I miss them terribly. I didn't care about the money for a long time. I'd rather have my parents back." He let out a loud sigh.

"Do you have siblings?" Maggie asked.

"No, unfortunately, my mother was unable to have more children after me. I guess it was a pretty rough labor. The only family I have remaining is my grandmama, and she just turned ninety-five. I wish you could meet her; she's something else."

"Does she live in Singapore?"

Wright laughed. "She would not step one foot into Singapore. She lives in Calcutta and thinks there are too many Limeys, Brits here. I'm afraid she's not very fond of them—including my father, who was one. My mother was to wed a proper Indian man, a doctor of royal blood, when she fell in love with the English scoundrel. He didn't have a title, not even a British one. My father was a good man; he just wasn't who Grandmama had picked out. My grandmama is a very proper Indian woman, but the heart feels what the heart feels."

"That's so true," Maggie said. "It's so funny to have you talk about Indians. I guess I'm always thinking Native American Indians when I hear the term, but you're right—India, Indians." She laughed.

"Maggie, what is interesting is when Christopher Columbus discovered the indigenous people of the Americas, he thought he was still in the Indies and therefore called them Indians, so both are right."

Maggie smiled at him. Her long black hair flowed in the evening breeze, and she shivered. He reached into a cedar box next to the chairs and pulled out a cashmere blanket and handed it to her.

"Nick, you want something to wrap up in?"

"I'm good, thank you."

They sat in silence and the clouds lit with pinks and yellows. The bay of Wright's island opened to the setting sun on the eastern horizon, turning the sea into a golden sheen as it sank slowly toward the world's edge.

"Nick, how are your eyes feeling?" Wright asked.

Nick nodded his head from side to side. "Still a bit blurry at times, but so much better. Maybe I need to hear more about your IGF-1 medication."

"Yes, I'm looking forward to that," Wright said.

"I think God has it all under control," Maggie chastised, causing them to grow silent again.

Wright stood up, began to pace, then sat down in front of Maggie and Nick in the sand. "I have been waiting for the right time to tell you something and now is as good a time as any, I suppose. This is for full disclosure." He scooped up a handful of sand and let it pour from one hand to another. "Maggie, have you ever thought about why the foundation picked the Hope Center?"

He looked straight into her eyes, and she shrugged at the question. "Well, I—"

"I mean no offense," he interrupted her. "We get thousands of applications each year. You had a slight advantage." He picked up another handful of sand. "Don't get me wrong, we love your ministry and your work, but I have to admit about knowing you before we received your application."

Maggie looked taken aback.

Wright decided to face the subject head-on. "My foundation was one of the biggest supporters of FOCO." As the acronym left his mouth, he could tell by their stunned faces that they recognized the Friends of Children Organization. The group that North Korean terrorists used to spread a virus that changed the world. They nearly killed Nick and his friends. More significantly, they were the group that murdered Maggie's husband.

Maggie gasped and Nick stood.

"What the…?" Nick started.

"Please, please know that I had nothing, absolutely nothing, to do with the North Korean conspiracy or what happened to you both in Guatemala." He looked at Maggie and thought she might be sick. Her eyes filled with tears and overflowed. "Maggie, Nick, please believe me. The Wright's Kids Foundation had no idea…and as you know, FOCO was doing some wonderful things around the world. They were simply hijacked by those hideous people."

Nick and Maggie looked mortified and unconvinced. "I know this news is difficult."

"Difficult?" Nick said. "I'll tell you about difficult! Those people killed my best friend and almost killed me," he said, wrapping his hands around his own neck. "They released their modified mumps virus that affected the entire population of the world." Nick picked up a stone from the sand and threw it hard into the sea.

Wright understood this conversation was going to be

complicated but wasn't sure where to take it from here, so he sat and let them process.

Finally, Maggie wiped at her tears and straightened her back and shoulders. "Mr. Paul…Wright…look, I understand. It's just that those wounds run deep. Even after four years, I have a difficult time forgiving those people. Believe me, I have worked and worked on forgiveness—prayed about it, been prayed over, had counsel…everything I know to do. Yet it's a moment by moment thing for me *still*," she said. "The crazy thing is, I know that forgiveness is one of the cornerstones of our walk with God. That the prisoner I'm letting out of the jail of hate is actually me." She let out a loud sigh. "Ew boy. Help me, Lord. I think this has caught me off guard. It's just like God, pulling at the scab that I think is healed—exposing it, putting on some more loving salve, and wanting it to heal once and for all."

"Then I ask that you forgive me as well," Wright asked. "Maybe I should have told you sooner. I don't know. Believe me, I have felt terrible about the situation all these years. We just simply had no idea what that group was doing and how they used the organization's name for evil."

They both seemed to understand. They weren't happy, but empathetic.

"Of course, we followed the news and the US Congressional hearings carefully, and even the foundation was scrutinized. We were as duped as everyone. I read about both of you during that time, and now I am hopeful I can make amends."

He waited. Maggie seemed to settle the matter in her heart, and her shoulders relaxed.

"You're right, this was not your fault," she said, nodding. "It's just that I thought I was looking so smart to receive this grant." The smile returned to her beautiful face.

"That, Maggie…that point has not changed one bit. You and the Hope Center are more deserving than anyone I know, and *that* is the truth."

A brilliant flash followed by an echoing boom exploded over the city as if to emphasize the point. The massive pyrotechnics display marked the beginning of the year of the horse.

* * *

The fireworks exceeded Wright's expectations. Remnants of the light show flashed in his vision when he returned to his room in the main house and turned on the control panel next to his bed. A large-screen TV rose from the dresser, and a full-color image appeared. It was not of any late-night show, but something better—Maggie was undressing for her shower. He was pleased when Nick and Maggie had only hugged, parted, and then went straight to their respective rooms.

He trusted that the oxytocin, continuously sprayed in her room, would work. Scented with the same men's musk cologne that he wore, it caused her brain to bond to him without her being aware of the attraction. A student of history, he loved the fact that musk was originally harvested from a small musk deer native to the mountains of the Himalayas. The gland sac contained a liquid that attracted mates. His tincture was much more sophisticated and potent.

His marketing executives at Zelutex called the company's oxytocin spray Confide. One member affectionately called it the 'cuddling cure' because oxytocin is naturally released in the human brain by touching and hugging. It's secreted in high amounts during sex, speeding up the attachment to one's partner—stimulating the brain to remember and bond with the smell, voice, and eye color.

Oxytocin took longer than the feel-good hormone, dopamine, to be released, but it achieved a deeper, safer, and longer lasting effect. Zelutex's research showed that their artificial oxytocin in Confide created the same relaxation and arousal in both men and women.

He could create the same level of trust and closeness in Maggie without touching her. He looked over at his nightstand at two pictures he held dear—the same picture that his Grandmama cherished of his mother, and a picture he had enlarged from Maggie's application. The two women looked like they could be sisters—two Indian princesses.

CHAPTER 15

THE HUNTSMAN RETURNS

Robert's seniority and financial security allowed him to work as the butler at the Zelutex Research Center only when Master Paul was present. He had taken the weekend to catch up on his duties as chief of their longhouse and drank a bit too much *tuak*, socializing with the other elders. Now he woke from a terrifying dream drenched in sweat. His heart pounded violently, and he struggled to catch his breath. *Was it real?* His body did not know the difference, and his mind tried convincing it that the terror was simply a nightmare. He gripped the sides of his hammock and wiped his brow. *A dream. It was only a dream.*

He tilted his head so his ear could capture any sound in the longhouse beyond the drumming of his heart. It was silent. Even the insects and the toads were silent. He lifted his head from the hammock and looked toward his wife's bed. She slept, and in the pitch black, he could hear the deep breathing of her slumber. He smiled to himself—how he loved that woman. Sixty-three years of marriage and they had never spent a night apart. He was sixteen and she was fifteen when they married.

When Master Paul bought the piece of land from him, Robert's first purchase was a soft mattress for his love. He still preferred the hammock except for those scarce nights of intimacy. They were getting rarer now that he was almost eighty.

He glanced around the rest of the room and could see and hear nothing. Their seven children were all long gone and lived on their own.

He rested his head back on his pillow not sure he wanted to think about the dream, but it had unsettled his spirit. It reminded him of the old days when all of life's actions and decisions spun around divination, augury, and omens. Before he was a Christian, he would have called this sort of dream a warning—an ominous, petrifying forewarning. But he knew now that Jesus in him was greater than the evils lurking in the shadows and around the dark corners of his mind. The missionaries of long ago had taught him that. He no longer had to fear every cloud formation, or a bird sitting on a post, or a deer licking at a tree. He remembered all the chanting, all the sacrifices, all the rituals, and the offerings that took up most of their days to appease their gods or ward off the evil spirits ready to devour them at any moment.

But still, he could not help but worry. He believed, like his ancestors before him, that there were good spirits ready to help him and evil ones eager to harm him. The missionaries had different names for them—the Holy Spirit and the demons. Even the missionaries told him that God still speaks to his people in dreams. *Is your Spirit talking to me, Father?*

As a Christian, he believed, like his ancient people, that he had a soul that would live on after death. His eternal life would differ little from his existence in the flesh, except he would be with God, the Father—the one his ancestors called the supreme God, *Bunsu Petara.*

Robert reached up and wiped his face, trying to rub out the image of the creature he saw. In his dream, he was still the chief of a great longhouse, the *tuai rumah,* and he lay in his hammock. The nightmare started with a faint sound like the rustle of the wind at their apartment door. He stood to investigate. He opened the door to one of the longhouse dogs wagging its tail. As he let the dog in, the dream morphed like only dreams can, and the dog mutated into a hideous beast—a lizard with the head of a dragon and putrid breath of rotting flesh. It dragged its deformed body into the apartment. The beast was covered in large scales that were sloughing off, exposing decaying tissue. His hind legs were useless, and they trailed behind like balls and chains. It had the tongue of a snake that flickered in and out, searching out its next victim. The creature's tongue wrapped around his leg and Robert lunged toward a large machete hung by the door. The dream ended there, and he woke up in sweat, not knowing if he had slain the beast or not.

The more Robert thought about the image, the harder his heart throbbed in his chest, giving him chest pain. He called out the name of Jesus, and he felt his body relax.

He thought of a story he had not pondered for years. His grandfather terrified him with the story of the evil Huntsman. Grandfather went on and on about *Telichu* and his younger brother *Telichai*. The brothers were mighty hunters, spending many days in the jungle away from the comfort of the longhouse. *Telichu* turned to evil, and his physical appearance changed until he transformed into a hideous demon—an *antu gerasi*, a demon that hunts the unfortunate souls of their people who disobey the warning revealed to them in dreams and omens.

The people banished *Telichu* from the longhouse, but before he left, the brothers divided up their hunting dogs. Those that went with the older brother into the demons' world turned into *pasun*—hideous lizards. Many Iban, even to this day, conclude that if they hear this *pasun* lizard nearby, the Huntsman is not far away. Robert tried not to believe. By ancient tradition, he should burn the bark of the *lukai* tree, but now that he was a Christian, he knew to pray. There was an evil approaching, and he didn't know what.

He was praying and almost back to sleep when the still of the night broke.

"AAAAAGH!" A woman's cry thundered through Robert's slumber. The shout turned into screams. As the cries grew louder and more desperate, the mongrel dogs howled, and the longhouse sprang to life in the darkness. Robert leaped from his hammock. He sprang for the entry, grabbing a flashlight and machete and flung open the door. He was not the first into the shared hallway of the longhouse, and flashlight beams bounced around the space as the screams grew louder and a crowd formed. Robert raced down the common area to the sounds of the anguish.

As he bound through the door to the last apartment, he pushed his way past the people. A woman held a man in her arms. It was his granddaughter holding her husband. Blood was everywhere, and the man's head decapitated.

CHAPTER 16

PHARMA

The helicopter rides were almost tolerable for Nick, especially when he realized what a fantastic tool it was for the rich and powerful to move from one spot to another. It was a beautiful day to fly from Singapore to Sarawak on the island of Borneo and besides, Wright was a competent and careful pilot. The only time Nick's anxiety returned during the flight was when Wright swooped down to show them a superpod of dolphins cruising through the South China Sea. Nick had given up the copilot's seat to Maggie so she could enjoy the view next to Wright. She seemed to be enjoying herself.

Wright had explained again that Borneo was shared by three countries, Malaysia, Brunei and Indonesia, making for a strange geopolitical region. They landed in the Malaysian portion of Sarawak after flying over the third largest city, Kuching. The total population of Borneo was slightly over twenty million people, Wright had explained. As the helicopter flew east, it rapidly left civilization, flying over a vast and ancient rainforest until it came to a huge lake. Landing at the research facility felt like dropping down into the Jurassic Park complex.

The Zelutex Research Center was everything Wright had described. They met Dr. Amy in the magnificent three-story atrium that overlooked the Batang Ai Lake with the sun illuminating the space.

"So, what do you think?" Wright asked.

"Amazing," Nick said. "Especially for being in the middle of the jungle. Is the only way to get here by helicopter?"

"Well, it's the fastest, but there is a road from Kuching," Wright said.

"If your back can stand the bumpy five-hour ride," Dr. Amy added.

"Yes, I'm afraid you've taken the trip too many times," Wright said and laughed. "You should get your pilot's license, Dr. Amy."

Nick wasn't sure if Wright was strictly teasing the doctor, but it was something he had always thought about doing. He wondered if it would temper his fear of flying if he were in control. Maybe with this break from medicine, it was a good time to fulfill that dream. He wasn't so sure he would pass the physical with his eye condition.

"What do you do here?" Maggie asked, looking at a massive sculpture in the middle of the atrium of two hands holding a brain.

Wright held out his hand to Dr. Amy to explain.

"Developing a new medication takes years," Amy said. "It obviously begins with the initial idea and then the test-tube work."

"That is done mostly at our facility in Singapore," Wright added.

"Once we establish the compound and develop it in the lab," Amy said, "we start with preclinical research such as animal testing to answer basic safety questions. That is done initially on mice, and then on orangutans."

"Orangutans' genetic makeup is similar to humans'," Wright said. "We share 97 percent of the same DNA. So they make splendid test subjects, plus the fact they are fun to be around."

"Once we determine that the drug is safe, we begin clinical trials," Amy said.

"They are given to humans?" Maggie asked.

"Yes. We start with minimal doses, increasing them gradually. The patients are monitored carefully for any adverse effects."

"Isn't that scary?" Maggie asked.

"Not really. We are confident in the results of the animal testing," Wright said.

Maggie laughed. "I meant for the patients."

"Yes, of course." Wright seemed slightly embarrassed. "The patients are well compensated, so they are very cooperative."

"Do you do the clinical trials here in Sarawak?" Nick asked.

"Yes, here and in South Africa," Wright said. "The regulatory laws are much more lax, and it keeps our costs down. To do the advanced clinical trials that we do for each drug would cost around fifty million US dollars. We can do it in Borneo or South Africa for half that. You have to understand that a new drug like Welltrex costs 250 million dollars...a quarter of a *billion* dollars to develop," he said.

Nick whistled through his teeth. "Wow, I had no idea."

"Yes, you and most of the medical community. However, most pharmaceutical companies report that it costs over two billion dollars to launch a new drug, so that estimate is a bit overinflated."

"A bit?" Nick asked.

"Well, they roll in all their costs for doing business. New buildings, payroll, marketing and such. Still, 250 million dollars is a lot of money."

"So, if it cost fifty million for the research, what about the rest?" Maggie asked.

"That's the sad part. A good third of that, around a hundred million, goes to all the regulatory work...getting approvals in all the different countries...and the lawyers."

"Don't you simply have to get approval from the FDA?" Nick asked.

"For the States, yes. But every country has its own regulatory body, and they all want their cut. And did I mention the lawyers? They're like sharks circling fresh bait." This caused everyone to laugh. "Once we get regulatory clearance from the governing bodies, we launch the product."

"When it goes to the general public, we start an intensive monitoring program for any side effects. It's called post-marketing surveillance," Dr. Amy said.

"We have to be careful during this phase because the regulatory bodies would love to find a problem with the drug. We might be forced to expand studies or design further research and then reapply all over again so they can require you to pay more money...did I mention lawyers?" Wright added.

"So how does your company make any money after all that?" Maggie asked.

Wright nodded and looked like he was trying to decide how to comment, then looked Maggie in the eye and confided, "We do okay. Welltrex is expected to be a two-billion-dollar drug."

"But if you spent a quarter of a billion to develop it and two billion to run the company, how does that work?" Maggie asked.

Wright smiled at her. "Two billion in *profits...a year*," he added. "And we got a nice bump in the stock market this morning after the launch. Zelutex is up 10 percent."

Maggie mouthed a *wow* and nodded in understanding.

"Gross profits," Nick said under his breath. "The grosser, the better."

* * *

The section with the mice looked like any advanced university laboratory in the States, boring and a bit smelly. They passed through the area without stopping.

Soon Nick and the rest of the group stood in an area that was nothing like he could have imagined. He had seen orangutans in a zoo, but this experience was like being transported to another time and space—the planet of the apes. The group gathered on an observation deck overlooking a jungle full of the large orangish-red, shaggy-haired beasts.

There were no concrete floors, tire swings or ropes. No fake ponds or food boxes. Just massive trees and plants—a thick jungle habitat full of orangutans looking as much at home as if the group had stumbled across them on a jungle trek.

"I would ask that you whisper out here. They know we're here, but we try the best we can to not disturb them," Wright whispered.

Within the large troop mothers fed their babies and juveniles raced and chased, making a racket. Two of the orangutans faced off and fought over a tree limb. The squabble only lasted a minute when the larger of the two snatched it away and headed for the top of the trees while the other complained loudly.

"Must be siblings," Maggie said.

"As a matter of fact, you're right. Only one year apart. We have five main families of orangutans," Wright said. "Maggie, do you know what you call a group of orangutans?"

Maggie shook her head.

"A congress."

"Really?" she whispered.

"Yeah, take a trip to Capitol Hill in Washington," Nick said, "And you'll see the resemblance." He covered his mouth to keep from laughing out loud.

"I think *our* congress is smarter," Wright added.

The biggest orangutan, with an enormous flat face, sat at the bottom of a giant tree eating a banana, oblivious to all the activity until a female nonchalantly strolled by. She stopped before passing completely and thrust her heinie in the air at the great ape. The male reached out to grab her buttocks, but the female slapped his hand away, bellowed loudly and ran off into the trees.

Nick covered his mouth again with his hand to keep from laughing. When the urge subsided, he whispered, "You're right; we're not much different."

"That's our oldest male, we named him King Louie after the *Jungle Book* character," Wright said. "We're very proud of what we have accomplished here. We have around two hundred apes on over a hundred acres of wild habitat. Our breeding program is the most successful in the world, and we have been able to release hundreds more into the wild."

"That's wonderful," Maggie said.

"We think of them as our co-researchers. Besides helping us, we are protecting these great friends of the jungle and ensuring their survival. Borneo and Sumatra, an island to our west, are the only remaining places in the world where the orangutans have survived. They were almost hunted to extinction."

Wright pulled his phone from his front pocket and looked at it. "Please, you all must be starving. Let's go have some lunch, and we can finish our discussion."

* * *

Before sitting down for lunch, Dr. Amy gave Maggie and Nick a quick tour of the clinical area. Decked out as completely as some of the world's most advanced health centers, it had amazing capabilities—the latest generation CT scanner, MRI imaging and even a Positron Emission Tomography unit. Dr. Amy explained to Maggie that the PET scanner used radioactive tracers able to map the brain in highly detailed images.

They finished their tour and Wright invited them to sit at a table in the third-floor conference room overlooking the lake on one side and the rainforest on the other. Situated like a sentry tower, the room sat on top of the complex, overlooking the jungle canopy teaming with aviary life. The view was magnificent, and the table they sat around appeared to be carved out of one of the trees of the ancient wilderness.

Two young women carried in trays of food, set them on the table and removed the silver cloches. One tray held a large, steaming tureen of soup and bowls, and the other, plates of fish and a green vegetable.

"Ah, I hope you're hungry," Wright said standing to serve the soup and having to fight his helper for the ladle. "I've got it." He smiled at the woman, who relented. "This is Sarawak Laksa… rice noodles, coconut milk, prawns, chicken and a slice of egg."

"It smells delicious," Maggie said.

After he had ladled a helping into each bowl, he turned to the other tray. "And this is salted *terubok* fish." He pinched off a chunk of the dried fish. "It's salty and crunchy…Borneo potato chips." He laughed. "And the green vegetable is *sayur manis*, sautéed in garlic and soy."

"You have quite the facility here," Nick said. "I know a little about your new medication, Welltrex, and the one that is in development, the IGF-1. What would you say is the heart of Zelutex?"

Wright put down his soup spoon, crossed his arms, and leaned back in the leather chair. "Dr. Hart, I'm not sure I've ever been asked the question quite like that, and I've been on all the business shows. They only want to know about profits, margins and such."

He spun his chair to face the jungle to think, and when he turned back, there was a tear in the corner of his eye.

"When I lost my parents, I was adrift. My whole world turned upside down. I didn't know what to do, so for a while I turned to drugs, and I almost got kicked out of university." He smirked. "They forced me into counseling. I guess it was helpful, but honestly, it seemed like all it did was identify the problem. They finally put me on an antidepressant, which was helpful, but I found the side effects intolerable." He pushed his hair back and sighed. "I guess I could sum up the heart of my company by this: Life is rough, and we are trying to level the playing field for people."

Maggie nodded. She knew how tough life could be and was grateful for Wright's passion for helping people. She admired that quality in a man.

"Pain medication is the second-largest pharmaceutical class globally after cancer meds. It alone is a twenty-four-billion-dollar market. The US and Canada combined consume 95 percent of the product. You think there's that much physical pain in North America?" he asked. "People are treating their emotional pain with opioids. But every medication has risks. For opioids, that risk is death. Over sixty thousand people died last year from overdose."

"Yeah, opioids are prescribed for one out of four Medicaid patients," Nick turned to Maggie and added.

Wright stood as his passion grew. "What if we can change that? What if we can treat pain, addiction, depression, and anxiety another way, with few side effects?" He repeated the company's slogan: "Better living through science."

"And how do you do that?" Maggie asked.

"We do it by manipulating the brain directly." He paused and looked Maggie and then Nick in the eye. "But the brain is the most complex organ in the human body. It's not easy. Two of the brain chemicals we research extensively are dopamine and oxytocin."

"The feel-good hormones," Nick said.

"Exactly," Wright said. "Maggie, get this: dopamine is critical in the reward centers of the brain. When your friend sends you flowers, what they are giving you is a big dose of dopamine in the feel-good center. Dr. Amy can watch this on all her fancy brain scanners. But the brain holds a fine balance—too little dopamine, and you have Parkinson's disease; too much, you become schizophrenic. We have to be very careful."

"And again, we try to minimize the side effect profile while doing so," Dr. Amy said.

Wright was about to add more when the door to the conference room opened, and an old man in an oversized butler suit came through the door pushing a tea cart. He looked frail and pale.

"Ah, Robert," Wright said. "I was worried about you. You weren't there to meet our helicopter." He sounded a bit perturbed.

"I am sorry, sir. We had an incident at the longhouse last night." The man said looking at the floor.

"Well, I'm glad you are well and here now. Everyone, this is my faithful friend, Robert. He is one of the last of the true Iban warriors. Robert, this is Dr. Hart and Ms. Russell."

The man bowed as much as his arthritic back would allow and began pouring tea, starting with Maggie.

"Ms. Russell, would you like cream with your tea?"

His withered hands tremored as he poured and she reached up and touched his sleeve. "Thank you, Robert. Yes, I would love some cream, and please call me Maggie."

Her touch and tone seemed to take the old man aback, but he smiled and looked into her eyes. In addition to gray rings of cataracts rimming his dark eyes, Maggie saw a great sadness. She squeezed his arm and whispered, "God be with you."

A tear formed in his eye and he turned away to his tea cart. She was about to say more when Wright interrupted her.

"In the morning, we will venture upriver to visit the jungle. Rest well tonight as tomorrow you will have the adventure of a lifetime."

CHAPTER 17

ANTU GERASI

"Yes, I saw him," the young woman cried out to the elders in the longhouse. Robert sat with a *manang*, on a bamboo mat, their backs against the wall. Her eyes pleaded with them as she told her story. Five more men sat on the floor in a semicircle behind his granddaughter.

Robert's wife supported their granddaughter from behind by her shoulders. The young woman was not yet twenty, and her whole body shook. "It was like a ghost…an animal," she cried and sobbed into her hands.

"Just tell us what you saw," Robert said gently.

"We were sleeping, and the creature attacked us before I knew what was happening," she sobbed. "I don't know what we did. The creature's eyes were as big as saucers and red like dragon's blood. It had to be *antu gerasi*. It had huge glittering teeth and growled like a rabid dog." The woman collapsed onto the floor. "It was awful. I'm so sorry."

Robert nodded to his wife to take her back to their apartment. As she did, he could hear his granddaughter weep the entire length of the long corridor.

All the men in the circle of elders were dressed in typical Iban fashion with only shorts. Each was heavily tattooed with the dark, handcrafted ink of their ancestors. Robert wore his characteristic long pearl necklace. The witch doctor chain smoked under his ornate headpiece decorated with bird feathers. The men sipped *tuak*.

Robert silently searched each man, all lost in their thoughts. A thick gloom settled onto the council. The elders were upset with him. They had been offended since he had sold some of his land to the white man and possibly as far back to the day he decided to follow Jesus. They were mad because he left that morning to go to work at the white man's medicine lodge and hadn't returned until the moon was high in the sky. They didn't understand why he would work at all. "Being chief of the longhouse should command your total attention," they had told him.

He had explained, "It is important to show the young people the value of work and how to get along with the whites."

Life in the jungle was challenging. It had been that way from the beginning of time for the Iban. The last forty years had brought changes, many unwelcomed, including a year when a flu epidemic swept through with a 30 percent mortality rate. There was a recent increase in late-term miscarriages and a continual drip of young people who lost faith in the old ways and moved to the city. Robert understood these had nothing to do with his family accepting Jesus into their hearts but knew others didn't have the same sympathies.

The *manang* blew a large smoke ring and then began chanting quietly under his breath the *mengap*, a long incantation to ward off evil that had been passed down orally from generations of long ago.

Robert swatted a fly from his bare foot and wiped his brow with the back of his hand. The evil had ushered in a stifling heat with no evening breeze. None of them, including Robert, could erase the image of the decapitated man, which resurrected memories of ancient times.

Robert was only two when World War II started. The last known headhunting in their area occurred when the Japanese occupied their land. At the time, headhunting was a treasured part of Iban culture. They believed if a man owned another person's skull, his victim would protect his family from the dark spirit world and serve him as a slave for eternity in the afterlife.

The elders had grown up with the heads given to them by their fathers, and these were stored safely as a valued commodity.

When Robert had become a Christian, he gave his family's heads to the witch doctor as a show of goodwill. Robert heard rumors that the people said it was a sign of weakness even though the *manang* had gladly accepted the heads.

"The only head I can remember being taken was twenty years ago on the southern Indonesia side of Borneo during a land conflict," Robert said to the men. "Why has the horrific practice returned?"

"I think you have brought this on our people," the *manang* said and blew another smoke ring. "You have ignored the omens and turned your back on the ways of augury. Your life is *mali*, bad, especially your belief in a foreign god. Maybe bringing this Christian god has angered *antu gerasi* and the evil spirit is attacking us. Maybe we have angered *petara*, the god of gods." He spoke without anger or malice.

Robert sat patiently and silently, letting the rest of the council process the witch doctor's words. When he thought they were done, he asked, "Do the rest of you agree?"

The elders sat stone-faced, sipping at their rice wine.

"Rentap," the *manang* said, using his given name. "You are the great-great-great-grandson of the warrior Rentap. The great Rentap refused to submit to the white man. He fought the first White Rajah, James Brooke, and saved our land and our people. You have betrayed your great-great-great-grandfather by befriending the whiteman...especially the White Rajah."

Robert let the man vent. After all, the young man that was beheaded was the *manang's* own great-grandson. Not everyone in the Iban people felt the same affection for Master Paul. They always showed respect face-to-face, but the hatred for James Brooke was a thick poisonous root that ran deep through their history.

"And what would you have us do?" Robert asked.

"Renounce this other god. Return to the ways of our ancestors." The witch doctor stared at him and the muscles of his jaw tightened. "We must ask each of the homes to provide the sacrifice of *piring*. Each home must prepare the sticky rice cakes and whatever else they can spare for food and prepare it for the spirits. I myself will furnish a *genselan*. I will slaughter a pig tonight and sprinkle the blood on the doorposts of our homes. If *antu gerasi* returns, he will see the offering, be satisfied, and his evil will pass by our homes."

Only half of the families in the longhouse had converted to the way of Jesus. The murder was not helping. Robert knew the pull of the old ways. When he first accepted Christ, he often thought about falling back or combining the two faiths. But he had seen and experienced God the Father too much to turn his back on Jesus.

Robert turned to face the *manang* and said, "You are a good man, my brother. You have served our people faithfully. I do not know why this evil has come to our village. You and I will agree that there is evil in this world and we must fight against it. You and I will also agree that the Great Father is always on the side of justice and what is right. But I now believe that the Great Father has sent his son, Jesus, to be the sacrifice for us. We no longer need the blood of animals. Jesus shed his blood for us, and he went to the evil place and defeated the devil. I cannot stop you from *piring* and *genselan*, but for me and my household, we will follow God the Almighty. I believe the ancient scripture that God in me is greater than the evil that is in the world."

The rest of the elders nodded but added no further comment. Each would have to decide for themselves.

"Have there been any other reports from up or downriver of this happening?" Robert asked. "Do we have any clue who could have done this?"

The men shook their heads.

Robert laid his head against the wooden wall and prayed silently. *Father, help us.* He knew an ancient evil had risen.

CHAPTER 18

ADAM AND EVE

Nick told Wright and Maggie that he would skip breakfast and meet them here on the dock. Even though the morning spread looked delicious, he had things to process, including the dream from last night.

Sitting on the waterfront below the research center, Nick watched the sun rising over the horizon, casting pink hues across the water. He was thankful he could see it. The morning was the perfect temperature, the sun warmed his face, and the air was brisk enough to require a light jacket. The hills of the jungle around the lake didn't hold a candle to the mountains of Montana. But they displayed themselves in a perfect image reflected in the lake. Never in his life would he have imagined sitting here in this place. *Thank you, God.*

It was the first time since losing his sight that he could be thankful for his life. If the North Korean incident had never happened, if Turkey's earthquake had never taken place, if losing his best friend or his eyesight had never occurred…he would not be sitting here. His mind tried to wrap itself around this truth. Was he catching a glimpse of God's goodness, His providence over Nick's life? *Your will Father, not mine.*

A small wooden longboat, similar to the one tied to the center's dock, sliced through the liquid mirror, sending a simple wake rippling across the lake. Nick compared the boat to the one tied to the dock. They were almost identical, except the one cutting across the lake was red. This one was bright blue. Its flat bottom was ribbed and, curiously, had no seats. A small outboard motor hung from the pointed end and the other, flattened out like a duck's bill, gave a backward appearance to the boat. It didn't matter; he couldn't imagine that they would take the small boat across the expansive lake. Wright told Nick and Maggie that the real adventure starts after the two-hour journey across the lake. He figured Wright would be zipping around the corner at any moment with a high-tech speedboat.

Nick stretched his back and yawned. At least he'd slept well.

The small apartments of the research center were elegant and comfortable—paneled floor to ceiling with exotic wood. A massive skylight in each room expanded the night sky and stars overhead. Although, at one point, he woke up to the full moon and thought he was at the operating table with a surgical light shining brightly in his eyes. During the last six months, he often had surgical dreams that were typically unsettling—looking down and realizing that he had forgotten to put on gloves, or finding himself halfway through a difficult operation only to forget the rest of the steps. Last night's dream was different; it was a happy scene, almost festive, as though the staff was celebrating. There were even balloons. *Ha! Balloons in the operating room.* Nick smiled remembering the dream. The operating table was gone and in its place was a buffet table full of party food, including an ornately decorated cake. It reminded Nick of when he'd graduated from medical school, and his family and friends celebrated his future—full of hope and promise.

Nick's memories were interrupted by amiable voices. He turned to see Wright and Maggie walking down the winding stairs from the complex to the dock. They were laughing, and Nick noted a twinge of jealousy as they made their way down, their arms full of supplies.

He had not found time to connect with Maggie since arriving on Borneo. It was confusing for him that Maggie had finally revealed her heart only to withdraw it again. Maybe he was making too much out of it and would trust Maggie's love for him. He heard Chang's words in his heart: "I believe you now have two journeys: the physical one with Maggie and your spiritual one of seeing yourself like the Father sees you."

Lord, let it be so.

"Good morning," Wright called to him as they stepped onto the dock.

Nick stood and went to them to help Maggie with her load. "Good morning."

"You enjoying the sunrise?" Maggie asked.

"Yes, it's something," Nick said relieving her of her bags. "You sleep well?"

"Oh, my gosh, those beds are like feather cradles." Maggie hugged her shoulders. "I had incredible dreams of home, sleeping under the stars on my parents' lawn." Maggie leaned in and kissed Nick on the cheek. "How about you?"

"I had pleasant dreams as well."

"Here," Wright said, "the chef made you this breakfast burrito, Sarawak style. It's local fish instead of beef." He handed Nick the foil-wrapped treat. "It's quite a journey upriver, so I wanted you to have something to eat."

Wright inhaled the refreshing lake air and stretched out his arms. "What a beautiful morning to go upriver." He walked to the end of the dock and surprised Nick when he set the supplies in the wooden boat. When he looked around for someone to bring a bigger boat, Wright read his expression.

"We're on our own from here," he said. "Those stairs are where I draw the line between my two worlds. That world"—he extended his hand toward the modern complex—"and that one." He turned and pointed to the lake and the jungle beyond.

Wright opened a supply box at the edge of the dock. He pulled out three wooden seats, designed like stadium chairs, and spaced them out on the bottom of the boat. He then took an old metal gas can that reminded Nick of the one his grandfather used to fill his lawn mower and placed it near the front.

"Life jackets?" Maggie asked.

Wright smiled and shook his head. "Sorry, not standard operating equipment in the jungle. Sometimes you just have to let go."

Maggie turned to Nick and shrugged.

"You guys ready?" Wright asked, stepping into the back of the boat by the small outboard motor.

Nick looked at Maggie and smiled. "Heck, yeah!"

* * *

Like the boat Nick saw earlier, this one cut through the flat water with ease. He wondered what the ride would have been like in a storm. The craft sat deep in the water, with only inches separating them from the waterline and disaster. Nick grew up around Flathead Lake, about the same size as Batang Ai Lake, and had seen mountain storms swamp large ski boats. He pushed those fears away and concentrated on the two-hour journey across the lake.

The day was warming, but as they motored across the water, the breeze made it comfortable. Nick turned back and smiled at Maggie, who sat in the middle of the boat to balance the weight. Her hair fluttered under a large brimmed hat that she held in place with one hand. She had shed her jacket, and her fuchsia tank top flattered her olive skin and athletic build. Wright had convinced them both to wear shorts. Maggie's eyes searched the horizon, and a wide smile wrapped her face—she looked as alive as Nick felt. Just like Wright had said, they were entering a different realm, and the cares of the world had been shed behind them. They were flying free into a new adventure. They had cast off the shore of one world to enter a new one.

As they came to the end of the lake, Wright steered the boat toward the mouth of a river.

"Hang on, the currents can get tricky here," he yelled.

As they entered the confluence of the lake and the river, the currents pushed the boat hard to the right, and the motor strained to keep them straight. A competent boat captain, Wright maneuvered through to a crystal-clear river that snaked into the jungle.

The river slowed and deepened, and in minutes they were in the ancient Borneo rainforest surrounded by lush jungle trees and greenery that created an emerald canopy overhead. Nick looked around in wonder, unsure he had ever seen anything as mystical or beautiful. The temperature dropped a few degrees with the disappearance of the sun but remained comfortable as musky humidity hit his nostrils and brow.

"This is the oldest rainforest on the planet," Wright said over the hum of the outboard. "There are fifteen thousand species of flowering plants, three thousand species of trees, over four hundred species of resident birds and freshwater fish. Since 2007, a hundred and twenty-three new species have been discovered. All our medical discoveries have come out of the jungle. Now you know the secret of Zelutex."

A massive reddish-brown and white bird of prey flew over their heads and screeched as it swooped over them. It circled once and then landed in a rain tree looming over the river. It eyed them carefully, cocking its head from side to side, and screeched again. The bird looked like a golden eagle except for its white head and chest.

"*Sengalang burong,*" Wright said.

"Senga what?" Maggie asked.

"*Sengalang burong,* the bird chief. The Iban believe that the red-back sea-eagle is the manifestation of their god of war. The Iban believe this god lived on earth as a man. It's why they worship birds."

"What a beautiful bird," Nick said.

"They also believe it is the god of headhunting."

Both Nick and Maggie instantly looked back, and Wright smiled and shrugged.

"Okay, that's twice you have mentioned headhunting. You're kind of freaking me out," Maggie said.

"The tribes of Southeast Asia were known for the practice. But rather than it being an act of war, like the current radical Muslim groups are doing, headhunting was usually a ritual activity for both joyous and sorrowful times. A warrior would take a single head for the coming of age or marriage or to signal the end of personal or collective mourning."

"Weird," Nick said, and added mockingly, "Here, darling, I can't wait to get married. Look what I got you."

"It doesn't make sense to me," Maggie said. "Take a life, to mourn a life?"

"Welcome to the Iban. They are mysterious people. Thank goodness they gave up the practice long ago."

"How long ago?" Maggie asked nervously.

"At least a few years." Wright flashed Maggie a grin.

Nick looked from Wright to Maggie. Was he flirting with her? Maybe he was being dramatic to impress her. But the thought of the ISIS terrorists that he battled in Turkey and the horrific pictures of the group cutting heads off was no joke—a barbaric act both now and then.

The thick jungle encroached on the river, but as they motored around a bend, the river widened. The trees opened to an area that held a handful of boats occupied by only a person or two. Wright slowed to navigate the traffic. Nick now understood the design of the boats with their flat fronts. Fishermen stood on the bow flinging large nets into the water. The fishermen threw them with the precision of a cowboy tossing a lariat. One man hauled in his net teeming with small fish flopping against the mesh.

When the fishermen saw Wright, they stopped what they were doing, smiled and waved. One man whistled, and another shouted, "The White Rajah!"

The other men followed and repeated the words in the round of chants.

Wright greeted them and waved as they passed, seeming to take the greeting as praise. But when one of the men frowned and looked away, Nick wasn't so sure. "Why were they calling you that, the White...Ra?" Nick asked.

"White Rajah." Wright grinned. "It's my heritage. I told you about my great-great-great-grandfather, Sir Thomas Stamford Raffles, who owned the island off Singapore. Well, another great-great-great-grandfather was James Brooke. James Brooke, also born in India, was a son of a British judge. Maybe I'll have the chance to tell his whole story this evening. James was a British naval man and entrepreneur that helped quell an Iban uprising here in Borneo. I'm afraid it was a bit of a rout...guns against spears...that sort of thing. But he brought peace to the island and was named the first White Rajah, abolishing piracy and headhunting."

"Piracy?" Nick asked.

"Yes, the Iban were scoundrels when the British East India Company was trading in this area. That's why the Brits sent him in the first place, to quash the looting of their ships."

"Crazy," Maggie said.

"Anyway, James had an illegitimate son, George, via an Iban girl. He's my great-great-grandfather. Because George was a bastard, the Brooke fortune and titles went to his sister's sons. It is why my father had no British title, and why I don't as well."

"It sure hasn't hampered you," Nick said.

Wright shrugged. "You are not British, my dear Dr. Hart. You would not understand. But you're right; those things don't matter much to me."

Nick had to wonder.

"And you want to know an even zanier part of this history? The old Iban man you met yesterday at lunch, my butler, Robert—we're related—through that Iban girl. Robert is my fourth cousin. I have Iban blood running through me...well 3 percent, that is."

* * *

It had been four hours since leaving the research center. The twists and turns of the river seemed to make the water collapse and expand like a living set of lungs. At one point, the river squeezed into narrow rapids that required the men to leave the boat and forge the falls—Wright pushed from behind and Nick pulled from the front.

Nick glanced at the blister on his palm and wondered if they would ever arrive at their destination. He sighed; the trek was his to endure. Then he remembered Chang's words of wisdom: "Our journey now is to be reborn into a new awareness and experience of what Jesus called the Kingdom of Heaven."

What a journey it has been so far. His recent journey flashed through his mind—images of Qodshanes, Turkey, and the Russians who speculated that the original Garden of Eden existed in what was now an abandoned high-mountain village. If Nick was honest with himself, the dense jungle they now traversed was closer to his ideas about mankind's origins. This mystic rainforest looked like where Adam could have walked with God in the cool of the day.

Still floating in his thoughts, Nick noticed an elderly couple on the high bank overlooking the river. They stood like apparitions amid the mist. Nick wondered if it was a jungle mirage until the old man smiled and waved to them. The man's weathered skin was covered in tattoos, and the woman was topless with saggy breasts.

"Oh yeah, I forgot to mention that," Wright said. "The Iban often don't wear much clothing and look at breasts as utilitarian food sources for the babies. They're not sexualized as in the modern world."

At first, Nick thought they were both naked, but as they motored past, he saw shorts on the man and a skirt on the woman. He smiled and waved. *Adam and Eve welcoming us to the rainforest.* It occurred to him that maybe that was how God saw humanity, stripped of all worldly things, naked and unashamed.

Nick wondered where the couple had come from, but as the travelers came around another bend of the river, they saw a community buzzing with life.

"Welcome to the longhouse," Wright announced.

CHAPTER 19

THE LONGHOUSE

Nick stepped from the front of the boat and back in time, landing on soil as foreign as the people gathering around him. His smile rippled out into reciprocating grins and prattle from the welcoming committee. Wright had told them that Robert's longhouse had twenty-five apartments, and it appeared that most, if not all, of the two hundred occupants had come down to the edge of the river. With every eye on him, the village's energy seemed full of friendly anticipation.

Nick wished he had asked Wright what the appropriate greeting was. He raised his hand like a Montana cowboy meeting a band of Indians. "Hi," he said.

His greeting was received with laughter and chatter. The heat of embarrassment raced up his spine and he wished he could take it back. But the people understood it as a friendly greeting and moved toward him and the boat. Thankfully, he recognized at the forefront the old man from the research center, even though he had shed the ridiculous butler's suit for a loincloth. His chest was bare and every rib showed, but what meat was on his bones was all muscle. His toned arms and legs were covered in dark, mysterious tattoos. One looked especially painful. It ran down his throat from the bottom of his chin to his sternum. But he smiled warmly and appeared to be one of the few men in the group with a full set of teeth.

"Dr. Hart, welcome to my home. Welcome to Sarawak," the man said and offered his hand to shake.

"I'm sorry. I've forgotten your name," Nick said.

"Robert," the man said, touching his chest. "I'm the chief of this longhouse."

"Well, Robert, call me Nicklaus," Nick said, not sure why he had used his given name. But it was too late. Robert had spoken to the villagers and then repeated Nick's name. It sounded like "Nickloss," with the emphasis on *loss*.

A wave of echoes rolled through the people: "Nickloss."

Nick smiled to himself. *I guess I am now Nickloss.* He turned to help Maggie. She handed him supplies, then took his hand and stepped off the boat. They looked at the crowd, a gathering of young and old, children and babies. Nick felt overdressed in his expensive shorts, T-shirt, hat and tennis shoes. The Ibans' attire was as simple and uninhibited as their surroundings.

Maggie focused on the children gathered in front. The kids were all barefoot, and most wore shorts and tank tops, except the youngest, who were naked. One boy wore a huge smile and carried a small bouquet of exotic-looking wildflowers. Maggie bent to greet the child. He shyly handed her the flowers and retreated into the crowd, creating giggles and more chatter.

"Hello, Ms. Maggie," Robert said, stepping up to her and embracing her with a warm hug. He turned to his people and waved to an elderly woman wrapped in a sarong, indicating that she should come forward.

"Ms. Maggie, this is my wife. She goes by the Christian name Ruth."

Ruth stepped toward Maggie holding a string of dark wooden beads to place over her head. Maggie removed her large-brimmed hat and bent to accept the beads. After situating the necklace around her neck, Ruth reached up, held Maggie by both cheeks, and then rose on her tiptoes to kiss her on the forehead. Maggie reciprocated by placing her oversized hat on the woman's head, and the crowd erupted in another round of cheers and laughter. Nick marveled at Maggie's ability to charm strangers. *She's a natural.*

Wright jumped from the boat, and two men waded into the river to push the boat farther up on the shore. Wright spoke to the people in their native tongue, which seemed to delight and excite them. Many of the children ran forward, clinging to him with affection.

While Wright entertained the children, Robert invited a group of men to meet Nick and Maggie.

"These are the elders of our longhouse," Robert said.

The men were similar to Robert, short in stature with wiry builds and covered in tattoos. Most held warm, toothless grins with graying dark hair and bushy brows. Nick wondered if handshaking was not their natural greeting. Their grip was more of a touch, and one man even held out his left hand. The final elder, a man without a smile, was highly decorated with tattoos and wore an ornate turban—a red wrap with large, exotic bird feathers arranged similarly to a Native American headdress. The man didn't extend his hand but rather gave a nod that seeped with aloofness.

"Welcome to paradise," Wright said, grabbing Nick's shoulders from behind. "What do you think?"

"I think I've fallen into the pages of *National Geographic*." Nick smiled and let his eyes follow the well-worn path from the bank of the river to a large wooden structure. It was situated on the ridge above the stream and supported by large log stilts ten or fifteen feet off the ground. Smoke swirled from stovepipes sticking from the roof, shrouding the structure in a shadowy haze. A massive jungle canopy overhung the longhouse with plants of various kinds, including large-leaved banana trees and other fruit trees that Nick couldn't identify. The complex sat naturally in the emerald-green rainforest.

"Please." Robert indicated the longhouse. "My home is now your home."

Nick followed behind the chief up the dirt path used for centuries, if not hundreds of centuries, to a set of stairs leading up to the longhouse. A large flock of chickens and three pigs scattered and ran under the longhouse for cover, squawking and squealing as they went. As he looked back, two young girls were holding Maggie's hands. Affection flowed from the Iban children, and they talked with her in Iban as if she understood what they were saying.

Nick started up the old wooden stairs, and several creaked under his weight. He had gained a few pounds the last six months, but even at his normal weight, he probably weighed more than twice the average Iban. He hoped the rickety stairs would hold. When they reached the top of the landing, they stepped onto a patio—an expansive platform of bamboo. The slats were lashed together in a manner that left an inch between poles, allowing Nick to see the jungle below.

The area was clean and plain with a few wooden benches and tables. Woven baskets and large clay pots hung from the walls or were arranged neatly around the area. It had the feel of Wright's tree house, but much more rustic. From the other side of the patio Nick noted three smaller outbuildings. The walls of the buildings were an eclectic mixture of bamboo, lumber and corrugated tin.

The crowd that gathered at the river followed them up into the compound, then dissipated, going on with their own lives. Robert scolded two mongrel dogs sneaking onto the porch and shooed them back down the stairs.

Nick looked at his wrist. He'd left his watch on the nightstand in the research facility. Then he realized he wouldn't need it because in the far reaches of civilization where cell towers and internet connections were nonexistent, time didn't matter. The afternoon sun faded somewhere beyond the canopy and shadows elongated. It had been quite a journey to the world of the Iban. Nick inhaled deeply and thought of Chang's talk about different kingdoms. The air was fresh, mixed with a tincture of smoke and earthen musk. He had no idea where he would find another reality as distinctive and as full of intrigue and wonder.

He smiled at Maggie, who was looking around with the same expression of marvel, while Robert and Wright discussed something in Iban. Robert made a slashing motion across his neck with his thumb. The discussion between the two became more animated, and Robert repeated the gesture. Maggie looked wide-eyed at Nick, and they both stared at Wright.

Wright chuckled after seeing the alarmed look on Nick's face. "No worries, mate. We were just discussing dinner." His grin widened. "And the good news is, you're not on the menu." He laughed loudly with Robert joining in. "Robert was telling me he has to go butcher some chickens for our dinner."

They all laughed together.

"I hope you see why I love Borneo. It's the natural order of things," Wright said. "I can come to the rainforest and leave the world behind…it's like I find balance here."

"A thin place," Nick murmured under his breath.

"Pardon?" Wright asked.

Nick hadn't meant for anyone to hear the statement and his face flushed with heat. "Oh, a friend of mine believes in thin places in the world. Where the separation between us and the divine thins somehow."

Wright nodded, looked around and shrugged, "Who knows?"

Either way, Nick was enchanted. The place was beautiful—primitive and definitely wild, but pristine. And he was astonished that in this day and age, people lived like this. He was so glad to experience this slice of heaven on earth.

CHAPTER 20

DRAGON'S BLOOD

Maggie sat cross-legged on the bamboo mat of Robert's apartment between Nick and Wright feeling more content than she had for years. She felt safe and protected by the two men. The Hope Center's future was secure with the financial backing of the Wright's Kids Foundation, and peace wrapped around her like a dream. She had to keep reminding herself of the reality.

As the sun set over the jungle and darkness descended around the longhouse, her contentment mixed with a smidge of fear. Guatemala was remote, but it seemed Sarawak was off the map. A sense of vulnerability swept over her, barely tempered by the flickering light of the candles and a small blaze in the corner fireplace. She was as far away from the comforts and safety of civilization as she'd ever been.

Robert and Ruth's apartment was a sparse, sizeable room, and Maggie assumed that the other living quarters in the longhouse were similar. Wooden beams supported rafters covered in tin. A hammock swung from two of the posts, and a queen-sized bed lay in one corner. Next to the bed was the only other piece of furniture in the space, an antique-looking dresser. In the other corner was a rudimentary kitchen, the small fireplace vented by a rock chimney. The guests and their hosts sat in a circle on mats in what Maggie decided was the apartment's living room. The apartment had no radio, TV, or electricity. The bathroom was across the bamboo patio on the "dirty side," as Robert called it. The Iban designed their complexes to open on the clean, river side. The back or unclean side was where sewage and garbage were recycled into the jungle below. Maggie wondered if the pigs, chickens, and dogs had a part in that, but she tried not to think about it as Robert's wife placed a large platter of fried chicken in front of them.

"Maggie, would you mind saying a blessing over the food?" Robert asked and smiled at her.

"It would be an honor," she said and bowed her head. "Father," she began, but a lump formed in her throat. There was so much to be thankful for. "I thank You for this precious couple that has invited us into their home. Bless them and their family. Bless them in their comings and goings. Father, I sense Your sweet presence here. Bless our time and bless this food. In Jesus's name, Amen."

Robert and Ruth loudly added, "Amen."

The meal included simple servings of rice, fried chicken, and bowls of fruit—bananas and something she didn't recognize. Robert handed the platter of chicken to Wright to start the feast. Wright took a couple of pieces and passed the platter to Maggie. She didn't recognize any of the chicken cuts and hesitated.

Wright came to her rescue. "They cut the chicken a bit different than you're used to. They lay the chicken down and take the machete and go, whack, whack, whack, down the chicken." He demonstrated with karate-chops.

Maggie grinned, nodded, and took a few pieces. It looked delicious however it was cut.

"Here, you have to have one of these," Wright said and grabbed a piece from the pile. "You normally have to pay extra for this." He grinned at her, as she stared at the fried chicken foot on her plate.

"Uh…thank you…I think."

As Maggie sniffed at the three-toed delight, something caught her peripheral vision. She looked up to see a huge spider dangling from a web, descending from the rafters. She screamed and sprang toward Wright, almost spilling the contents of her plate.

Robert scrambled to his feet, grabbed a broom from the corner of the room and swatted at the spider. It fell onto the mat next to Maggie and wiggled to regain its footing. She screamed louder and jumped, practically into Wright's lap.

With one hard whack of the broom, the spider lay flattened and dead.

"Oh my Lord. Is that the typical size of spiders you have here?" Maggie asked. Her voice still an octave above normal. She spread out her fingers and held her hand over the dead spider to judge its size. Its body and legs were huge, much bigger than her hand.

"Bad, bad, spider," Robert said, shaking his finger at the dead arachnid.

Ruth scooped the corpse into a plastic dustpan and walked out the door. Maggie assumed she would dump it on the dirty side.

"Pleasssse tell me that is the only one of those I'll see on this trip," Maggie said, realizing she still clutched Wright's arm.

"Okay, that is the only one left on the entire island of Borneo," he teased her.

She let go and slapped his arm.

Heat rose in her neck as she scooted back to her seat. "I'm so sorry, you all, I didn't mean to make such a fuss. I didn't know the world held such creatures." She laughed, and everyone laughed with her.

She glanced at Wright to make sure he'd taken her outburst in stride. She loved how he smelled—earthy and animalistic. He was handsome to be sure, with his luscious hair, enchanting eyes, and inviting smile. And it wasn't just his unfathomable wealth, but his natural confidence and relaxed manner, Maggie imagined, that caused women to swoon. She wondered why he was still unattached. Arousal—an emotion she had long disregarded— was percolating within her and it confused her spirit. After hours of prayer and contemplation, making a romantic attempt with Nicklaus had seemed right and proper. Then in strolled Wright, looking very much like a handsome Blackfeet warrior. Maggie pushed the awakenings from her thoughts.

* * *

Dinner was simple and delicious, and afterward they sipped *tuak*.

"I put a little honey in yours, Ms. Maggie," Robert said and smiled at her. He must have seen her turn her nose up at the thought of drinking the alcohol, but the men were thoroughly enjoying themselves, swapping stories and drinking too much of the wine. The candlelight danced off their animated faces and the walls of the longhouse room. She kept a wary eye open for another one of the hand-sized spiders.

"Dr. Nickloss," Robert turned to Nick. "I have been hesitant to ask you for a favor."

"What can I do for you?" Nick sipped his *tuak*.

"As you can imagine, it is very difficult for my people to get medical care. Would you mind putting on your doctor's hat and seeing a few people in the morning?"

Maggie was interested in how Nick would respond, knowing that after the injury to his eyes, he thought his doctoring days were over. She knew him well and watched him struggle. He took a large swig of his wine.

"I suppose I could see a couple of people. You do know I'm just a dumb bone doctor…and I've been out of the business for a while…I'm a little rusty."

"Thank you, Dr. Nickloss. I appreciate it."

Out in the common area, Maggie heard people talking and walking around. Over the last hour, the commotion in the hallway had grown, and she turned her head to listen. The walls were far from soundproof. She imagined that living here, one would get to know her neighbors well.

"How have the Iban survived financially?" Nick asked.

"My people have traded with the Chinese for thousands of years—gold, camphor, hornbill ivory, rhinoceros horn, bird nests, and of course, dragon's blood," Robert said and looked at Wright.

"Dragon's blood?" Maggie turned back to Robert.

"Yes, dragon's blood," Wright said and looked a bit disapprovingly at Robert. He said something harsh to Robert, who said something equally severe back. Maggie could not tell if the men were joking, serious, or had too much wine.

Wright cleared the air. "Sorry, Robert's telling secrets, and I was cursing our shared heritage. Mostly out of fun."

Maggie was not so sure.

"We share a great-great-great-grandmother, *Lenyou Aiwong*, Lost Waterfall. She was one of the wives of the great warrior, Rentap. Rentap—his great-great-great-grandfather—is Robert's lineage. James Brooke, my great-great-great-grandfather, had an affair with Lost Waterfall and my lineage was born. Rentap and Brooke were mortal enemies for more than one reason. We love to remind each other of it."

Wright held up his wine glass to Robert, and they toasted in friendship.

"This dragon's blood...is it true blood?" Nick asked.

Wright tilted his head back and forth as if trying to decide how much to tell them. "Well...the ancients believe it arose from the blood of elephants and dragons that died in mortal combat. Today, we know it's not blood, but men have spilled much blood over it." He looked again annoyed at Robert. "It's the resin of the dracaena tree."

Maggie chuckled nervously. "Sounds like the Dracula tree."

"No, *dracaena*. It's Greek for a 'female dragon.' The bright red resin has been used in medieval ritual magic, alchemy, and Chinese medicines for centuries." Wright took a sip of his *tuak* and looked from Maggie to Nick and back again. "We found one of the keys to preventing the downregulation of dopamine in the resin for our new drug, Welltrex." He threw back the rest of his cup of wine. "I guess I'll have to kill you now."

As they laughed together, the noise from the common area increased and caused them all to turn toward the door. To Maggie, it sounded like someone was upset. It was a mixture of uproar and shouting that developed into rhythmic chanting. Even Wright appeared concerned, and they all looked at Robert, who sat unfazed. Wright said something to Robert in Iban, and he chose to answer in English.

"There is nothing to worry about," the old man said as he straightened and crossed his legs in front of him. "I told the people of my longhouse that Dr. Nickloss and Ms. Maggie were visiting us and they are Christian. Our witch doctor and his followers are not happy that you are here."

Maggie looked at the door, wondering if they should barricade it, then back at Robert.

"Do not worry, Ms. Maggie. They are out there doing their silly chants and such. Truly, 'No weapon formed against us can prosper.'" He quoted what was one of Maggie's favorite scriptures. "After all, greater is Jesus in me than the evil that is in the world."

Maggie searched the old warrior's eyes and saw no hint of fear or worry. His faith and confidence in who he was extended beyond worldly strength.

"They will be done soon. Probably they have been drinking too much *tuak* and will go sleep it off." He smiled at her. Then his expression turned serious, and he looked at Maggie and Nick. "But to be on the safe side, please do not go anywhere tonight and do not accept anything they might offer you to eat or drink."

Maggie swallowed hard. She had experienced her share of spiritual warfare but sensed they had arrived at the devil's doorstep. Her dream of the horse with a large handprint on its right hip rushed back to her mind—the pat hand signifying that the horse had brought the rider home unharmed from a dangerous mission. It reminded her to pray fervently.

Robert spoke to Wright in Iban and told a prolonged story. Maggie did not find the behavior rude; after all, where else would they go in the small space to have a confidential conversation? Maggie watched Robert make the same slashing motion across his neck. She wondered if they were discussing what to have for breakfast, but looking at Wright's eyes, it seemed to be something of far more significance.

Wright listened intently, nodding occasionally, then crossed his arms in thought. He finally blew a puff of air through pursed lips and looked seriously at Maggie and Nick.

"They have had a most unfortunate incident here at the longhouse. Two nights ago, someone murdered a man in his sleep. The man was married to Robert's granddaughter."

Maggie saw the alarm on Nick's face. "Do they know who did it?" Nick asked.

Wright asked Robert again in Iban, and the two seemed to have a longer discussion. Wright finally answered Nick's question. "No, they are still searching."

Robert turned to Nick and Maggie. "The man's head is missing."

CHAPTER 21

MIRACLE

Nick opened his mouth to scream, but nothing came out. He was powerless against the hand clutching his throat. He could no longer suck air in or vocalize words out. His arms were useless.

Run! his brain screamed at him, but he couldn't shake the death grip or coax his arms and legs to move. The man morphed into a giant creature squeezing the life out of him.

Fight! his brain screamed again.

The massive beast, ten times the size of a man, was covered with shaggy hair so coarse that it cut Nick's hands as he clawed at the grip around his neck. The monster laughed through sharp, glittering teeth and pierced him with blood red eyes.

"Help me!" Nick yelled, finally finding his voice.

"Nick. Nicklaus, it's okay," another voice said in another corner of his brain, but the monster was pulling him back into the night terror. "Nick, wake up. You're having a nightmare."

Like a high-speed elevator coming from the depths of a mine, his mind ascended into the reality of the here and now, and he gasped for breath.

"Nicklaus, you're okay. Everything is all right." It was Maggie's voice.

He opened his eyes, but everything was pitch black, and he thought he had gone blind again.

"Something is wrong with you," he thought he heard the

monster sneer.

"Someone, get me some light," Maggie yelled.

The longhouse was in chaos. Nick's brain not only registered Maggie's voice but the howling dogs and squealing pigs underneath the longhouse.

A bright light flashed in his eyes and Nick tried to cover them with his arm. *My arm*...it was dead asleep and tingled as the blood returned to the tissues. He tried moving the other one, but it had fallen through the weaving of the hammock and tangled in the rope.

"It's okay, mate." Wright's voice cut through the night. "You've had a night terror. Everyone is okay." He was shining a flashlight at Nick and helped him sit up in the hammock.

Nick rubbed his eyes, disoriented. He flicked his wrist back and forth as the blood returned.

Robert had joined them and held a flickering candle to Nick's face. "Dr. Nickloss, you okay?"

Nick looked around at his friends lit in eerie shadows. His brain finally fired on all cylinders, and he laughed. "Well, that was some dream."

Maggie put her hands over her chest. "Oh, my Lord, Nicklaus. My heart is pounding outside my body. You woke us all up with a blood-curdling scream, and then the dogs and the pigs joined in, and we thought you were being murdered."

"Yes, you gave us quite a fright." Wright handed him a small cup of water.

Nick took a sip. "Okay, I confess. Whatever was attacking me was ferocious...and ugly."

Robert's expression in the candlelight turned ominous and sober. "The Huntsman—'be alert and of sober mind. Your enemy the devil prowls around like a roaring lion looking for someone to devour.'"

"Who is the Huntsman?" Maggie asked.

"It is the Iban term for the devil. He is called *antu gerasi*."

"Then, we pray the rest of First Peter that you quoted," Maggie replied, "'Resist him, standing firm in the faith.'"

"Yes, 'Submit yourselves, then, to God. Resist the devil, and he will flee from you,'" Robert added from the book of James.

* * *

The day was beautiful. The warmth of the sun was burning off the lingering effects of the nightmare and Nick's vision of the creature. They had slept in hammocks in Robert and Ruth's apartment, but he wasn't sure anyone got much sleep after he'd woken the entire longhouse with his screams. But now everything was calm. Long gone was the chanting witch doctor, the bad dream, and even the spider. Of course it was no wonder he had such a frightening dream when he'd gone to sleep with tales of dragon's blood, headhunting, the recent beheading, and the witch doctor's clan ready to do away with the Christians.

Ruth fed them fresh eggs and the sweetest mango that Nick had ever tasted. He could get used to this simple life with none of the often unused formal dining or sitting rooms found in the developed world. Every inch of space in the Iban dwellings was used for life's daily activities. Very little went to waste. They unhooked their hammocks from the poles in the apartment and sat for breakfast exactly where they'd slept. Nick had no idea what time it was, and he didn't care.

Voices and activity rose out in the common area and Nick looked at Robert, concerned the chanting might begin again.

Robert looked at him and smiled. "You mind doing some doctoring this morning?"

He had hoped that after a little more rice wine Robert would forget Nick's promise to see a few people. Being a physician seemed to be far from his thoughts now. After his blindness, giving up his sheepskin, his doctorate diploma, was a certainty. Not only did he feel inadequate as a physician, he imagined that whatever they wanted him to look at was something completely unrelated to orthopedics. He wanted to say no but instead said, "Uh…sure."

They stood, and Robert led them into the communal area. Nick was surprised at what greeted them—not one or two people, but the entire community lined up in an organized queue. Anxiety filled in his mind, and his heart began to race. He wanted to run back into the apartment and away from his calling. He wanted to catch the next boat home and lock himself in his dark apartment. He was especially intimidated because the person at the front of the line was the witch doctor dressed in his regalia—the man that was said to want to slip him a deadly poison or kill him outright. The witch doctor sat cross-legged with his arms folded in front of him. He had the same sour expression that had greeted Nick and the others yesterday.

Maggie put her hand through the crook of Nick's elbow. "I'll help," she said and squeezed his arm.

"Where are we going to do this?" Nick nervously asked Robert.

Robert indicated the bamboo mat in front of the witch doctor. "Here, of course."

Nick looked at him, then at Maggie and shrugged. "I think I've been set up."

"Kind of reminds you of Guatemala," she said and laughed. "You'll do great."

Nick sighed loudly and allowed Maggie to lead him to the front of the line, where they sat on the floor across from the witch doctor.

"Do you speak English?" Nick asked.

The witch doctor didn't change his expression and shook his head.

Nick looked at Wright and Robert. "Who's going to translate?"

Robert happily volunteered and sat down next to them.

Nick thought about extending his hand to shake. Instead, he asked, "What can I do for you?"

Robert interpreted and the witch doctor launched into a long story. Nick was immediately relieved when the man didn't point to his stomach or head or some other body part that he knew little about; instead, the man grabbed his shoulder and winced, demonstrating that he was only able to move it ten degrees in each direction.

"Ah…he has a frozen shoulder," Nick whispered to Maggie before Robert could interpret.

"See, you can do this."

Nick looked down the line of patients. He estimated more than two hundred. "Maybe frozen shoulders are epidemic," he said, grinning at her.

"How long has his shoulder been like this?" he asked Robert to ask the patient.

"He says over one year," Robert said and added without asking, "He fell out of a tree."

"Can I examine your shoulder?"

The witch doctor must have understood some English, because he scooted closer to Nick. Nick held the man's wrist with one hand and put his other on the man's shoulder. The muscles in his arm tensed like a snake ready to strike, and Nick wondered if the tension was caused by pain or because he was being examined by a Christian. In any case, he confirmed the witch doctor's limited movement.

"How do you say *relax* in Iban?" Nick asked.

"*Belelak*," Robert said and added in English, "Relax."

The witch doctor smelled of tobacco and alcohol. As Nick moved the man's shoulder, he inspected the tattoos. His skin, leathery from decades in the sun, was covered in them. Both shoulders displayed tattooed flower blossoms, but the tattoos everywhere else seemed symbolic of some creature or animal. There was a large bird in the center of the man's chest with a great horned beak. A dragon or snake with multiple heads covered his entire back. Tatted writing adorned the man's arms.

The witch doctor grimaced and tensed as Nick tried to find the extremes of motion of the shoulder. Forward, backward, side to side, Nick could only move the shoulder a few more degrees in any direction than what the witch doctor could do on his own. Nick led the man through some hand movements, verifying the nerves in the arm were working properly.

Nick rocked back on the mat, leaned against his extended arms and nodded. He relied on Robert to interpret. "You have a frozen shoulder and may have torn your rotator cuff in the fall. The tendons that support your shoulder and the capsule that holds the ball in the socket have scarred down."

Robert told the witch doctor and then turned to Nick. "What can you do for him?"

The same hopelessness that Nick felt in Guatemala when he'd sat in front of the children with clubfeet fell again on his own shoulders and he sighed. A frozen shoulder in the US was hard enough to treat. It often meant multiple surgeries to cut the scarring, hard manipulation under anesthesia to rip the adhesions, and months of intensive physical therapy to keep it from freezing down again.

"Well, frankly, nothing." Nick straightened his back and crossed his arms. Why would he help a man that in the least didn't like him or at most wanted him dead?

Robert didn't translate and stared at Nick like there had to be something he could do.

Nick shrugged and raised both hands in defeat.

"Would you pray for him?" Robert asked.

The question shocked Nick but lifted his spirit. His mind flashed with memories of sitting with Chang in Glacier Park, listening to Running Eagle Falls thundering over the rocks. He remembered Chang praying over him "to being strengthened with power by the Holy Spirit." Chang's words, "deep calls to deep," resounded in his heart.

Go deep, Nicklaus, he heard God's Spirit say to his heart.

Nick looked at the proud old man. The early stages of cataracts clouded his dark eyes.

"Can I ask you about the rest of your health?" Nick took the path of least resistance.

"He thinks he is in good health," Robert interpreted.

"What about your drinking?" Nick took a turn to the road less traveled.

The man's eyes burned with anger. "Did Robert ask you to say that?"

Oh, he does speak English. Nick looked at Robert, who remained silent. He looked back at the witch doctor. "No…I sensed that the God of heaven wanted me to ask."

"What else would this god tell you to ask about me?"

Nick arched his back and stretched his neck from side to side, trying to hear the Spirit. "That you no longer have to be an orphan. That He hears you. He sees you," Nick repeated what the Holy Spirit was telling him.

The witch doctor's head drooped, and tears filled his eyes.

Maggie must have sensed the Spirit stirring and put her hand on Nick's back.

Heat filled his hands like he'd stuck them in a fire, and he looked at his palms, making sure he hadn't set them in something.

"Would you allow me to pray for you, my friend?"

The witch doctor nodded, and Nick laid his hands on his frozen shoulder. "Father...show Yourself great. Show Yourself as the great physician. To this shoulder, I speak restoration. Let every tendon and muscle come back to normal, as You made it. Loosen the scarring and Your healing on the shoulder." Nick paused. "I especially pray the same for his heart." He laid a hand over the man's heart. He could feel it pounding. "Amen."

Nick removed his hands, and the witch doctor stared at him with the shock of disbelief.

"How do you feel? How is your shoulder?" Nick asked.

The witch doctor's hand shot straight up over his head. It surprised Nick as much as the man. Nick was flabbergasted. He had seen miracles, but none that had been ushered in under his own hands. His scientific mind wanted the witch doctor to run through all the motions and strength of the muscles. His shoulder moved normally. Robert and Maggie praised God, and a cheer erupted from the villagers.

Nick and the witch doctor stared at each other, not knowing what to do or say. One thing was clear, the witch doctor was smiling for the first time.

"I can see your Christian God is very powerful," he said, taking Nick's hands in his. "Can you teach me how to follow this Jesus?"

* * *

After spending the morning seeing the occupants of the entire longhouse, it was bath time, and Nick needed a good scrub more than anyone. He had never bathed with two hundred people, but here they were, in the deep, crystal-clear water of the Batang Ai River. The afternoon sun elevated both the temperature and the humidity of the jungle. Nick floated on his back in the cool water watching birds flutter in the canopy overhanging the river. A sense of contentment and peace flowed over him like the currents.

With Robert's and Maggie's help, Nick had explained God's plan to the witch doctor and led him in a prayer of repentance and salvation.

Fortunately, the rest of the villagers were remarkably healthy, and most just wanted to shake Nick's hand or have him and Maggie pray over them. Some of the older women suffered from back pain from carrying large water jugs up the path to the longhouse, and Nick showed them exercises to ease the hurt. And there were a few rashes that he had no idea how to treat, but Maggie suggested applying coconut oil.

The people were a shy and modest group—during his examination and now bathing—washing discreetly under their shorts or sarong dresses. But most of all, they were joyous. By the world's standards, they had nothing, yet where it really counted, they had everything. Probably the reason they were so healthy was that there were no pesticides or herbicides, no cell phones or other electromagnetic energy changing their DNA, and no air pollution or water pollution. They had their health, fresh food from the jungle, clean water, and joy. *So this is what joy looks like.*

Nick sat up and then dunked under. As he came out of the water, he wiped his eyes. He looked around at this community living in harmony with the land. The people splashed playfully with their children or rested in contentment. It was a glimpse of God's design and His Kingdom—full of joy and peace. *The renewal of all things.* It held more serenity than the hundreds of beautiful sunsets or mountain passes that Nick had experienced. He surveyed the people and asked in his heart, *Was it for that one man that You sent me, Father?*

"*Yes, Nicklaus, I will go to the ends of the earth for the one.*"

CHAPTER 22

THE OFFER

After the communal bath, Robert had motored them an hour upriver to where Wright wanted to show Nick and Maggie a set of waterfalls. When they arrived, Maggie took Wright's hand, and he helped her step out of the boat. She loved how he smelled and wished she knew his brand of cologne. She'd love to get Nick some but was embarrassed to ask Wright. He held her arm and guided her onto the slippery rock ledge below the falls.

It was just as Wright had described, but even his words didn't do it justice. The river tumbled over shelves of red rock, coating the cliffs in a strong mist. Lime-green moss grew between the rust-colored shelves as the water cascaded into a deep pool. The crystal-clear water poured out of the heart of the jungle and disappeared downstream into the rainforest.

Robert secured the boat to a large tree with a rope. He looked every bit the Iban warrior wearing only a loincloth, a leather pouch hung around his neck, and a large machete strapped to his waist. He carried a hollow staff two meters long.

On the journey upriver, they had paused at another longhouse at the confluence of the Batang Ai and a tributary. Robert asked if it would be okay to stop for a short time. He had local business to discuss with the chief and asked them to wait in the boat. When he returned to the boat, he was uncharacteristically quiet and remained so, motoring up to the falls, only telling them that he had asked the chief if any orangutans were in the area. The Iban wore their emotions on their face, and Maggie understood there had to be more to the story, but she didn't know if it was appropriate to ask, and Wright didn't pursue it.

"You ready to find dinner?" Wright asked Maggie and Nick.

"Uh…can I say no?" Maggie smiled. "Lions and tigers and bears, oh my," she said and looked at the men. With all the discussions of sun bears, clouded leopards, and the fox bats with a wingspan of over four feet, she already had her fill of jungle adventure.

While Nick and Wright had gone native and seemed to be in their element, Maggie thought that Wright's tree-house mansion with its soft bed, satin sheets, and French soap sounded better by the moment. Yes, she had agreed with Nick what a simple and earthy existence it was here in the rainforest. But she'd also seen how hard the women of the village worked—lugging water from the river and caring for their families. They bore all the same cares as a modern woman but without the help of electricity or refrigeration. The men probably didn't see it.

"You okay?" Wright asked and extended his hand to help her up the steep trail that disappeared into the jungle.

She fanned herself with her hand in the jungle humidity. "Lead on," she said, not wanting to be the buzzkill.

They had traveled less than a mile on the trail when she grew more anxious. "If we see a leopard, is Robert going to fend it off with that stick of his?"

Wright laughed. "That's not a stick. It's a blowpipe, a blowgun."

"Oh, I feel so much better." She rolled her eyes.

"Besides, all those animals are more afraid of us than we are of them." He smiled and added, "Normally."

"Yeah, great," Maggie said.

"We'd be lucky if we see one," Wright said.

"A blowpipe? For real?" Nick asked.

Robert stopped to show them the weapon and handed it to Nick to inspect. "It was my father's and his father's before him. It's been handed down through many generations," Robert said proudly.

"What kind of dart do you use?" Nick asked.

Robert reached into the leather pouch around his neck and lifted out a large folded leaf, which he carefully opened, revealing five long wooden darts. They resembled long toothpicks with a cotton plug on one end.

Nick started to reach for one, and Robert pulled the packet away. "Oh no, Dr. Nickloss. You should not touch. They are very poisonous."

"Really? I'm so sorry. I always thought that poisonous darts were urban legend."

Wright put his hand on Nick's shoulder. "The poison is made from the latex of the *Antiaris Toxicara* tree. We have isolated the chemical in the research center—beta-antiarin, a cardiac glycoside. In small, healthy doses these substances decrease the heart rate and increase the output force of the heart. We developed a leading heart medication for congestive heart failure and another for cardiac arrhythmias from that tree—billion-dollar drugs."

"You made a billion from a poison?" Maggie asked.

"Well, two hundred and twenty billion, so far, to be exact," Wright said. "But, like in all of life, too much of a good thing is bad. The amount of the chemical on the tip of one of those darts would stop your heart in seconds."

"Wow," Nick said. "Thanks for not letting me touch it."

"If you received a simple scratch from the dart, it wouldn't hurt, but you would keel over dead," Wright said. He still had hold of Nick's shoulder and turned him toward himself. "And speaking of medical discoveries, I have wanted to ask you something, my friend. I suppose there is no better place than in the middle of the jungle."

"What's that?" Nick asked.

"You know the new drug that we are experimenting with, IGF-1, the one that helped heal my eye so fast? We think it has great orthopedic applications. Would you ever consider coming to work for Zelutex?"

Maggie saw the shock on Nick's face, as he searched for a response. "Well...I..."

"Nick, I don't want you to say anything now. Maybe we can

talk about it more tonight over some *tuak*?" Wright placed a hand on Nick's neck. "I wanted you to think about it before we talk."

Maggie read Nick's face. Over the last six months, he had been fighting a lack of confidence and purpose in his life, and now, one of the richest men in the world was telling him he was valuable. Nick looked at Wright with gratitude. "I don't know what to say, but I look forward to hearing about it."

Robert interrupted by holding up his hand. "Shhhh," he whispered and crouched.

Maggie stooped with Nick and Wright but didn't see a reason for the alarm. Her heart raced. What was it? A leopard? A bear? Or worse, one of the megabats whose image sent chills down her spine? She could not see anything but remained frozen with the men, wondering how many steps it would take her to get back to the boat.

Robert took two steps forward, loaded one of the poisonous darts into the blowpipe, and raised it to his mouth. Something in the foliage rustled. Maggie grabbed the closest arm to her and dug her fingernails into the flesh.

She heard it before seeing it. A branch snapped and a leaf moved, and in a flash of a millisecond, she saw color…reddish-brown. Then it was gone. A leopard?

Robert held his hand out to make sure they didn't come any closer, as he silently took three more steps forward. A small animal appeared from the bush, looked at them and froze. Robert aimed the blowpipe.

"Ohhhh, he's so cute," Maggie said loudly.

And in a flash, it was gone. Robert's dart missed its mark.

Maggie tried shrinking behind Nick and Wright, on whose arm she had left marks.

"I'm sorry, you all," she said and grimaced. "He was so cute."

"He was supposed to be dinner, so I guess we'll have fish tonight," Wright playfully scolded.

"Now you know why my father never took me hunting in Montana," Maggie said. "What was that anyway?"

Robert turned, stood up straight and smiled at her. "A tender heart, along with that beautiful smile." All was forgiven. "It is called a mouse-deer."

Maggie thought it looked like neither a deer nor a mouse. It stood only two feet off the ground and was covered in orange-brown fur like a fox, but shaped like a small goat. The feature that she noticed most was its beautiful dark, Bambi eyes.

"They're delicious," Wright said.

"Well, I couldn't have eaten it anyway. I think I've had enough jungle adventure for one day. I'll be waiting in the boat for you men."

* * *

Of course, they were not going to let Maggie walk by herself to the boat. The jungle was full of things that were ready to hurt or eat her—deadly plants and insects, poisonous snakes and, of course, the carnivores.

"This was not the way we came," Maggie said nervously as they made their way down a trail.

"We have a special treat for you, Maggie." Wright pointed through the trees to the stream.

When they emerged from the jungle, they stood at the top of the waterfall, thirty feet above the crystalline pool and the boat. "I'm afraid, Ms. Maggie, it is our only way down," Robert said with a growing smile.

"Oh, no…there is no way in heck that you're getting me to jump." Maggie shook her head and crossed her arms. "No way, no how. Besides, I have my cell phone in my pocket," she said, pretending that she did.

"Come on, Maggie. You can do this. It'll be fun," Wright taunted her.

Nick stepped to the edge, peered over, turned, and smiled at her. "Just like med school days, when you and John and I would jump off the old bridge into the North Fork of the Flathead."

"You mean when I was young and dumb and had a little too much beer," she protested.

"Come on, Mags, for old times' sake," Nick said. "We can jump together."

She sighed with resignation and took a step to the edge. Nick held out his hand to help her to the rim of the cliff, but she pulled her hands back and shot him a playful perturbed look.

"Don't you dare. If I'm going to do this, it's on my terms." She stepped carefully to the precipice and peered over. "Oh, hell, no. There's probably piranha or some woman-eating monster in that pool."

"You're thinking of the Amazon," Wright said, joining them on the ledge. "I promise you there is nothing here but beautiful clear water."

Before Wright could do more convincing, Robert shot past them over the cliff, giving a primordial yell as he went. He splashed down and then bobbed to the surface with a laugh.

"You're not going to let an eighty-year-old man best you?" Wright asked and leaped off the edge.

When he came to the surface, Maggie yelled. "Oh, I see the plan, leave the defenseless woman on top of the falls so she has no other choice." She grabbed for Nick's hand. "Don't leave me here." She looked wide-eyed at Nick.

"I'm not going anywhere. I'll lead you down the trail if you want."

Maggie looked over the lip again. Robert and Wright had swum to the boat. "Well, I guess when in Rome..." She held tight onto Nick's hand, and they both leaped. Maggie screamed all the way down.

They came up out of the water at the same time, and Maggie grabbed Nick's neck, almost pulling him under water. "I did it!" she yelled. "Now get me out of here."

* * *

They were almost back to the longhouse when a buzzing came from a small bag that Wright had tucked under his seat in the boat. He looked at Nick and Maggie apologetically and sighed deeply. They both looked at the bag in wonder. "I'm so sorry, you all. It's my satellite phone. It's an unfortunate part of leading a company. They know not to call unless it's an absolute emergency."

Wright pulled the bag from its resting place, opened it, pulled out a sat phone, and extended a large antenna.

"Yes," he said into the phone.

"Hello," he said louder. All he heard was rustling. He was about to get mad that someone might have pocket-called him. "Hello?"

He heard shouting and chaos and then sobbing. "Oh my God."

"Amy?"

"Just do it!" Amy shouted to someone in the background.

"Amy, what is happening?"

She said something garbled and sobbed louder.

"Amy, settle down," Wright yelled into the phone.

"He...he went berserk," Dr. Amy cried. "I've never seen anything like it. Oh my God, I don't know what to do."

"Amy, please calm down and tell me what happened. You are not making any sense. Who went berserk?"

There were more sobs and heavy commotion on the other end.

"We need you here, Wright," she screamed into the phone. "He went crazy and tore into Joseph and then killed two females. We had to shoot him...we just had to shoot him."

"What? Who? Joseph?"

"King Louie, we've killed King Louie."

There was a loud gunshot that resounded in the phone just before it went dead. Wright looked at the face of the sat phone.

"Damn. Amy, Amy!" Wright yelled into the phone until he realized it was useless—the connection lost. He immediately hit redial but got only a busy signal. He hung up and dialed another number.

"Leah...Wright. Get to the research center, now!" he yelled. "I have no idea what is happening, but the shit has hit the fan." Wright looked at the time on the phone and calculated the distance. Going downstream at full speed would make the trip much quicker. "I'll be there in four hours."

CHAPTER 23

SEPARATION

"I am so sorry that I'm cutting our time in the jungle short," Wright said as the longhouse came into sight. "There is so much more I wanted to show you."

"I hope everything is okay back at the research center," Nick said.

"Dr. Amy can be a bit on the dramatic side, but I better check on things. I'm just sorry I have to leave."

Nick was disappointed as well. There was something about this place, and he wanted more of it. He knew of all the dangers and peril, even the murdered man. But the Iban seemed to take it all in stride as the cycle of life. If someone from another longhouse had taken the head, it was probably a one-time occurrence. Whoever did it would be exposed and punished. Rumors swirled over an argument between the victim and a man downriver over a fishing hole. They would know the truth soon enough.

"Whatever is brewing at the research center can be dealt with quickly, I'm sure," Wright said. "There is no reason that we can't come back out tomorrow morning."

"We are supposed to fly out in two days anyway," Maggie said, sounding unhappy to be leaving. "I was hoping to do a little shopping in Singapore before we left."

Nick smiled at her. *Ah, the real concern.*

"I've been thinking about your return flight," Wright said.

"With the kind of money we spent on tickets, the airlines are pretty flexible on switching dates if they can...you guys interested?"

"Yeah!" Maggie and Nick answered together.

Nick added, "We don't want to impose, but I'm not sure I'll ever get a chance to see this part of the world again...and you still owe me that *tuak* and work discussion."

"That would be brilliant," Wright said. "For now, you're both welcome to stay here or go back to the research center. I should be back tomorrow sometime."

"I would love to stay with Robert and Ruth. If that's okay with you, Robert," Nick turned to the man, who nodded enthusiastically. Nick turned to Maggie.

She looked at the bottom of the boat. "Sorry, Nick. I'm looking forward to a hot shower and that cozy bed."

"Well, you can each have your way. Nick, stay and enjoy the rainforest, and Maggie, come back with me. I'll have the chefs prepare a delightful meal for you."

Nick regarded Maggie. He was surprised and a little hurt that she was nodding in agreement with Wright's plan. Nick hoped she'd stay at the longhouse, and they might get a little time alone under the stars—as much as that was possible among two-hundred people separated by thin walls.

"Nick, you don't mind?" Maggie asked him.

What was he going to say? *Yes, I mind,* or *I've changed my mind and I am going to go with you.* Either way, he looked like a schmuck. "No, I suppose not. I think you are in good hands."

* * *

Nick waved to Wright and Maggie as the longboat pulled away from the dock. Something in his spirit was unsettled, and he didn't know why. Wright had assured him that he knew the river like the veins on the back of his hand. They'd get home shortly after dark. They debated who should keep the satellite phone. Wright offered to leave it with Nick, but Nick won the argument, wanting them to have it in case they had any problems getting back to the research center.

When they had returned to the longhouse they learned that Ruth had a five-year-old boy in their apartment with a large piece of wood stuck in his hand. It required a doctor's attention, and this sealed Nick's decision to stay. Nick was still sore at Maggie for bailing on their chance to spend time together, but he understood that she wouldn't cherish another night in the hammock with visions of spiders descending from the rafters.

In Robert and Ruth's apartment Nick smiled at the five-year-old. The boy sat on the floor stoically before the white man, holding out his hand to be examined. The boy reminded him of Ibrahim and wondered how he was getting along in the States. Ali and Astî made loving parents for the child and would give him every opportunity to succeed. Maybe he'd even become a doctor—his hands held God's power of healing.

Nick focused his eyes, the eyes that Ibrahim had touched, and he thanked God for the return of his vision. He was sure he would never have adjusted to being blind. The wood in the boy's hand was embedded deep within the thenar eminence, the pad of the palm under the thumb. In Memphis, Nick had removed larger penetrating objects—knives, bullets or the frequent penny nail. A pneumatic nail gun could drive a large nail through a bone as smoothly as it did a two-by-four, and because the nails were often coated with adhesive, they could be difficult to extract.

The splintered piece of wood didn't penetrate nearly that far, but wood was tricky. Its rough edges gripped the tissues like Velcro. If the splinter wasn't removed, it would fester and be infected by morning.

Nick opened the small first-aid kit that Wright left with him. It wasn't much, but it did contain some disinfectant, a syringe, and an eighteen-gauge needle.

He looked at Robert. "Let's lay him down so I can work on his hand."

The boy reclined on the floor mat, and Robert turned the child's face away so he couldn't watch. Robert laid a loving hand on his head for reassurance.

Nick laid prone onto his stomach and took a flashlight in one hand and the needle in the other. It was the first time doing surgery lying down. He rested his arms on the bamboo mat as his normally rock-steady hands shook. His muscle memory had faded and he was amazed how unconfident he felt. *Have I ever been a surgeon?* He was thankful he wasn't trying to reattach a finger, delicately suturing the tiny nerves and arteries together. He was unsure he could ever do that or any other surgery again. Maybe his tenure as a surgeon was truly over. He wished that Wright had explained his job offer more thoroughly; perhaps there was life outside the operating room.

He opened two disinfectant pads and swabbed the area. Nick knew the disinfectant burned, and the child winced. Through trembling hands, he picked at the skin overlying the chunk of wood. The child's hand stayed steadier than his own. Using the sharp end of the needle, he unroofed the splinter and gently pulled at the wood. Breaking it off would be unfortunate, and he decided a bit more dissection was needed, but going deeper would be painful.

He looked at Robert and then the boy, who had a tear falling down his cheek but remained still. Nick had forgotten how much he detested hurting people. *Why does pain so often precede healing, Father?*

He slipped the needle along each side of the wood, trying to release its grip. The trick worked, and the piece of wood lifted out with the needle. He held the three-inch splinter up to the light and then showed the boy, whose eyes widened, and he smiled.

"Robert, tell him I'm going to wash the wound with some soap and water, put a dressing on and then we're done. I'm not going to put any stitches in so as not to get it infected. It's better to leave it open. We'll clean it every day while I'm here."

The child sat up and took the splinter from Nick, chatting happily.

"He wants to show his friends," Robert explained.

Nick patted the boy on the head and the boy smiled at his hand without the wood sticking out.

Nick was as relieved as the boy.

* * *

Wright looked out the windows of the conference room as Leah handed Dr. Amy a glass of water. The CEO had the situation under control before they had reached the research center. He wasn't surprised, as he had little doubt in her ability. He told Maggie she should go enjoy a long bath and gave his chef instructions to prepare something delicious for her. Then he went about settling Dr. Amy's nerves and finding out what had happened.

Amy was ashen, and mascara smeared her face. He'd always hated dealing with emotions. Leading a company of eight thousand would be easy if not for the weak and sensitive people. *Needy people helping people in need*—maybe that should be the company's real slogan. Dr. Amy was one of the worst. She was brilliant and a valuable researcher but always needed reassurance. He sighed and pushed his anger down.

"What do you think happened?" he asked her.

"Bloody hell, I have no idea. King Louie and the younger male have squabbled a few times in the past, but they always worked it out. We saw no signs of this coming," Amy said, her bottom lip quivering. "Two females were caught between them. Then Joseph, one of the caretakers, went to separate the two, and Louie attacked him. When we got there, Louie was standing on top of Joseph, enraged. There was nothing we could do to coax him away." She put her face in her hands. "I've never seen Louie or any other orangutan behave like that. His eyes were ablaze. Joseph should never have gone in there alone." She wept audibly.

Wright looked at Leah. "Joseph has severe facial and upper body wounds. He is already in surgery in Singapore," she said without emotion.

"Will you do an autopsy of the orangutan?"

Amy wiped at her tears. "Of course."

"And the younger male?" Wright asked.

"Once...Louie was dead"—she stumbled over her words—"and we got Joseph out of there, the younger male went berserk as well. He slammed himself against one of the walls." She started to cough and gag on her emotions. "There was nothing we could do. We had to shoot him as well." She looked at Wright through inflamed red eyes. "I am sorry, I am so sorry," she said, then dissolved into tears again.

"Any thoughts?" Wright looked at Leah, who took a step away from the emotional woman.

"They are wild animals you know," Leah said. "The younger male was challenging the dominant, and the females and the boy got in the way. It's over and cleaned up."

"Okay, let me know if you find something unusual on the autopsies," Wright said and left the room.

* * *

The knock on her door surprised Maggie. She was lying on the bed, not expecting company, and was wearing only an oversized T-shirt. She quickly sat up and covered herself with the bed sheet.

"Come in," she called.

Wright opened the door, and any embarrassment she might have felt evaporated when she saw the baby orangutan in his arms. "Oh my Lord, that has to be the cutest thing I've ever seen in my life," she gushed.

"Sorry to disturb you. I was hoping you were still up so we could come for a visit." Wright bounced the small ape on his hip as though it were a young child. He poked the ape's fat belly and held out his hand. The little ape grabbed his finger. The baby stuck out its tongue and leaned backward so that it hung upside down, clowning for Maggie.

The baby was so ugly it was adorable. Its dark forehead resembled a bald-headed old man with tufts of hair sticking straight up in back. It blew raspberries at Maggie from big lips and a tan mug. The baby's dark, inquisitive eyes searched her up and down. Apparently satisfied, the baby ape somersaulted out of Wright's arms onto the floor. It made endearing hooting sounds as it waddled to Maggie's bed, its gangly arms held over his head for balance. The baby ape's reddish-brown fur was fine and frizzled, as though its keepers had blown it out with a hair dryer.

Maggie threw off the sheet and leaped off the bed to receive the baby. It took two quick skips and jumped into her arms. It was heavier than she expected, but it buried its face in the nape of her neck and purred like a contented cat.

"I think he likes you," Wright said and smiled.

"I have never seen anything as delightful, I swear." Maggie cuddled into the baby orangutan. "Does he have a name?"

"Well, LT-4, but say the word and you can give him a proper name."

The ape reached up and caressed her face. Then he took a strand of her hair and ran it between his nose and his upper lip, creating a black mustache. Maggie and Wright laughed. Their approval animated the baby even more, and he puckered his face at Maggie, staring deeply into her eyes. His eyes were like black onyx gems that searched the depths of her soul.

"They're like little humans, aren't they?" Maggie said.

"At least the closest thing to it."

"I'm going to have to take you home, little one." The baby seemed to understand and wrapped his arms around her neck. She patted his back and turned seriously to Wright. "Everything else okay? I've been worried."

"Yes, it's all fine now. A bit of a rouse with a couple of the males, but everything is back in its place."

"I'm so glad." Maggie pulled away from the baby to look at his face. "I think we should call him Larry. He reminds me of a Larry, don't you think?" She turned the orangutan toward Wright.

The baby grabbed the edge of Maggie's long T-shirt, and before she could react, pulled it up, almost exposing her breasts.

She shrieked and tried pushing the baby away from her, but his arms were as long as hers, and he wouldn't let go of her nightshirt. Wright came racing to her rescue and pulled the baby away. The orangutan protested loudly.

"This little guy must be hungry," Wright said. "I'll take him back."

Maggie bristled and pulled her shirt back into place, laughing with embarrassment. "Sorry, Larry, you won't find any dinner there." Then she added, "Larry. He's definitely a Larry."

CHAPTER 24

FISHING

Nick didn't know how the Iban did it. There were too many things to think about, like not falling off the end of the boat or knocking himself in the water with the net. With his pale white skin and lack of fishing skills, the only reason he came close to fitting in was that he was bare chested and wearing shorts like all the other men fishing on the river. Robert had found some shade from the jungle canopy at a fishing hole and was laughing.

"I think you have frightened the fish to death, Nickloss. They should be floating to the surface any moment." He then gave an even louder snort.

Nick stood on the nose of the boat, peering into the water of the fishing hole, and pulled the weighted net up by its rope. Of course it was empty. It had hit the water like a chunk of concrete with a loud splash—a complete belly flop.

"Let me show you one more time," Robert said and joined him at the front of the boat. The near-eighty-year-old moved with ease in the longboat. Taking the net from Nick, he stepped to the very lip of the boat, like he was hanging ten on a surfboard. Nick estimated that the casting net weighed less than fifteen pounds, so it wasn't the weight that was the problem; but once expanded, the net was almost fifteen feet in diameter with yards of nylon to hold onto. Robert took part of the weighted line into his mouth and showed Nick once again how to separate the net, fashion it around his arms, twist his body at the waist, and let it fly. Robert's throw made a beautiful circle in the air before touching down on the top of the water and sinking to the depths below. He let the lead line sink for a half a minute, then pulled it all in. There were two small fish wiggling in the net as he brought it up. He opened the net, and the two fish fell into the bottom of the boat and flopped around.

"It's like that, Nickloss," Robert said, smiling and handing the net back to him.

"You know, when I would go fishing with my dad in Montana we would always have to give each other a dollar for the first, the most, and the largest fish. So far, I owe you three dollars."

Nick took the net and stepped to the front of the boat. He wasn't sure about putting the net in his mouth, but the Iban had done it from the beginning of time, and they were healthy. He hoped giardia wasn't going to be part of this adventure. He mimicked Robert's hold on the net as best he could, turned his body like a discus thrower, then unwound, twisting hard and fast, and let go.

It wasn't pretty. Part of the net caught on itself, but the worst part was, he forgot to let go with his teeth, and the net pulled him over. He kept from falling into the water but smacked his forearm hard against the side of the boat.

Robert was at his side in an instant. "You okay, Nickloss?"

Nick pushed himself up and inspected a large scrape down his forearm. But at least he hadn't let go of the hand rope and lost the net. Robert helped him sit back on the side of the boat as Nick nursed his arm.

"You will get it. It takes years of practice—I started before I can remember," the old man said and patted him affectionately on the head. "Come on, give it another go." Robert pulled on the hand line, but as the net came up out of the water, it held a large fish.

"Look at what we have here!" Robert cheered in excitement. "An Empurau."

The flopping fish looked something like a carp with large greenish-blue scales and weighed in at three to four pounds.

"Nickloss, you have caught dinner for us tonight and a delicious one at that."

"Really?" Nick said. His arm stopped hurting as much.

"Oh, yes. My people eat very little of these fish anymore because they are so valuable at the fish market in Malaysia. This guy would probably be worth a few months' salary, maybe three hundred dollars."

"Well, then you should take it, Robert, and sell it."

"Oh, no, Nickloss. Some things are more valuable than money. Tonight, we eat like kings."

Robert dumped the fish at his feet, and Nick reached in and grabbed it by the gills. He held it up to Robert with a huge smile, but as he did, the fish shook so hard it came off of his fingers. It hit the bottom of the boat, bounced once, bounced twice and was almost over the side before they could react. Nick dived for it and smacked his forehead against the edge of the wooden seat, but it was Robert who saved the fish from going overboard. He thumped it on the head and threw it into a bucket of fresh water behind his seat.

"That was a close one." Robert laughed.

Nick rubbed both his forehead and arm. "I didn't remember fishing being such a contact sport." He laughed with his friend. "I went fishing once with John and Maggie and her dad. Her dad was so competitive; he would have let the fish go over and said it didn't count."

Robert smiled and sat facing him. "Maggie is a very special lady."

The statement surprised Nick, and he looked at the old man. Robert's smile disappeared, and he turned serious. "You know, Nickloss, God will give you what you need, but you have to fight for what you want."

"You mean Maggie?"

"Of course. I was surprised when you let Master Paul take her away."

Nick's heart sank. *Was it that obvious?*

"He can be very persuasive," Robert said.

This was not helping. If he knew where to go, Nick would point the boat downstream immediately and go to get her back.

What was I thinking? He didn't even have the sat phone to call her; he'd relinquished that as well. He shook the thoughts out of his head. She loved him, she'd told him so, and he'd have to trust in that fact and trust her.

"Is that why you sold the land to Wright? He made you a deal you couldn't pass up?" Nick said, changing the subject.

Robert watched a bird with a bright red head and chest and long colorful tail wing by. "That is a hard question, Nickloss. Many of my people were upset at me and still are." A shadow of somberness crossed his face. "The Iban are the guardians of the rainforest. We believe that if there is no rainforest, there is no more earth. This is the oldest rainforest on the planet. The scientists have told us that it is one hundred and forty million years old."

The old man closed his eyes like he was praying or tired. A tear formed in the corner of his eye. "I am going to tell you something that only my wife and the elders know. Part of the settlement was that I would not discuss the deal with anyone else, and I have kept that part to this day." He glanced around as though the forest were listening. "There was a battle raging over the land that I sold to Master Paul. A logging company was challenging our ownership of that portion of land and threatened to take it by force. Mr. Paul came to our rescue and overbid the loggers, and his lawyers chased them away. I had to sell. My comfort is that the land is used for research and not clear-cutted."

"Well, that was good of him."

Robert nodded but bit his lower lip.

"And?" Nick asked.

"And...I have told no one else this, not even my wife." Robert lowered his voice even though they were alone on the river. "I do not know if I should even say this, as I have no proof and my people have reasons to distrust Master Paul as it is."

"It's okay, Robert. You don't need to tell me either."

Robert seemed to straighten his back with resolve. "I think Master Paul may own the logging company as well."

Nick nodded. Relinquishing the secret seemed to take a burden off the old man's shoulders. "He was going to get the land one way or another. You had no choice."

Robert leaned back, scooped a handful of water and splashed it over his head. "Yes, I suppose you're right."

"Why don't some of the men like Wright? They always are polite to him to his face."

"Of course. That is the Iban way. But that animosity has run its course for many generations. It goes back to Rentap and James Brooke. Forgiveness is not natural for those of us in the rainforest. Some hold on to bitterness and are unsure why."

A raindrop hit Nick's shoulder and then his arm. Rain dimpled the water as the clouds above the canopy let loose their volley. The shower was a welcome relief from the heat and humidity of the afternoon, and instead of motoring for cover, Robert raised his arms in celebration and scrubbed his face and chest in the downpour. Nick followed suit, and the rain finished almost as soon as it started.

"I guess that's why they call it the rainforest," Nick said.

"It is what keeps us all alive," Robert said and smiled. "Master Paul told me about the injuries to your eyes and that you may give up being a doctor. What do you think you are going to do with yourself now?" he asked. "I saw what you did for the witch doctor and that little boy. I think you are a very good doctor, Nickloss."

"Thanks, Robert, but it's pretty complicated. I have been out of surgery for a while and I'm not sure I can go back. It's like I'm all thumbs now, even doing something as simple as taking that wood piece out of the boy's hand. Besides, medicine in the US is a mess. It's all based on profits and production. Doctors have become a commodity for the medical system to use, and they are spending less and less of their time taking care of patients."

"Can't go back or don't want to go back?" Robert asked.

"Well, that's a good question. I wish I could take all the things I love about medicine and make a living at it. A surgeon is required to do a certain amount of surgery just to pay the bills, and the mountain of bills keeps growing. A lot of doctors have given up and sold out to the hospital where they become a mere pawn of the system."

"But I see healing in your hands. I saw how the miracle for the witch doctor surprised even you. You need to know that in

Him we are far more loved and powerful than we can possibly imagine."

Nick smiled to himself and heard Chang in Robert's voice. "I'm not sure what I'll do," Nick told Robert. "I have to make a living somehow."

Robert laughed. "Yes, our lives are laid out before us like the twists and turns of our river. As we move through it, we are given choices—and we are not smart enough to know what is good and what is bad for us...therefore we need the Holy Spirit to guide us and then to say, 'Your will, Father, not mine.'"

Nick nodded.

"Look at my people. We do not have much, but we have everything we need. I'll tell you what, you can stay here and be a doctor, and we will pay you in chickens."

Both men laughed.

"You heard Wright asking me to consider working for his company. Do you like working for Wright?" Nick asked.

Robert only nodded and looked beyond the river in contemplation. "It would not be my first choice, but I feel like the Holy Spirit has asked me to do so. I still do not see the reason why."

"Was your longhouse part of the clinical study for this latest drug?" Nick asked.

"No. I have told my people that we will not be a part of the drug testing. We do not need the money from it. Besides, I have never heard of such a thing...taking a pill to make you happy." He searched the jungle. "After all, this is all we need." He stretched his arms. "But Dr. Amy told me that many people around the world suffer and the medication would help them not be miserable."

"And what do you think?" Nick asked.

"I think the Iban people have endured much throughout time." Robert gathered his thoughts. "But somehow the suffering that we go through is important...there are no shortcuts. I think God is preparing us for eternity."

Nick contemplated Robert's words as two large black birds flew into the trees overhead and barked out their calls. The birds sounded and looked prehistoric with gigantic, hooked bills and secondary bright orange horns that jutted out from their foreheads. The birds' blinking blue eyes seemed to judge the men.

"My ancestors thought these birds, the Great Rhinoceros Hornbills, served as intermediaries between man and God," Robert explained. "Even before we came to know Jesus, we understood that we must have a connection to Him. It is the only way to understand life and the suffering that we endure…it is our only hope…to abide in Him."

"What do the villagers who are participating in the drug study say about the medicine?"

"They are happy to get the white man's money. Most say they don't feel any different. But the witch doctors are calling it *mali*…bad."

"Really? Why is that? Do they see side effects?"

"No, not really, but some are saying that they can no longer hear from the spirit world. Even the witch doctors know there is a cost…taking a shortcut always costs something."

Nick nodded and sighed deeply, watching the hornbills overhead. When he looked back at Robert, the old man was smiling and holding up two fingers.

"What, Robert?"

"You may have caught the largest fish, but I caught the first and the most," he said looking at the two small fish still flopping in the bottom of the boat. "You owe me two dollars."

CHAPTER 25

PINECONE

Wright frowned at the haggard-looking doctor with her stringy, oily hair hanging around her face. Amy wore no makeup and had an annoying piece of food caught in her front teeth. Leah didn't look much better, standing behind them with her arms crossed.

"You get any sleep at all last night?" Wright asked them.

They ignored his question, and Dr. Amy continued with her findings. "The autopsies on both King Louie and the other male were unremarkable except for their injuries and the gunshot wounds." Her voice trailed off. "This whole thing is buggered up—even their brains were unremarkable. I'd almost hoped I'd find a tumor to explain the change in behavior."

"Nothing?" Wright asked.

The doctor turned to her computer and typed on the keyboard. Instantly images of brain MRI scans filled the large monitors hanging over her desk.

"Fortunately, we have prestudy cranial MRIs on both of them." She pointed to the screen on the left. "And postmortem scans." She indicated the right.

Wright bent to look closer. He knew what the grainy black-and-white images of the brain represented and searched between the screens for differences. There were none.

"I don't see any changes," he said.

"Exactly. I didn't either." Amy nodded. "I ran the new program we recently purchased to measure the exact size of each portion of the brain." She typed a sequence of keystrokes, and the scans disappeared, replaced with 3-D images of the brain. Each section of the brain was clearly marked in different colors. She took a joystick off her desk and manipulated the images, rotating the brain and splitting it into pieces. The cerebrum divided into its right and left hemispheres and then into the four lobes of each. She separated the brainstem into its three regions. Amy pushed buttons on the keyboard. The outer portion of the brain faded, and the deep structures expanded into view—the hypothalamus (the master control of the autonomic system), the pituitary and pineal glands, the thalamus, and the limbic system (the center of human emotion).

Wright studied the models and nodded in approval. He glanced at Leah, who looked away in boredom, then back at Amy. "See anything?"

"Nothing significant," she said, adding, "there is one tiny difference."

She began typing again, and spreadsheets replaced the images, listing every portion of the brain and revealing the exact size of each. "You would expect to see discrepancies here…the difference between a living brain and one with no blood circulating through it. In this column, I adjusted for the variations, then compared each region again." She pointed to one line of the sheet. "This is the *only* difference I could see. There is a 30 percent reduction in the size of the pineal gland, and even that's reaching." She threw her hands up. "I'm beached. I have no idea."

"The pineal gland?"

"We have not talked about this very small gland." She replaced the spreadsheets with the MRI scans. She zoomed in to an area in the very depths of the brain. "The pineal gland is the only midline brain structure that is azygous."

"Azygous?" Wright asked, irritated that she was being obtuse.

"It's a single entity…it's unpaired. Every other area of the brain has two of itself, a left and a right. The pineal gland is one-of-a-kind and stranger; it is the only part of the brain that is not isolated from the body by the blood-brain barrier. Amazingly, this small gland has a great deal of blood flow, second only to the kidney."

"Where is it?" Wright asked, looking at the scan.

"This is it." The doctor pointed to a tiny dot on the screen. "In the human brain, it's the size of a grain of rice."

"Geez, no wonder we couldn't see any changes. What's it do?"

"That's a very good question. It's a bit of mystery. For sure we know it produces melatonin."

"That regulates our sleep?" Wright asked.

"Exactly. But this tiny structure does much more. It also produces a type of serotonin and, crazy enough, the gland contains photoreceptor cells."

"Photoreceptor cells? Like the cells in the retina of the eye?" Wright straightened his back and rubbed his head. "Why would that occur in the depths of the brain where there is no light?"

Dr. Amy laughed. "The pineal gland holds an exalted status in pseudoscience. A Greek physician named Herophilus described the pinecone-shaped structure in the third century BC. It's where it got its name. The New Agers call it the third eye, and throughout the years, theories have popped up now and again that it's the center of our spiritual experiences...like some antennae to the divine."

Wright laughed and shrugged. "What do you think?"

"Who knows? To make it more interesting, the staff that the Pope carries, the papal ferula, has a pinecone between his hand and the Christ—the connection between God and man. The Vatican even has a huge pinecone statue connecting the palace to the Sistine Chapel."

"The Fontana della Pigna? I've seen it," Wright said excitedly to Leah, who just shrugged. He turned back to Amy. "The portal between the seen and the unseen?"

"Yes, even the Maya have statues of pinecones." Amy smiled at him. "Plato may have been a believer in the pineal gland when he said, 'The soul through these disciplines has an organ purified and enlightened, an organ better worth saving than ten thousand corporeal eyes, since truth becomes visible through this alone.'"

"You're right, who knows," Boxler grumbled, starting to fidget with talk of the divine. "I guess the important thing is we don't see a reaction to Welltrex. I can't imagine a small decrease in a rice-sized gland caused all this."

Leah's phone rang, interrupting the discussion.

Wright watched her expression change to concern as she listened. He could tell she was serious when she pulled on a random hair on her chin.

"What's up?" he mouthed.

"Yes, I'm standing here with him. I'll tell him."

Leah ended the call and looked at Wright. "It's your grandmother. She has fallen and broken her hip. She is with the surgeon now."

"Is she okay otherwise?" Wright asked, annoyed at her lack of empathy. "Did she hit her head?"

"No, she's fine. Her staff called the ambulance straight away. Her surgeon is one of the finest in Calcutta."

Wright was about to push for more information when Amy interrupted them.

"Bloody hell," Amy said and pushed away from the computer. "I'm sorry about your grandmother, but maybe I was too pissed-up to think straight. I've been looking for something that the medication did, some structure change, some reaction, some side effect." She put her hands on top of her head. "Oh my God, Wright. What if this is withdrawal? I stopped the medication last week, both for the orangutans and in the human trials…I've got to get upriver."

* * *

Maggie's world had shrunk. A month ago, she couldn't have imagined being in Singapore, never mind the mysterious island of Borneo, but now here she was in the heart of Calcutta.

Wright gave her a choice to stay at the research center or accompany him. He convinced her he needed the moral support and reassured her their visit would be short. They'd be back by morning to travel upriver and join Nick. He was positive Nick wouldn't mind and was being well cared for and having a wonderful time with Robert and his wife. Dr. Amy was heading upriver. She would tell them of his grandmother's injury and to expect them to be late, so Nick wouldn't worry.

Maggie hoped Nick wouldn't be upset. After all, he understood broken bones better than any of them.

Maggie had always wanted to visit Calcutta, the home of her hero, Mother Teresa. The saint worked, lived, and showed the love of the Father to the outcasts like no one else. Maggie thought how amazing it would be to visit the very streets and mission where Mother Teresa worked. She didn't ask, however, because Wright's grandmother was their focus.

The trip in Wright's sleek jet took only two hours, and it was thrilling to watch him fly it. He sounded so official when he talked with the towers in Singapore and Calcutta. But she could tell he was nervous. He admitted it was the fastest he'd ever flown the jet, just under the speed of sound, and he seemed worried about their fuel consumption.

After they landed, a courteous man in a silver Bentley chauffeured them to the hospital. Maggie saw the power of money. Everything was so convenient—staff and other amenable people were always present. One staffer offered to carry her purse so she wasn't burdened, but that was where she drew the line.

They walked into Calcutta's modern Ruby Hospital, and even there, a young woman was waiting to escort them to the post-operative area.

"Your grandmother is quite well. Dr. Gupta, her surgeon, who owns this hospital, I might add, will meet us promptly," the woman said in broken English.

"How long has she been out of surgery?" Wright asked.

The woman looked at her watch. "Fifty-three minutes."

Maggie smiled at the staffer. *Yes, there is power with money.* Maggie watched the numbers in the elevator click until it reached five. There was a loud ding, and they exited.

"Dr. Gupta has put your grandmother in our finest suite. I hope that suits you," the woman said, bowing and extending her hand toward the hallway. "Mr. and Mrs. Paul, may I offer you something to drink while you wait for the doctor?"

Heat rose into Maggie's cheeks, and she flushed with awkwardness. "I'm not...we're not..."

Wright came to her rescue. "This is my friend Ms. Russell, and please, I think we could use some water." He smiled at Maggie, seeming to enjoy her blush.

"Please forgive me." The embarrassment transferred from Maggie to the young woman. "I'll get the water straight away."

As she turned away, a portly Indian man in scrubs and a white coat strode down the corridor. "Oh good. Here is Dr. Gupta now," the woman said and bowed out.

Dr. Gupta appeared to be a jolly man. He was licking his lips and wiped something greasy from his chin, then without cleaning his hand on a handkerchief offered it to Wright and then to Maggie. He was as full of himself as he was of his meals. "Your grandmother was in quite capable hands, I can assure you." He thrust out both of his hands to emphasize the point. "She is doing very well. She sustained a fracture of her hip that required us to replace it," he said.

"A hemi or a total?" Maggie asked, surprising the doctor.

He bobbed his head from side to side, seemingly bothered to be questioned by a woman, and looked over the top of his glasses at her. "We prefer a total here at Ruby. We replaced both the ball and the socket, so no arthritis develops in the joint," he said with some annoyance.

"Dr. Gupta, this is Maggie Russell from the US. She is well aware of medical procedures."

"Are you a surgeon?"

"No, I run a mission hospital in Guatemala."

"That's nice." He smiled at her as one would smile at a small child, then spoke to Wright. "Well, please, let me show you to your grandmother's room, and then I must get back to surgery."

The surgeon led them down the hallway, and Wright whispered into Maggie's ear. "More like back to his lunch… pompous ass." He imitated the surgeon's waddle, and Maggie choked back a snicker.

They entered the room where two nurses attended Wright's grandmother.

"She had a spinal for surgery, so she is awake but groggy," Dr. Gupta said. "Now if you would please excuse me, I am required back in the operating theater."

Wright ignored the man's extended hand and went straight to his grandmother.

"Grandmama, it's Wright. You have given us quite a fright. How do you feel?" He held one of her hands and put his other on her forehead where a washcloth lay.

The old woman, looking fragile and pale, opened her eyes at the sound of his voice. Even in her state of semiconsciousness, she smiled. "Mowgli, how good of you to come, my dear. Bless your heart."

"Grandmama, how are you doing?"

"I will be fine, dear. I got a little off-kilter is all." Her eyes drifted closed.

Wright indicated to Maggie that she should come forward. Before he could introduce her, his grandmother's eyes opened, and she turned toward Maggie, looking surprised.

"Kumārī, my daughter. You are here. Oh, my lovely Kumārī." Her eyes closed again.

One of the nurses stepped forward. "She is still waking up from the pain medicine. If you would kindly give us a moment to take her vitals, you can talk with her in a moment." She smiled with compassion.

Wright and Maggie stepped to a corner of the room.

"Poor thing. She has been through a lot. She is so sweet." Maggie whispered and grinned at Wright with her newly acquired secret.

"Yes, yes…she still calls me Mowgli. It was my nickname growing up."

"That's so precious," Maggie said. "She called me something. I think she thought I was someone else."

Wright grinned. "I think she thought you were my mother… Kumārī."

CHAPTER 26

TRUST

"Do you trust me?" The voice in Nick's heart said again.

Nick floated on his back in the cool river water. It had been a peaceful morning: breakfast, harvesting bananas with Robert for lunch, and now bath time. Maggie and Wright should be back any moment. Maybe his life had just slowed enough to listen, but God was speaking to him like never before. Perhaps this was a thin place and the water, a river of transformation. With his ears below the waterline, he heard the muffled sounds of the visible world and the people around him, but the unseen world seemed amplified in this place. The message was clear—the Holy Spirit was speaking to him.

He decided there must be two problems causing the worry and fear that chased him all his life—either he didn't believe in God's promises, or he didn't believe in general. *Father, forgive me.* He was growing in the former, and the latter was fading.

Nick reached his arms behind him and pulled himself along the surface of the water, the sun warming his face. *Father, what am I to do with my life now?*

"Do you trust me?" the Holy Spirit said again.

"Yes, Father, I trust you," Nick said aloud, still trying to believe it in his heart. "But can you make it a little clearer for me?"

He felt Robert tapping his legs and let them sink to the bottom of the river so he could stand. He hoped it was a signal that Wright and Maggie had arrived at the longhouse. A boat was motoring around the bend of the river, but there was only one person in the vessel. Nick wiped the water from his eyes and focused. It was Dr. Amy.

She steered to the landing area, and a young man swam to the boat and pushed it up on shore for her. She disembarked from the front.

Nick paddled to shore and grabbed his towel from a tree branch; he wrapped it around his neck as Robert joined him. Amy did not look well. Anxiety pumped through Nick's veins.

"Do you trust me?" Nick heard in his heart.

He pushed the voice away and stepped toward Amy. "Everything okay?"

"No, it's terrible," Amy said and looked at the ground.

Images of tragedy filled his mind, and his heart pounded.

"We've had quite a 'mare…two of the male orangutans had to be put down."

"And Maggie and Wright?" Nick asked fearfully.

"Oh, they're fine," she said. "Wright's grandmother has fallen and broken her hip and required surgery yesterday. They went to visit her in Calcutta," she added nonchalantly. "They're as good as gold."

"India?" Nick's voice came out an octave higher.

"Yes, but they should be back tonight or tomorrow, aye."

Nick's heart sank. He shouldn't have let her go, or at the least he should have gone with her. Self-condemnation rose in his heart and with it, sinister voices shouting. They fought to replace the still, small voice of the Holy Spirit.

Robert must have sensed his angst. He put a hand on Nick's back. "Everything will be fine." He turned to Amy. "What males?"

"King Louie and RT-13," Amy said, wiping a tear from her eye. "It was awful, Robert, just awful."

"Oh, that's bad," Robert said and stepped closer to her. "What happened?"

"I don't know for sure. It's the danger of working with wild animals, I suppose, but I worry about the apes having a reaction to the medication. Early in the animal trials of Welltrex, we occasionally encountered aggressive behavior at higher than therapeutic doses. But the apes have been off the medication for a few days. My gut is telling me there is something more. My fear and working hypothesis are that one or both of the apes were having withdrawal reactions from Welltrex." She wiped her face with the back of her forearm. "If that's true, I need to get to the longhouses that were in the clinical trials."

"We'll go with you," Robert said.

* * *

The first longhouse sat an hour up the Batang Ai River and another half hour along a tributary. A rain shower met them along the way, and the clouds remained low and grew thicker as the longhouse came into view. A mist hung over the structure like a shroud. Something inside Nick screamed danger.

The longhouse was half the size of Robert's. It was intact but dead quiet. Robert guided their boat past it, turned off the motor, and let the current carry them slowly past the village. Robert watched the longhouse and scanned the jungle. He was on high alert, bearing the same affect he did when stalking an animal.

There was an occasional call from an animal or the bark of hornbills far in the distance.

"There are no fires," he whispered and gripped the handle of his machete. "They should be preparing dinner."

The boat drifted to the shore where five empty boats tied to the trees bumped against the mud.

"What do you think?" Nick asked.

"I think something is terribly wrong," Robert whispered.

"Do you suppose we should go back and get more men?" Amy asked loudly enough that Robert shushed her.

A sound came from the longhouse, and Robert crouched.

"See anything?" Nick whispered.

Robert shook his head and stepped in front of Amy and Nick to pull the longboat onto the mud. He didn't tie it off.

He motioned for them to stay in the boat and turned to the looming structure.

"Robert, wait. You can't go in there alone," Nick whispered, stepping out of the boat. "I'll go with you."

Amy was on his heels. "I don't think it wise to separate, aye."

They crept up the path, stopping every few feet to look and listen. There was that sound again. Robert's bare feet made no noise in the dirt, but Amy's flip-flops made plenty. Nick turned and eyed her feet.

"Sorry," she mouthed and slipped them off.

Robert made it to the base of the longhouse and scanned in every direction, peering up and over the closed gate to where the animals were kept. Nick made his way silently to Robert's side.

The old man whispered in his ear, "The gate is closed like it was night, but there is not one animal here."

There was a thump overhead, and the two men ducked, fearing something was coming at them, but there was nothing. Robert pointed up to the floor of the complex. He moved to the stairs and stealthily took the first few steps.

Nick tried to follow, but each step creaked under his weight. *Crap.*

Robert made it to the top and signaled for him to continue despite the noise. By the time Nick and Amy reached the landing, Robert had his machete unsheathed. They stood on the patio and listened. The sound had stopped.

The silence of the surrounding jungle was unnerving, but the absence of the usual, vibrant Iban community was even more ominous.

They crept across the open patio to the side of the longhouse. There were no windows to peer into and no way to find out what was happening inside except to go through the front door. As they stepped to the entrance, Nick's sense of smell awoke and transported him to his first day of anatomy lab with a cadaver—it was the smell of death.

He grabbed Robert's shoulder and pointed at his own nose. Robert nodded and grimaced. The old man's muscles tensed as he pushed open the partially ajar front door.

The common area was pitch black, and Nick was about to look beyond Robert when it hit him.

* * *

A Calcutta taxi driver laid on his horn and cut in front of the Bentley, missing the front fender by a fraction of an inch, but clipped the wheel of a rickshaw they were passing. The drivers all exchanged words and finger waves.

Wright's driver looked into the rearview mirror. "Forgive me, sir." He said and bobbed his head. "Calcutta taxi drivers are crazy men."

Wright nodded and smiled at Maggie.

She smiled back and said, "I'm just glad he is driving."

Wright looked out the side window and watched the traffic zoom past. He was thrilled with the effects of Confide. The oxytocin-packed cologne was already on the market and doing well, but he was especially fond of the version he was wearing because it was custom-made for him. His scientists had added another molecule exclusive to his bottle. They called it the "Right Stuff," making a play on their boss's name and the astronaut movie. Wright couldn't smell the change it made, but the men promised it was there. When they exposed a person to the spray, the oxytocin excited all the feel-good neurons like regular Confide did. But because it contained the exclusive molecule corresponding to his natural scent, the affection of that person would be directed to Wright alone. What an advantage it gave him in business when his adversary's brain was tricked into trusting him.

Now it was working its magic on Maggie. He could see it in her eyes. When she came close to him, he believed he could see her almost animalistic attraction. He had not made a move on it, wanting to keep her arousal maximized until the timing was perfect.

"Thank you for coming with me to see Grandmama." He turned and smiled at her. "She's all the family I have left. Thank you for understanding. I don't feel comfortable leaving her here alone."

Maggie smiled at him, and he had a peculiar sensation of wanting to hold her close. He wondered if the oxytocin was affecting his own brain.

"I certainly understand, but I hope Robert and Nick are

getting along without us," she said.

"I'm sure they're surviving," Wright said. "Amy would have arrived at Robert's longhouse this afternoon, and they'd know by now what is happening. I'm sure they'll understand. Amy took the satellite phone...they should be checking in with us soon."

Wright twisted the yellow rose in his fingers and held it to his nose. "These are Grandmama's favorite. I'm hoping it wakes her brain up."

"Poor thing, she's been pretty confused," Maggie said. "It has to be frightening for her. From my experience at the mission hospital, confusion is common for the elderly after big surgeries."

Wright nodded. "The brain is so complex—it has fascinated me since I was a little boy."

She looked at him with a sparkle in her eye. "Mowgli," she teased.

He chuckled with her. "That will only be fair if you share your childhood nickname." He said, poking her in her ribs.

Maggie looked out the window from the back of the Bentley at the towering hospital. She turned to him, zipped her lips with her fingers and tossed an imaginary key over her shoulder.

"Please." He pleaded with his eyes.

"Okay, just don't laugh at me."

Wright held up his hand as if taking an oath.

"Only my dad called me this...well, sometimes my mom as well when we were fighting, and she wanted to be snarky... Princess. He calls me his Princess," Maggie said, blushing.

The nickname shocked Wright, and he tried to hide his emotions by turning to the window.

Maggie touched his shoulder. "I'm sorry, Wright. Did I say something to upset you?"

He looked at her, trying to decide if he should confide in her. She was touching part of his soul that few had.

"You know how Grandmama called you by my mother's name, Kumārī?" He paused, struggling to get the words out. "It is no wonder that you remind her of my mother with your beautiful complexion and long black hair." He smiled at her. "*Kumārī* is the Bengali word for 'princess.' My father called my mother...Princess."

CHAPTER 27

BEAST OF BURDEN

The animal hit Nick with such force it knocked him to the ground. But it wasn't attacking; it was escaping. The leopard took three long strides across the patio, sprang over the railing and was gone. Amy screamed, and Robert froze, then rushed to Nick's aid.

"Nickloss, you okay?"

Slightly dazed, he sat up. "Man-oh-man, that scared the crap out of me." Nick rubbed the back of his head.

"Are you hurt?" Amy asked.

"I don't think so." He felt his chest where the large cat hit him. His shirt was torn. Through the tatters he saw sizable scratches across his pecs.

Amy knelt to look at his injury. "Thankfully they're superficial," she said.

Robert gave him a hand up. As frightening as the big cat was, the smell reminded them that more horror was inside. Nick brought the top of his torn shirt over his nose and nodded at Robert to enter.

The common area was pitch black, and the three stood inside the threshold allowing their eyes to adjust to the darkness.

Robert picked up a kerosene lamp from a table near the door. He found some matches next to it and lit the wick, illuminating the area with an ominous glow. It appeared to be empty except for a crumpled mass near the far end.

Robert looked at Nick and then at Amy, his eyes wide with fear. Instead of stepping toward the body, Robert pushed the first apartment door open and held the lantern up into the room. It was deserted.

As was the next and the next.

They made their way down the row and finally to the end of the common area to the body—a half-eaten pig carcass lying in a bloody mess of bowels and flesh, the leopard's bloody tracks all around it.

Robert checked the last room and held the lantern to Nick's and Amy's faces.

"We should leave. It is not safe here," he said.

* * *

The Calcutta Polo Club could have come straight out of Kentucky, Maggie imagined. Horses grazed on rolling hills of lush, green grass. Wooden fences framed them all. She had never been to the Bluegrass State, but she'd seen photos that matched this beauty.

Their driver followed the tree-lined lane to a massive white wooden barn with copper cupolas topped with weather vanes. This was not the Calcutta that she had pictured. Where were the jammed streets and begging poor—the filth and destitute that Mother Teresa had poured her life out for? There were obviously two sides of the city. A conflict and confusion grew inside of her that she couldn't quite put her finger on. She took a sip of the sweet strawberry lemonade that had awaited them in the Bentley as they exited the hospital.

"I was surprised that they had Grandmama sitting up in a chair already," Wright said to her, interrupting her thoughts. "One day after surgery…it seems a little much."

"I know it seems harsh, but it is so much better for the patient to get out of bed. It aids in battling complications like blood clots and pneumonia."

Wright nodded. "She still seems pretty confused."

"Let's hope that clears up in the next day or so." She smiled at him.

The driver pulled into the circular drive of the stables and stopped beside two horses that pulled at their reins. A tall Indian man in a vest held them steady. The driver hopped out and opened Maggie's door before she could open it herself. Wright had already exited the car. He was anxious to meet his new polo pony. She stood by the fender of the car watching him.

"Oh, he's a beaut, mate," Wright said, walking to the front of the horse.

The horse genuflected its neck and pawed at the ground. His loud whinny rolled across the field. Apparently the pony was just as anxious to meet his new rider.

"You've got some spirit, boy," Wright said, not yet touching the horse, letting him examine his human. "He's a perfect match to Smoothie, the horse I just lost," he said to Maggie. "Same build, similar coloring."

The black-and-white gelding had one white sock up the front right leg and a splash of white along one side. It appeared that an artist had tossed the paint from a bucket, splattering it down its side, giving the appearance that the horse was going fast yet standing still.

"Where did you find him?" Wright asked the trainer.

"Argentina. Your friend Poncho suggested him. He's young, only three, but runs like the wind."

The horse thrust its head up and down and whinnied again as though he agreed.

"How is my friend Poncho?" Wright asked.

The trainer looked down as if embarrassed. "He told me to tell you that he was going to keep the horse for himself but thought you could use the advantage...sir." The man added the formality but acted perturbed to be stuck in the middle of the jab.

Wright put his hand on the man's shoulder, "Now that sounds like Poncho. Anything else?"

"Well...he said, maybe the horse can teach you to ride." He grimaced.

Wright laughed. "You can tell that young punk that this *señor* is going to teach him some manners." He laughed again.

Wright moved closer to the horse but didn't touch him. The

animal raised his head and flared his nostrils. His ears cupped forward to scan Wright like radar antennae.

"It's okay, boy, don't let a little banter frighten you," Wright said softly. "What do they call him?" he asked the trainer.

"King Commit…they call him King."

"King, what a royal name for you, boy." He stepped closer. The horse huffed air in and out of his nostrils and then nudged Wright with his nose. The muscle in the horse's neck relaxed, and Wright stepped alongside and ran his hand across his neck. "Oh, you're beautiful."

He turned and smiled at Maggie. "You up for a gallop?"

"I haven't ridden for over fifteen years," she said.

She hadn't considered until now why there were two horses saddled. She assumed the trainer was riding the buckskin mare with the groomed tan coat and black mane. The mare stood contentedly like a well-seasoned horse. "How about a slow trot?"

The trainer gave Wright a foot up to his saddle and then boosted Maggie to hers. The trainer must have been informed of her height beforehand because the stirrups fit perfectly.

Wright's horse danced side to side but soon calmed. Wright looked back at her. "How's that feel?"

"Fun," she said. "Lead on."

Wright urged King through an open gate and onto one of the green fields, and Maggie's horse followed without command. It looked like they were walking on a groomed golf course, and Maggie's buckskin came apace with King in a smooth gait.

"Wow, I miss this. I grew up with horses." She reached over and patted her horse's neck and ran her fingers through the black mane. "She's beautiful."

"We call her Sandie. She was a tremendous polo pony years ago, but now I'm afraid she can't keep up with the big boys."

"Sandie, that's okay. We girls will stick together." She patted the horse's neck again. "I'd forgotten how amazing these creatures are. I had a horse growing up that was afraid of its own shadow. One day I was riding her, and a couple of ducks flew out from the stream next to us. You would have thought she'd seen a grizzly bear. She almost tossed me and headed for the barn."

Wright laughed. "Yes, they can be big sissies. That's why they need us. As the horse comes into alignment with its master, the two can become one. But it is a battle of wills...the more the horse resists, the more struggle it will have."

Maggie didn't agree and said nothing.

"You don't agree?" Wright looked at her.

"Uh..."

"It's okay, Maggie. You can speak your mind."

"I think God has made the horse one of the most commanding creatures on earth...you have to wonder what they would really be like if they only knew how powerful they are," she said.

She watched him process her words before continuing. "It's kind of like us. Most people I know don't understand how God has made them." She looked at his face to judge his reaction. "Now you don't seem to agree."

"Yes, powerful is right. I consider horses as beasts of burden, and I'm just not sure of the whole God thing. I have been all around the world, and all I see is a lot of bad things happening in the name of some god."

"Then maybe you need to come down to Guatemala and see God doing some good things."

"Maybe I should do that," Wright said.

"Do you believe in God?"

Wright pursed his lips. "I don't know. I guess I believe in the human spirit and what it can do. I haven't had much need for God in my life." He seemed to grow agitated with the conversation. "You ready to give them some gas?" he asked her, then gave King a sharp kick in his side.

CHAPTER 28

CURSED

Nick didn't feel much like eating breakfast. The mystery of the deserted longhouse with the images and stench of rotting swine was enough to addle his brain and turn his stomach. Neither Robert nor Amy had an explanation, and the trio, filled with trepidation, headed to another longhouse the next morning. They had gotten an early start, and the sun was beginning to warm the rainforest. Three boats of fishermen floated at the confluence of the main river and the tributary leading to the second longhouse.

Robert turned off the motor and drifted among the fishermen, causing them to pull their nets out of the river. They seemed friendly enough and greeted the trio with smiles and waves. Robert and the men had a lengthy discussion in Iban. It wasn't until Robert pointed upriver that the fishermen looked at each other and shook their heads.

"These men are from a longhouse downstream and have heard nothing about the deserted house we visited yesterday," Robert said.

Robert turned back to the men, and his tone grew solemn. When he made a slashing motion across his neck, there was an audible gasp from two of the men, one making the sign of the cross over his chest. The men used a phrase that Nick recognized, *antu gerasi*, the devil.

The men questioned Robert, but the discussion seemed to disturb the fishermen, and they folded their nets and motored down the river.

Robert pulled the starter rope on the engine, and it leaped to life. He turned the boat up the tributary.

"I don't know, Robert, the mystery of it all is freaking me out," Dr. Amy said. "What in the world is this all about?"

Robert only shook his head, but his fearful eyes searched the jungle watching as if the evil Huntsman might leap out at any moment.

Around the bend, a canoe filled to capacity was heading downstream. Water lapped at the edge of the vessel. An old man steered the craft, and a middle-aged woman supported the head of someone wrapped in a blanket and lying in the bottom of the boat. An old woman sat at the very front of the boat, and six children squeezed between the adults. The passengers appeared to be a family of three generations. The old Iban driving the boat used a paddle to bring their canoe alongside, then stood to talk with Robert.

Nick feared that the body wrapped in the blanket was dead until the two boats bumped together. The person under wraps murmured something and shook as if suffering tremendous chills and fever.

Robert listened to the old man's story and interpreted for Amy and Nick.

"This family is from the longhouse where we are headed. A curse has fallen over them."

The old man told another long story until Robert held up his hand to stop him.

"You must understand something about my people," Robert said to Nick and Amy. "They believe in the seven omen birds. Their god of war and headhunting lived on earth as a man. They call him *sengalang burong,* or the bird chief."

"Yes, we saw that magnificent bird with Wright when we first got into the rainforest," Nick said.

"Yes, it is quite beautiful. Iban legend says that *sengalang burong* and his wife had seven daughters. Their sons-in-law all manifested themselves into omen birds. To this day, the people watch and listen carefully for them. The people who believe in such things find direction based on where the birds are seen, or what actions they're doing, or from which direction their call is heard. The birds affect many aspects of life—hunting, farming and health. The man is telling me that they have encountered the *Embuas*, the Banded Kingfisher. It is a beautiful bird with a bright red beak, a neon-blue striped body, and an orange chest, but despite its bright colors, it is known as the bird of mourning."

Robert encouraged the old man to continue his story, and as he did, the middle-aged woman covered her mouth and wept. After a few minutes, Robert stopped him again.

"They found a Kingfisher nesting outside the wall of their apartment. When this happens, it's called a *burong tau enda*. The occurrence is a mixed blessing as it indicates that the family will accumulate much property, but later, the child who should inherit it will die," Robert said.

The old man indicated the body wrapped in the blanket and continued with his story.

"This is his son, and he's been deathly ill," Robert interpreted. "When they tried to shoo the Kingfisher away, it circled inside their house and perched on the old man."

Robert pointed to the old man, who understood and patted his shoulder to show where the bird had landed.

"That is a very bad omen for the Iban. It foretells of great distress by the deaths of many close relatives."

Dr. Amy leaned across the boat. "May I examine your son?"

Robert asked the man. Amy's request created tension between the old man and the woman who cradled the body. The old man finally relented, and Robert interpreted, "He and his wife worry that the curse would fall on you."

"Tell him I'm a doctor, and I am immune to these curses," Amy said.

The old man looked skeptical but yielded.

Dr. Amy pulled the blanket away from the sick man's face, but he jerked it back over his head, shouting and screaming, causing his entire body to seize. Amy tried to feel his forehead and take his pulse at the wrist, but the patient became agitated.

She looked at Nick. "He doesn't appear to be feverish, but his pulse is quite tachycardic."

"What is he yelling?" Nick asked.

"Most of it doesn't make sense," Robert said, "but he thinks we are *antu*...ghosts."

Amy turned to Robert. "Ask the old man how long his son has been sick."

Robert asked and then repeated what the man said. "Ever since the bird."

"How many days?" Amy asked.

The old man discussed the question with his wife and held up four fingers.

"Four days," Amy said. "Ask if he was taking the heart medicine."

While Robert, the old man, and his wife conferred, Amy turned to Nick. "We call Welltrex heart medicine because the pill is heart-shaped."

"Yes, he was part of the trial," Robert said.

"Has he stopped it and if so, how many days ago did he stop it?" Amy asked.

Robert interpreted, and the old man shook his head, conferred with the wife again and held up six fingers.

"Where were you taking him?" she asked.

Robert answered for the old man. "They were taking him to the research center for care."

"Is there anyone else sick in your village?" Nick asked.

Robert and the couple discussed the question, and Robert finally said, "There are two other men that became ill, but they recovered after two days and are now fine."

The old man said something to Robert who translated, "He says that those men did not have the Kingfisher visit them."

Nick turned his hands up to Amy, wondering what she was thinking.

Amy shrugged. "I don't know, could be viral encephalitis or another infection. Maybe even something unpleasant they ate or some psychedelic plant. We won't know until we do a complete work-up."

Nick nodded and looked at the six children crammed around the sick man. They appeared to range in age from five to fifteen. The oldest had her head wrapped in a scarf; she held an edge of the scarf over her nose and mouth and stared at him through sad eyes.

"Is something wrong with her?" Nick asked Amy, nodding at the child. They looked to Robert for an answer, and Robert asked the old man.

"This child is *menawa,* deformed. She has been that way since birth," Robert interpreted. "Her father slaughtered a pig during the seventh month of his wife's pregnancy. How do you say...she had an open lip?" Robert pointed to his own upper lip.

"A cleft palate?" Nick said. "May we look at her?"

The girl's mother said something to the child, who covered her face and turned away.

"What is her name?" Nick asked.

Robert answered without asking the old man. "She is nameless. She is only known as *menawa.*"

Nick's eyebrows went up.

"Children with congenital deformities are often thought of as cursed...the living dead," Amy said.

The old man was talking to Robert.

"He said that when she was young, they made it to Brunei, and a doctor did surgery on her in his clinic. It was all they could afford."

Robert grimaced at the old man's next statement and hesitated to translate. Finally he said, "They tried to sell the girl in Brunei, but no one would buy her."

Nick's heart lay heavy in his chest, and he blew out a long sigh. "You've never seen this child during your visits to the longhouse?" he asked Amy.

"Never. It's pretty buggered, aye. But a lot of these kids are hidden away in shame. She's probably only out because the whole family is here. Tell the mum the only way we may be able to help her is if we can examine her."

Robert had no sooner interpreted Dr. Amy's request than the girl's mother forcibly grabbed the child's arm and pushed her toward them, removing the scarf from her face.

Nick was shocked. Whatever surgery she had was plainly botched. The surgeon had crudely closed the cleft in her upper lip and done it at the expense of the skin that extended from her cheeks and up to her lower eyelids. It looked horrendous. No wonder the poor thing kept her face covered. The girl's lower eyelids were scarred down. It was the face a child would make in jest by pinching her cheeks hard enough to show the undersides of her eyelids and the whites of her eyes. But in this case, there was no humor.

As Nick studied the unfortunate face, he saw an even more critical issue—the girl could not close her eyes. With no tears to moisten her eyes, corneal scarring was already advanced.

Anger raged in his belly. How could someone do this to a child? The surgeon obviously had no idea what he was doing and probably charged them a year or two of their income.

He looked at Amy. A tear was rolling down her cheek. "What do you think?" he asked her.

"I think we need to help this poor child. My God, it breaks my heart. Since the whole family is headed to the research center, we'll do a work-up on the couple's son, and I will check with Wright or Ms. Boxler to see if we can send the girl to Singapore. There has got to be something the plastic surgeons can do."

The old man must have read their frustration at the situation and spoke to Robert.

"That is why the family agreed to the medicine trials," Robert said. "They thought they could raise enough money to have the child evaluated."

Nick felt helpless. Even if the deformity were orthopedic in nature, there would be zero he could do out here in the jungle. Worse, the deformity was out of his specialty, and because he was no longer practicing medicine, there was nothing, absolutely nothing he could do to help. He looked at Robert, who was staring at him.

"Why don't you lay hands on her, Nickloss, and pray for her?"

As incompetent and inadequate as he felt as a surgeon, Robert's request multiplied his angst.

Robert must have recognized the hopeless anxiety in Nick's eyes. "You know, Nickloss," he said, "nothing is impossible with God." He turned to the old man and asked if it was all right if they prayed for the girl.

The old man nodded.

CHAPTER 29

MOTHER TERESA

"How is Grandmama?" Maggie asked, looking at the passing sights from the Bentley.

Wright smiled at her; he loved how she said Grandmama with such endearment and tenderness. "She gave her doctors a bit of a fright this morning. They thought she had developed pneumonia in her right lung, but they caught it early and put her on the appropriate antibiotic."

"I'm sorry that I didn't go with you," Maggie said.

"It's all right; the doctors seem to have it well under control. I wanted you to enjoy your breakfast and massage this morning," Wright said. "How was it?"

"Honestly, I'm struggling with all the pampering. The people in the hotel are so kind and generous," Maggie said. "A two-hour massage with two masseuses—who would have thought?" She blew air through her lips. "I was such a limp noodle by the end, I was surprised I could get off the table. Then they did my nails and my makeup." She showed him her perfect fingers and flipped back her hair.

He smiled at her. "You look refreshed, pretty as a morning lily."

Maggie blushed. "I was really sore after the horse ride yesterday, but they worked out all the kinks. I feel like a new woman."

Wright looked at the Maps app on his phone and told the driver to turn left at the next street.

"So, where to today?" Maggie asked.

"Since we need to stay for another day to watch over Grandmama, I thought I'd take you to the fanciest restaurant in Calcutta for lunch. I hope you don't mind? It's very popular."

He read the conflict in her eyes, and it made him smile inside. It was nice to see her struggle with the opulence while being kind and grateful at the same time. Maggie was a breath of fresh air. His usual companions were either employees or business associates with an agenda. Yes, his foundation had just endowed her mission, but with her, he perceived no ulterior motive.

"I'm a bit concerned that we haven't heard from Nick," Maggie said.

The statement irritated Wright, not only because she was thinking of Nick, but also because he had misread her conflict. Maybe his scientists could develop a cologne that would break off attraction. He smiled to himself. He would name it Repel.

He hid his disappointment and said, "I'm sure they are having so much fun that they have just forgotten. We can call them after lunch if you would feel better."

"I think that would be good."

*Yes, Repel…*that's what he'd call it.

He looked at his phone again and told the driver to take the next left and then a right.

"I hope this place has small salads. I'm still full from…" As Maggie was finishing the sentence, the driver pulled to the front of a worn, gray building with a crowd of Bengalis huddled around the entrance.

"See, I told you it was quite popular."

She looked at him, confused, still not registering where they were.

"Come, I have reservations," he said, taking her hand and guiding her out of the back seat of the Bentley.

Wright led her toward the crowd, which courteously stepped aside, creating a pathway to the entrance.

"সলামালিকুম, Welcome," many of them warmly greeted in Bengali.

"Good afternoon, শুভ সকাল," Wright answered back. "এক্সকিউজ মি, please excuse us."

Wright led Maggie through the multitude, keeping a firm hold of her hand. He glanced at her and smiled, enjoying her bewildered expression. A guard at the wrought-iron gate saw them, opened the access and let them pass through to the entryway. Wright stopped to allow Maggie to catch her breath and gain her bearings. Above the archway was an iconic picture that Maggie recognized immediately, and she teared up.

She let go of his grip and covered her mouth. Speaking through her hands, she said, "Oh my God...Mother Teresa." She studied the portrait. "That's one of my favorite pictures of her."

Wright looked at the picture of the saint in her trademark sari with three blue stripes. She knelt at the bedside of a frail man, sponging his face with a cloth. Under the picture hung the charity's mission statement: *To serve: the hungry, the naked, the homeless, the crippled, the blind, the lepers, all those people who feel unwanted, unloved, uncared for throughout society, people that have become a burden to the society and are shunned by everyone.*

Maggie stared at Wright but said nothing until he looked at her.

"Wright, how did you know? I mean it...I've so wanted to visit her mission. In fact, I was praying for the nuns last night as I was going to bed."

"I had the feeling that with your heart for people, you'd want to visit the mission. I guess great minds think alike." He grinned. The truth was he had watched last night when she prayed. Technology had made it so easy for a bouquet of flowers or other inanimate objects to hold a wireless camera. Of course he would never tell her that.

"I can't tell you how much this means to me."

"Are you happy?"

"Oh, my gosh, Wright. I am *so* happy." She hugged his arm.

Three sisters in their white saris and veils edged with the same three blue stripes came toward them. The oldest one, in the middle, extended her hand to greet them. "Mr. Paul, Ms. Russell, welcome to the Missionaries of Charity. Thank you for joining us today. I'm Sister Caroline."

* * *

The long line of people concerned Wright. He wondered if it would ever end—three hours had never lasted so long. The most unpleasant part was many of them stank of body odor, urine and worse.

Finally, Wright and Maggie sat down to the same soup and crusty hard bread that they had just served to the throng. Wright didn't feel much like eating. He looked at Sister Caroline sitting across from them; she seemed happier than he'd ever been, as did Maggie. He let the women chat, thankful there were people in the world that enjoyed this sort of thing.

"Mr. Paul, thank you for your very generous donation today, but most of all, I thank you for your time and bringing this special lady to join us." Sister Caroline said, then turned back to Maggie. "It has been such an encouragement to hear about the Hope Center and your mission in Guatemala. May God richly bless you."

"Oh my gosh, Sister Caroline. It's you I must thank." Maggie said. "I read Mother Teresa's book in college, and it inspired me to go on my first missions trip. It is such an honor to be with you. How long have you been in Calcutta?"

"If I tell you, you will know how ancient I am." Sister Caroline hooted. "Like you, I was looking for something more out of my life. Mother Teresa started the Missionaries of Charity in 1950, and I came to Calcutta a year after that—I was eighteen. I never left, there was so much work to do…still is." She smiled sincerely. "I walked in the first day expecting some sort of orientation, and all I got was a mop. These days, we try to be a bit more accommodating to our guests."

"How does one go about volunteering?" Maggie asked.

"Honestly, most just show up. To become a Sister of Charity now takes nine years. You have to earn your stripes, we like to say." She hooted again. "Not everyone is cut out for this kind of work, nor the vows of chastity, poverty and obedience." She then smiled at Wright. "We need very little in our lives. Our possessions include three saris, a veil or two, a girdle, a pair of sandals, a rosary, and a crucifix." She put her hand over the silver cross hanging around her neck. "We are very content with our love of Christ."

Wright's thoughts drifted as the women talked. He didn't understand how these nuns could be so devoted to something unseen. Love was a difficult concept for him anyway, but to be so in love with a religious icon was beyond his comprehension. After the death of his parents and a couple of incidents of drug-induced rebellion, he was sent to a shrink by the university.

His jaw tightened as he thought about that psychiatrist. The doctor had told him that his personality made it difficult for him to understand love. Maybe that's when his contempt for others began, especially those who knew love. In the past, he considered affection to be unattractive and a form of weakness. The psychiatrist suggested that being a pampered only child had molded his mind for egocentrism. He'd even gone so far as to use the word *narcissistic*. Wright had hated the man for saying that, especially after Googling the word that was typically associated with psychopathic personalities. Wright understood that many highly successful people, including CEOs, tended toward narcissism—craving control and using others for their gain—but he didn't consider them psychopaths. That term should be reserved for serial killers and terrorists. His doctor had begged to differ.

Could I learn to love? The closest thing to affection he'd ever felt was when the news of the North Korean incident broke, and the media plastered Maggie's picture across the news. He had an instant fascination with her. Her beauty matched her charity and her ability to articulate the Hope Center's mission. Maybe he wasn't so atypical as the psychiatrist suggested. After all, Wright had always thought that being unique was a good thing.

"Don't you think so, Wright?" Maggie asked. She was looking at him with concern.

"Uh…I'm sorry. What was the question?" he stuttered, jerked from his thoughts.

"Sister Caroline was saying that their simple lives of devotion, prayer, and service to others are keys to joy. I was just saying that we found similar joy in the lives of the Iban. Their lives of simplicity are inspiring."

"Yes…true." Wright searched for words. "There are days when I long for the simple life. I would love to give up the stress and responsibilities of my businesses, but I also appreciate the opportunities my position allows for philanthropy. I'm thinking about some of my contemporaries, Bill Gates and Mark Zuckerberg. They seem to have found a balance between their wealth and benevolence." He looked into Maggie's eyes and smiled. "But they also have wonderful wives that ensure that balance."

* * *

Maggie knelt at the railing of the Missionaries of Charity's chapel. Sister Caroline had invited them to stay for the service that was as pure and unassuming as the sisters shepherding it. Their worship was supernatural—their voices joining with angels and archangels and all the company of heaven as they sang, "Holy, holy, holy Lord, God of power and might, heaven and earth are full of your glory."

The sisters celebrated their life with Christ solemnly but joyfully, then left Wright and Maggie in the chapel alone. Maggie had excused herself to go to the front of the small sanctuary to kneel before the altar and her God. A simple wooden crucifix hung behind the altar lit with two old beeswax candles. The agony of Christ, so well captured by the carving, brought tears to her eyes. *Yes, you paid the price for all my sins.*

"*Tetelestai*, it is finished," Maggie said out loud to the cross. "Jesus, thank you for loving me…for laying your life down for me."

She identified with the nuns' consecration to the poor and admired their steadfast devotion to their vows. First and foremost, Maggie held an unwavering love for Jesus in her heart, but she was not sure that she had reached a level of piety that would cause her to swear off intimate relationships.

Maggie glanced at the back of the chapel where Wright sat comfortably in the last pew, his arms stretched out on each side. His handsome face gazed at the rafters in contemplation. She could almost see his hazel-green eyes, which seemed to captivate her heart.

Suddenly it occurred to her: *What did he mean by that crack about wonderful wives? Was he suggesting I should be his balance between wealth and benevolence?*

She forced her eyes back to the cross. Sure, she liked him. How could she not? There was an ease about him that made her feel relaxed. His cologne kind of turned her on. But marry him? She whacked her head gently to keep her thoughts from short-circuiting her brain. Wright was too fetching for his own good.

Maggie sighed, took a deep breath and exhaled. *How can I even be thinking like this?* After all, she'd just kissed Nick on the lips in the airplane, and she'd known Nick a long time. They had a history. And then this guy comes along.

Was she that starved for love and affection? It had been years since a man held her in his arms. *Why does my head say yes while my heart says no?*

"Father, help me. Help me love you more." She prayed aloud but not loud enough for anyone else to hear.

CHAPTER 30

THREAT

Not even the invigorating water could squelch the flame of failure that burned in Nick's heart. His prayer had done nothing to heal the girl's deformed face. Parting ways, she looked as sad and pathetic as when the scarf had fallen from her face. She simply stared at him with haunting sorrow, not knowing why she'd been rejected.

Amy chose to go with the family to the research center and had already climbed into their overloaded boat. There was no room for Nick to go with them. He would stay with Robert, further investigating the longhouses.

Nick and Robert interviewed the two men that had fallen sick but recovered. Both had been on the heart medicine, but both blamed omens and curses, not the medication. They had stopped taking the pill a few days before falling ill, experiencing uncontrollable tremors and sweats. One claimed to have had visitations from a dead grandfather and other deceased family members. But the men thought they were back to normal now.

Amy left the satellite phone with Nick so when she got back to the center she could communicate her findings. Judging the position of the sun, Nick thought they would have been back at the center for only a few hours, too briefly to learn anything.

He had called Maggie and now wished he hadn't. She seemed only too happy to relay her excitement on being in India, visiting

Mother Teresa's ministry, and meeting Wright's grandmother. Nick tried to sound excited for her. *Isn't that what love is?* But he was consumed with a growing sense of uneasiness. Obviously, Wright had no control over his grandmother's health, but Nick wished he'd chosen to go with them or, better yet, convinced Maggie to stay.

Nick floated in the river's current, trying to make sense of his life. It was impossible. At one point he was a talented, well-respected surgeon at a level-one trauma center, and now he was a nobody. Right now, he floated in a river with people who had never stepped outside the rainforest of their remote and mostly unknown island. He had no clear direction about what he should do with the next few days, not to mention the rest of his life. The love of his life was flitting around the world with a man with whom he couldn't compete. Nick was losing the battle for her and was defenseless to fight. None of this made sense, and the more he tried to figure it out, the more confusing it became.

A strong hand grabbed Nick's ankle. He pulled his torso out of the water to see Robert smiling at him. The old man's face was peaceful, unscathed by the events of the last few days.

"I was thinking about the young girl with the deformed face and thought I better check in with you, Nickloss. You seemed pretty upset that your prayers had no result."

Nick knelt on the river bottom and tread water with his arms. "The girl has to be one of the saddest creatures I have ever seen. Is it not God's will to heal her?"

Robert floated next to him and offered no answer.

"Look at what happened to your surly old witch doctor, or even the miracle I received," Nick said. "I would think a benevolent Father, a good God, would give healing to that little girl." His neck burned with anger. "She should be the first in line."

"Yes, the Father must have mercy for her...like He does for all of us. We are all equally loved by Him. I, too, was disappointed that we did not witness a miraculous change to her face, but the Lord did not tell us that we would understand all things. He told us to have faith and to pray and to keep praying. I'm afraid, Nickloss, I do not have answers to your questions."

Nick nodded, knowing life would always have its mysteries.

"I know in His Word, Jesus promised that healing is His will," Robert said. "But I also have a sustaining grace when healing doesn't come. It takes me through my unbelief, so I don't quit."

"Maybe my faith is too small," Nick said. "As I was praying, I'm not sure I believed my petition would be answered."

"Possibly, but I doubt your faith was much stronger when you prayed for the witch doctor."

"That's true. Maybe even less…smaller than a mustard seed."

"Nickloss, we are always growing and advancing into God's Kingdom. You are moving from faith to faith. Don't let your disappointments rise above God's Word. The missionaries explained to me that faith is both a fruit and a gift."

"I'm not sure I understand, Robert."

"Faith as a gift is a sudden installment…like what happened with the witch doctor. Bam…it just happened." Robert smacked the water. "Faith as a fruit grows with use and hearing—hearing the Holy Spirit and obeying. Faith sees, and the greater the faith, the clearer your sight."

Nick splashed his face with water as if trying to wash away his disbelief.

"Nickloss, you can lose a battle, but know the war has been won. I have to believe that the Lord will make a way for that little one."

* * *

Wright shut down his laptop and the camera feed from Maggie's room. She was putting the finishing touches on her make-up and they would be leaving the hotel soon for the airport where he would fly her to Hong Kong for dinner.

It was hard enough to listen to Amy's prattle through the phone without the distraction.

"She was born with a congenital cleft lip and palate," Amy explained. "As far as I can tell the local surgeon buggered the job, not only failing to close the palate but closing the lip at the bloody expense of the skin on her cheeks, causing her lower eyelids to be pulled down. If something's not done soon, she'll go blind."

When Amy had asked Boxler to join them on the phone, Wright figured there was more to this call than the child. He tried to be patient.

"Unfortunately," Amy continued, "she needs to see a plastic surgeon or a maxillofacial surgeon if not both, plus an ophthalmologist to determine if any surgery is needed for her eyes."

"Can she wait until I get back and can fly her to Singapore?"

"Yeah, nah," she said in her Kiwi indecisiveness. "She's got a pretty nasty sinus infection from food passing through the palate into her sinus cavity. It's plenty dank. I could start her on antibiotics, but that brings me to the second issue."

There was clicking over the sat phone, and Wright looked at it to make sure he hadn't dropped the call.

"You still there, Doctor?" he asked.

"Yes, I was saying that the family that brought her downriver came to the center because her father is sick. He's one of our patients."

"And?" Wright asked, his irritation growing.

"I have worked him up from head to toe and honestly didn't find much of anything except for dehydration and malnourishment. He hasn't had anything to eat or drink for days."

"How many days?" Boxler asked.

"Well, the family tells me four. But the real issue is that the man has had a real psychotic break. I'm afraid we don't have the facilities to handle him here. We had to restrain him even to examine him."

"Leah, go ahead and send one of the planes down to pick up the family. The foundation will cover it. Just make sure to strap the man down. I don't want him going nuts at thirty thousand feet." He cleared his voice. "Is that all, Amy?" He was anxious to get off the phone and dress for dinner with Maggie.

"Well…"

It was a bad sign; her voice always got nasally when she was upset or afraid to speak.

"What is it?"

"When I was training, we cared for many heroin addicts. They would withdraw after they were in the hospital after a few days."

"And this has to do with what?"

"When we were looking at the MRI scans of the orangutans, I told you I suspected withdrawal from Welltrex was the culprit." She paused and Wright imagined she was biting her lower lip. "But now I am convinced."

She had just dropped a bomb in their laps.

Wright heard Leah huff. "What makes you come to that conclusion?" she asked.

"Nothing absolute, but a gut feeling," Amy was quick to say, but then added, "there is zilch in this man's history or current exam that would explain a sudden psychiatric event. Plus, they had two other men at the same longhouse with similar symptoms that thankfully were temporary. And, of course, we had the incident with the orangutans."

There was a long silence on the phone that Amy tried to fill. "I know what this news could mean. Remember, I have a stake in this as well." She apologized. "I just thought we should talk about it. Objectivity is what you pay me for."

Wright took a deep breath and cracked his neck side to side. If it was withdrawal, it was a serious, reportable event to the regulatory bodies, including the most stringent, the FDA. And a reportable event this early in release could place a black mark on the drug or worse, trigger a recall. Either would spell financial disaster.

Fortunately, Leah took the lead.

"Doktar, let's look at this critically," she said, her German accent thickening. "You have one man in your clinic sick from an unknown origin. You have two others that might have eaten rotten fruit, and two monkeys that got into a fight."

"Apes…they are apes," Amy said defensively.

"Yes, of course, dear," Leah said and tried a more pacifying tack. "But we have to be absolutely confident before we make those kinds of leaps. Do you have anything else?"

"Well…four years of medical school plus six years of specialized training."

Wright could tell the discussion could go south quickly. He couldn't afford that. "Amy, we appreciate everything you are saying. We hear you, but I would have to agree with Leah on this one. Do you think you could get more proof?"

"I could find you more crazed Iban or dead orangutans."

Wright didn't have to see her face to know it was crimson. "Leah, let's say this is withdrawal. What could we do for damage control?"

There was a long pause. "I guess you could make a case that, once started, Welltrex is a lifetime drug…like insulin. After all, would the patients want a life of addiction, depression or chronic pain when they could take a little pill every day and feel better? I suppose there would have to be a caution label on the packaging…the crap that nobody reads."

"Hmmm," Wright contemplated.

"Requiring patients to take it forever is not a terrible thing… for sure, not for Zelutex," Leah snorted. "If, and that's a big if, this is truly withdrawal, why didn't we know about it before now, Doktar?" She thrust the accusation deep.

"Oh, piss off, aye. Ms. Boxler, you know exactly why. *You* were the one that moved up the release date!"

"Yes, but we also ran it by you, Doktar. *You* were the one that said the trials were going amazingly well."

Wright was getting a migraine. "Now, ladies, please, let's not fight amongst ourselves or rush to conclusions. Leah…Amy, we will find the answers. But first things first, Leah. Send the plane over for the family. Maybe we'll get more answers from the man once he's in Singapore, and let's get the girl taken care of."

Wright didn't often get stern with the people that worked for him, but he was feeling uncharacteristically angry.

"Amy, the reason we can pay you as well as we do and can afford the kind of expenses that this deformed girl will cost the foundation is because of the resources fueled by our products. Are you asking us to choose between defending our medication and helping the girl?"

He was generally good at talking her off the window ledge, but this time he pulled the wrong strings.

"Don't you think I understand that, Mr. Paul? I would not even be bringing this up if I didn't feel strongly about it. I let you bury the reports from the witch doctors on problems with the medication, but I'm not standing by to watch innocent people get hurt. My reputation as a physician is on the line here."

"What are you threatening, Dr. Amy?" Wright asked.

"If we don't get clear answers by Monday that this is *not* withdrawal, I'm calling the regulatory bodies myself. I don't have to remind you that I know our FDA examiner by name."

"Well, Amy…you have to do what you see fit," Wright said, trying to hide the boiling rage in his voice. He stared at the phone and ended the call. He glanced out the hotel window and then at the clock on the wall. He would meet Maggie in thirty minutes.

He pushed a series of keys on the sat phone, and Leah answered on the first ring.

Before he could speak, Leah said, "I know what needs to be done."

CHAPTER 31

FIRE

"What are you thinking, Maggie?" Wright asked.

She looked toward the skyline of Hong Kong. *This is how the jetsetters live. Singapore one day, Calcutta the next and now Hong Kong.* As they floated in the iconic Victoria Harbour, Maggie watched the city ablaze with lights and colors that reflected off the sea. Water lapped at the side of their Chinese junket, and a breeze rippled the red fan-shaped sails above them. *How do I answer that impossible question?* What do you say to a man that stirred emotions long ago buried? Or one who flew her to Hong Kong on a whim to have a picnic on a restored junket? Finally she replied, "I'm thinking my mind is jumbled with emotions."

"Don't you think it's beautiful?" he asked, waving toward the city.

"Like nothing I could've ever imagined," she said. Never in her life would she have thought that she would be visiting some of the most exotic places on earth with one of the richest and kindest men on the planet—it was a fairy tale come true.

"Maggie, I am so grateful to be here with you."

Maggie smiled at him and sipped her champagne. He was the sincerest man she'd ever known.

"There is no one else I'd rather be with right now," he added.

How did this happen? Why does he have this affection for me? Oh, God, help me!

Wright scooted close to her on the blanket and reached for her hand. "This okay?"

She didn't resist. The last time she was pursued by a man was when John awkwardly asked her to dollar night at the local movie theater. *John, I'm so sorry.* Her heart pounded in her chest and she wasn't sure she could catch a complete breath. Nick had courted her, but often it seemed more out of duty and concern. Sure, he'd made comments about them getting married, but always sideways and never actually acting on it. This was a head-on blitz.

"Ever since I saw you on the news, I pictured this moment in my mind," Wright said.

Maybe a head-on collision. Was she dizzy because it was happening so fast or was that caused by Wright's intoxicating cologne? What in the world would she say to Nick?

"Maggie, please say something. I hope I'm not embarrassing myself."

She cleared her throat and sat up straight. "Wright, I'm just a farm girl off the reservation," she began. "I imagine that you could have any amazingly beautiful and smart woman you desire. This has taken me by surprise…I…uh…think you're pretty swell."

His cheeks blushed beet-red, and he diverted his eyes to the picnic basket.

"Oh, my gosh, Wright, I sound like a bumbling idiot. I don't know where that even came from." She laughed. "I've been out of the game for a long time…I've forgotten even how to play." Laughing at herself seemed to defuse his angst. "Sorry, let me try again."

She ran her fingers through his hair, pushing it back from the breeze. "You are honestly one of the most amazing men I have ever met. I'm feeling a bit out of my league. Wright, we don't even live on the same planet. I guess I feel pretty inadequate," she said, stopping her hand on his cheek.

He grabbed her hand and kissed her palm. "That's what makes you so extraordinary. Any of the other women I know think they deserve all this. You don't take a moment of it for granted, and I love you for that."

Love? Maggie wondered if she was going to vomit. *Now that would make an impression.*

He sat up straight, put his hand behind her neck, pulled her close and kissed her deeply.

* * *

Nick woke with a start. *What was that?* His heart pounded in his ears, and he lifted his head and grasped the sides of his hammock. He wondered what loud sound had awakened him from a deep sleep, but all was quiet in Robert's apartment. The rhythmic breathing of Robert and Ruth came from the corner where they slept. Nick's neck dripped with sweat at the stagnant air of the night. *How long was I asleep?* When he heard no racket from the mongrel dogs and feral pigs, he guessed the thump had been in his dream.

He lay his head back against the pillow in the hammock and tried to remember what he'd dreamed. *Nothing.* He'd often dreamed of arriving at a class only to have forgotten an impending test. Sometimes a tumultuous surgery had triggered such nightmares. Robert's wife murmured something in her sleep. Nick turned on his side and closed his eyes to try to get back to sleep.

Maggie! Her name was almost like an echo, or a feeling so deep within his soul that shouted and repeated it through his every cell. His eyes snapped open with overwhelming dread. There was only darkness and silence. He sniffed an unusual, unpleasant smell. Was his memory regurgitating the smell of the rotting pig? Perhaps it was the lack of air flow that caused the garbage and sewer to waft from the back of the longhouse.

Nick glanced over the side of his hammock toward the corner but saw nothing. *That smell.* It seemed more real than imagined—real enough that he sat up on the side of the hammock and reached for his headlamp.

His stirring roused Robert. "Nickloss?"

Words started to come, but not before chaos struck. The dogs woke a millisecond before the hogs—frantic barking and squealing filled the night until the real danger struck—

Fire.

Robert shot past him out the door before Nick's feet hit the floor. As soon as Robert pushed open the door, smoke billowed in, followed by screams and shouting. Light from the fire danced around the room. As a surgeon, Nick had always run toward danger, but now, he was frozen. Screams from Robert's wife snapped him out of his shock.

Headlamp in hand, Nick leaped from his hammock, wheeled around the post and grabbed Ruth by the arm, helping her out of bed and to the front door. The fire engulfed one of the outbuildings. It shot flames into the night sky, filling it with glowing embers. The occupants poured out of their apartments and into the fray. Shirtless men began chopping at the porch, frantically trying to separate the compound from the fire. Others tossed buckets of water from storage barrels along the wall.

Robert's wife shook off Nick's grip and jumped to help the bucket brigade. Nick stood immobilized and searched for Robert. He was nowhere in sight. With no machete to chop at the bamboo patio, Nick remained frozen in place.

The village's firefighting efforts appeared to be making headway. But just as they gained the upper hand on the blaze, a man shouted and pointed to the other end of the compound. Fire climbed up the corner of another outbuilding and lapped at the thatched roof.

How the fire had started made no sense to Nick. He had watched as the community members diligently put out their fires in the kitchens before going to bed. Two fires in different buildings didn't add up. *How did this happen?*

The separate fires grew; the community was losing the battle. Flames hit the thatched roof of the second outbuilding, and it ignited like a Roman candle. The heat scalded Nick's face and forced many of the men to dive for cover.

That side of the compound was ablaze in terror. The overhanging jungle canopy shimmered from the heat. Smoke and sparks choked the air.

Out of the corner of his eye, a fast-moving presence ran up the stairs to Nick's left. The phantom screamed a battle cry and charged, wielding a weapon overhead. Nick jumped back, but not in time to avoid a searing pain in his upper left arm. His knees buckled, and a flash of steel blade arced over his head, missing him by the length of his cropped hair. His brain accelerated in overdrive. Something or someone was trying to kill him.

Fearing the flash of another blade, Nick dived to his right and somersaulted out of harm's way. The blade stung his heel, but his awkward escape had succeeded because he seemed out of the reach of the machete.

The phantom screamed wildly, wielding a machete in one hand and a lit torch in the other, forcing Nick to move farther away. He could make out the form of the attacker and centered his balance, holding both arms in front of him for defense, as they circled one another.

The ghoul's outline was the shape of a man, but his form was hunched and dirty like a rabid animal's—its eyes ablaze with fire. Nick didn't know the local language but had heard enough the last few days to know that whatever venom the creature spewed was not Iban. It lunged at him with the steel, missing Nick's abdomen. It was relentless and charged again.

Nick tried to regain his balance but was hit with such force that he tumbled backward with the madman on top. Nick grabbed for its wrists, but the maniac's strength surged. Nick knew he wasn't going to hold it for long. The creature hissed obscenities—its breath smelling of rotten flesh.

Fight! Nick's brain screamed. A primordial cry came from deep within as he pushed the creature's arms back, concentrating his strength to force the point of the blade away from his throat. The maniacal manifestation seemed to enjoy the fight, toying with Nick—smiling through gnarled teeth. For an instant, its arms relaxed, but his rotten fangs opened wide to bite Nick's cheek.

Nick released one of the creature's arms and clawed at its face, stopping the attack for a moment. Like a wolf reevaluating his strategy, the creature's spine straightened to attack again, but as it did, a machete slashed its throat. The blow startled the beast. It dropped its weapon and grabbed its neck. For a second, it stared Nick in the eyes, and then, like an extinguishing fire, its burning gaze disappeared to be replaced by confusion. The creature's eyes rolled completely back into its skull, and it fell over dead.

The creature's killer kicked the dead carcass off Nick and

stomped out the burning torch.

As if the heavens had decided to punctuate the extinguishing of evil, a torrential downpour fell, causing what was left of the fire to sizzle, sputter and die after a few more buckets of water snuffed it out. The villagers erupted with a cheer that segued into joyous singing. Their lives and their homes had been saved.

Nick pushed himself up to sit and examined his wounds, both superficial. The machete had grazed his upper arm and sliced the heel from his shoe and a layer of skin but nothing more. He breathed a sigh of relief when a scream broke the jubilation. The cries grew below the platform, and a young woman raced up the stairs, shrieking in Iban. Two men pulled Nick to his feet, and they flew down the steps. There at the bottom was Robert, hunched over the threshold, his throat slashed.

CHAPTER 32

CRICOTHYROTOMY

The men rolled Robert onto his back. Blood poured over his face. The wound ran from below one eye, through his nose and ended below his chin, causing him to gurgle in pain. Other men turned helplessly to Nick, who stiffened for a moment until instinct jumpstarted his brain. *ABCs…airway, breathing, circulation. Crap. All three compromised.* Robert struggled to move air through his damaged airway while blood streamed from the gash.

Airway. Nick grabbed Robert and rolled him onto his side. The wound and flowing blood were blocking his airway. He started yelling as if he were back in the emergency room and his staff would understand. "Light! I need light. Get me a shirt or rags. I've got to stop this bleeding!"

He clamped his hand over Robert's chin to try to close the wound while allowing some air movement through Robert's mouth.

The villagers stood around Nick and his patient, understanding nothing and staring wide-eyed and frozen.

Breath. Robert gasped a few short breaths. Yes, it was helping, but barely. Finally, someone shined a flashlight beam on Robert, illuminating the wound. It was ugly. The sharp steel had cut into the sinus cavity, the upper palate, tongue, and cleanly through the mandible. Blood oozed down Robert's throat, further compromising the airway. He needed intubation, a tube inserted down his throat to save him. *Impossible.* Nick didn't have a laryngoscope or an endotracheal tube to insert for an airway.

Circulation. Nick jerked Robert's upper body off the stairs and positioned his face lower than his chest. He couldn't stop the blood, but at least he could keep it from running down his windpipe and drowning his lungs. Someone else pushed a white towel in front of Nick's face. He grabbed it and wrapped it around Robert's jaw and face, keeping a space for air to move. The cloth saturated quickly but stemmed the tide of blood. It was a knife-edge balance—too much pressure and he would stop breathing, not enough and the blood would soak through.

"My God, help us!" Nick screamed. This was why he hated medicine. He cursed his helplessness. Supporting Robert's head and neck with both hands, he looked up to the eyes of the men around him and saw blank stares. He recognized one teenage boy that knew English. "A tube. I need a tube." He let go with one bloody hand and made a small okay sign. "It has to be about this big," indicating a half an inch. "Like a rubber tube…and a knife. I need a sharp pocket knife."

The boy translated the needs and men fled to search.

Cricothyrotomy. It was the only way to save his friend. If Robert was to survive, Nick had to establish an airway. He would cut a slit in the throat and insert a tube directly into the trachea. It was tricky at best and fraught with complications: slicing through the vocal cords or creating uncontrollable bleeding. He had never done one, never even seen one.

The EMTs would talk about cricothyrotomies, the ER docs hated them, and only a handful that had attempted one either wore the merit badge with pride or didn't want to talk about the disaster that followed—watching the patient die in agonizing suffocation.

"More light!" Nick yelled. He had to see what he was doing. The only possible way to do the cric was to roll Robert onto his back, giving Nick a fraction of time before Robert was smothered by his blood.

More flashlight beams illuminated the patient, followed by a small pocket knife and the best gift of all—a water bottle with a large plastic straw. The water container advertised a chicken restaurant. Nick was never so thankful for fried chicken.

"Pull the straw out!"

The boy did what he was told. If Nick could carefully cut through the skin below the Adam's apple, the cricothyroid membrane, and into the trachea, the plastic tube would be perfect. It could have been a few millimeters bigger in diameter, but it was ribbed and sturdy enough not to collapse.

"Open the blade." Nick nodded toward the pocket knife. What he wouldn't do for some alcohol right now—this was not going to be sterile or pretty. He had one chance. The man holding the knife opened the blade.

"Oh great!" Nick cursed loudly. It was rusted.

He swallowed his disappointment and went into action.

"When I roll him over, shine as much light as you can on his neck. Then hand me the knife, another towel, and the tube. We have one shot at this," he yelled.

The boy interpreted, and Nick waited to make sure they understood.

When Nick rolled Robert onto his back, his breathing stopped and the timer on Robert's life started. Nick pushed Robert's chin up and away, stretching his neck, tenting the trachea and hoping the old man's Adam's apple was easy to feel…it wasn't.

There, I think that's it. Maybe.

Robert was drowning in his blood and started to flail his arms. The men held him down.

If Nick didn't do it now, all was lost. He grabbed for the knife, and his hand shook violently. Adrenaline surged through his body and brain. His heart beat in his ears, blocking out the cries of everyone around him. He wished he was back in an operating room with a diamond-sharp scalpel. He pressed the knife edge to the skin and drew back, trying to carefully make a longitudinal incision. He lifted the knife away. *Not even a scratch.*

"It's dull." He shot a glance at the boy. "You got me a frickin' dull knife?" he yelled. "Aaaagh," he screamed, trying to stop his hands from shaking.

He ran his thumb over the knife. It couldn't have been duller. *The tip, try the tip,* his brain screamed.

He felt again for the thyroid cartilage and plunged the tip of the blade through the skin into the trachea. A rush of air bubbled the blood. He held the handle of the rusted knife in his fist and withdrew it hard and fast, slicing the skin and windpipe, hoping it was enough.

It was.

He grabbed the tube the boy handed to him and thrust it into the trachea, worrying whether it would fit, believing it would follow the trachea down and not up, praying it didn't collapse.

It worked. Robert gasped a deep breath. And then another and another. Coughing around the tube, sending blood splattering. It was a marvelous sight.

* * *

Nick made sure Robert was not moved an inch until the villagers found a ball of string so he could secure the tube in place. He lassoed the twine around the tube and tied it tight around Robert's neck, adding a second strand for good measure. If the tube was dislodged or knocked out of place, their heroics would be wasted. It was a lucky insertion to begin with, and that kind of luck happens only once.

With an airway established, Nick stuffed Robert's mouth with rags and stopped the bleeding. *ABCs restored.* Robert was alive and for a moment he had even opened his eyes.

The boy who spoke English had found the sat phone and brought it to Nick, who wiped his hands on a towel and tried to remember Dr. Amy's instructions. Fortunately, she had programmed her number on speed dial. Nick hit the series of keys.

"Hello," the New Zealand doctor's voice crackled through the phone.

"Amy, this is Nick. We're in trouble."

"Nick…what…call," the phone sputtered.

"Amy…help," Nick yelled. It was all he could think to say before the phone squawked a series of beeps that ended the call.

"Damn," he yelled.

He looked at the phone and tried again, but there was no connection.

He set the phone down and was about to tell the men to help him carry Robert to the longhouse when the phone rang.

"Nick, this is Amy. I'm calling you back from the plane's satellite phone."

"Amy, we're in a whole pile of dung here. We need you or Wright or someone to come get us, *now*!" Nick screamed. "There has been an attack on the longhouse, and Robert's injured. I had to cric him," he added, trying to catch his breath.

"Did you say cric…like cricothyrotomy?"

"Yeah, one and the same. He's stable for now, but we need to get him to care."

There was silence and Nick cursed loudly, thinking they had lost the call again.

"Nick, sorry…I am still here. Criminy, I have no bloody idea what to do. I'm at thirty thousand feet on my way to Singapore with the family."

"Well, then call Wright and have him jump in his frickin' whirlybird and come get us."

"Nick, let me call you right back."

The phone clicked off.

The realization that he was in the middle of nowhere and was not going anywhere quick collided with Nick's desire to provide proper care for Robert. He wanted to scream or run, but he'd already screamed, and there was nowhere to run. Panic was about to overtake him when a hand grabbed his arm…it was Robert's. Startled, Nick turned to his patient. Robert's eyes were open, and he was trying to talk around the tube and the mouthful of dressings.

"Robert, it's okay," Nick said. "No, don't try to talk. I put a tube in your throat to help you breathe." He put a reassuring hand on Robert's chest.

Robert pleaded with his eyes.

"Are you in pain?" Nick asked.

Robert shook his head and tried to speak again.

"Robert, please hold still. You don't want to dislodge your tube or start the bleeding again."

Robert nodded slightly, squeezed Nick's hand, and lifted it to his own forehead. He put his other hand over his heart and patted his chest like Nick had seen him do when he prayed. Nick thought he understood what Robert was asking.

"You want me to pray for you?"

Robert's lacerated mouth lifted at the corners, and he nodded.

Nick's chest heaved with emotion, and his shoulders quaked. "Oh, God…oh, God." No further words came. His mind was empty. Only the words of Chang filled his head: "Sometimes emptying precedes filling."

Sure enough, as those words swirled in Nick's consciousness, a prayer filled his mind and heart. It was the one he had prayed as a child with his mother after his friend drowned. He closed his eyes and prayed out loud.

"Our Father, who art in heaven,
hallowed be thy name,
thy kingdom come,
thy will be done,
on earth as it is in heaven.

Give us this day our daily bread.
And forgive us our trespasses
as we forgive those who
trespass against us.

And lead us not into temptation,
but deliver us from evil.

For thine is the kingdom,
and the power and the glory
for ever and ever…Amen."

Nick opened his eyes to see Robert's eyes tearing as he squeezed Nick's hands hard. Nick couldn't remember ever praying with such intensity. All these years, never understanding its power.

The sat phone buzzed at Nick's knee, and he grabbed it and answered. "Yes?"

"Nick, I wish I had good news," Amy said. "Even if we could

turn back, there is obviously nowhere to land near you. I have tried Wright several times, and, strangely, his phone is off—it normally never is. I have talked with Boxler, and she was her usual unhelpful self. Nick, I'm so sorry. The best thing I can recommend is that you get Robert to the research center and I will have someone meet you there. I'm sorry."

"Amy…that's not acceptable. What other options do you have?" Nick yelled. He was about to curse at her, when two of the men interrupted him, trying to tell him something. He looked to the boy to translate.

"They are trying to…" the boy began. He turned to the men to ask more questions, then back to Nick. "The man that attacked us is from the abandoned longhouse. A human can't kill the devil, so the attacker had to be a man, and they recognized him when a woman cleaned his face. They said his name was Rajang…Rajang Bok."

Nick ignored the boy's words and turned his attention to Amy.

But before he could speak, Amy, who had overheard the boy, gasped, "Rajang Bok? I spoke with Rajang at that longhouse three weeks ago. He was very distraught. He is one of the witch doctors I told you about. He'd lost his connection with the spirit world and was beside himself. He was on the medication, and I told him to stop it."

Nick shook his head. "Look, Amy," he insisted, "we need to take care of the living right here. Help me out. What are you going to do about this mess?"

"I'm sorry, Nick. Please tell the men to get you downriver."

CHAPTER 33

REGRET

Regret and shame, typically fueled by tequila and bad decisions, hadn't flooded Maggie's spirit since her college-day shenanigans before she'd met John.

She rolled over in bed, pulling a pillow over her head. At least this time she was alone. *What was I thinking?* She'd kissed him back. It was one thing to let him kiss her, but she'd kissed him back. She tightened her grip on the pillow and listened to her stomach gurgle with regret.

After the kiss they returned to the airport in Hong Kong and flew back to Calcutta, where they were chauffeured to their hotel. This extravagant life was exhausting. The worst part of the long night was that Maggie knew she'd hurt Wright's feelings. After she'd kissed him, he held her tighter and tried kissing her again, only to receive her firm no. It was her heart that stopped her, though her mind and body were willing.

The kiss was more than pleasant, his lips warm and soft. He seduced her with those hazel-green eyes. But the passion halted there. Her heart wasn't leaping out of her chest. The earth didn't move. There were no sparks, no fireworks. To tell the truth, it was kind of mechanical and Wright kind of robotic.

Back in her hotel room, she closed her eyes and buried her face in the pillow, where she imagined Nick smiling at her. *Oh, God. Nick. What am going to tell him? Am I going to tell him?* And what would she say to Wright when she saw him this morning? They planned on meeting for breakfast at eight and going to see his grandmother.

She sat up in bed. Her room was dark. No light showed through cracks in the window shades, and the digital clock on the nightstand read three thirty. She'd gone to bed at midnight and didn't sleep at all. She fell back onto the feather pillow. In three and a half hours she'd have to pull herself together, and she knew she was going to look as terrible as she felt.

Maggie stared at the dark ceiling. Wright had said her reluctance was perfectly okay, but his body language betrayed his frustration. The color of his eyes changed, and she noticed the shadow of defeat. When they arrived at the hotel, he said he would be patient and didn't even try to kiss her good night.

Maggie was startled by a loud knock at the door. She sat up straight and wrapped the blanket around her.

BAM, BAM, BAM! The knock was relentless. Then she heard a familiar voice.

She sprang from the bed and put her ear to the door.

"Maggie, it's Wright."

"Wright?" she replied behind the closed door. She was not about to open the door in her pajamas.

"Maggie, there's been an incident!" he yelled.

She grabbed the door handle and pulled, forgetting the security chain was in place. When the door refused to open more than an inch, Maggie peered through the crack to see Wright, fully dressed and asked, "Wright, what is it?"

"There has been an attack on Robert's longhouse. I'll be downstairs waiting in the car. We're leaving immediately." Without another word, he turned on his heels and left Maggie in shock.

* * *

Maggie's head spun as the Bentley raced down the empty streets. She held onto a leather strap hanging by the door when the car squealed around a corner.

"Damn it!" Wright cursed. "I never turn off my phone." He glowered at her, suggesting it was all her fault. "I only turned it on because I couldn't sleep." He accentuated his scowl with a frown directed at her.

"Wright…I'm so sorry." She stumbled over the apology.

"When I turned it on, there was a phone full of urgent messages from Leah and Amy. A crazed man attacked the community, tried to burn the place down, and Robert was nearly mortally wounded."

Maggie looked out the window at the dark landscape. Was all this her fault? "I am so, so sorry…was anyone else hurt?"

"No."

She glanced at him, and his countenance darkened.

"Your friend is okay."

After a minute, his look softened, and he stretched his chin forward. "Dr. Hart saved Robert's life. But if we don't get to the research center, this will be all for naught."

* * *

As the Bentley wheeled up to the jet, Wright answered his phone on the first ring. It was Leah.

"Tell me some good news," he told her.

"You're not on speakerphone, are you?" Leah asked cryptically.

"No." He covered the phone with his other hand and turned away from Maggie.

"The threat has been eliminated."

That was indeed good news, but not what Maggie would want to hear. Wright shot a stony glance at her. She was staring at him, anxiously awaiting the news. He said nothing. He would have to act.

Anger burned in his stomach as he remembered the last of the many messages left on his voice mail by the frantic Dr. Amy. "The crazed man was one of our patients, Wright. Do you believe me now or do you need more blood on your hands?" she had screamed.

How dare she talk to him like that, even if she was upset? No one talked to him like that. His knuckles tightened around the handset, and he put it back to his mouth.

"When?"

"The good doctor's plane dropped off the radar as she headed back to Borneo," Leah said without emotion. "I just got the call from authorities. It was a fatal event."

A twenty-million-dollar-jet event, he wanted to say. That was the benefit of having insurance. Knowing there were more jets where that came from buoyed his spirit. But this wasn't the time to show relief. He had to play the grieving employer. He put his hand to his forehead and sighed. "Oh, my God."

Maggie put her hand on his arm. "Wright, what is it?"

He put the phone in his lap and said softly, "One of our planes headed to Borneo has gone down. Dr. Amy was on board."

CHAPTER 34

THE SAVIOR

The research center was all but abandoned except for skeletal housekeeping and cooking crews. Nick could have been fed royally and tucked between fresh, sweet-smelling sheets, but food and sleep were the last things on his mind. He needed first-class medical care. Dr. Amy was supposed to be here to meet him. *Where is she?* She'd promised they would drop the family off in Singapore and get the plane right back to the center. Nick cursed loudly. He hadn't signed up for any of this. He'd made the trek downriver, and now it was Amy and Wright's responsibility to do their part.

Three men from the longhouse carried Robert into the clinic area. It was dark until Nick found a light switch that flooded the space with fluorescent lights. They laid Robert on an exam table.

"You okay, my friend?" Nick asked. Robert nodded, but Nick could see the pain radiating from Robert's eyes and across his brow. The horrendous gash through his face screamed silently of Robert's repressed agony.

During the boat ride, Nick had comforted Robert, coaching him through episodes of panic as the old man sucked life in and out through his straw. Terror struck when a sticky fly, balancing precariously on the edge of the breathing tube, thought he'd found a new home in the warm, moist environment. It could have had an unimpeded entry into Robert's lungs, but, to everyone's relief, it decided to fly away instead.

While they waited in the clinic, Nick rummaged through the drawers and cabinets looking for supplies. Robert had lost a lot of blood. Exactly how much was hard to tell, but Nick estimated at least a third of his tank. He was tachycardic both from the pain and the blood loss, and his near-eighty-year-old heart could not be happy from the taxing. Nick refocused on the ABCs.

He found a gauze bandage in the drawer and taped a piece of it over the tube to filter out any undesirable elements. He made a mental note to check it soon, as the moisture of Robert's breath could create a waterboarding effect.

Oxygen. Robert needed some *Os* to help his breathing, but there were no oxygen connectors extending from the wall. Nick walked across the hall to the MRI scanner room, where he found a portable bottle of oxygen, tubing and a mask. Nick knew that with the claustrophobic effects of the MRI, patients often took comfort in extra air flowing across their face.

Nick brought the supplies back to Robert's side, turned the bottle to three liters of flow and placed the mask over the tube and gauze. Robert coughed but settled, drawing in the oxygen.

The clock on the wall read six thirty. *Where the hell is Amy?*

Wright and Maggie should be here soon. Nick was glad when Wright finally called him shortly after three, but it would take them some time to get there. Wright had said he was headed to wake Maggie and they would leave promptly. *At least he didn't say that he'd roll over and let Maggie know what was happening.* It would take them two hours to get to Singapore on the jet and an hour from Singapore to Borneo in the helicopter, plus transition time between. The chopper would be fueled and running when they got to the airport in Singapore. Best-case scenario, they would arrive at seven thirty. It was the best they could do. "Dr. Amy should be there before that," he'd told Nick.

Yeah, right.

Nick held Robert's arm. Shock made the texture of his skin cool and clammy. Robert's face wound had coagulated miles upriver. He'd lost no more blood but he needed an IV to help his circulation and antibiotics to stave off infection. Pulling the rags out of the wound and putting on a clean dressing might be more sterile but also ran the risk of dislodging the clots and stirring more bleeding. He also needed some pain medicine.

Nick's adrenaline still surged, putting his knees in danger of buckling at any moment. He wished Dr. Amy were here. She didn't have much experience in surgical matters but at least would know where all the supplies were. *Where would she keep medications?* Probably under lock and key—*her office.* He didn't recall seeing it during the tour but assumed it would be in this part of the building.

Robert's eyes drifted closed from exhaustion. Nick let go of his arm, signaled to one of the men to watch over him, and walked into the deserted hallway, glancing up and down in each direction. Walking toward the back of the clinic, he found her name on the last door—AMY ANDERSON, MD—and it was locked.

Nick thrust his shoulder hard against the door, and the trim gave way. Apparently security was not a major concern. As he pushed the door open and flicked on the light, he saw why her office was not part of the tour. Every bit of the floor and desk space was full of stacked textbooks, files, or other clutter.

Behind the untidy desk was a beautiful sight—a large glass-and-steel medicine cabinet full of supplies. Nick found a narrow pathway through the mess and twisted the cabinet's handles. *Damn.* It was locked as well. He peered through the glass and saw what he was looking for, vials of morphine on the top shelf and a selection of antibiotics on another.

She wasn't going to like his intrusion, but at least his status as an orthopedic surgeon and the specialists' reputation as bulls in a china shop would remain intact.

He grabbed a textbook off the nearest stack and crashed it through the cabinet windows. He took multiple vials of the needed medications and put them in his pocket.

* * *

There was still no sign of Amy when a staff member came into the exam room and told them Wright had landed. Nick had marked time with the dripping of the IV fluid from the bag into Robert's arm: 8:06 a.m. He hoped Wright's connections could get Robert to care in the Singapore hospital quickly.

Nick wrapped his fingers around Robert's wrist to palpate his pulse. It bound under his fingertips and had slowed, indicating both an adequate restoration of his fluid status and titration of morphine to keep him comfortable. Robert weighed no more than a hundred and twenty pounds, and Nick hoped his kidneys could handle the slug of antibiotics. Sending Robert into kidney failure from too high of a dose would make matters worse.

Wright popped his head around the corner, startling Nick. "You guys ready to roll?"

Nick frowned. He'd said it like they'd been sitting around doing nothing. Wright didn't even ask how Robert was doing. Heat raced up Nick's neck. He looked at the three Iban men that had been his guides and companions during this night of horror. They smiled back, knowing Wright, the great white savior, had come. Nick shrugged and nodded to them. "Okay, let's go."

The men picked up Robert from the table. Nick put the IV in Robert's lap and positioned himself as guardian of the breathing tube. Holding the bottle of oxygen under his arm, he left the room in procession. When he saw Dr. Amy again, Nick would suggest that she get a stretcher or two for the facility or at the very least, a wheelchair.

Wright reached between Nick and one of the other men and patted Robert's arm. "We're getting you to care, old man. Hang in there."

Maggie stood outside the room with her hands over her mouth. She looked as exhausted as Nick felt. He tried to smile at her, but he flushed with anger instead and covered his feelings by looking at Robert and his tube. Nick would have to deal with those emotions another time. Maybe Maggie sensed his frustration, because she didn't seem to want to look at him either.

"I've already contacted the hospital, and the staff is awaiting our arrival," Wright said as he walked alongside Nick. "He'll be in very capable hands."

Thanks, great savior.

Nick was exhausted, physically and emotionally, and decided

he'd better keep his mouth shut. He looked back down the hallway and saw he'd left the light on in Dr. Amy's office. "You'll have to give my apologies to Dr. Amy for my intrusion," he said, looking at Wright.

Wright looked away. He glanced at Maggie, whose face lost all color.

"What?" Nick asked.

"Dr. Amy is missing," Wright said. "That's why she's not here. Our plane carrying her and the pilot went down over the South China Sea."

CHAPTER 35

DAISY

Yes, you can certainly do a lot more with money than without, Nick decided. A team of maxillofacial and plastic surgeons waited for them at the medical center's heliport. Granted, they were all residents, but the lead attendings for both services met them promptly in the emergency department. The entire staff was both efficient and competent. With a complete work-up, including three-dimensional CT reconstructions of Robert's face, they wheeled him to surgery an hour after his arrival. That sort of efficiency was unheard of in the US, unless you were the president. Even the CEO of the medical complex came down to check on them and to thank Wright once again for his generous donation of the Wright Wing. Yes, money opened doors.

Both attendings graciously invited Nick to scrub in. After all, they might need to harvest bone from Robert's pelvis to help in the reconstruction. Nick declined. He was beyond exhausted and afraid they'd ask him to do something he was not yet ready to attempt. Even though bone was involved, orthopedics never ventured above the neck. Besides, that was then, this was now, and Nick didn't want to make a fool of himself with his hands and mind trembling. He had lost his surgical mojo.

They were all too kind in praising him for saving Robert and for his resourcefulness in performing a cric in the dark in the middle of the jungle. They showered him with more honors than he thought he deserved, but he had been sanctioned by their benefactor, Wright Paul, and if Nick was good enough for Mr. Paul, he was good enough for them.

While the residents prepped Robert in the operating room, the plastic's attending invited Nick, Wright and Maggie to visit the young Iban girl with the deformed face. The plastic surgeon had time, as the first chore of the operating room team would be to decide what to do with Robert's airway. The anesthesiologist would make the call, likely by inserting a regular endotracheal tube down his throat and having the surgeons close the hole in the throat. No use inviting pathogens to gain easy access to the lungs. This step was one of the most important and would take some time.

Chief of Plastic Surgery, Dr. Fang seemed young for the title, but Nick was feeling old and tired and noncompetitive in every way, especially since the Chinese surgeon didn't have a gray hair on his head. Dr. Fang and the CEO led them through the new third-floor pediatric wing. As they entered, Nick recognized the Wright's Kids Foundation logo—the handprint over the blue and aqua earth. He couldn't miss it; the logo had been reproduced everywhere.

"She is in here." Dr. Fang pointed to the fourth door on the right. He extended his hand to allow Wright, Nick, and Maggie to enter the room first.

The modern room smelled of fresh paint and had a spectacular view of the Singapore harbor. But sitting in the middle of the bed was the young girl, looking pitifully out of place. Her horrendous facial deformity couldn't mask her embarrassment at being seen, and Nick thought if she still had her scarf she would have covered her face. Her mother sat in the corner, willfully unattached to the child but carrying a similar woeful affect.

"She is quite the interesting case," Dr. Fang said. "Awfully tragic and preventable. We will be discussing the case this afternoon and hope to correct the deformity later in the week." His tone was nonchalant as though such cases were commonplace.

Wright, Nick, Dr. Fang, and the CEO stood before the child with their arms folded as though they were examining a turnip.

Maggie pushed through them to the girl, and Nick recognized her exasperation.

"Oh my, dear child. Don't let these men frighten you," she said, sitting on the side of the bed and pulling the girl's oversized hospital gown up to cover her shoulders. Then she stroked the girl's black hair and smiled with compassion and love. Nick realized what she was doing and felt guilty for assuming his doctor stance and forgetting the human being.

Maggie's actions may have been the first expressions of love the girl had ever experienced. Her scarred face could barely express emotion, but a tear rolled down her cheek, and she seemed entranced by this strange woman who gently wiped it with her fingertip.

"What is her name?" Maggie asked. But the girl's mother sat unresponsive, and the plastic surgeon snapped his fingers at a nurse to fetch her chart. Wright started to translate Maggie's question, but Nick interrupted.

"She's called *menawa*," Nick said. "But don't call her that. It means 'deformed.' She has no other name."

It was Maggie's turn to wipe a tear from her own cheek as she nodded. "It is the same everywhere in the world—deformed children are treated like second-class citizens." Maggie cleared her throat and glanced around the room. Colorful wildflowers had been painted all over the walls. "Daisy. I am going to call you Daisy," she told the girl.

Wright interpreted for the girl. She appeared overwhelmed by the attention. She looked at the flowers on the walls and nodded at Maggie but did not smile. Nick thought she wasn't sure how to accept a compliment.

Maggie looked at the girl's mother and smiled. "Does she know what is happening?"

"Yes," Dr. Fang said. "We will keep both her and your team closely informed."

"Dr. Fang," Wright interrupted. "I'm afraid in my fatigue I have not properly introduced you and Ms. Russell. Ms. Russell leads a mission hospital in Guatemala. She represents the heart and soul of what the Wright's Kids Foundation is all about. You both would get along smashingly."

Dr. Fang bowed slightly. "I am honored, Ms. Russell. I am at your service."

Maggie laughed. "You all give me too much credit. I so appreciate what you are doing for these children." She rubbed the back of Daisy's neck.

"Now, if you would please excuse me, I will go attend to my staff in the operating theater," Dr. Fang said.

The CEO, Mr. Kwek, thanked the doctor and spoke to Wright. "Mr. Paul, I was also hoping to show you the baby you saved ten days ago—the one with the congenital heart condition. I think you will be pleased."

He led them down the children's wing to the pediatric cardiac ward. They entered the central nurse's station with rooms arranged around it like spokes in a wheel. The area was full of medical machinery—blinking, beeping and breathing in a chaotic choir of life-saving measures, surrounding their tiny patients in a sea of medical miracles.

Mr. Kwek escorted them to the farthest room. It was full of balloons, flowers, and toys and, unlike Daisy's room, it was filled with joy. The baby's mother jumped from her seat and ran toward Wright, embracing him around his waist, hanging on, full of gratitude. In the crib was a healthy looking pink baby with one arm immobilized by a board to protect an IV, heart leads stuck to its chest around a large dressing, and a pulse oximeter wrapped around one big toe—a fraction of the tubes and monitors that adorned the other sick children.

"We are moving him to a regular room today. I'm thankful you could see him," Mr. Kwek told Wright.

With the grateful mother still clinging to Wright, he turned to Maggie and Nick and said, "The little nipper had Tetralogy of Fallot, a hole in his heart. Looks like the cardiac surgeons have done a splendid job." He peeled the mother from his waist, held her by the shoulders, and said something to her in Iban.

The mother loosened her grip from Wright, and like a magnet drawn to anyone accompanying the great savior, attached herself to Maggie and Nick, hugging them both, even though they had nothing to do with her baby's care. She was expressing happiness that he was alive.

"The Kangdang Kerbau Hospital, the KKH, is the largest hospital specializing in healthcare for women and children in Singapore," Wright said. "One of the best in the world. You both would fit in here like a hand in a glove."

* * *

Wright convinced Nick and Maggie to leave the hospital shortly after Robert was out of the operating room. The doctors would keep Robert heavily sedated with his new endotracheal tube in place until the swelling around his mouth and throat subsided and his own airway stabilized. The residents would keep them well informed.

Nick thanked God that Robert's six-hour surgery had been successful. His exhausted mind couldn't stand one more assault. He was in complete denial and shock about the news about Amy, but when Ms. Boxler called Wright as they were in the helicopter on their way to Wright's island home, she told him the plane wreckage and the bodies of the pilot and Dr. Amy had been found and were being recovered as she spoke. It appeared to be a critical engine failure, she said. They didn't stand a chance.

He had no words.

Nick hadn't been this tired since a twenty-four-hour stretch on call. Since the injury to his eyes, not having to be on call for trauma duty was the one thing he was thankful for. But that was a lifetime ago.

Nick stood with Wright and Maggie overlooking the infinity pool that stretched out to the sea. A clock in the house chimed midnight. The last time they were together in that spot, they had been about to embark on an adventure to the rainforest of Borneo.

"I know you both are exhausted," Wright said. "Please sleep for as long as you can and ask anything of the kitchen staff. They are at your service." He paused as if trying to decide whether to continue. "The news of Dr. Amy is...devastating, to say the least," he finally said. "Nick, as you rest, I propose that you consider my invitation. I know we have a lot to discuss, and we're all too tired now. But, Dr. Hart, I need you now more than ever. I would like you to consider becoming my chief medical officer." He looked Nick in the eyes and must have caught his glance at Maggie. "With modern technology you can work from anywhere in the world."

Wright filled in the missing puzzle piece for Nick. He didn't understand how he could take a job in Singapore and wave good-bye to Maggie and his life in the US.

"I'm afraid the loss of Dr. Amy has caught us at an unfortunate time, and that puts you in the driver's seat. I will give you whatever you ask." He put his hand on Nick's shoulder and squeezed. "Within reason, of course. I do have a fiduciary responsibility as well."

* * *

When Nick and Maggie reached the top of the stairs of the guest house in the trees, he turned toward his room. All he wanted was to plod to his bed and crash, but Maggie grabbed his arm and spun him around.

"Nicklaus...I'm so sorry." Tears filled her eyes.

He searched them. She had been so distant since the rescue at the research center, through the travels to and from Singapore, and in the hospital waiting room. But now that she wanted to connect, he was too tired.

"Maggie..." He sighed, showing no desire to talk. His heart was clouded with anger and weariness. Then he tried to soften his tone and held her shoulders. "Maggie, whatever it is that we need to talk about should wait until we both have half a functioning brain."

"Nicklaus, I'm sorry this has been so awful. I can see it in your eyes."

She had no idea.

Maggie stood on her tiptoes and kissed him on the cheek. "I'm not going anywhere without you ever again."

* * *

Wright watched her kiss Nick, then threw his glass against the TV monitor, shattering the glass and cracking the LED screen. He was as mad at himself as he was at Maggie. He'd miscalculated Maggie's resistance to the oxytocin and her feelings for the doctor. Her room in India had not been filled with the feel-good compound, but he'd thought she was already smitten. The effects had worn off and her affection had faded. That would change.

Jealousy was a new sensation that weighed heavy on his chest. The closest he'd ever felt to this was losing control in a business deal. He'd never experienced jealousy over a person before, and he analyzed it with contempt. No wonder he didn't have time for intimacy—it was too big a burden.

He looked at the bottle of medication on his nightstand. For months, he had considered starting on Welltrex. He believed in the research and his own motto, *Better Living Through Science*. Maybe the psychiatrist was wrong; people with narcissistic personality disorders weren't supposed to suffer from depression, but the blues he'd felt the last couple of years had to be just that—depression. If it was, he didn't want to feel this way any longer and he knew Welltrex was the answer. He opened the pill bottle and dumped the heart-shaped pills into his palm. So tiny, but so powerful. Dr. Amy was wrong. This drug would change the world, because the world had lost hope and Welltrex was the answer.

He put a tablet into his mouth and savored the taste. It was bitter, but he closed his eyes and tilted his head back, letting the medicine make its way to the back of his throat.

Images of Maggie reaching up to kiss the doctor tried to override his joy. He was not going to let that happen. He would see not only that her room was filled with oxytocin, but he would also start Maggie on Welltrex…she just wouldn't know it.

CHAPTER 36

DECISION TIME

"Grasshopper! How goes the high life?" Chang asked. Nick knew it was early in the morning in Montana. The man sounded like he'd just awakened but was still glad to hear from Nick.

"Master Chang, you drowning anyone today?"

Chang snorted.

How Nick missed that laugh.

"No, but the day is young, my dear Nicklaus. How are you? You have been on my heart and mind all week."

Nick didn't know exactly where to start. The foundation award dinner, the pharmaceutical company, the Iban, the Huntsman, or Maggie?

"She kissed me…" The words just fell out, and then he regretted them—they sounded foolish.

"Oh, so you're one of those kiss-and-tell kind of guys."

Chang's reply didn't help. Nick sighed and began again. "God, Chang…I'm pretty exhausted. A lot has happened since we got to Asia. I guess I didn't realize how much she's been on my heart. But, yes, Maggie kissed me and told me that we had a future together. Now…I don't know. She has played hard to get and is quite distracted by her rich benefactor."

"Oh, the game is afoot, huh? There's another suitor?"

Heat instantly filled Nick's belly. "Well…I…" He didn't finish the sentence. He knew it was true, but hearing someone say it out loud made him angry. "The guy is ridiculously rich and good looking. There is no way I can compete."

"I didn't know love was a competition. It either is or it's not."

"Come on, Chang, you know how these things work," Nick snarled. Why was this man bringing out the worst in him?

"Okay, okay," Chang relented. "I see you're still pushing on that anger boulder. I know Maggie loves you. I heard it in her voice. Sometimes, you just have to relax and let these things run their course. Let her find her own heart."

"But she has been so on-again, off-again it makes me crazy. I don't understand women."

"I'm afraid I can't help you there. I've been married twenty-five years, and I learn something new every day." Chang laughed. "How are your eyes?"

"The fog seems to be clearing…they're doing pretty well," Nick said. There was an awkward silence until Nick understood what Chang was after. "The fog over the eyes of my heart is lifting as well." Then he remembered what he wanted to tell Chang, and his spirit leaped. "Chang…the most amazing thing happened. I saw a true miracle. I prayed for an Iban witch doctor, and God healed his shoulder. It shocked us both." Nick laughed.

"I bet." Chang laughed with him. "That's wonderful, Nicklaus. May you continue to see the truth about yourself and the people around you. Are you now giving up medicine and moving to the jungle?"

"Well, that's why I called, Chang. I've been offered a job. Maggie's benefactor owns a pharmaceutical company and has offered me a position."

"Maggie's suitor? That's interesting."

"Oh stop, Chang. It's not like that." Nick said but wasn't sure what was the truth. "His company has developed some pretty amazing medications. Most of their work has been on the brain, but they have a new drug that has the potential to revolutionize healing, especially in orthopedics. It's based on IGF-1…the growth factor."

"Interesting. I've read some of the research on IGF-1."

"Yes, and this company apparently has found a way to stimulate the body's natural production and turn off the downregulation. It's like a rheostat that can finely tune the person's IGF-1 levels."

"What is the Holy Spirit telling you to do?"

Nick chuckled to himself. Before calling Chang, he knew the man would ask him that very question. He didn't have a good answer. "That's why I'm calling you."

They both laughed.

"Are you ready to give up the surgical knighthood? In the death of the ego, its cries aren't easily silenced."

"You know, I've enjoyed not feeling the pressures of surgery. It's a long story, but I had to fall back on my surgery skills recently, and it was awful. Plus, I can't imagine staying up every third or fourth night and washing out gunshot wounds and nailing tibias."

"I'm not saying that you shouldn't. I just want you to prepare yourself for the lament of your ego. Maybe God is moving you into a new season of medicine. I don't know—time will tell. But you can probably help more people with this new medication— if it truly has the potential that you say—than with the surgeries you will do until you retire."

"True."

"I guess I'm sensing a warning," Chang said. "You know big pharma wants disciples instead of free thinkers. They need people who think the same way they do. It's how they make their zillions of dollars. But maybe you can be the difference."

"Well, thanks, Chang. I knew you would have some good advice." Nick's ear was getting hot from the phone. He still wasn't sure he knew the answer and had hoped Chang would just tell him what to do. Chang must have sensed the same.

"Nicklaus, my friend. You know who you are and Whose you are. Now abide in Him, Who gives life."

"Thanks, Chang. I'll let you go and torture more fellow journeyers."

"Good to talk with you, Nicklaus. I'm praying."

Nick hung up the phone and decided to make one more call—to his dad. His father had retired from medicine and was consulting for a medical company. He would have some good advice.

The phone rang and his dad answered, "Hello."

"Hey, Dad, it's Nick."

"Nick. It's so good to hear from you. Your mother and I were worrying about you. How are things on that side of the globe? The world still round?"

"As far as I know." Nick laughed. It was good to hear the ol' man's voice, and he explained his situation and the job offer.

"Yes, it's true. You can do a lot more with money, but there is more to live for than that."

Nick was confused. Wasn't this the man who had been pushing him so hard to find work?

"How much are they offering you?"

"We haven't gotten there yet. Recently, some events have happened, and they need my immediate help. I have no idea what to ask for."

"Well, remember you're a physician…a surgeon. Don't sell yourself short. What's the average pay of an orthopod these days, mid to high six figures?"

"Yes, for the most part."

"Most of these companies want to pay their professional people—researchers, engineers, and the like—under a hundred thousand. You know, the whole bottom-line responsibility to their investors. Gotta maximize profits. Don't sell yourself short."

Nick nodded. "Thanks, Dad."

"Here's the other thing. If you decide to go to the dark side of the industry—remember, it's called the dark side for a reason. You are entering a whole different world. Most of the business guys I know will smile and pat you on the back as they thrust in the knife. They'll act like you're their best friend and then gleefully betray you and not think twice about it. Get everything in writing. Contracts instill trust, not the other way around."

"Thanks, Dad. Sure love you. Give my love to Mom. I'll call you all soon and let you know what I decide."

Nick hung up his phone and tossed it behind him on the bed. Maybe he should throw out a number to Wright that was so ridiculously high he couldn't possibly accept, in which case, Nick would grab Maggie, head back to the States, and put all this nonsense behind him. Right about now, a job at Starbucks sounded pretty good.

He'd slept most of the day away and wondered if Maggie was still sleeping. He was excited to ask Maggie what she thought about the job offer. If he could perform his duties from anywhere in the world, why not Guatemala? His stomach growled and rumbled. Maybe he should get out of bed.

* * *

Nick peeked into Maggie's room and was surprised to see it empty—with her bed neatly made. He heard laughter coming from outside and went to the railing to see Maggie and Wright in their swimsuits lounging by the pool and a wave of jealousy and doubt swept over him. A thought stabbed in his heart. *Does she still desire me?*

He tried to push himself back into the shadows, but it was too late.

"Dr. Nick. Good morning, sleepyhead. I guess I should say good evening," Wright said, and he and Maggie laughed. "Please come join us."

Nick waved and looked out toward the bay. It appeared that there was only an hour or so of daylight left. He plodded down the steps to the pool, feeling like the walking dead. The chaos had turned his circadian rhythm upside down, and he wasn't sure when he'd last eaten. His whole body ached.

Maggie was still laughing from something Wright had told her as Nick met them poolside.

"How are you feeling, mate?"

Nick stuck out his tongue like an ailing man. "As if I've been drugged…I guess I slept the day away."

"Well, you must be famished. Please, the staff has laid out quite a feast for us. Help yourself." He indicated a table in the shade.

"You guys going to eat?" Nick asked.

"I had a huge breakfast in bed a few hours ago," Maggie patted her belly. "I'm still full."

As Nick served himself, he thought they both seemed rather chipper and wished he wasn't acting like a zombie, but that's how he felt.

He poured a large glass of lemonade, drank it down and poured another before joining the pair. Maybe he was just dehydrated.

He chose the chaise lounge next to Maggie and smiled at her. She looked trim and sexy in her two-piece black bikini, like a fashion queen in a large sun hat and round sunglasses.

She smiled back. "I'm glad you joined us."

"I don't know where you guys got the energy. I feel like a truck ran me over."

"I was feeling bad as well, but I had an amazing breakfast, and now I've got all the energy in the world," she said, flexing her biceps and laughing.

Nick glanced at Wright, who seemed fit and rested as well.

"The best news first," Wright said. "I just got off the phone with Dr. Fang, and Robert is doing smashingly. They think they will be able to remove his breathing tube in the morning. You made quite the rescue, Dr. Hart. Robert owes you his life. The Iban don't forget."

Nick smiled around a piece of pineapple in his mouth. *Better lucky than good.*

"Now, it's your turn, Nick. Please, tell me you've made an affirmative decision."

Nick played dumb. "About eating? Yes, I'm all for it."

Wright looked away in disappointment.

Maybe he isn't used to being teased, Nick thought and changed tactics. "Yes, of course. I've given it much thought. You still sure you want me to work for you?"

"No, Dr. Nick. I don't want you to work for me. I want you to work with me. Tell me what it's going to cost me."

Nick inhaled deeply. *Okay, here goes.* "I know the industry standards. I've looked them up. There are not many surgeons who give up their careers to work with industry, so there is not much of a precedent. You may know what most orthopedic surgeons earn." He emphasized surgeon. "I'm afraid I won't change streams without significant incentive." He paused, looked at Maggie and then at Wright. "Three-hundred thousand."

Nick was surprised at Wright's poker face. He didn't flinch.

"Done," he said, thrusting his hand past Maggie to shake Nick's.

An awful feeling swept over Nick. *Did I just say three? I meant six.* But he shook Wright's hand. "And flying lessons," he quickly added. "You mentioned to Dr. Amy that you would help her get her pilot's license. That's what I'd like."

Nick glanced at Maggie. He couldn't read her reaction to his decision.

He turned back to Wright who smiled. "Yes, of course. And you need to be thinking about your retirement. We will have to come up with a number that is satisfactory for that."

Wright stood up and shouted toward the house. "Christian, bring us some champagne. We have much to celebrate." Smiling, he turned back to Nick and Maggie.

Nick still had hold of Wright's hand. "And, I would like it all in writing," he said.

Wright squeezed his hand. "Of course, mate…don't you trust me?"

CHAPTER 37

IGF-1

Even though Nick was involved in medicine and had seen people recover from severe physical trauma, it was hard not to marvel at the resilience of the human body and spirit. Gathered in Robert's hospital room, the doctors, nurses, Wright and Maggie could not avoid the obvious—the old man had made a brilliant recovery. It was a miracle. They shook their heads in wonder to see Robert sitting up in his hospital bed and smiling. The sutured wound still looked as angry as the madman who'd inflicted it, but the surgeons had done a masterful job in reconstructing Robert's face.

Bruising was already spreading, settling below his eyes and down his neck; it would look worse before it got better. Robert's lips had swelled to three times their normal size, and with his jaw wired shut, he could only communicate with his eyes and hands. He touched his nose and winced, objecting to the nasal tube in place to keep a clear airway. The endotracheal tube down his throat had been removed.

"The tube is an irritating necessity, Robert," Dr. Fang said, guiding his hand away from his face. "As soon as some of the swelling decreases, we will remove it."

Robert lifted his hand again, drew a circle in the air around his face and made a sound through his teeth. When no one reacted, he repeated the gesture and stared at his audience through hemorrhagic eyes, trying to make them understand. When no one guessed, he did it again with frustration. Then he held his hands palm side up. He didn't know how else to say it.

A nurse pushed through the doctors and handed Robert a pad of paper and a pen. He scribbled a word and handed the pad to Nick.

"Uh…" Nick shrugged. "I'm sorry, Robert. Your handwriting is worse than a doctor's."

Anxiety creased Robert's brow, and he pointed to Maggie. Nick handed her the note.

She studied it and finally asked, "Beautiful?"

Robert nodded and circled his face again.

Everyone laughed, and Wright said, "Oh, yes, mate. It is a vast improvement."

Robert gave two thumbs up and reached for the pad again. He scribbled more words and handed it back to Maggie.

Maggie frowned. She looked at Robert and back to the note. "Iban head…hunter?"

Robert nodded, pointed to Nick, and made a slashing movement across his neck with the back of his thumb as Nick had seen him do before.

"Yes, the man is dead." Nick thought Robert was asking about his attacker.

Robert shook his head. He pointed to Nick, then to where Nick had sliced Robert's neck, then reached for the notepad.

Wright caught on. "I think he is telling you that you have become an honorary Iban headhunter."

Robert nodded enthusiastically, making everyone laugh again.

"I think I could have used a sharper knife," Nick joked.

Robert grabbed Nick's hands and kissed them.

Wright turned to Dr. Fang. "Dr. Fang, my company has developed a new medication that stimulates IGF-1, promoting rapid healing and tissue regeneration. We plan on going to market within the year." He put his hand on Nick's shoulder. "Dr. Hart has agreed to work with us on its launch and research. The potential is quite something. Looking at Robert here, I'm wondering if you would help us with some clinical trials on wound healing."

"Of course, Mr. Paul. Whatever assistance I can offer would be my honor."

"There is no time like the present," Wright said. "I will have the good doctor here arrange for Robert to get started on the medication this afternoon."

The declaration seemed to surprise Dr. Fang. It certainly did Nick. Typically, these kinds of experimental trials took months, if not years, of committees, discussions, and regulatory approvals. But Dr. Fang said, "Yes, that would be fine. I will talk with Mr. Kwek to fast-track the approval."

Nick glanced at Robert and couldn't tell how he felt about being a guinea pig, but he was too distracted by Wright's hand on his shoulder to think about it.

"We are sending you over to Zelutex later this morning," Wright told Nick, "where the team will fully bring you up to speed on the medication. I will leave it up to you and Dr. Fang to work out the trial."

Nick's mind flashed to *Star Trek*, one of his favorite shows growing up, and Jean-Luc Picard telling Riker, "Make it so, Number One."

"Sure," Nick said. He thought he should salute and say *aye, aye, sir*. Instead, he chalked it up to another glimpse of how quickly the power of money opened locked doors.

"In fact," Wright added, "since your team will be operating on the girl with the deformed face, we might as well add her to the trial, don't you think, Dr. Fang?"

The plastic surgeon hesitated but said, "Yes, that would be splendid."

Nick figured it was hard to say no to the man who had paid for the hospital wing they stood in.

* * *

Nick and Ms. Boxler sat in an expansive conference room. Though only the two of them sat at the massive mahogany table, Nick felt strangely claustrophobic. Wright called her Leah, but she never offered Nick the same familiarity. He thought it strange that she'd chosen to meet here when a small office would suffice. Maybe it was a show of power.

"So, you were a surgeon?" Ms. Boxler asked Nick.

"Well, I am a surgeon…I guess." Nick tried not to sound defensive.

"You have decided to give up surgery for this?" She raised her hand in a gesture that included Wright's entire domain.

"Yes." He wanted to remind her that Wright had pursued him, not the other way around.

"Interesting," she said, looking down at the papers in front of her, reading and nodding occasionally. "Your résumé is quite impressive. We will call you if someone falls and breaks their leg."

He couldn't tell if she was snarky or attempting humor.

"I hope you don't feel like a fish out of water here," she continued. "The business world is different from what you're used to."

"So I've been told."

She continued to read Nick's CV, seemingly word for word. Nick observed her while he waited. He thought Ms. Boxler was as strange in affect as she was in appearance—an unfortunate cross between Michael Jackson and Joan Rivers. She'd apparently spent thousands on plastic surgery, but as so often happens, the more the surgeons did, the more alien she appeared. A pinched nose sat uneasily upon engorged red lips. Her tattooed eyebrows sat too high. Her hair might even be fake, but Nick decided he'd already stared too long. Whether it was real or not, it was jet black, short and curly. Her affect brought to mind an Auschwitz guard—her tone clipped and cruel.

She turned to the last page. It was a hand-scribbled note from Wright that included the salary Nick had requested. It made her eyebrows go up, even though Nick didn't think that was possible. She nodded, then stared at him with cold gray eyes.

"Doktar, Mr. Paul has offered you a most generous salary. You will be the third top money maker at Zelutex."

Nick figured after Wright and herself.

"The other eight thousand employees are not going to be fond of the fact that you are so highly paid."

"I thought those sorts of things were supposed to be confidential," Nick said, fighting his irritation with the woman.

"They seem to have a way of escaping."

Like the children you torture in your basement? He bit his tongue.

"Doktar, please follow me and I will show you to your office." She stood abruptly, then led him out of the room and down the hall.

It was hard to believe that she and Wright existed on the same planet, not to mention in the same company. *She is his right-hand person?* Maybe she was the alter ego, the bad cop. It was a good thing Wright had warned him; otherwise, Nick might have turned around and walked out the door. "She has the personality of a sour lemon, but she has one of the most brilliant minds for business," Wright had told him. "I promise that you won't have to interact with her much…unless you get in trouble," he'd said. Nick wasn't sure what that meant.

"Doktar." He hated that she did not use his name and he didn't care for her harsh German inflection.

"Doktar, Mr. Paul is the visionary and I'm the realist. I know he has told you that you can work from anywhere in the world, but I'm sure I don't need to remind you that the company is here in Singapore and the research center in Borneo. You will be required to do extensive traveling—teaching, lecturing, and marketing events, but after that, you should have time to go visit your family on occasion in the US." She said the last two letters with disdain.

Definitely the bad cop.

Partway down the hall, she stopped, turned and squared off to him, forcing him to hit the brakes so as not to touch her. She didn't move.

"Doktar, I know you are used to being the god of the operating theater. I'm afraid we don't tolerate that size of ego here at Zelutex."

Nick was sure her ego was big enough for the whole company. He hated the comparison to God anyway. Very few doctors that he knew, including surgeons, even came close to feeling that way about themselves. Most were just trying to navigate one of the most challenging callings in the world. He crossed his arms, wondering if he'd made a mistake in taking the job. Was it too late to say no? *Probably.* Okay, he'd collect his salary, have an ironclad contract for shares in the company, and see how it went. *What's the worst that can happen? They fire me?*

"I understand, Ms. Boxler. I'm just happy to be here."

* * *

Nick was sure everyone would have to remind him of their names again. His team, scattered throughout the building, included marketers, sales reps, regulatory folks, attorneys, and scientists. An impressive number of people were assigned to the new medication, and this was only the tip of the iceberg, Ms. Boxler indicated.

She also told him she hoped he had the intelligence to get up to speed quickly. She didn't want him to be an encumbrance. He must move into the leadership role. She made no attempt to hide her doubt. The team was cordial and treated him with respect, but he could tell they had a twinge of skepticism. He understood. After all, he was an outsider and a complete unknown. They talked fondly of Dr. Amy, and he even saw a tear or two shed for her.

He thought it poor form that Ms. Boxler chose to give him Dr. Amy's old office. The shadow of the removed nameplate lingered solemnly under his new shiny plaque. Nick entered tentatively. This office compared to the one at the research center was heavily sanitized, or she'd rarely used it.

Ms. Boxler shut the door behind her, leaving Nick with a young biochemist who set her laptop on his desk, unwound a power cord and plugged it into the wall outlet. He offered her a chair and she adjusted the computer so both of them could see the screen. "Kerri Kim," he said, observing the thin, attractive Chinese woman with impressive credentials.

She waited until after they could no longer hear Ms. Boxler's heels clicking down the hallway. "Never mind the mother of dragons." She smiled warmly at Nick. "We've all had to endure the initiation. Cut a wide circle around her, and you'll do well."

She pushed a button on her computer and the computer screen lit with the Zelutex logo.

"Yeah, thanks. I was beginning to think it was just me."

She laughed easily, putting him at ease. *Maybe I can do this after all.*

"Dr. Hart, I want to brief you, but please don't let me offend you. How much do you know about IGF-1?"

"Kerri, you better start from the beginning…biochemistry 101."

She seemed pleased at that and started her PowerPoint.

"Insulin-Like Growth Factor-1, IGF-1 has a molecular structure similar to insulin, which is how it got its name." The projected illustration showed the two molecules side by side. "Unlike insulin, it has a weak effect on glucose levels and is more of a somatotropin—a growth hormone secreted by the anterior pituitary gland. But instead of being secreted by the pituitary, it is mostly manufactured in the liver. However, part of our research has demonstrated that most tissues manufacture it as well, only in smaller quantities. You might be most interested to note that IGF-1 is highly involved in the formation of bone."

Nick nodded, leaned back in his chair and rubbed his head. He had the same overwhelming feeling he had experienced the first day of medical school.

"IGF-1 has an uncanny number of properties, including anabolic—critical in tissue growth and regeneration; antioxidant—it's a true anti-aging hormone; and anti-inflammatory and cytoprotective action. Among others," she added.

"Doesn't a congenital lack of IGF-1 cause dwarfism?" Nick asked.

"Yes, you're exactly right, one form of it."

"So, is the new medication a replacement for IGF-1?"

"No, that's the beauty of it. That's where my research began, but we learned that just giving more IGF-1 was fraught with issues, including some pretty horrendous side effects, including tumor growth. If IGF-1 can stimulate tissue growth, it can also stimulate cancer growth. It was pretty ugly," she said, looking at the floor.

"So how does this new medication work?"

"The medication stimulates autogenous production…the body's own IGF-1."

"I seem to remember that the pituitary gland secretes growth hormones to stimulate the manufacturing of IGF-1 in the liver. Once you increase IGF-1, doesn't that have a feedback loop to stop the secretion of the growth hormone and therefore slow the production of IGF-1?" He straightened and leaned toward the screen.

"Yes, good. Now you are thinking like a biochemist. Remember, Dr. Hart, these hormones are like keys, unlocking pathways to turn on processes throughout the body. In other places, hormones lock pathways to turn them off. It is highly regulated. But think of it this way: what if a patient needs bone laid down in a fracture of their leg? What if we can tell the body to turn on IGF-1 in that particular bone without affecting the rest of the body or shutting itself off?"

"And you…it can do that?" Nick's excitement was palpable.

"Yes." She smiled coyly. "We are using epigenomics to tap a patient's individual DNA expression so we can target where the IGF-1 is specifically needed…Skin? Bone? Heart? You get the picture."

"Yes, but I need some coffee. Where can I get coffee?"

CHAPTER 38

SILENCE

Wright walked with Maggie and Dr. Fang toward Daisy's room. He was pleased to have Maggie to himself, or at least he would soon. He was full of energy from the medication and wondered if Maggie felt the same. He wished they could talk about it, but for now, the Welltrex would stay hidden in her morning coffee. She appeared energetic.

"I thought Robert looked remarkable. He sure is in good spirits," Maggie said. "You did an amazing job, Dr. Fang."

"Well, we have an accomplished team of doctors and nurses here, Ms. Russell."

Wright tilted his head as if to shake off the jealousy he was unaccustomed to. He'd hoped the medication would eliminate the feeling, but it was only his second day on Welltrex. *Give it more time.* Should he up the dose? Maybe both?

"Wait until we start him on my IGF-1 drug. You will see an accelerated recovery," Wright said.

Dr. Fang smiled and nodded as they entered Daisy's room. Nothing had changed. The mother still sat detached in the corner, staring out the window, and Daisy sat in the middle of her bed, staring at the door, looking pitiful and lonely.

Maggie started right for Daisy, but Wright grabbed Maggie's arm and opened his briefcase. "I have something for her, but I would love for you to give it to her." He pulled out a teddy bear and a short stack of coloring books and pencils.

"That's so sweet," Maggie said and hugged the soft bear. Holding the gifts behind her back, she walked to the child. "Hi, Daisy. Guess what dear Mr. Paul has brought you?" She leaned in to kiss the child's forehead. But as she did, the child cowered as if Maggie was going to strike her. Maggie backed off, looking at the mother, who ignored them. She turned to Wright. "Does the mother speak English?"

Wright asked the mother in Iban. She finally acknowledged them but shook her head.

"This poor child has been abused," Maggie said. Color moved up Maggie's neck. Wright knew the issue had hit a hot button. "I've seen this look before with some of our kids coming off the street. She needs more than the reconstruction of her face; she needs a full spiritual transformation."

Maggie handed the teddy bear to Daisy, who stared blankly at it. Universally, children would reach out for the toy and cuddle it. She finally reached for the stuffed animal. She looked at it, then dropped it to her side without acknowledging the toy any further. Daisy did not know how to show the cuddly bear affection because no affection had ever been extended to her.

"You have someone working with her?" Maggie asked Fang.

The doctor shook his head. "I'm afraid, Ms. Russell, we have no street children in Singapore. There are no orphans. We are ill-equipped to deal with such a case."

"Your case is a little girl," Maggie shot back but then flushed. "I'm sorry, Dr. Fang. I have no right. I'm just a little sensitive about this issue. Please forgive me."

Wright interceded. "Ms. Russell is right. This child needs some support." He turned to Maggie. "Dr. Fang is correct, Singapore has few social problems because of its economic stability. Dr. Fang, I'm sure your staff and Ms. Russell could have a splendid exchange of ideas…Grand Rounds or the like?"

"That's a splendid idea. We have Grand Rounds at 5:30 a.m. tomorrow morning. Her case…er…the child is on our agenda. Please, will you join us, Ms. Russell?"

"Certainly, Dr. Fang. It would be my honor."

* * *

Wright had taken Maggie to a noodle shop a few blocks from the hospital. They'd sat at a table in the shade of a large oak tree. Wright was not exaggerating when he said that Singapore did not suffer from the same ailments as other large cities. It was the cleanest and most beautiful she'd seen—a far cry from Central America. Even the hole-in-the-wall Chinese wok kitchen was spotless. She had to laugh when Wright told her that selling bubblegum was outlawed in the city with penalties of up to two years in jail or a one-hundred-thousand-dollar fine. Feeding pigeons was a five-hundred-dollar penalty, and not flushing the urinal a hundred-and-fifty-dollar fine.

They'd returned to Wright's island retreat, and now Maggie sat alone on her bed. She pulled her cell phone out of her purse and turned it on. The screen saver was a picture of her and John in front of the Hope Center; it was pouring rain the day the picture was taken, and they were soaked. John had his arm around her, and they were laughing in the deluge.

Strange. Typically, emotions welled up whenever she studied the picture…tears of great joy and sorrow. But now her emotions were flat, muted somehow. She shrugged off the sensation and dialed the international number to Guatemala.

It rang seven times. She was calling before sunrise, and everyone was probably still sleeping.

"Hello?"

It was Joseph, one of the faithful guards at the Hope Center, who answered in a sleepy voice. She could almost smell the smoky warmth of her home and her family.

"*Hola*, Joseph, *Cómo estás?*"

"Ms. Maggie! We are well, thank you. Missing you of course. How are you?"

"It is so good to hear your voice. I'm sorry I am calling so early. Is everyone still sleeping?"

"Yes, even the roosters." He chuckled.

"How is everyone?"

"Oh, they are doing very well, thank you…*no hay problemas.* We have often thought of calling you but didn't know what time it would be there and worried the call might cost too much."

Maggie sighed. What a strange feeling. Here she was, jetting around, eating at banquets that would feed her orphans for weeks, and sleeping in places that could house hundreds more. She smiled at her staff's frugality—recycling their stale bread into bread pudding and making do by mending the kids' socks time after time. If they only knew how she was living.

"I miss you all so much, Joseph. Please give my love to everyone."

"When will you be home, Ms. Maggie?"

"I hope within the week."

"I hope you get some rest. You sound *cansada*."

"I am a little tired, yes. Thank you, Joseph. I will see you soon."

Maggie hung up, put her phone on the bed, and knelt beside it. "Father, bless them all."

Her thoughts were at war with themselves. She'd made up her mind in India that Wright's advances would have to stop, but ever since getting back to Singapore, she didn't know if she still wanted that. She'd never been this indecisive or confused in her life, except for maybe when the hormonal rage of adolescence hit her.

Wright was everything a woman could ever want in a man, yet there seemed to be a missing piece. She would occasionally see a glimpse of it. *What was it?* She tried to catch it in her mind, but then she would think about him and see his smooth muscular chest under his linen shirt, and the thought of any shortcomings would disappear.

It was as though every part of her was loving his company, except maybe the most important part of all, her heart. *I don't get it.*

"Oh God, help me…Papa, help me."

Her head fell against the bedspread, her hands folded in prayer. God would speak to her. "Lord you are my deliverer, my rescuer and comforter. You say that You reach down from on high and take hold of me, and You draw me out of deep waters."

Maggie trusted His faithfulness. Yes, she had endured many things in her life—the painful experiences of her teenage years;

the blood, sweat and tears of building a ministry; and of course, John's death, her one true love ripped from her. But God was always with her, walking with her, talking with her, guiding her. She didn't know how people without faith could possibly manage, how they could make it through a single day without hearing His voice.

"Papa, even though I walk through the darkest valley, I will fear no evil, for you are with me. Your rod and your staff, they comfort me," she prayed from the book of Psalms.

She sat back on her heels and lifted her hands to Him. "Speak to me, Papa, through your Holy Spirit."

She quieted her heart and her mind as much as she could. She knew the Father of heaven would help her, would give her a word in her heart or a nudge in her mind. She took a deep breath and waited.

There was nothing.

CHAPTER 39

A TURN FOR THE WORSE

Ugh. It still felt like the middle of the night for Maggie as Grand Rounds started promptly at five thirty in the morning. She seemed like the only one who wasn't quite awake. She didn't know how these people accomplished all they did while keeping these crazy hours. *They should be wearing Superman capes instead of white coats.*

There was no doubt that Daisy's surgery was going to be complicated and fraught with technical issues. Maggie marveled at the expertise and resources available to the young girl. The doctors and the care team pondered the technical details of reconstructing her face. Dr. Fang led the discussion, broadcasting Daisy's deformed face, along with three-dimensional CT reconstructions of the bony structures that supported it, on a huge monitor at the front of the room. Dr. Fang could manipulate each bone and demonstrated the insertion of bone that they would take from her hip to close the palate. The lower eyelids would be the most difficult to correct. The ophthalmologist made it clear that they had to be rebuilt with the suppleness to close or the child would soon go blind.

Dr. Fang showed in graphic detail how the skin of her face would be lifted off—detaching all the adhesions and scarring, down to the muscles controlling her expressions. The procedure would be similar to a facial transplant. They would know, as their team was one of the first in the world to have successfully attempted such a task. Once the skin was elevated, it would be gently laid in place. The absent skin in the most critical areas would be replaced with full-thickness grafts that they would harvest from her forearm or inner thigh.

Maggie was certain that Daisy was in the best of hands, but it was also clear that Maggie's presence transformed Daisy from a case to a child in the eyes of the surgical team. Even Dr. Fang announced that they would need a heavy dose of luck and a touch from the divine to be successful.

Maggie prayed under her breath. *Papa, hear our prayers.* She took a sip of hot coffee. She was having trouble staying awake—she had not slept well, filled with anxiety at being around the talented surgical team. She felt inadequate and out of place. Worse, she had been asked to speak to them, and her turn at the podium was coming.

"I have asked Ms. Russell to join us this morning to discuss the child's psychological issues," Dr. Fang said, introducing her and inviting her to the podium.

The group of forty doctors, attendings, residents, and medical students, along with nurses and other ancillary staff gave her a warm applause. The group in their pressed white coats embroidered with Doctor this or Nurse that or Chief of Plastic Surgery or Director of Nursing and the like attentively leaned toward her.

"Good morning," Maggie began.

They all responded, and the room quieted.

"I must say, I am truly blessed to be here this morning. Your work and talents are something remarkable. Dr. Fang told you that my late husband, John, was a surgeon, and he would have given anything to have the technological advances that you all have at your fingertips…and the camaraderie that you enjoy. Thank you for making me part of Daisy's care."

She cleared her voice and readjusted the microphone.

"Emotional trauma comes to us in all sorts of ways." She paused. "It comes in different shapes and sizes, but the reality is, no one escapes it. Maybe it starts early, like in Daisy's case, from abuse or physical issues. Perhaps it hits later in life with war or natural disaster. Or maybe it occurs from aging, loss or illness. But the research is clear, we all experience it to some degree and must walk through it."

Maggie lifted her hand toward the enlarged picture of Daisy behind her. "Sometimes the pain is much more obvious," she said. "And sometimes we carry the pain invisibly. But the circuit breakers of our soul can handle only so much voltage until they become overloaded, and the emotional stress comes out in all sorts of ways—depression, anxiety, physical pain, or as in Daisy's situation, the psyche shuts down."

The director of nursing raised her hand. "Ms. Russell, is it possible to heal from such trauma?"

Maggie smiled at her. She could see the pain in the woman's eyes. "That's the beauty of the latest research. Yes! I wish my friend Dr. Hart was here with us this morning, as he would love this analogy. As an orthopedic surgeon, he knows that often, as a bone heals from a fracture, it becomes stronger than the original. I like to think of these traumatic experiences as the broken bones of the soul. When the person is encouraged into the healing process of these emotional wounds, they often come out stronger."

Maggie took a sip of coffee to wet her dry mouth.

"We have experienced this firsthand at our mission in Guatemala. Many children come to the orphanage with awful stories...terrible things..." She stopped and redirected her thoughts. "Through the healing and rebuilding process, most of these kids go on to lead very productive lives. Two of our orphans are currently in medical school."

"Then they obviously needed more healing," Dr. Fang interjected, causing the group to laugh. Maggie was thankful for the humor.

"Yes...remember, I was married to one," she said, causing more laughter.

"How do you accomplish so much with your children?" another doctor asked.

Maggie nodded thoughtfully. "Our psyche has a tremendous capacity for reclamation and growth, but recovering from a traumatic experience necessitates that the painful emotions be thoroughly processed. They cannot be repressed or forgotten. We deal with them head-on, little by little, day by day. We are not afraid of them and don't let them have power over us."

Maggie straightened her back. "Look…Daisy has a long road ahead of her. She must find a person or two that she can trust. She has to understand that there are people she can trust and others she cannot."

The group was nodding when a voice filled her heart. *Who can you trust?* Suddenly her mind was filled with thoughts and images of Nick and Wright. She'd have to deal with the conflict another time. She cleared her mind and continued.

"The point is that Daisy must find people who will love her above all else—people who are not afraid of her wounds, physically and emotionally. People who will help her feel those feelings and express them…and people who will teach her ways to deal with them constructively. Love is the salve that heals all things."

* * *

After she had spoken and the doctors filed out, a group of nurses swarmed around her, hungry for more. One of them showed a great deal of courage and vulnerability as she shared her story of being sold into the sex trade at age ten in Thailand. Rescued by a ministry at fifteen and raised by a loving family in Malaysia, she could attest to the healing power of love. The other nurses had no idea their colleague had endured this, and for a moment, they removed their masks of stoicism and expressed empathy. Maggie was suggesting a support group when she saw Wright enter the back of the room looking pale and sullen.

"If you would please excuse me," Maggie said and started toward Wright, but not before the director of nursing stopped her.

"Ms. Russell…Maggie, thank you. Would you ever consider joining me and some of my staff one evening to share more? Our culture is not one that typically goes deep into our emotional pond. We could use a guide."

"I would love that. It may have to be soon, as I am hoping

to head home before the week is out," Maggie said and excused herself.

Wright stood with his hands thrust deep into his pockets.

"I just got a call from the hospital in India. Grandmama has taken a terrible turn for the worse. They suggested that if I want to say good-bye, I better hurry."

He crossed one foot over the other and stared at the floor, more like a preadolescent boy than the king of a vast empire. "Maggie, I need you. Will you go with me?"

* * *

Nick sat in Amy's empty office at Zelutex. He needed to catch up on all her projects, but the vast majority of the information sat in her office at the research center. He could ask the staff there to ship the contents of her office to him, but the most expedient thing to do was for him to go and spend a day or two on Borneo sorting through the most relevant files. Maybe Wright could take him and Maggie would come along.

He picked up his phone to call Wright, but the phone rang in his hand before he could dial.

"Wright, I was just about to ring you."

"Nicklaus, it's Maggie."

His stomach churned.

"Nick, I'm calling from Wright's phone."

Yes, I know that.

"Nick, Wright is distraught. His grandmother is dying, and he needs to get to India. Nick, I'm so sorry, I told you I would not leave you again. Nick, I've prayed to know what to do, and I do not hear anything…I don't know what to do…I think I need to go with him, Nick."

How many times is she going to say my name?

"Nick, are you there?"

"Maggie, I'm here. I'm sorry to hear about his grandmother. I was about to call to see if you wanted to go back to Borneo with me."

"Nicklaus, I'm so sorry, we are already at the airport."

I guess not!

CHAPTER 40

LETTING GO

"Ms. Boxler, Dr. Hart here."

"What can I do for you, Doktar?"

"I'm in Dr. Amy's office, er…my office, and there are huge gaps in what I need to know about the projects in which she was involved. I need to go to the research center and look through her files and information. I'm not sure how to get there. I was going to see if Wright could take me, but I hear his grandmother is not well and he is on his way to India."

There was silence. He wondered if the news had caught her off guard. More likely she was bristling because he'd called her, asking for a favor.

"No, I did not know that. I've been trying to call him." She sounded perturbed.

"What do you suggest?" Nick asked.

"What information are you looking for, Doktar?"

"Just about everything to do my job." It was Nick's turn to be irritable. "The staff has been very kind to catch me up on the IGF-1 drug. But I don't find any records of the animal studies or the early clinical trials, except for what the individual staff members could provide me. There are too many gaps. Also, I think I should follow up on the issues we may have seen with Welltrex."

"Issues?"

"Yes, like the crazed person in the jungle and the man Amy took to Singapore. I have not heard any reports about him."

There was a long pause, and Nick thought she'd disconnected the call.

"Doktar…I know you have a very steep learning curve and we don't want to overload you. I would suggest that you focus on the IGF-1 drug before you follow any rabbit trails. We hope to launch the new medication in six months. That leaves you very little time."

"I think I owe it to Dr. Amy to complete her work on Welltrex."

"That is very kind of you, Doktar. But I have assigned another division for that."

Nick's hand tightened around the receiver and heat rose in his ears. "As medical director, doesn't *all* research fall under my authority?"

"Yes, Doktar, but you fall under my authority." The tone of her voice remained steady. "I'm only looking out for your well-being. There are only so many hours in the day and we need you to focus." Her voice turned almost kind. "It is our tradition that you name the newest drug. Dr. Hart, think long and hard about what you want to name the new IGF-1 drug. It will be your legacy."

Nick sighed. He hated her patronization, but he was too new to argue. "Will do, Ms. Boxler."

"Dr. Hart. Let me release one of our planes to get you to Borneo. I'm afraid you will have to take a car from Kuching."

"Hopefully it's one that flies well." He knew it was a bad joke, but he didn't care.

* * *

Maggie was relieved when they landed safely in Calcutta. Wright had seemed to throw all his safety checks out the window as they sped down the runway in Singapore and set the jet down hard in India. She wasn't sure if he was in any shape to be at the controls, but when she mentioned that maybe someone else should pilot, he ignored her.

Maggie had trouble keeping pace with him as he marched through the hospital and down the hallway. The surgeon anxiously waited outside his grandmother's room to discuss her condition, but Wright ignored his outstretched hand and marched past him into her room.

A nurse was mopping his grandmother's brow with a wet cloth. The smell of death and loose bowels hit Maggie's nose, and she realized they had barely made it in time. The old woman was in the final stage of her life here on earth.

Wright sat on the side of the bed and held her bony hand. "Grandmama, it's Wright. I'm here now. Can you hear me?"

Her consciousness rose out of the depths and her eyes opened and focused on Wright's face. "Mowgli, how good of you to come see me," she said in a wispy voice.

"Grandmama, how are you feeling?" Wright asked.

She smiled, and her eyes drifted closed. Wright looked back at Maggie for support, and she stepped forward to put her hand on Wright's shoulder. Maggie had seen this before—the elderly holding on to this world with as much strength as their frail bodies could muster.

In the end would she be any different? Even with her unwavering faith and belief in eternity, would she let go so easily to the unknown? She hoped that peace would flood her mind for that last breath and the ultimate letting go that released her into the arms of God and the loving embrace of all who went before her.

Maggie had heard stories of the dying holding on until their loved ones arrived to escort them into death, or having a brief moment of clarity before taking their last breath.

"Grandmama, please don't leave me. You're all I have," Wright whispered.

A smile broke across her wrinkled face. "Oh, Mowgli, how I love you. I'm afraid…" She winced, trying to hang on to her thought.

Wright held her hand to his cheek as though trying to receive comfort as much as give it. "Grandmama, please." He looked frantically at Maggie.

Maggie took over for the nurse, claiming the washcloth and dabbing Grandmama's cheeks with the cool cloth. The old woman was burning up. Maggie supposed an infection of some kind had come to claim its victim. It could be from the surgery itself, but more likely from her lungs or kidneys. Sometimes the body just gives up the fight.

Grandmama's eyes fluttered open, and she stared into Maggie's eyes. Maggie stared back and saw pain, fear, and pleading.

"It's okay, Grandmama, it's all going to be okay," Maggie reassured. "You can let go. You don't have to fight any longer. A better place awaits you."

The woman nodded, and Maggie could see her body relax.

"Father, we give this wonderful woman into Your loving arms."

As Maggie continued to pray, Grandmama's breathing became agonal and disjointed. Her spirit left, but the neuronal circuitry was discharging independently, firing its last few impulses to the heart and lungs. After a few moments, the heart monitor above their heads began to signal the slowing of the heart and then lost all myocardial activity.

Wright grabbed Grandmama's shoulders, laying his head against her chest. "No, Grandmama, no."

* * *

Nick was angry. His back throbbed as much as his head. Not only had Maggie broken her promise not to leave him, she had gone with Wright. And Nick was bouncing down a rutted, pothole-filled dirt road on the equivalent of a Guatemalan chicken bus. Ms. Boxler had arranged for his flight to Kuching, but there was no car waiting for him at the airport. Her only suggestion was to take the bus to the Batang Ai public jetty, where she would have one of the staff from the research center pick him up by longboat. The mother of dragons could arrange all that, but not a car. *She's messing with me.* Nick knew she was not about to make his transition to the business world easy.

He wasn't sure how much more of the seven-hour trip he could take, especially since the bus driver was blasting Katy Perry through the large woofers overhead.

God, is this what You meant by trusting You?

How could he let Maggie slip through his fingers? He loved her, but she obviously had eyes for the rich guy. *Who can blame her?* He didn't know what else to do besides throw himself into this new job, as he'd done before with medicine. He hadn't talked with Katelyn or AK for a while. Maybe he'd give one of them a call. AK was always threatening to show up on his doorstep with a bottle of cognac and a smile, but he always discouraged her advances. Perhaps now he'd take her up on the offer, but he wasn't sure he was man enough to handle the Russian lioness. He smiled to himself. *She'd be a handful for sure.*

Nick was holding his head in his hands when the bus swerved. He looked up. An old Iban man sitting across the aisle and a seat ahead had turned to face him, smiling a toothless grin. Nick nodded and smiled back, even though a migraine threatened to settle in.

"You, Dr. Nickloss?" the old man asked.

It surprised Nick, hearing his name and in a voice like Robert's. "Uh…yes."

"You save Rentap?"

Nick tilted his head, unsure of who he was talking about.

"Robert," the old man said. He made the slashing motion across his neck with the back of his thumb and grinned, showing his gums.

Nick nodded and smiled. He was shocked how fast news could travel in the rainforest. "Yes." *Great.* His legacy would be that of slashing a man's neck.

The old Iban flashed an enthusiastic thumbs-up. "You pray for wife and me," he said in broken English and pointed to the old woman sitting beside him. "We want to know this Jesus."

CHAPTER 41

SANITIZED

A young man who said he was one of the people that cared for the orangutans picked up Nick at the deserted pier. He was relieved as he was beginning to wonder how he was going to find a place to spend the night.

The young man hoped Nick hadn't waited too long. He was told to be at the pier by six, and he was only ten minutes late. Nick didn't mention that he'd been waiting since three. Ms. Boxler's message came loud and clear: *I'm not your travel agent.* He wouldn't make that mistake again. First on his agenda: find out what it would take to get his pilot's license. It was almost dark when they arrived at the research center.

Anxiety filled Nick's mind as he walked down the hallway to Dr. Amy's office. What a tragic ending to a talented woman. He wished he knew more about her. They hadn't discussed family, but he assumed she was unmarried. He had no idea what kind of life she'd left behind. She was kind and smart and wore large shoes that he could never fill.

Her office door was open and Nick entered, flicking on the light switch as he'd done a few nights ago, expecting to see stacks of books and files and the broken window panes of the medicine cabinet.

Instead, he was shocked. The entire office had been sanitized. The books had been neatly put on shelves and a small stack of files left on one corner of the desk, and the broken glass had been replaced.

He glanced around the office, and any trace of the doctor was gone. None of her diplomas hung on the walls and no personal items sat on the bookshelf.

Nick went to the metal filing cabinet in the corner and pulled out the top drawer. At least it wasn't locked—but it was empty. He opened all four drawers and found them barren. *Strange.*

He walked around to the desk and sat in Amy's chair. The top drawer contained some fresh office supplies—pens, two yellow pads, a stapler, and some sticky notes. The other drawers, including one for hanging file folders, were empty.

A growing sense of confusion mixed with anger filled Nick as he reached for the only stack of papers left in the office. The twenty or so files were neatly marked and arranged by labeled color flags: animal studies, biochemistry, development, scientific articles, and so on. They all had one thing in common—a large red IGF-1 stamp.

There was not one shred of paper about Welltrex or any other drug. Nick sighed deeply. He knew when he'd been duped and felt the sharp knife that his dad had warned him about piercing his back. Ms. Boxler had thrust it in deep.

One of the young women that he'd met the first time he'd arrived at the center knocked at the frame of the door, put her head in, and smiled. She wore a sarong.

"Dr. Hart, would you like some tea or something to eat? I can show you to your quarters anytime you desire."

Nick's first thought was to wave her off in anger. But she was not the problem, and he was starving. "I would love some soup or ramen or something…and some water, please."

"Yes, right away," she said and started to leave.

"Oh, excuse me," he said, and she reappeared. "Did you clean Dr. Amy's office?"

She smiled politely. "No, I'm afraid not. Ms. Boxler was here with three men and cleaned it this afternoon. I hope you find it to your liking."

Nick looked around the sanitized office. "Yes, thank you." She was not the enemy, but he sure knew who was.

CHAPTER 42

DUST TO DUST

Wright required only four to five hours of sleep each night. He didn't need more than that and got most of his work done early in the morning when there were no distractions. But last night his mind seemed to be on what the computer guys called "fatal loops"—the dreaded color wheel spinning and spinning, with no way to stop it. His brain swirled with memories of his childhood, his parents and Grandmama. Wright had never felt this alone, even when he received word of his parents' deaths and that tragedy had whirled him out of control.

Now he felt adrift and afraid.

At one point during the night, he thought Grandmama had come to visit him and was physically present in the room. The image was neither peaceful nor comforting. Thankfully, the apparition disappeared.

Now he stood naked at the window of the hotel as the early glow of first light lit the eastern sky. Good thing he was already on Welltrex or this crisis might spin him off axis and into a nervous breakdown. Now he felt numb, as though his heart was crying out behind a veil of false security that the medication provided. It could stay veiled; he didn't want to feel the pain ever. He had Maggie to give him safety and comfort. She could never leave, he would see to that. He wished she was with him now and had been with him through the night, but there was time for that.

At least he'd had his wits about him enough to bring his trusty cologne. He'd find some way to make sure her room was thoroughly sprayed with Confide. The Welltrex was easy; he had only to slip it into her coffee. He thought she loved him anyway, but he wasn't about to take any chances. *Why do that?*

The glow of the eastern light pushed back more darkness. They would escort Grandmama's body soon and fulfill her Hindu wishes to be cremated on the Ganges River. There she would join all the generations before her. It was his sacred duty as the *Karta*, the eldest male relative, to see it through. He knew it was customary for only men to attend the cremation, but he would be thankful to have Maggie at his side. He thought the whole ritual silly but would have shot Grandmama to the moon if she'd requested.

* * *

Maggie was uncomfortable being the only woman near the base of the Hindu temple. Wright continued to reassure her that it was okay in spite of the other men's disapproving looks. He said he didn't care what they thought but instructed her to stand by a massive concrete pillar, out of the way of the crowd. Maggie thought the ritual was fascinating, but the smell was horrendous.

A Hindu priest dressed in white pants, a smock, black vest and dirty brown shoes had met them at the hospital's morgue. He spoke rapid Bengali and wiggled his head side to side as he spoke. He not only gave Maggie the same disapproving look but engaged in a heated exchange with Wright until a roll of money crossed his palm and smoothed his attitude.

The shadow of the temple fell over them and down the expansive set of stairs that extended into the Ganges River, where boats floated and men waded to their chests. Huge stacks of wood lined both sides of the stairs. Heavy smoke choked the air with three cremations already in process. Large groups of men mulled around, performing various duties or observing.

Maggie thought it was a strange affair, more like a social gathering, a men's club: talking, smoking and even laughing, as though meeting on a street corner, discussing the news of the day in casual conversation. Death in Calcutta seemed to be as natural as everyday life.

She brought her scarf over her head and across her face, protecting herself from the stares and stench. She watched the priest and the men Wright had hired take Grandmama's simple pine casket from the hearse, escort it down the steps and place it upon the wooden pyre—a carefully constructed tipi of logs. The priest waved Wright over and told him to circle the body three times counterclockwise while sprinkling holy water from the river on the pyre. The priest then handed Wright a lit torch to ignite the stack of wood. An accelerant quickly ignited the pyre.

Soon the blaze licked the casket, then engulfed it. Wright joined Maggie, and she put her arm around his waist. "I'm sorry, Wright. I know how much she meant to you." She could see the flames dancing in his eyes and was surprised by his lack of tears.

"Grandmama would tell me that spreading your ashes on the Ganges frees you from the cycle of death and rebirth as the spirit ascends to *Moksha*, Nirvana."

Maggie held him and nodded. "What do you think?" she asked.

"I don't know. I guess every religion has their beliefs in the afterlife. I guess Grandmama can rest now."

"She was a beautiful lady. She loved you very much."

Wright nodded. "Let's get out of here. The smoke is ghastly. I think we need to get away."

CHAPTER 43

REVIVERE

There was no reason to stay at the research center, but Nick was not about to call Boxler for logistics on getting back to Singapore. He was more than happy to take the bus back to Kuching and then a puddle jumper to the Singapore International Airport. He was not going to let Boxler mess with him again he decided, as he unlocked the door to his office at the Zelutex complex.

Nick set his briefcase on the desk, took a seat and turned on his desktop computer. This transition from clinical medicine to the medical industry was going to be hard enough on his ego, but he couldn't shake the image of her smirking when he showed up at the office in the research center. *What a jerk.* Maybe she had an underlying disdain for doctors; she certainly had the right to be angry at the plastic surgeons that plasticized her face. He'd heed the warning from the young biochemist, Kerri Kim, and steer clear of her.

He slipped a yellow pad from his briefcase, set it on his desk, and tapped on where he had written notes about naming the IGF-1 drug. Regenerate? Rejuvenate? Nick thought about all the ads he'd see on TV for drugs and wondered how they got their names. Some made sense, others not. Often, they were names that were difficult to pronounce or remember.

He liked the name Revive, but upon Googling it he had to laugh—it was the name of a trademarked caffeine pill. He leaned toward his computer keyboard and typed into the Google search bar: *what is Latin for revive?* The search engine found *revivere* and defined the Latin word as a verb made up of *re*, in English "back," and *vivere*, in English "live": "to bring back to life."

"To bring back to life. Yes," Nick said aloud, thinking of the healing potential to revive tissue.

He searched the trademark website, and nothing came up. *Perfect.*

He wrote it on the yellow pad and circled it twice as his cell phone rang. He pulled it from his pocket hoping it was Maggie. The caller ID said unknown. *It better not be that witch, Boxler.* He reflexively covered his writing as if she might be watching. She'd find a way to nix his idea or take credit for it.

"Hello, this is Dr. Hart."

"Dr. Hart?" the caller asked.

Nick practically fell out of his chair. The New Zealand accent sounded like Dr. Amy.

"Yes," he said tentatively.

"Oh, thank God. Dr. Hart, you don't know me, but this is Allison Anderson. I'm Amy's sister."

There was a long pause.

"Dr. Hart are you there, aye?"

"Oh, yes, of course. I'm sorry. Is it Allison?" Nick moved the phone to his other ear. "Allison, I'm sorry to hear what happened to your sister. We are all devastated."

"Thank you, Dr. Hart. Her service was yesterday here in New Zealand…it was very difficult for my family," she said, trying to find the words. "Dr. Hart, I'm sorry to bother you, but I got a strange packet by FedEx today. It was from Amy. It was full of scientific reports and other things that make no sense to me, and I have no idea why she would send it here, aye. There was a handwritten note on the front that read, 'Going upriver with Dr. Hart.' Do I have the right person?"

"Yes, Allison."

"Unfortunately, it didn't have your contact information. I've practically called every Dr. Hart in the US, and they all probably think I'm bonkers. But I finally called one in Montana, and it turned out to be your father. He gave me this number. I hope you don't mind me calling you."

"Of course not, I'm glad you found me. Is there anything else written on the note?"

"There's a name circled in red ink…Welltrex."

Weird. Why would Amy send that information home?

"Dr. Hart, did I lose you?"

"No, Allison, I'm still here. Just thinking is all. Was Amy planning a trip home soon?"

"She was coming home in a month." Her voice broke. "Should I send this back to her workplace?"

"No!" he said too forcefully. "I'm sorry, Allison. Would you do me a favor and hang on to it for now? I'll think about this and call you back in a few days. Please tell your family that I'm sorry for their loss. Amy was a really good person."

"Thank you, Dr. Hart. I will look forward to hearing from you again." She gave him her number, and he wrote it down on the yellow pad.

Nick hung up and slid his phone onto the desk. *Strange.* Something is rotten in the kingdom and with Welltrex. Zelutex wouldn't be the first company to hide or destroy unflattering research data. He didn't know what to do about it except bypass Boxler and go straight to Wright. He wrote Welltrex on the pad and circled it twice.

* * *

With the help of Kerri Kim, Nick calculated the dose of Revivere for Robert. She liked the name. He figured if he got the team calling it that, Boxler wouldn't have a voice in the matter. For now, he could only administer the drug intravenously, but the team was close to producing it in pill form.

He stood at Robert's bedside with two nurses working on the IV setup. Robert was in good spirits, although his incisions appeared raw and angry. The surrounding tissues were swollen and his nasal tube still in place.

"Robert, this medication is going to help with the swelling and inflammation. It should focus your immune system on healing the bone of your face and jaw, as well as the skin. It will help with growth and regeneration of the tissues."

Robert tried talking through his wired jaw.

Nick thought he was trying to say, "Safe?"

"Yes, Robert. I believe it is. From all that I've read and talked with the team, it appears safe." Nick knew he was wearing his company hat. "But you know, Robert, every medicine can have adverse reactions."

Robert pointed at him and tried to say something through his clenched teeth.

At first, Nick didn't understand, but Robert persisted until Nick asked, "Would I use it on myself?" to which Robert nodded.

"That's a good question, my friend." Nick stopped to think and answered honestly. "Robert, knowing the amount of healing that needs to happen to your face and knowing the results of the trials so far…yes, I would."

Robert gave him a thumbs-up and held out his arm so the nurses could insert the needle into his IV line.

Nick, Robert and the nurses watched as the medicine slowly dripped in. The small bag of medication took fifteen minutes to empty into Robert's system while the nurses kept track of his heart rate, blood pressure, and temperature to monitor for any reaction. The procedure went smoothly.

When one of the nurses unplugged the tubing, Robert shrugged and gave another thumbs-up.

"We'll give you another dose this evening and two more tomorrow," Nick said, then turned his back to pack up his things.

He heard Robert's breath through his teeth quicken, and he snapped his attention back to the man. Robert was thrashing about with his hands around his throat. Nick felt the blood drain from his face and heart, but before he could react, Robert stopped and smiled with his eyes.

"Oh, my God, Robert. You joker!"

The old man laughed as much as he could around his wired jaw and laceration and pointed at Nick.

"Yes, you got me, ol' man. You practically gave me a heart attack."

CHAPTER 44

KUMĀRĪ

Maggie sighed with relief as Wright touched the jet down safely in Singapore. A helicopter ride to his island and she would be back with Nick. He had not called her and vice versa. She wanted to talk with him face-to-face. She still had no idea what to do and continued to pray, but it seemed like the more she prayed, her only answer was overwhelming silence. How had she lost her connection with God in a handful of days? *Father, are you mad at me? Did I do something wrong?* But she knew that was not how her heavenly Father worked. She had experienced God's silence only a few times in her life. She would have to trust in Him and her faith.

The turbines of the helicopter roared to life, spinning the blades overhead, and the chopper started its slow lift from the landing pad. Wright flew the usual path past downtown, but instead of veering left over the Singapore Straits and to Raffles Island, he abruptly turned south and then east. She glanced at him to make sure he was okay. He'd certainly been acting out of sorts.

Finally, looking out the side window and realizing they were over the South China Sea, she turned to him and asked, "Uh… you okay?"

"Maggie, I told you we were going to get away," he said without turning to look at her.

"I thought you meant away from the temple. I didn't…"

"I don't think I'm doing very well, Maggie. I don't think I can face the world right now. It's like I can't stop the voices in my head. I need to go where the world stops spinning...to the rainforest."

* * *

Wright slipped off his shirt. He was already feeling better. Moments before stepping onto the longboat and heading upriver, he'd popped another Welltrex into his mouth. Maybe that was the reason for his calmness, or maybe it was the fact that he was returning to where the world spun in peace and harmony. Everything was going to be okay; he'd been through this before, pulling himself up by his bootstraps and forging ahead. He was in control.

The water on the lake was glassy smooth. As he steered the boat toward the entrance of the Batang Ai River, the evening air temperature dropped slightly. It was a perfect evening, and there was no one else with whom he'd rather share it. The sun was beginning its descent in the west, and a beautiful waning gibbous moon rose in the east.

"Are we headed to Robert's longhouse?" Maggie asked.

"No, somewhere more private. I have been building my own home away from home out here and wanted to show it to you," he said, then whispered the Bengali word for princess: "*Kumārī.*"

After they landed at the research center, it had taken a considerable amount of convincing to get Maggie to go back into the jungle. Wright reminded her that the Huntsman was dead and the forest had reclaimed its tranquility. He promised to protect her from the spiders and other creatures that would have them for dinner. She insisted on calling Nick, but the call would not go through.

She didn't know Wright had switched off the Wi-Fi and the cell tower. He offered no explanation and smiled to himself. He sensed her fear, but that only heightened his sexual energy, filling him with life.

He observed her beautiful black hair fluttering in the breeze along with her silk blouse, which accentuated her breasts and her dark skin glowing in the fading sun. He was excited and he thought the feeling must be love. The psychiatrist had told him he might never love—that control did not equate to affection. But Wright knew the man was wrong. He had found his *kumārī*, his princess.

* * *

"I've built it practically myself," Wright said as they pulled the boat onto the shore. "My little hideaway."

Maggie was relieved to see the A-framed structure jutting out from the hillside, supported by sturdy beams. The roof framed large-pane windows covered in shutters, and a deck hung near the water's edge, surrounded by log railings. This was no thatched-roof longhouse; it was a beautifully constructed home, something you might find on a million-dollar luxury lake property on Flathead Lake in Montana.

"Okay, I had a little help." He smiled, as she admired the home. "The best part is that it is off the grid. Solar panels line the roof, and I don't know if you can see"—he tried to look around the overhanging foliage—"the wind generators at the crest of the hill. The cabin has a deep water well and septic system, even a flush toilet."

Maggie smiled at him.

"See, I told you you'd love it."

Wright led her up the concrete steps to the first landing, unlocked a metal box on a post, opened the door and flipped on switches. Shutters on the windows unfolded automatically and two fans with large leaf-shaped blades began to turn on the deck. Lights flickered on, both inside the home and around the eaves. Twinkling white lights came to life on many of the trees surrounding the deck. The effect was magical.

"It's beautiful," she said.

"Now do you trust me?"

"Of course I do."

"It's my true Robinson Crusoe getaway. I figured if the world keeps spiraling down and one of the rogue nations decides to drop a nuclear bomb or two and the world goes crazy, my fortune would be worthless. I would come here and live out my days in peace."

He put his arm around Maggie and pulled her close. "I would not want to be here with anyone else but you."

CHAPTER 45

ASYSTOLE

Nick had not slept well; it seemed like his spirit was battling the tide. He'd awakened in the middle of the night full of anxiety and worry, and his only remedy was to pray. He prayed over his parents, over his work, over Maggie, wherever she was, and over himself. *Let go*, his heart told his mind. "Father, I trust You," he said over and over until his spirit took hold of it.

He thought about the old couple on the bus and how easily they'd put their faith in Jesus. Their faith was childlike. "Let me trust you like that, Father. Am I doing the right thing by taking this job? It sure doesn't feel like it."

A familiar voice rose from Nick's heart with a kind and loving intonation. It seemed to be slowly but surely replacing the dark tone that had always been quick to remind him of his failures—the one that brought depression and self-loathing.

"Nicklaus, I am with you. I will never leave you. You are exactly where I want you, son."

"Father, I'm not sure what I'm to do. Have I lost Maggie for good? Is there nothing I can do?"

"There is power in your prayers," God's voice rang in his heart.

A verse came to Nick. He wasn't sure if it was John or Maggie who had taught him the scripture. Maybe it was one of his friends, Buck or Anna: "Call to me and I will answer you and tell you great and unsearchable things you do not know." Nick wasn't even sure where in the Bible the verse came from, but he repeated it in his head until he drifted back to sleep.

* * *

Robert's rapid healing had to be the result of the Revivere. Nick was sold on the drug's potential. After only two doses, the effects were remarkable. Robert's incision was less angry and it no longer tugged at the stitches. The swelling resolved to the point that his surgeons had removed the nasal tube.

His stabilized jaw would stay wired shut for at least six weeks, unless the Revivere sped that up as well. Even the cric wound appeared to be well on its way to healing, and Robert continued to try to talk through clenched teeth.

"I am certainly thankful for what I'm seeing, Robert. You almost look human again." Nick smiled and squeezed his arm.

"Not you, Nickloss," Robert said through the hardware closing his jaw.

"Yeah, I'm afraid I didn't sleep well last night. But this is not about me. You ready for another dose?"

"Sure," he shrugged.

"We'll give you this dose and another after lunch, and if you're feeling okay, your surgeons said you could blow this pop stand."

Robert tilted his head and frowned.

Nick laughed. "You can get out of the hospital. They figure since I am staying in Wright's home, you can go there with me for a night or two, and then we can get you upriver."

Robert gave a thumbs-up.

"But no antics today. No more heart attacks." Nick nodded to the nurse to give the medication.

The fluid started dripping from the bag. Zelutex and Nick would be rich. Hundreds of thousands of patients underwent surgery daily around the world, and if Zelutex provided the medication to a fraction of those, the financial potential was more than he could imagine.

Still, he tried to imagine. Like any person buying a lottery ticket when the jackpot was in the hundreds of millions, it was impossible not to dream. But this was a real possibility; he'd seen the numbers. When he'd sat with the witch lady, she showed him an example of the stock options that Wright was set to offer him. At first he thought it was a ridiculous fraction of what it should be—until she ran the numbers. If the IGF-1 medication turned out to be half the success they hoped, his options would be worth millions. No wonder people put their whole lives into these companies—big risk, big reward.

Plus, if patients responded as well as Robert had, it would be a saving grace for each and every patient. Nick thought of the burn patients he'd cared for throughout the years. If the drug prevented grotesque scarring, he could make dispensing it his life's mission. On the personal side, if he cashed in his options, he would be completely out of debt and have plenty to live on. He and the medication could do so many good things.

The last of the bag emptied. "I'll be back later to administer your last dose," he told Robert. "We're starting Daisy on the medication as well."

Robert looked confused.

"Oh," Nick explained, "the little girl we met upriver. Maggie named her Daisy. She had her surgery yesterday."

Robert nodded. "She okay?"

"I'm going to see her next, and I'll let you know."

Robert waved his hand to the negative and shook his head. "Maggie?"

Nick understood and sighed. "That's a story for another day. I'm afraid it's just you and me tonight. We'll go over to Wright's on a boat unless you know how to fly a helicopter."

Robert looked shocked and tilted his hand as if to say, "What?"

"I'll tell you all about it tonight. I'm afraid I haven't made the cut."

* * *

Dr. Fang, his residents, and the medical students were all in Daisy's room discussing her surgery and care plan. He introduced Nick to the group. Fang was kind to introduce him as a colleague rather than someone who had gone to the dark side of the drug industry.

"This is Dr. Hart, an orthopedic surgeon from the US. He works at a Level One trauma hospital—at the Elvis Presley Medical Center."

That wasn't exactly what they called the Memphis Medical Center, and Nick no longer worked there, but he wouldn't make the correction in front of all the other doctors. It was better than being introduced as a damaged man who no longer practiced medicine and had sold his soul to the devil. *Yes, I recognize that voice of darkness.*

"Dr. Hart is helping us with a trial of a new medication that increases the body's healing process by increasing secretion of IGF-1."

The group of young doctors nodded approvingly.

"Yes, we are giving Daisy her first dose," Nick said. "What I have seen so far with our other patient, Robert, is that its effectiveness is pretty impressive."

The doctors parted for Nick to get to Daisy's bedside. Images of Daisy's deformed face flashed through his mind, and he looked forward to seeing the surgeon's work. But Daisy's face was completely covered—wrapped like a mummy, with only her breathing tube coming through the gauze.

Of course. She'd have to be intubated and placed on a respirator until the swelling around her mouth decreased. Poor thing, it was probably more humane to keep her comfortable in a medically induced coma. Her chest rose and fell with the sounds of the respirator next to the bed.

Dr. Fang stepped alongside of him. "Her surgery went very well, maybe better than expected. We hope her skin grafts will take. We're encouraged by how well the old man responded to the medication."

Nick nodded to Dr. Fang and then to the nurse that held the bag of Revivere. As he did, a sense of dread and danger rose in his solar plexus. *"Don't,"* the voice of God called to his heart. He pushed the sensation away—the young doctors were watching him.

He nodded again to the nurse to insert the line into Daisy's IV, and she started the drip. Had he imagined the voice and the slight hesitation of the nurse? *Oh well. She'll be fine.*

Maybe the medicine went in too fast, or there was an interaction with another medication, but whatever it was, she was not fine.

It started with a slight increase in her pulse, then a decrease in her blood pressure. Dr. Fang and Nick missed the fluctuations as they casually conversed. The surgeon was asking where he should visit in the States.

Fortunately, a brave medical student with a short white coat stepped forward to interrupt them. "Uh…" was all he got out when Nick and Dr. Fang turned to see Daisy's blood pressure dropping. Nick hadn't gotten the words out of his mouth to stop the infusion when Fang yanked the needle out of the tubing and yelled back to no one and everyone, "Get the crash cart! Now!"

Daisy's pulse slowed until it stopped.

The resident closest to Daisy threw the sheet off her and started immediate chest compressions. Thank God, she was already intubated. An anaphylactic reaction would not only stop her heart but would likely close her throat, making it impossible to insert a breathing tube. Even a cric would be useless.

The crash cart was bedside in less than a minute, and another resident yelled that the paddles were charged.

Fang held his hand over the chest. "Asystole," he said, looking up at the monitor. "We've got to have a rhythm to shock," he said calmly. "Continue chest compressions and give one amp of epinephrine, please," he ordered. "Open her fluids to full and slow push ten milligrams of dexamethazone."

Nick was frozen. He'd killed the child in front of the whole team. *Come on, Daisy.* Her heart was not even quivering, and her blood was not pumping. From the allergic reaction, her arteries were dumping fluid into her tissues. Hopefully, the epinephrine would spark the heart into activity and constrict her body's arterial system. The steroid should reverse the allergic reaction. *Hopefully.* If her heart restarted, they would administer antihistamines. Right now, they were useless.

The two minutes of chest compressions seemed to last an eternity but circulated the epinephrine to her heart and tissues.

"Stop chest compressions," Fang ordered. Every eye was on the monitor.

Nothing.

"Ready another amp of epinephrine, please." Fang looked at his watch. Nick knew it could be repeated at three minutes. "Resume compressions," he ordered, but then recanted and grabbed the young doctor's arm to stop.

The monitor flickered. It was beautiful, but deadly—ventricular fibrillation. Daisy's heart was quivering.

"Shock now, please."

"Clear," the resident yelled and placed the paddles on the young chest and discharged the voltage.

WHOMP. Daisy's body spasmed, and there was an audible exhale through her tube as her chest compressed.

Beep…beep…beep—sinus rhythm.

"Yes." Fang fist pumped the air and the residents high-fived.

Thank you, God. Nick's knees went weak.

Fang grabbed Nick's arm. "Well, you win one, you lose one."

Nick shook his head; he was speechless.

CHAPTER 46

PSYCHOSIS

The inside of the river lodge was even more attractive than the outside. Exotic woods framed the living area in cozy comfort. The kitchen looked like the set of a cooking show with every gadget possible, including an Italian espresso machine. The bathroom really did have a flush toilet and included a marble inlay shower with multiple heads that bathed a person in waterfalls. And best of all, as far as Maggie was concerned, it was highly unlikely that a spider could find its way into the space. At least that's what she told herself.

This was no cabin in the woods; it was a luxurious get-away. Except for the bathroom, it held an open, spacious design as one large room with the bed in the corner. After they'd arrived and settled in, Maggie showered. Wright made her a decaf cappuccino, and they sat on a plush couch sharing their drinks and thoughts.

Maggie noticed only one problem with the lodge—it had one bed, and she broached the topic head-on. "I haven't shared a bed with a man since John died," she said. As much as her head and body desired Wright, sleeping with him wasn't okay. "I don't believe in sex outside of marriage."

Even though he tried to reassure her that they could share the bed together without the sex, Maggie thought it was too slippery a slope. Maybe she trusted him, but she wasn't sure she trusted herself.

But whether to share the bed turned out to be a moot question. Their conversation turned to religion and morals and then to business, and they ended the evening in an argument. Wright slept on the couch, and Maggie slept in her clothes on top of the bed's comforter. In the morning, she woke to an empty cabin. Wright and the boat were gone.

* * *

Wright cast the fishing net into the water. *What am I going to have to do to make her love me?* It wasn't fair. He'd done everything he knew to do. Given her things and showered her with kindness and affection, even though those concepts were foreign to him.

He pulled in the net, and it was empty. *A statement on my romance.* He could have anything in the world that he wanted, and he was offering her the same. Why wasn't she happy? He'd tripled his own dose of Welltrex that morning, and maybe he'd do the same for her. He knew dopamine could increase a woman's sexual response.

In spite of advances in scientific research, so much of the brain was still unknown. They knew the limbic system, the structures deep in the brain—the thalamus, hippocampus, amygdala, the corpus callosum, and the cingulate gyrus—controlled emotions like happiness, sadness and love. Would they ever be able to control a specific emotion instead of relying on randomly flooding the area with different neurotransmitters?

Wright wrapped the net around his arms in the Iban way, then cast the net in a perfect circle onto the water. *Robert would be proud.*

Wright was certainly proud of Zelutex's research. It had won the Novac Award last year at the Neuroscience Convention. Their paper, titled "Proof That Women's Brains Differ from Men's," was received with laughter, cheers, and accolades. Everyone knew it, but they had proved it. Everyone understood there was no single emotional center in the brain, but different emotions involved different structures. Most importantly, their paper demonstrated that the brains of men and women generate certain emotions with different patterns of activity. Their advanced research imagery allowed them to take snapshots of the brain in action. Emotions are fleeting, and so the snapshots had to capture them quickly. When a woman felt sad, high-speed PET scanners showed increased activity in the limbic system closest to her face and more activity in the left prefrontal cortex than in the right. It might explain why women wore their emotions on their faces more than men.

Maggie certainly did last night. She'd even scoffed at his answer to her question on how to solve the world's dilemmas: "Better living through pharmaceuticals."

Wright pulled on the hand line of the net and brought in a nice-sized Asian Banjo fish. The locals would have eaten the ugly fish, but he wasn't interested in eating a fish that released mucus that was poisonous to their prey and caused instant death to other fish nearby. He threw the unappetizing fish back.

The brain was a marvelous thing. Even the little almond-shaped structure, the amygdala, deep inside the brain, played an important role in major affective activities like love and affection. When scientists destroyed the tiny amygdala in animals, they became tame but sexually nondiscriminatory. Humans with lesions of the amygdala lost the ability to process the meaning of external information, such as the sight of someone they knew well. They could remember the person but were unable to remember if they liked them or not.

An even smaller and seemingly insignificant group of neurons in the brain stem related to gratification. When a patient had a genetic error and a reduced number of dopamine receptors, they were incapable of gaining gratification from common pleasures in life and sought atypical alternatives, such as alcohol, drugs or a compulsion for sweets. Wright often wondered if he carried this genetic abnormality. He understood Zelutex's medications were trying to affect brains that were different from male to female and from person to person. He realized the wiring of the human brain was not static, not irrevocably fixed—brains were also adaptable—so they were shooting at a moving target. Maybe someday, with the new pharmacogenetics, they would develop individualized treatment for patients. Wright had recently okayed twenty million dollars for a project to examine how the cortical and limbic systems worked together.

Maggie had expressed the puzzle last night. She worried about being of two minds in her feelings for him—her head told her one thing and her heart told her something different.

He'd said she didn't understand that the rational cortex could tell a person one thing and the instinctive limbic system another. That's when the fight started. She was adamant that scanners, microscopes, and brain chemistry couldn't explain every mystery. When he argued that we truly are double-minded, she insisted the Bible knew that long before all the fancy instruments said so. She believed that emotions and pain couldn't be cured by pills but could only be understood and healed through a relationship with God.

"You think you can find the answers to all of life's problems in medication," she'd said. "I don't have a problem with using medications when they're needed. Sometimes they can be life saving. I have many friends who've been helped with antidepressants, but there are no shortcuts—there is always a cost. Look at all the side effects of so many of the medications. Even when you're using prescription drugs, you still have to work through the pain."

He had to admit, with some of their medications, patients suffered a higher than 25 percent incidence of significant side effects. When he'd jokingly replied, "I can live with that, especially when the company is making money," she really got angry.

"I could never be with a man that believed that!" she'd yelled, then threw some biblical mumbo-jumbo at him and stopped talking. It had made him angrier than he'd been in a long time. That's when he stormed out, slamming the door so hard that it broke part of the frame.

Her words seemed to reverberate off the jungle canopy. Negative internal dialogue grew louder in his mind and seemed impossible to shut down.

Wright wondered if he heard an audible voice and scanned the thick jungle. Then he thought he heard laughing from the trees. He dropped the net to the bottom of the boat. Was he having a breakdown?

"Wright," a dark voice said, and he spun around looking from side to side.

"Ha, ha, ha," the voice called from one side and then the other.

Wright picked up the large machete that leaned next to his seat and flashed it through the air.

"You'll never get what you want," the voice screamed in his ears.

He twisted left and then right, looking for a wild fig tree or a hilltop. He knew the Iban believed that was where good and evil spirits built their invisible habitations.

"You've lost control of the situation," the voice yelled. Now it seemed to come from inside his head.

"Stop!" Wright yelled at the jungle, dropping the machete and covering his ears with his hands. "Stop."

His head spun, and he sat down hard, bumping his back against the handle of the engine. "Grandmama, help me. Why did you have to leave?"

He was hyperventilating, so he focused his mind to slow his breathing. The screaming decreased and he lowered his hands and looked around. *Nothing.*

He reached back and pulled the starter rope on the outboard. It sprang to life.

He would apologize to Maggie and beg her forgiveness. He could not live without her. She had to understand that. And if she didn't, he knew exactly how to convince her. It was time to pull out his secret weapon. He knew it was just a matter of time, and he'd been waiting for the right moment. He knew her faith was everything to her.

His father had given the small book to him as a child. He hadn't been impressed and had never even opened the cover. But today was the day. He still had no interest in the book, but he knew it was important to Maggie, and he would put on a good show of its value to him. The book was tucked away at the cabin where she was fast asleep—his Bible.

CHAPTER 47

WITHDRAWAL

Nick sat in the family waiting room at the hospital and dialed Maggie's number for the fifth time. She must be out of cellphone range as his calls went straight to her voice mail. He didn't know whether to be angry or worried. Even if she chose Wright as her mate, they would always be friends, and he needed to talk with her. Daisy's cardiac arrest shook him to the very core. Why had he not listened to the sense deep down inside of him, warning him about giving Daisy the medicine? If he acted on every "bad feeling" he had, he would have never operated on anyone. But this time, in retrospect, it felt like the Holy Spirit had told him not to give the dose.

What in the world was he doing? He had prayed and sensed that God gave him the green light to take the job, even though he was full of self-doubt. Had he really heard from the Father? Right now, he thought he'd been listening to the deceiver. He really was a fish out of water. If he wasn't going to continue with this job, then what? He felt like an amoeba floating in space and time with no skeletal structure.

"Trust me, Nicklaus."

He sat up straight and listened. "Yes, that is definitely your voice, Father." He was aware he'd spoken aloud. He glanced around the waiting room and was relieved to be alone.

Chang's discussion of Abraham's "hope against hope" floated through his mind. "God is looking for people that can look beyond the horizon," Chang had said. Nick nodded. *Better to look beyond because the foreground looks bleak right now.* "Father, help me see past all this crap," he said aloud.

At least Daisy was doing okay after her reaction to the medication. The residents would, of course, watch her closely over the next few hours. Fang did not expect her care plan to change, except for the obvious—she would receive no more Revivere.

Nick's winning lottery ticket numbers seemed to evaporate just as he was counting his fortune. If Revivere caused that bad of reaction in even a handful of patients, it would kill the drug.

Nick dialed Kerri Kim's office number, and she answered on the second ring.

"Dr. Hart, how are the trials at the hospital going?" she answered cheerfully.

"Not well. The medication about killed the little girl."

There was a long pause.

"What happened?" she finally asked.

"Her blood pressure dropped out, and her heart stopped."

"Oh, my…"

"Yeah. It wasn't pretty. Thank God the team was able to resuscitate her."

"Is she going to be okay?"

"Except for a little burn on her chest from the cardioversion paddles, yes."

"Thank goodness."

"In the original clinical trials did you all see anything like this?" Nick asked. "I don't remember seeing any severe reactions in the report."

Kerri didn't answer. Finally, she said, "Dr. Hart, let me call you back later tonight. It will be from my cell phone. I'll have to leave the building."

* * *

Nick was hesitant to give Robert his final dose. *But he's done so well.* Nick prayed and thought he got an affirmative to administer the drug. Thankfully, Robert did fine.

Nick had one other item on his to-do list before he helped get Robert home, and that was to track down Daisy's father. It wasn't easy. The doctors had admitted him to the psych ward, and Nick had to get clearance from the hospital administrator to get through the locked doors.

A young female resident at the nurse's station was happy to help. She took the patient's chart and escorted Nick to the room. They passed many patients sitting outside their rooms in various states of drug-induced stupor. Nick wondered if the treatment for psychosis had changed from his days as a medical student rotating through psychiatry. Back then they administered heavy doses of Thorazine or Haldol. The drugs that combatted hallucinations, paranoid delusions, and thought disorders left patients with drool dripping from their chins.

The resident stopped at a locked door with a small, thick window and opened the patient's chart. Nick looked through the window to see a man resting comfortably on his bed. The room looked more like solitary confinement in a maximum-security prison than a hospital room; there was nothing the patient could use to harm himself, not even a sheet on the mattress.

"This man suffered an acute psychotic episode, with hallucinations and passivity phenomena," the resident said and smiled at Nick.

"Remember, I'm a bone doctor...help me out. Passivity what?"

"It's when they have delusional beliefs that others can control their will or feelings, even their limb movements and bodily functions."

Nick nodded.

The young doctor flipped a few pages of the chart, studying each one.

"The note from this morning says he is being weaned off Haldol and may come out of lock-up tomorrow. He seems to be doing much better."

She flipped the page. "His history and physical says he was on some pharmaceutical trial?"

"Yes," Nick said.

"Well, all his admission labs were within normal limits," she adjusted her glasses and looked at Nick. "It says here they postulate that the medication increased his dopamine levels to the point that sent him into schizophrenia. Either that or the medication was stopped abruptly, and he was having symptoms of acute withdrawal."

* * *

Nick and Robert took a cab to the docks and a boat taxi to Wright's island. It wasn't as stylish as the helicopter and took longer, but Nick thought Robert handled it well. He was helping Robert up to the house when Kerri Kim called back. He smiled at Christian who met them on the path and handed Robert off to him as he answered his phone.

"Dr. Hart, I'm sorry about the delay. I hate to sound paranoid, but I didn't want to talk about any issues over my office phone."

"What am I missing here, Kerri?" he was anxious to get to the point and to get Robert inside.

"The first clinical trial of IGF-1 medication, Revivere, had a 15 percent autoimmune reaction, sometimes severe. We thought a protein in the medication's carrier was to blame. We removed it and hoped that would stop the reaction. This is the first trial since that adjustment."

"Why wasn't I told about this?" Nick tried to not put too much heat into his words.

Again, there was a long pause. "Dr. Hart, I'm sorry. The team thought we'd solved the issue."

"But the reactions in the first trial were not in the reports."

Kerri blew out a loud sigh. "Dr. Hart, we need to talk about this. All I can say is that Ms. Boxler's office filters all reports."

Nick nodded. He was getting the picture. "And reactions or withdrawal symptoms from Welltrex?"

"I was not on that team." She hesitated. "But I've heard rumors. We need to talk about this face-to-face. You need to understand there are huge amounts of money on the line."

"Understood." Nick disconnected the call and stared at his phone. *What in the world have I gotten myself into?*

CHAPTER 48

MADNESS

The mighty fisherman brought no dinner home. Wright returned to the cabin like a dog with his tail between his legs, looking sheepish, and apologizing for his failure. Fortunately, the refrigerator, freezer, and pantry were fully stocked, and he set to work preparing a delicious shrimp pasta dish, continuing to apologize until Maggie insisted he stop.

After dinner, when he pulled out the Bible, he knew he had hit the mark. As soon as she saw the book, both her spirit and her eyes lit up, and now they sat comfortably on the couch together sipping tea and chatting.

"Wright, everyone has faith in something," Maggie was saying. "It's how we're hardwired. Most people around the world have faith in the divine, in God, but even the atheist believes in something—even if it's themselves or their organic garden or the crystal hanging around their neck. I don't think I've ever met a person that doesn't hold something dear. It's just not possible."

Wright sipped his tea. He would have to agree with that. He did not believe in a supreme being, but he had faith in how the human genome came from the sea and continued to evolve.

"Whether you want to believe it or not, there is a spiritual world," Maggie continued. "Every religion acknowledges that. I remember when I went on my first mission trip to Guatemala. Next door to where we were staying there was a witch doctor of sorts. We would sing and pray each morning and night. He got angry with us because he could no longer cast his spells and do his magic. We believed our worship had changed the atmosphere and ushered in the Kingdom of God—pushing away the darkness."

Wright frowned and shrugged.

"What so many people need to understand and think about is what spirit they listen to—the Holy Spirit or an evil spirit," Maggie said.

"But I'm not a religious person," Wright said.

"See, that's exactly where people get hung up. It's not about religion. They pick apart something about a church or organization, or they get offended by a street-corner preacher or televangelist and miss Jesus's whole message. Yes, yes, yes, there have been terrible abuses in all religions, including Christianity. But the truth remains the truth, whether you believe it or not."

"How do you believe in someone we don't even know existed?"

"You mean Jesus? Oh, come on, Wright. That argument always gets me. Do you question the existence of Abraham or Moses? Everything in history tells us they walked the earth and no one seems to dispute that, but they want to say Jesus was some myth. That argument doesn't hold water."

"Okay, I guess I'll concede and say Jesus existed, but I think of him more as a great moral teacher, like Buddha or Muhammad."

Maggie shook her head. "But there is a great and important difference. None of the other people you or anyone else like to equate with Jesus ever said they were divine…that they were God Himself." Maggie leaned forward and set her teacup down.

"We all have to decide if Jesus is truly who He said He is. I love how C. S. Lewis debated this point to those that wanted to accept Jesus only as a great moral teacher. Lewis told people that Jesus made it very clear; He was the Son of God. He leaves us with no other choice, either you believe He was a lunatic, or He is the Messiah—Jesus left us with no other choice."

Wright wanted to argue but decided to back off and not start another war. He hoped he wouldn't be sleeping on the couch again tonight.

* * *

The question of sleeping arrangements didn't come up because Maggie and Wright had fallen asleep on the couch. When she awoke and realized this, she was glad she hadn't had to make a big deal about not sleeping with him in the bed. She sat up and discovered she was wrapped in a soft blanket and Wright was standing over her with a steaming cup of mocha. It smelled delicious.

"Good morning," she said and stretched.

"I've made you a special coffee with Mexican chocolate. I hope you enjoy it." He handed her the cup.

She blew at the steam rising off the top and took a sip. The cinnamon chocolate was rich and soothing.

"Thank you. How did you sleep?"

"Uh, not so well," Wright said. "Like not at all."

"Sorry to hear that," Maggie said, watching him pace up and down the floor. She wondered why he was so agitated, rubbing his head as though he was shooing flies away.

He caught her quizzical look and said, "I thought we could go out this morning and look for some of our ancestors."

Maggie tilted her head, confused as she watched him place a holster and pistol through his belt and slap it in place.

"There is a family of orangutans that live in this area. I thought we could go out looking for them."

"Are you okay this morning?" Maggie asked. "You look a little pale." She wasn't sure what else to say, but he was definitely off. Even his beautiful eyes seemed dark and disoriented.

"I'm fine. Finish your coffee and let's go." His voice registered anger.

* * *

Before Maggie's father had found peace in his relationship with God, he was an angry drunk. Like so many of her Blackfeet elders, he lived in hatred of the white man and was ireful at his lot in life on the reservation. Alcohol was his drug of choice, but it worked poorly, only making him more belligerent and angry.

As Maggie followed Wright into the jungle, she fought the feeling that she was ten again and walking on eggshells, afraid to say or do anything that would throw the man she was with into a rage. Wright seemed to take everything she said the wrong way. She suggested that she take a shower and get cleaned up for him, but he told her that was a stupid idea. They were, after all, about to get dirty and sweaty. She could shower when they got home.

They had walked for over two hours, and now he was ten steps ahead of her, almost tempting her to fall behind and get lost. She stumbled over a large root and fell. He didn't turn around to help.

"Wright, please, I'm so sorry for whatever I've done, but I can't keep up."

Maggie felt tears coming on and tried to blink them back. She remembered how they made matters worse with her father. Memories of him slapping them away made her shudder, even though she'd worked through the abuse a long time ago and fully forgiven her father.

Why am I struggling so? She picked herself up and held her head, trying to regain her balance. Since drinking that delicious coffee, her head had spun and her equilibrium was off. It wasn't like her to be so unsteady. Was it too much caffeine and chocolate?

Wright had disappeared, and Maggie realized she was alone and helpless. If he left her there, she would be lost. Worse yet, he carried the backpack with their water and food. She was totally dependent on him. Why didn't he turn back to check on her? He'd been so accommodating. *Is he doing this on purpose?*

She reached for a branch to help herself over another gnarled root system.

"Ouch," she yelled. A large thorn had stuck in her hand. She pulled it out and shook her fingers.

"Wright, please," she called. "Don't leave me alone!" Suddenly her mind was filled with images of slithering snakes and snarling leopards.

"Wright!" She could continue no longer. She stopped, covered her face with her hands and began to sob. Her world was collapsing around her.

"Oh, stop it!" Wright yelled, making her jump. He had circled back behind her. "Stop it." He grabbed her shoulders and spun her around. "Don't ruin this." He shook her. "You trying to ruin this?" He shook her harder.

Maggie's hands dropped to her side. She stared into Wright's eyes and saw madness. She whimpered as his hand raised to slap her.

"UOOOF!"

Something bellowed behind Maggie, and Wright froze, dropping his hand. "Kumārī, look," he said, slowly turning Maggie around.

A large male orangutan stood on his hind legs, ten feet from them. "UOOOF," the animal bellowed and beat his chest.

CHAPTER 49

UNVEILED

Nick startled awake to see Robert standing at his bedside in the guest room of Wright's home. He thought he'd slept through his alarm, then he remembered it was Saturday.

"Nickloss, I brought you some breakfast," Robert said through his teeth. "You looked pretty tired last night. I thought you could use something to eat."

"Oh, Robert! You're the one we should all be waiting on," Nick said and stretched.

"Old habits die hard, I guess," Robert said. He put the tray of food and coffee on the table by the sliding glass door that overlooked the sea.

Robert looked anemic but spry for an eighty-year-old man recovering from a near-deadly attack. After the assault, Robert had come close to requiring a blood transfusion, but he'd declined it. Nick wished the old man's stamina and resilience were contagious.

"I tried all night to reach Maggie," Nick said as he got out of bed. He pulled a T-shirt over his head and tucked it into his scrub bottoms. "I was worried enough that I finally called Wright's phone. He didn't pick up either. Their phones are turned off, or they're out of range."

Robert nodded. "That is quite unusual."

"What do you think we should do?" Nick asked, sitting at the table and admiring the meal.

Robert sat in the chair opposite Nick and took a frozen smoothie from the tray. He would be eating through straws until his jaw was healed and unwired. He took a long draw of the liquid and looked thoughtfully out the window at the calm sea.

He looked back at Nick. "Mr. Paul's helicopter is not in the heliport here, and the staff at the research center told me he went upriver. I guess they could have gone to my home or…" He looked out the window again.

"Or, what?"

"Mr. Paul has a lodge in the rainforest that he recently completed."

Nick huffed. "That figures." Nick leaned back in his chair hard and crossed his arms. "Robert, I don't understand what Maggie is doing." Pain rose in his chest, and he put pressure on it with his fingertips.

Robert shrugged. "I as well, Nickloss. I saw how she looked at you. How she cared for you. Even Iban women are hard to understand sometimes, but this…I don't know. Maggie is not the kind of person who would throw away her heart to have the trappings of this world."

They sat in silence.

Nick picked at the fruit and granola but didn't have an appetite.

He finally let out a loud sigh. "I may not be much different; I don't know."

Robert looked at him with surprise.

Nick raised his hands in surrender. "I really don't know, Robert. I jumped at this job because I thought it would give me security, but it seems to be packed full of heartache. I thought as I prayed I got the green light from God, but maybe it was my own desire for a comfortable life. No more being on call, no more emergency-related stress. But now I'm thinking the money's not worth it." He puffed air out his lips. "Geez, look at me. I'm working for the guy who stole Maggie from me. Don't I look like a total loser?"

Robert shrugged, then nodded.

Ouch! Having Robert agree didn't help. Nick rubbed his chest. "And now I see these problems with the new medications."

Robert's eyes brightened. "Perhaps you are supposed to be here after all. Maybe you are not here for the money, but to be the voice of reason. I have been quite concerned about Welltrex. My people do not like it."

"Why haven't you said anything?"

Robert smiled with his eyes. "I am only the humble butler."

Nick understood. He was supposed to be the medical director and had zero influence over anything. Certainly he had no say over Boxler.

Robert got up, opened the slider door, and let a fresh sea breeze drift in. "Nickloss, maybe we are looking too close."

Nick didn't understand and tilted his head.

"Sometimes we don't understand or see God's long-term plan. Do you remember the scripture in Matthew where Peter declares that Jesus is the Messiah? Jesus blesses Peter and tells him that he is the rock on which He will build the church."

"Yes," Nick said.

"In the very next verse, Jesus tells His disciples that He must suffer many things, and Peter tries to convince Him otherwise. Jesus rebukes him and says, 'You are a stumbling block to me; you do not have in mind the concerns of God, but merely human concerns.'"

Nick immediately caught on. "I've been too short-sighted... looking too close, as you say. I haven't been trying to see the whole picture. Maybe we need to be looking beyond what we see right now."

Nick walked to the nightstand and opened his Bible to Matthew 16 to read through what Robert had just paraphrased. He nodded.

He traced the scripture with his finger until the end of the chapter and read Jesus's words aloud: "'Whoever wants to be my disciple must deny themselves and take up their cross and follow me. For whoever wants to save their life will lose it, but whoever loses their life for me will find it. What good will it be for someone to gain the whole world, yet forfeit their soul?'"

Would I give up my soul for the millions that were promised?

* * *

Nick was sitting poolside after breakfast, reading through a stack of reports. Voices inside the house broke the morning tranquility, and Nick looked up to see Robert escorting Christian, the muscular Iban servant, out the door.

"Nickloss, please…" Robert all but dragged the young man behind him.

Nick set the files on the table beside him and sat up on the side of the lounge chair.

"Nickloss, you must listen to what Christian has to say," Robert said, pulling the servant close.

"Tell Dr. Hart what you just told me," Robert's face was beet red and his eyes angry as he forced Christian to square up to Nick. "Tell him." He shook the young man's arm as Nick stood.

Christian looked at the granite decking. "Dr. Hart, I am sorry. Mr. Paul threatened me if I told anyone, but I asked Robert what I should do."

"Tell him!" Robert yelled through his teeth.

"Mr. Paul asked me to put the heart medicine in the lady's coffee before I served it."

Heat and alarm instantly shot up Nick's back. "And did she know?"

The boy's shoulders drooped, and he shook his head slowly.

Nick looked at Robert. "What the hell? Why would he do that?"

"I do not know, Nickloss."

Nick back-kicked the lounge chair he had been sitting in and sent it tumbling over.

"There is one more thing," Christian nervously said, looking at Nick and then at Robert.

"What?" Robert asked, still shaking the boy's arm.

"There is a canister in her closet I am supposed to change every day."

"A what?" Nick didn't understand his accent.

"A canister, a spray," the young man repeated.

Nick looked up at the balcony of the guest rooms and took off in a sprint up the stairs with Robert hauling Christian behind him.

Nick flung open the door to Maggie's room and went straight to the closet. Maggie's evening dresses hung from the rack, and she had neatly placed the fancy shoes that Wright bought her on the floor. Nick pushed the clothes from side to side but did not see a canister.

Robert and Christian came in behind him, and Robert pushed the boy forward to show them where it was. The young man took a step inside the closet and reached for a small door next to the door frame. He opened it, took out a small aerosol can and handed it to Robert.

Nick snatched it from Robert. He turned it over. Written on a piece of tape was THE RIGHT STUFF. "What the hell is this?" he demanded.

Robert looked at Christian, and they both shrugged.

Nick smelled the top of the can for hints, and rage rumbled in his gut. "What the hell…this smells like him!" he yelled. Nick gave the canister to Robert to confirm, then took Christian by the throat.

"Is there anything else?" The terrified young man's eyes widened, but he shook his head.

"No, nothing, Dr. Hart. I promise."

Nick let go of the boy. No use taking his anger out on him. Instead he tipped over chairs, threw off the bed coverings, and dumped drawers frantically searching for any other secrets Wright hid in Maggie's room. In the top drawer was the fancy jeweled necklace that Wright had given Maggie. Nick threw it against the wall with such force that pieces came flying off it.

He felt like a madman, but every piece of furniture he toppled and every drawer he emptied was cathartic. He remembered raging against the waterfall, but now he could see…oh, could he see. That monster in sheep's clothing was drugging Maggie.

Nick's catharsis continued until his mind and body were exhausted, and he sat down on the now bare mattress. He tried slowing his breath until he could look at Robert and Christian without rage in his eyes.

"What are we going to do, Nickloss?" Robert asked.

Nick's focus shot past the pair, and he ignored the question. He sprang up, went to the desk, righted it, and slid it across the floor to the middle of the room. Jumping on top of it, he stretched toward an air vent and pulled off the cover with his bare hands, taking plaster with it. The vent stopped at shoulder level and dangled by a black cord. Nick ripped the cable from the vent and inspected the end. The eye of a miniature camera peered back at him.

He threw the vent across the room and into a picture, shattering its glass.

"Maggie's in trouble."

CHAPTER 50

ATTACK

"Don't look him in the eyes, Kumārī," Wright whispered. In slow motion, he gripped her shoulders and turned her back toward him. He forced her to her knees and held the back of her neck, bending her face toward the ground. "If he attacks, ball up and protect your head and neck with your arms."

The orangutan stood only five feet on his back legs, but he had a muscular body twice as wide as a man's. He was a gorgeous specimen, one that Wright had never seen before, and that was bad. Even the wild beasts that knew him could be unpredictable, but this huge male must have moved in by force and taken over the congress of orangutans. Wright watched him out of the corner of his eye, tucked his chin to his chest and reached for his gun. The .357 Mag would stop the creature, but only if Wright hit it square in the chest or head. He withdrew the weapon slowly from the holster and raised it to his side.

The beast grunted again, grabbed branches from a nearby bush, and began ripping them apart.

Not a good sign.

As the orangutan shook the branches at Wright and Maggie, his massive facial disk and double chin wobbled like an angry fat man. He stretched out his arms to their full eight-foot span and grabbed small trees on each side of the trail to use as poles. He bounced up and down with agitation.

Wright covered the back of Maggie's head with his hand.

This movement incited the creature, and his rage intensified, turning into a two-minute roar amplified by his mammoth face.

Maggie whimpered, wrapping her arms around her knees. Her cries roused the beast further. He roared again and charged.

Wright pushed Maggie to the ground, protecting her with his own body, and at the same time he fired the gun. The enormous beast smacked into them and sent them tumbling into the foliage.

They landed hard, and something snapped. Wright wasn't sure if it was branches or bone, but darkness filled his vision.

* * *

SNAP. Maggie heard the sound. She thought it came from her body, but her world was spinning and she couldn't be sure. She heard the bellowing orangutan. *Is he going to attack again?*

She squeezed her eyes shut as if that would make the terror disappear. The jungle around her swirled with the intruder's rage. She thought Wright's shot must have missed its mark but antagonized or possibly wounded the beast, making it more ferocious.

In Montana, grizzly bears attacked much the same way when surprised—charge, knock the danger to the ground, use their massive jaws and claws to subdue the challenge, then posture over their victory with huffing and roars. When hiking the wilderness she had always carried bear spray, and she wished she had a canister now. The best thing to do was play dead, act like she no longer posed a threat.

She could not feel Wright beside her. Had the monster dragged him off? Was he getting mauled? She risked danger and tried to assess the situation through squinted eyes. *Little movements. Silent little movements.*

She turned her head to the right and saw the beast standing on top of Wright's limp body, jumping up and down on it as though trying to pound the carcass into the ground. The angry orangutan swung its enormous arms wildly, howling as it did. Wright had told her that an orangutan has seven times the strength of a man. The creature could easily snap Wright's spine.

The big male's agitation continued to grow, followed by roaring vocalization. Maggie opened her eyes wide when a large female wandered into view. A riotous exchange erupted between the two apes. The male jumped from Wright's body into a tree, climbed effortlessly to the top, and swung two times to another tree.

The female sniffed at Wright's lifeless body, picked up one of his arms and dropped it. She grabbed the pistol by the barrel and inspected its end. As soon as she touched it, she screamed as if the barrel was burning hot, and she tossed it into the brush. She searched the area and spotted Maggie. Maggie averted her eyes, but not before she saw the orangutan headed her way.

Maggie tried rolling herself into a ball but found her right arm was tucked awkwardly behind her back and she couldn't move. When she attempted to free herself, excruciating pain shot through her upper arm into her shoulder. The attack had broken her humerus.

She felt the hot breath and low vocalizations of the orangutan sniffing at her. A calloused hand wrapped around her neck, and she braced for the worst. But instead of attacking, the orangutan pulled Maggie to a sitting position and off her trapped arm. The pain was agonizing, and Maggie held her arm to stabilize it, bringing her forearm to her lap in one motion. She couldn't help but whimper, which triggered more vocalizations from the ape that supported her. The animal put its white fuzzy mug to Maggie's face and sniffed at her hair.

Maggie wrapped her left hand around where she knew the bone was fractured on the right, trying to stabilize it and stop the muscle spasms. The ape sniffed at Maggie's arm and gently mouthed it with her big lips. She startled Maggie when she turned and scolded the bellowing male overhead. Spasms and pain shot through Maggie's arm, and she panted through the agony.

The orangutan held Maggie's face like a mother would comfort a hurt child. She kept her chin tucked and avoided eye contact, but the beast forced her chin up and her eyes forward. Maggie looked into the creature's sad, dark eyes. The animal stared at her as if trying to read her mind and stroked Maggie's cheek with concern.

Even in her pain, Maggie had to smile; the great ape was

tending to her with the compassion of a nurse—communicating with her using touch and eye contact. Shaggy red hair framed its leathery face. The mother ape made a low, guttural grunt, followed by a kissing, sucking sound. It looked back over her shoulder as the rest of the ape family wandered into the area.

A young male approached Wright's body and sniffed at him. Unafraid, the ape sat beside him and inspected Wright's hair. It was then that Wright shifted, bending a leg.

"Thank God!" Maggie exclaimed. *He's alive.*

She scooted herself back with her legs and leaned against a tree. She breathed through the pain and repositioned her arm. Nothing else seemed to be broken.

The female ape continued to minister to her. A small face appeared over the shoulder of Maggie's nurse and regarded her with curiosity. *Her baby.* The little one's hair stood straight up, and its coal-black eyes examined Maggie and made a funny expression.

Maggie couldn't help smiling. *All things in perspective.* Then she looked beyond mother and child to see the entire congress of great apes sitting quietly, observing, chomping jungle grasses, and chatting among each other with grunts and chirps.

Then her eyes fell on the quivering human body, and the harsh reality of the situation hit her square on. Her arm was broken, and Wright was severely hurt. They were somewhere in the jungles of Borneo. She had no idea where.

CHAPTER 51

RESCUE

Nick was beside himself. It had taken them all day to get to Wright's lodge. The sun had set hours ago, and the moon was the only light in the sky. He'd strong-armed Boxler into releasing a plane to fly them to Kuching. She resisted until Nick told her about Wright drugging Maggie and putting a camera in her room. He also threatened Boxler with jail time. He had no idea if it was possible, but he told her that if she didn't cooperate, she would be considered an accessory to a crime. Whatever tripped her trigger, Boxler quickly became helpful. Then, once in Kuching, it took four more agonizing hours to get to the lodge.

When they arrived, it was empty.

The door was locked, but Nick threw a chair through one of the large windows and forced his way inside. Maggie's bag and clothing were there, but there was no sign of her or Wright and no indication of a struggle. Nick's shoulders drooped, and he sighed with helplessness.

On the journey Nick had wished for a firearm or some weapon. Robert had stopped a passing boat and convinced the occupants to loan him a blowgun and darts. He also asked them to motor to his longhouse and ask some of his young men to meet them here.

As they had approached the lodge, adrenaline surged through Nick's veins, and he'd readied himself for a fight. But once they arrived, there was no brawl. But maybe that was fortunate. Nick was so angry, he might have killed Wright with his bare hands.

"Now what?" Nick turned to Robert. He could see determination and anger in the old man's face. His gentle eyes had become as fierce as any Iban warrior's.

"His boat is here," Robert said. "They must be out there." He waved his hand to the jungle. "We need to look for them." He sniffed the air as if he could sense peril. "There are greater dangers out there than Mr. Paul."

"Where would they go?" Nick asked. "Why would they go out there?"

"Hunting or adventuring, I suppose. We must be careful. Mr. Paul often carries a sidearm into the jungle."

Nick followed Robert to the porch. "Lead the way."

"Nickloss, there are many trails leading into the jungle. We have no idea which one to take. My men should be here in an hour or so; maybe we should wait?"

"Maggie may not have the luxury of time."

Robert nodded. "Then we must pray and hope we choose wisely."

Nick dropped to his knees. He knew Robert was correct—they were lost without divine guidance. "Father help us. Show us the way we should go. Father, protect Maggie."

Robert joined him in an amen.

Nick stood, then walked to the back of the lodge. As Robert had indicated, many trails branched off from the main pathway. Nick took his headlamp off the top of his head and shined it at the dirt, looking for prints. The trail was hard, compacted clay, and there was no clear sign of which way to go.

Left? Right? Straight? "Which way, Father?" Nick prayed.

The logical way was to go straight on the widest path.

Take the path less traveled, the voice in his heart said.

His mind wrestled with his heart. *I hope that's you, Holy Spirit.*

"I think we should go this way," Nick said and started down the trail to the right, the narrower, more overgrown path. Robert followed, using his blowgun as a walking stick.

They had gone a quarter of a mile, and the night was getting darker and darker. Then, as if by a miracle, Nick's headlamp revealed a beautiful sight in the middle of the dirt path—Maggie's scarf.

* * *

Maggie shivered in the cool night air. Fear had already made itself at home in her mind, and now shock was settling in. The orangutans had moved into the trees for the night, out of harm's way. Maggie tried to splint her arm as much as possible to prevent the ends of the bones from grinding together and sending violent spasms through her body. She inched closer to Wright. She was able to roll him over and was glad to see he was conscious. He blinked at her, dazed and confused.

"Kumārī, what happened?" he murmured. "Where are we?"

"Wright," she said firmly. "It's Maggie." She wanted to tell this man who had raised his hand to slap her to stop calling her his princess, but chastising him made no sense. He was her only lifeline out of the jungle. "Where do you hurt?"

Wright winced and hugged his ribs. Maggie thought the orangutan must have broken them. She knew it could be worse. If his spleen had ruptured, he'd already be dead. A large bleeding gash on the side of his head was matted with clot and dirt.

Supporting her broken arm, she made it to her feet and staggered to where she thought the orangutan had tossed Wright's gun. She found the pistol on the ground and then tore a large leaf from the foliage. She'd use the leaf to compress Wright's bleeding head. But, holding both the plant and the pistol, she was unable to support her broken arm. Horrific pain shot up and down her limb. She panted through the spasm. Then she made her way back to Wright and collapsed by his side. Forcing herself through the discomfort, she put the leaf on the wound and pulled his hand up to hold it.

"Wright, do you know where you are?"

He uttered a strange, incoherent sound.

"Wright?"

He cleared his throat and said, "Kumārī, we must get out of the jungle. We are not safe."

"Do you have any idea which way is the lodge?" In the dark, nothing looked familiar.

"Lodge?" He looked at her with unfocused eyes.

Maggie knew it was up to her.

A light rain began to fall, and lightning flashed in the night sky. They would die of hypothermia if she couldn't get them to shelter. She hesitated, then leaned against his body for warmth. How could she have gotten so lost and trusted a man who was clearly unstable? *Father, help me.*

She heard a sound from the jungle and glanced over her left shoulder. She heard it again. Were the orangutans back? She squinted, trying to pierce the darkness. Something was there.

The rain began to fall harder, making it difficult to hear the sound. It was not the grunt of the orangutans—it was a low growl of a predatory animal. A lightning strike lit the area and momentarily she saw a flash of the animal—a leopard.

Ignoring her pain, she reached for the gun that she had set down beside her. She was an excellent shot with her right hand. Since she couldn't use it, she'd have to rely on her left. She awkwardly picked the pistol up with her left hand. The large bore gun was heavy, and her hand shook with the weight.

The leopard disappeared, then reappeared at her right, then disappeared again.

The leopard was stalking them—gauging its approach, looking for the best attack. It could take its time and toy with them—a cat with a mouse. The predator had been drawn by the scent of blood.

Maggie glanced at Wright. He would be no help. She could move away from him and let the big cat feast on the madman's body. She immediately thought better of that. She couldn't live with herself, even if Wright had gone mad.

She aimed the gun toward where she'd last seen the leopard. If the .357 had the usual six bullets in it, she had five left, but with the predator's speed, she would only get one or two shots off before the leopard was on top of them. Then she saw it.

The big cat slinked out from the bush probably ten feet from them. Lightning flashed, showing its marbled spots. *A clouded leopard. Beautiful, but deadly.* It hissed at them as though smelling the threat of the gun. Then it paced one way and the other.

Then it stopped. Maggie saw it winding up to pounce. She had to shoot it, but her hand shook so violently she could not get it in her sights. It leaped, and she shot, knowing she had missed the mark.

The leopard was hovering in midair when a roar and flash of movement burst from the jungle. The leopard was grabbed and ripped from its trajectory. The huge male orangutan had returned, not to harm them, but to save them. The ape caught the predator with one of his enormous arms, swung it over his head like a rag doll, and threw it against a tree trunk, ending its life.

The orangutan roared in victory and beat his massive chest. Maggie collapsed over Wright, and her world went to black.

* * *

Nick heard the shot and took off on a dead run with Robert at his heels. They hurtled over tree roots and ignored thorns tearing their skin. The rain fell harder, coating the trail with slick mud. Nick went down hard on his back but ignored the pain. He jumped up and pushed through the night. Lightning flashes illuminated the jungle in light and shadows. His lungs burned, and his legs filled with lactic acid, putting them in danger of collapsing as they raced through the night and storm.

"Maggie!" he yelled at the jungle and rain and lightning. "Maggie!"

They sprinted another hundred yards, and Nick stopped, thinking he'd lost their way. Then he heard something, something human. The rain hit the foliage hard, obscuring the sound and saturating the rainforest with the sizzle of white noise.

"This way!" Robert yelled and darted south.

Nick caught up to Robert, who held out his arm to stop him.

"Maggie!" Nick called breathlessly. He strained forward, but Robert held him. Nick stared at the sight in the light of his headlamp. Maggie lay crumpled over Wright's body. Nick tried to break free of Robert and lunge toward her, but Robert continued to hold him back. He tried shaking off the old man's grip until he heard the roar of a gigantic animal standing over Maggie.

Lightning flashed through the canopy and showed the massive beast; his enormous black face roaring and revealing yellowed fangs. He stood upright on his hind legs, swinging his arms aggressively overhead. The monster's eyes flashed red in the light of the headlamp, and Robert knelt, pulling Nick with him and covering Nick's headlamp with his hand. The beast radiated intimidating power. It bellowed again, trying to decide if the humans were friends or foes. Having decided in the affirmative, it took one long leap into the tree overhead, swooped over them for one last acknowledgment of who was king of the jungle, and fled the scene.

Nick raced to Maggie and knelt at her side. "Maggie!"

Her hair was matted and soaked over her face, and her body shook with hypothermia and shock, but she was alive.

"Nicklaus. Thank God."

"Maggie, I'm so sorry." He tried pulling her close, but she cried in pain. "Where are you injured?"

He let go of her shoulders and instantly saw the deformity of her upper arm. "Are you hurt anywhere else?" Water dripped from her face as she shook her head.

"Nicklaus, I am so sorry."

It was just like Maggie to take the blame. He smoothed her hair back from her face. "It's okay, Maggie. We're here now."

Wright moaned and shifted. A confluence of emotion flooded Nick's mind. He was glad Wright was alive but wanted to bash his head in with a rock.

He turned back to Maggie. "What happened?"

She could barely get words out of her chattering jaw. "The orangutan...he saved my life...our lives. Wright's hurt pretty bad...broken ribs...head."

Nick felt the pulse on Wright's neck. It was weakened but present. He looked up at Robert, who stood over them. "We have to get them back to the lodge."

Robert nodded and looked around as though looking for a phone to call 9-1-1.

"Robert?" Nick asked.

"Listen." Robert held up his hand for silence.

At first, all Nick could hear was the storm. Then he heard something else. Men's voices calling through the rainforest.

Robert pointed into the darkness and cried out.

His yell was answered with more calls.

"How did they find us?" Nick asked.

"We are Iban," Robert said proudly. "We are the guardians of the rainforest."

CHAPTER 52

REVENGE

Robert's men helped transport Wright and Maggie. She tried to walk the first mile, but her legs grew weak and it became necessary to carry her the rest of the way. Nick took his shirt off and wrapped it around her arm and chest to support the fracture. It only helped a little with her pain, but it was all he could do at the time.

Bouncing Wright down the trail on the back of one of the men was not the safest or healthiest mode of transportation for his broken ribs and head injury. One of Robert's men who was not fond of Wright suggested leaving him, but Robert scolded the man and told him it was not the way of Jesus.

As soon as they arrived at the warmth and protection of Wright's lodge, Robert turned on the heat. They set Maggie on the sofa, wrapped her with blankets and gave her warm fluids. Wright was laid on the bed, dazed but slowly regaining consciousness.

Nick tended to Maggie's injury by cutting off the end of a sock and sliding it up her arm. He found two bamboo sushi rollers in the kitchen drawer and wrapped them tightly around the break. He secured them with a stretch bandage from the first-aid kit he'd found in the bathroom. He fashioned a sling and swath from one of Wright's shirts. During the process, she winced a few times, but for the most part, he was able to stabilize her arm without causing her too much pain.

Mission accomplished, Nick smiled at her. "That okay?"

She nodded.

He couldn't tell if she was still in shock, hurting, upset, or all the above. He wanted to tell her what he'd learned about Wright, but when he started to do so, she cut him off.

"Nicklaus, I am sorry. I…" Tears streamed down her face. "I have been so stupid. I don't know what got into me."

"Well, start with some Welltrex," Nick said. He could no longer keep his anger to himself.

Maggie looked at him with confusion.

"That jerk has been slipping you Welltrex," he said, pointing at Wright.

She looked shocked.

"In your coffee," Nick exclaimed.

"Are you kidding me?" Color and anger rose in Maggie's face.

"And spraying your room with some sort of spray," he added defiantly.

"Spray, what do you mean?"

"Maggie, I don't know what it means, but we'll get to the bottom of it."

Maggie glanced in horror at Wright and back at Nick.

Nick hesitated, but she had to know. "Maggie, there is more."

"What do you mean?"

"He's been spying on you…in your room…with a camera."

Maggie covered her chest with her uninjured arm and moved away from Wright's direction toward Nick. Then dropped her shoulders and started to cry.

"Oh my God, what have I done?"

Nick put his arms around her and pulled her close. "It's all going to be okay, Mags," he said and tenderly kissed her forehead. "He will not hurt you again. That I promise you." He looked out the windows. It was still pitch black. "Get some rest. We'll head downriver at first light."

* * *

Wright could barely open his eyes. He squinted, recognizing the interior of his lodge. Then he remembered. He'd regained consciousness on the back of one of Robert's men. After a mile or so bouncing along, he recalled what had happened. It was Maggie's fault. He had been so angry at her he almost hit her. He thought he would never hit a woman, but she had infuriated and dishonored him. Her disrespect had to be set straight. He'd raised his arm to strike her. Then the orangutan hit them like a bullet train.

He was lucky they were still alive.

His head throbbed, and he sucked in shallow breaths to protect his broken ribs. Something told him to play possum. How did they get here? How did the men find them? Why were they here? He didn't understand until he'd heard Nick talking to Maggie.

Damn.

Wright was a trapped animal in his own home. Adrenaline pumped through his brain, giving him clarity. If only he could call Boxler, she would make it right, as she'd done so many times before.

His gun. Where was his gun? He wondered if he'd killed the beast. It deserved to die; it had attacked them. He felt no remorse about killing it. He felt no remorse for anything. He'd never understood that emotion; his brain didn't allow it. To him, it was as abstract as intimacy.

He saw Nick and Maggie cuddling on the couch and rage throbbed in his chest. *How dare she, after all I've done for her?*

He lifted his head and saw Robert asleep on a chair and the other Iban men scattered around the room, asleep. His mouth was dry with thirst and revenge. How was he going to survive this? He had no other guns. Where was his machete?

He would let the men get him back to his island, where he had control. His army of attorneys would work their magic. It might cost him a few million to silence Maggie and Nick, but that would be easy. He'd made a mistake in giving Nick the job. He'd thought it was the best way to control Maggie—keep your friends close and your enemies closer—and Nick was his enemy. He thought he could manipulate the situation by having influence over Nick's destiny.

Well, he still had control. He would throw money at the Nick and Maggie problem until it went away. Money made everything right.

He lifted his head again until he could see early light coming through the top of the window. *Water.* His throat ached with thirst. As he pushed himself up on one arm, ever alert, Robert stirred and opened his eyes. Seeing Wright move, he leaped off his chair and went to his side.

"Mr. Paul, how do you feel, sir?"

"Robert, my friend…how did you find us?" Wright said, struggling to sit up.

Robert bent to help him sit and smiled. "Only by God's grace, sir. Can I get you something?"

"My throat is parched like the Sahara. Could you please get me some water?"

"Certainly, sir."

Wright supported his ribs with his hand and breathed as deeply as he could. He hadn't seen Robert since he'd left for Calcutta and was amazed at how rapidly he'd healed. The IGF-1 medication would make him billions. He swung his legs off the side of the bed and held his pounding head. His hair was matted, and he felt for the wound, trying to judge its severity.

Robert was about to hand him a glass of water when Nick pushed it away and grabbed Wright by the throat. "You son of a bitch. You think you deserve any mercy?" The grip around Wright's neck tightened to the point that air stopped moving. "I'll show you mercy."

Wright clawed at Nick's hand, and his eyes shot wide. He tried to choke out words. "Nic…" His aching brain screamed for oxygen.

A black curtain of unconsciousness started to fall over his vision just as Nick let go. Wright found himself on his back, gagging and coughing, shooting pain through his broken ribs. His muscles flexed to strike back, but he had no strength.

"How could you do that to Maggie?" Nick now had him by the shirt. "She trusted you. We both trusted you!" he screamed in Wright's face.

As he'd done when the orangutan attacked, Wright let his body go slack. Maybe Nick's rage would pass, but the pressure on his chest squeezed his broken ribs, and he gasped for breath. "Dr. Hart. I'm sorry. Maggie…" He glanced at her. Her eyes were wide and dilated. "We can work this out, I promise."

"You'll be lucky if I let you live," Nick screamed. Spittle shot from his mouth.

Robert interceded by squeezing his body between the two men. "There will be justice, Nickloss. Please, do not take it into your own hands…please," he begged.

Nick stood upright, crossed his arms, and glared at Wright. "I bet you know about the problems with your drugs, don't you?" He started to go for Wright's throat again, but Robert pulled him back.

"Dr. Hart…Nick…please," Wright pleaded. "I'll make this right. You know these medications will help millions of people." He tried to scoot back on the bed and looked at Robert, remembering how his wounded face had looked. "You gave Robert the IGF-1 medication? My god, look at him. Just look at him. See how well it worked?"

Nick relented and looked at Robert. His face softened.

"Nick, you're going to ease the suffering of countless people," Wright said. "You know the value of this medication."

While Nick's wrath waned, Wright saw what he was looking for—his .357 Mag on the coffee table in front of the couch. But the doctor's anger returned.

"That medication almost killed a little girl," Nick said. "I've talked with the biochemist. You are hiding data from the FDA. You and Boxler are going to be exposed. I'll see to that."

"Nick, come on. We can solve this. Help us unlock the riddle of this powerful drug. You know every drug has issues. Just watch any advertisement on the television for medications, and you know that. Don't throw the baby out with the bathwater. Come on, Dr. Hart. We can do this together."

Nick glanced at Maggie and his face flushed with fury.

"This will be your drug—your legacy," Wright pleaded.

Nick fumed, his temples pulsed with rage.

Wright had no clue why his statement infuriated the doctor.

"My legacy is going to see to it that you are stopped," Nick said. "You and your dragon lady are going to jail. I'm putting a stop to your dangerous medications. I took an oath: 'First, do no harm,' and that is exactly what I am going to do. I am not going to let you harm anyone else. You and your empire are going down!" He turned his back to Wright. "Let's take this asshole to jail."

Wright thought the tempest was over, but Nick swung around, his fist catching Wright's jaw, snapping his head back.

Stars filled Wright's vision as he slumped to the bed.

"That was for Maggie," Nick shouted, shaking out his hand. "Let's go," he demanded again.

Two of Robert's men grabbed Wright by the arms and heaved him off the bed onto his feet. Wright staggered, trusting his entire weight to their hands.

They dragged him toward the door. As they pulled him through the living room, Wright mustered his strength and pushed one man to the floor, grabbed his pistol off the table, turned and shot the other man. The bullet hit him in the shoulder and spun him to the floor. Wright reeled to face Nick, who had stepped forward.

"Back off!" Wright yelled at Nick, then turned to Robert, who was already at the door. "Robert, you and your men should go." He indicated with the barrel of the gun that the one on the floor should help his injured friend. "The doctor and I have business to discuss."

Robert hesitated, but Wright did not. He aimed the gun and shot. Wood splintered the door frame. "The next one is for your chest, old man. Go!" he yelled.

Wright's mind was clearer than it had been for days. Power and control surged like high-voltage electricity through his brain.

Robert and the other Iban supported the wounded man out the door. Wright kept the gun pointed at Nick's chest while he stepped toward the window to watch Robert and his men climb in the boat, start the outboard, and leave.

"You stupid, stupid man. You think this will end well for you?" Wright said, stepping toward the doctor and leveling the gun at his head. He sidestepped, grabbed Maggie by her broken arm and yanked her to him. She cried in pain.

"Now, Doctor, you have one of two choices. You can work with me or work against me. One, you save Kumārī's life, the other…well, let's not go there."

"I'm not your princess!" Maggie yelled at Wright.

Her strength surprised him. She punched him in his broken ribs, and he heard the bones crunch. The pain threatened to bring back the darkness. He saw the doctor moving toward him and got off a shot that stunned and stopped Nick. Wright then whirled toward Kumārī and smacked her hard across the face with the butt of the gun. She collapsed.

"You two are not making this easy for me. This could have been so easy." Madness returned to his brain.

Voices. The voices were back—laughing at him. "You're done," one yelled into his ears.

He pressed the pistol to Kumārī's head. "If I can't have her, no one can have her." He cocked the hammer back.

"Wright, no!" Nick screamed. "Let's figure this out. You're right. We can work this out." He took a step forward with his palms up in surrender.

"Back off or she's dead," Wright yelled and straightened his arm to pull the trigger.

"NO!" Nick yelled.

Wright felt a prick to his neck like the sting of a bee. He straightened, trying to get his balance. "Hmm," he whispered. His body felt strange as it disconnected from his brain.

* * *

Nick's knees went weak. He watched Wright straighten his spine and saw his eyes go wide with confusion and resignation. Wright dropped the gun and his body collapsed in a heap.

Robert stood inside the door holding his blowgun.

"Agi idup, agi ngelaban," Robert yelled.

CHAPTER 53

SAD VICTORY

Nick felt for a pulse at Wright's neck. There was none. He hesitated. Why should he help this monster? But his natural reflexes followed the Hippocratic Oath ingrained since med school, and he flipped Wright onto his back and started chest compressions.

Robert put a hand on his shoulder.

"It's no use, Nickloss. The poison is irreversible," Robert said sadly.

Nick continued for another half a minute but knew in his heart that Robert was right. It was a feeling he recognized, having helped with multiple futile resuscitations. Wright was dead…his spirit had left, not to return. Nick collapsed on the floor next to the body, exhausted—confused—relieved.

Robert's men broke through the front door and burst into celebration when they saw Wright, cheering and repeating Robert's battle cry.

"*Agi idup, agi ngelaban,*" the men shouted. "*Agi idup, agi ngelaban.*"

"Rentap finally is victorious over James Brooke," one man shouted. "The battle cry of Rentap's warriors will be sung in the villages. *Agi idup, agi ngelaban*—Still living, still fighting."

Nick looked at Robert, who averted his eyes to the floor in sorrow and shook his head. "This victory gives me no life," Robert said.

"We should head downriver," Nick said. He got up, went to Maggie and wrapped his arms around her. "We need to get care for Maggie and your man with the gunshot wound to his shoulder. What should we do with Wright's body…leave it here?"

"No, we will care for him, like our brother," Robert said solemnly. "He was deranged but still one of God's children. Like all of us, he had his demons to fight. Now his battle is over."

Robert sat next to the body. "We will prepare his body and get him to the research center. I do not know what his last wishes were, but I suspect he will want to remain in Borneo. We'll have to contact the authorities and Ms. Boxler when we get to the center."

Robert reached to Wright's face and swept his dead eyes closed. "God have mercy on your soul, Mr. Paul."

* * *

Boxler dropped the harsh attitude and became a southern peach, flying over personally to make arrangements for Wright's body. Kuching's authorities demanded the body be brought to the capital of Borneo. The investigation would start in their jurisdiction. They also required an autopsy for the homicide inquiry. Nick suggested they perform a thorough examination of the man's brain. After all, brain tumors could often throw a person into madness.

For now, Nick and Maggie were back in Singapore at the Ruby Hospital. He smiled at Maggie as they wheeled her into the pre-operative area. There was a lot to process, but it could wait. Her care came first. "How are you doing?"

She shook her head. "Nicklaus, I'm so sorry…"

"Okay, that's enough of that. I know we have lots to talk about, but there will be time for it." He put his hand on her cheek and adjusted the bouffant surgical hat on her head. "This is cute." He grinned.

"My God, Nicklaus, how do we get into these messes?"

"Just lucky, I guess."

She sighed. "I'm kind of nervous. I don't think I like being on the patient side of things. How long will my surgery take?"

"Probably a couple of hours. They'll plate the humerus."

Maggie nodded. She looked him up and down. "You know, you look good in scrubs."

"So I've been told."

She finally showed a semblance of a smile. "Nick, I know you must feel like a rusted scalpel, but I'm sure glad you'll be in there with me." She reached for his hand.

"Well, it was nice of the surgeons to invite me in. I think the best thing I can do in there is pray for you."

"And the most important thing," Maggie added.

CHAPTER 54

JUSTICE

Maggie slept soundly. Nick stood at the large window of their top-floor room of the Marina Bay Sands Hotel, grateful she was recovering well. The large shopping area, casino, and ArtScience center sprawled below. No wonder the Singapore officials and even the US Embassy hesitated to investigate Wright's business dealings further. He practically owned the city—even though he was dead.

This was the hotel where he and Maggie had been scheduled to stay while she accepted the grant. Nick shook his head and fought the anger that kept trying to settle into his soul. He looked at the ArtScience Center that Wright had built and where the foundation party had been held. Everything that had happened in the past week flooded his mind and he fought back his rage.

Nick was livid that Wright had used Welltrex to manipulate Maggie and how he modified the Confide spray to trick her brain. At the heart of the mixture was oxytocin, the love hormone. *Funny way of showing love.*

After collecting everyone's statements, the Singapore police ruled that Wright's death was clearly a case of self-defense, and they would not pursue charges against Robert, Nick or Maggie. It made Nick angry that the cops had even said that, as though Wright's death was somehow their fault.

He knew he had to find a way to put it all behind him.

At least the Borneo homicide investigator had talked to Nick, something that the Singaporean officials seemed hesitant to do. The investigator told Nick that the autopsy revealed high levels of Welltrex. So Wright had been dipping into his own medications. Dissection of his brain revealed no tumor, but a significantly undersized pineal gland.

Nick's phone vibrated. He pulled it out of his pocket and looked at the caller ID—Kerri Kim. She was calling from her cell phone. He answered it with his mouth covered to keep from waking Maggie. "Hi, Kerri," he whispered. "Give me a minute."

He walked out to the balcony and closed the sliding door behind him.

"Hey, Kerri, thanks for calling me back."

"How is your friend?" Kerri asked.

"She's okay…her arm is probably the least of her concerns," he said and turned right to business. "I imagine my office is already cleaned out?"

"I'm afraid so, Dr. Hart."

"Well, that was my shortest employment since a two-day stint at McDonald's when I was a freshman in high school." He laughed.

"What can I help you with, Dr. Hart? I have to get back to the office shortly."

He could hear either angst or annoyance in her voice. "Kerri, I know you are taking a chance in calling me, but I'm just looking for some understanding. I heard from the investigator in Borneo this morning about Mr. Paul's post-mortem. He had high levels of Welltrex."

There was a long pause. "And?" she asked.

"Do you think this had anything to do with his descent into madness?"

"Hard to know," she said. "Remember, Dr. Hart, I was not on that team."

"Come on, Kerri, throw me a bone here. I need to understand this. And if there's a problem, don't you guys need to know?"

He could hear her sigh.

"Dr. Hart. I don't know if you remember back to neurophysiology in medical school, but too much dopamine can cause schizophrenia. I'm not saying the Welltrex caused this. I don't know. I'm probably saying too much."

"The dissection of his brain showed shrinkage of his pineal gland. I don't remember much about that area of the brain."

"I don't know, Dr. Hart. I still work for Zelutex, remember?"

Nick's stomach churned with anger. "You know I'm going to have to report all this to the FDA."

There was a long pause, and Nick worried she'd hung up on him.

"Dr. Hart…you'll have to do what your conscience tells you, but remember my warnings from before. There is a lot of money at stake. Please watch your back. I was involved in something like this at another company. They usually find some low-level marketing person to throw to the wolves, and the top people go unscathed. You also must understand that these big-pharma companies have the FDA and all the other regulatory agencies in their back pocket. They send millions to the FDA every year."

It was Nick's turn to sigh.

"Will you help me with this?" he finally asked her.

"I'm afraid I need this job, Dr. Hart. They pay me well." Kerri paused. "Dr. Hart, everyone always says they like whistleblowers, but the reality is they really don't. You must understand there are eight thousand other people just like me counting on their paychecks from Zelutex every week. Boxler will make you out to be some crazed, disgruntled employee that only worked there for less than a week and doesn't have his facts straight."

Nick nodded. She was right. "Kerri, thank you…maybe in a different life, we would be friends."

"Maybe so, Dr. Hart. Maybe so."

Nick hung up the call and rested his arms on the balcony railing. He wanted to scream and throw his phone over the edge. Yes, they would make him out to be the crazy one. It just wasn't fair. The injustice of the world bubbled in his chest—his next call would be to Amy's sister, Allison. He would tell her to hold onto the files Amy had sent to her. He may need them to protect himself.

CHAPTER 55

GOOD-BYES

Life in Borneo was unchanged. It was as if a storm had passed through, then the sun had reemerged.

Maggie encouraged Nick to go and say his good-byes to Robert and his longhouse family. Nick was happy to do that. He doubted he would see Robert again on this side of heaven. Besides, getting Robert's man home from the hospital gave Nick a great excuse. Wright's bullet had shattered the head of his humerus, which had been replaced with a metal ball. The man seemed to take it all in stride and smiled widely when they turned the corner and the longhouse came into view.

He explained to Nick the best he could in broken English about the long-standing battle between Rentap and James Brooke, Robert's and Wright's great-great-great-grandfathers. The score had finally been settled. Brooke's enslavement of the Iban was broken. "Still living, still fighting," the man said proudly.

When they arrived, Nick smiled at the grand welcome. He had no idea how the Iban communication network operated, but the entire village stood on the bank of the river as they had when he'd first met them. The excitement in the air was electric.

Nick aimed the longboat at the muddy bank and docked it perfectly. Robert was the first in the water to stabilize the boat.

"Well done, Nickloss. We may turn you into an honorary Iban yet."

The crowd cheered when the wounded man and Nick stepped from the boat. They were instantly surrounded by the people, hugging them, slapping them on the back, and praising God.

* * *

"How is Ms. Maggie?" Robert asked as they floated in the river, bathing with the entire village.

"Good. Thanks to you, Robert."

"I was not about to let anything happen to her."

Nick dunked under the cool water and wiped his face when he came up. His hair was growing out, and he pushed it back. He felt cleansed of anger and anxiety, having let the river water carry it away. It seemed so easy in this thin place. Its rhythm flowed naturally like the sun and the moon and the currents of existence.

Nick felt reborn with a new awareness of the infinite goodness of God. *It must be like this in the Kingdom of Heaven.* His perception had shifted, and his eyes had been opened to the truth of who he was in God's eyes. He was God's beloved child. It was always there—his awareness had adjusted, the truth had not—it remained the same. He realized how blind he'd been to the truth—how he'd forgotten Jesus's core teachings.

"So, what will you do now, Nickloss?"

Nick smiled at the old man. "I have no idea…and that's okay."

Robert laughed and nodded. "I think you see the world through new eyes—you see what was there, in the beginning. And there is far more to you than what your eyes showed you—it is Jesus, who lives in you."

Nick smiled and nodded. "You know, Robert, I may not see you again until we get to heaven."

Robert smiled a grand smile. "Yes, Nickloss, that is true. Won't that be a glorious day! Hope against hope. Isn't that what we carry? The eyes of our hearts have been opened to the hope of resurrection."

"Until then…I'm going to miss you, my friend."

"You as well, Nickloss."

* * *

Nick waved at the Iban as his boat drifted downstream in the current. A great sadness overwhelmed him, but he realized for the first time in his life that great joy could coexist with sorrow.

He gave the villagers one more wave and one last glance. How he'd miss them. Life somehow felt like a continuous series of good-byes. Where could one find hope through that pain? In the lesser comforts or a medicine bottle? *No...we find it only in God's promises,* Nick thought. *When we live in the hope of heaven and the renewal of all things, we know that the good-byes are only temporary. We will see our loved ones again.*

EPILOGUE

6 MONTHS LATER

LOVE

Nick drummed his fingers on the arm of the chair. With his legs crossed, his right foot bounced. Adrenaline flooded his cerebral cortex. He tried pacing again, but that didn't help either. His necktie tightened around his throat, and he pulled at his collar, trying to give his neck more room. A deep breath was impossible.

At least the rumors of storms turned out false, and the sun shone through the large picture windows of Glacier Park Lodge overlooking the majestic mountains dusted with snow. The lodge would close for the coming winter in two days.

Kerri Kim had been right. People didn't like whistleblowers. Boxler had threatened to sue Nick, and when that didn't work, she did everything she could to smear his reputation. "You'll never work in the industry again," she'd finally said, and the words echoed in his head.

He smiled to himself and shifted his legs to cross left over right. Now his left foot bounced. The courts had recently indicted Boxler on fraud, but her attorneys had so far managed to keep her out of prison. Nick hoped that would change. He suspected, as did others, that she had a hand in Dr. Amy's death, but there was not yet any evidence to prove it.

At least Nick had gotten the FDA to delay the release of Revivere until Zelutex solved the problem with the acute reactions. He honestly hoped they'd figure it out, as the potential to help people was huge. With no contract signed before he resigned—or was fired, depending on who you asked—he would personally see no windfall. Kerri Kim would not return his calls. *I guess I don't blame her.*

He'd turned Amy's files on Welltrex over to the FDA as well, but just two days ago, he saw Zelutex's new marketing campaign on TV during prime time. A shapely blond woman smiled serenely and said, "I got my life back." People of every color and creed repeated the slogan over and over. Then the ad's volume dropped and, almost like an afterthought, listed the potential risks and side effects while showing videos of people playing with puppies and running on the beach. The portion of the advertisement discussing the side effects was longer than half the ad. It finished with: "Call your doctor right away if you have any reaction to the medication. Welltrex should not be stopped unless directed by your physician."

Yeah right…call your doctor if you start hallucinating or going crazy. Nick sighed deeply. Kerri was probably right—the FDA was in the pocket of big pharma.

His thoughts were interrupted when the door to his room opened. He was glad to shake them from his head. He was still learning about forgiveness.

Nick's father came through the door, "You ready?"

Nick nodded solemnly and pushed himself out of the chair. Was he ready for this?

His father held the door for him to enter the expansive gardens of the lodge. Nick paused outside the door as the warmth of the sun and the crisp fall air met his face. He was overwhelmed with the sense that he was opening a new chapter in his life. Hope against hope—when all things seemed impossible—he was celebrating new life.

He glanced at the Rocky Mountains blanketed in snow, starting their great slumber into winter. The tamaracks and aspen were gilded against the forest green of the pines. The colorful gardens of the lodge had either put on their fall colors or withered into brown tones. Nature was rolling itself back, awaiting the great lethargy of winter, during which it would gather its strength to reemerge next spring. Death and life. Sorrow and joy. The cycle of life and the great hope of all things renewed. Someday, when Jesus returned to fulfill His promises to make all things new, when all sorrow and tears are halted, the cycles of death and rebirth would stop. Until that day, Nick was learning to hope against hope.

He took a deep breath. His friends were waiting, probably wondering if his feet had grown cold. He didn't know all the mysteries of God, but he had a feeling that John was cheering for this day.

His dad put a hand on his shoulder. "You okay, son?"

Nick wiped a tear from the corner of his eye. "Just missing John is all."

It made his stoic father tear up as well. "Me too, son. Me too."

"You think this is okay?"

His father looked out over the eastern range and nodded. "Yes…if anyone is going to care for Maggie…I know he would want this. He knows you'd lay down your life for her."

That was certainly true. Nick's nerves popped, seeing the rows of chairs filled with his friends anxiously waiting on him. It was supposed to be a small family affair, but when marrying someone from the reservation, you tended to marry the entire rez. It looked like the whole town of Browning had shown up. Maggie had laughed when he suggested they steal away to Vegas. She'd told him that everyone wanted to celebrate with them, that they all held a stake in it.

His knees went weak as his father pushed him forward to stand with the men who meant everything to him. He shook their hands as he passed them, Maggie's two brothers along with Ali, and Buck, his best man. Buck gave him a bear hug that brought whoops from the Blackfeet nation. Then Nick hugged Chang who, as an ordained minister, had agreed to officiate the wedding. Nick turned to face the cheers of the gathered crowd.

Music started, and another door off the lodge opened. Maggie's proud parents, Cliff and Mary Black Elk, emerged. And then came Maggie.

Buck patted Nick on the back as if to say, *Wow*. She had chosen a traditional Blackfeet wedding dress of supple buckskin. Fringe edged the sleeves and hemline, and delicate blue-and-white beading in intricate designs adorned the shoulders and neckline. Matching beaded leggings and moccasins covered her calves and feet. Her long black hair fell over her shoulders and down her back, and she held a fan of eagle feathers.

Her parents escorted her down the aisle. She was radiant, smiling warmly and receiving hugs and well wishes as she passed friends and relatives. When she finally locked eyes with Nick, his heart melted. Another mystery of God. How could love go so deep?

Nick smiled back at her and took two steps forward to receive her from Cliff and Mary, who hugged him. Cliff whispered in his ear, "Thank you for loving my little princess. We bless you with everything we have and everything we are."

Nick hugged Maggie. "You are so beautiful," he said and led her to stand with him in front of Chang.

Chang cleared his throat. "I'm sure this will not surprise all of you who know Maggie and Nick, but they wanted to keep this short and sweet." His statement brought chuckles and more cheers from the crowd. They were ready to party.

"Go ahead, Nick." Chang motioned to him.

Nick readjusted his hold of Maggie's hands. "Maggie, I love you with my whole heart, with every part of my being. I am so honored, but somehow feel so inadequate to fill this role of being your husband. I promise to love you. I promise to protect you. I promise to comfort you in times of need and sorrow and to share with you in all of life's joys. I ask for God's help to be all that you need."

"Maggie," Chang said.

"Nicklaus, only the mysteries of God have brought us together. I never thought that I would be able to love someone again, and I stand here before you promising you my heart. I know that John is here with us in spirit. It is in our love for John and our unity with the heavenly Father that we can love each other freely. God's love binds us together into oneness. I promise to love you and care for you through hard times and joyous times. I love you, Nicklaus Hart."

Nick wrapped his arms around Maggie and held her close. The crowd cheered with approval.

Chang raised his arms to the crystalline blue sky, inviting the blessing of heaven. Then he said, "Ibrahim, come on up here, boy."

Ibrahim left Asti's side and made his way to the front. Chang held out his hands, and Ibrahim placed the wedding bands in them. Ibrahim then positioned himself in front of Maggie and Nick and stood wide-eyed. Ali tried to beckon him to move from the center of attention, but Nick gave him a reassuring nod to stay.

Chang handed Nick a ring.

Nick held Maggie's hand to place it on her finger.

"Maggie…with this ring, I thee wed."

Chang then gave Maggie the other ring.

"Nicklaus…with this ring, I thee wed."

Another loud cheer rose from their guests.

Chang put his hands on their shoulders. "Then, with the power vested in me by the church and by the Holy Spirit, I bless you in the name of the Father, His Son, Jesus, and in His Holy Spirit. I pronounce you husband and wife. Nicklaus and Maggie, you may kiss."

Nick smiled at Maggie, took her in his arms, pulled her close, and kissed her long and deeply.

A WORD FROM TIM

I hope you enjoyed The Rusted Scalpel. It was great fun to write and remember my time in Borneo...a magical place indeed. The issues with big pharma are ones that I feel very strongly about. Nick and Maggie will be back soon in the next novel which is percolating in my mind as I write this.

Building a relationship with my readers is the most amazing thing about writing. I occasionally send newsletters with information about new releases, special offers and video-podcasts about various subjects. I hate getting bombarded with spam emails, so when I say occasionally, I truly mean it. If you join my Readers' Club today, I'll send you a taste of my next book.

You can get your free content by visiting my website at AuthorTimothyBrowne.com. I look forward to getting to know you.

* * *

ALSO BY TIMOTHY BROWNE
IN THE DR. NICKLAUS HART SERIES

MAYA HOPE

A doctor stumbling through life. A North Korean bioterrorist plot. The two collide in an unforgettable tale.

THE TREE OF LIFE

A massive earthquake hits Eastern Turkey, the ancient area of Mesopotamia, unveiling hidden secrets and opening an epic battle between good and evil.

*Watch for the next adventure of Nick and Maggie in the 4th
installment of A Dr. Nicklaus Hart Series
and for Browne's new historical fiction 2019.*

THE GENE

Combine Artificial Intelligence and Gene Therapy…What
could go wrong?

* * *

LARIMER STREET

Larimer Street is a historical novel based on the true story of
my great-grandfather, Jim Goodheart. To quote an article in the
Bloomington News in 1936; "The story of Jim Goodheart reads like
a novel." Yes, indeed!

Jim was a tall and handsome man, born in 1871 and most well
known as the charismatic leader of the Sunshine Rescue Mission
in downtown Denver (on Larimer Street). The Mission served the
destitute and "bums" in an era that there were no safety nets of social
programs. He grew the ministry to a program that had an annual
budget of $60,000/year and served thousands and thousands of
people; feeding, clothing, and sheltering them. But Jim was a man,
like all of us, that walked with a significant limp and had life battles
to fight. His war was against demons of alcoholism and impropriety
that brought him to the point of losing everything, except the two
things that were the most important to him, his wife, Ada and his
faith.

Larimer Street is a story of courage, faith, redemption and the
greatest of all—love.

AUTHOR'S NOTE

My Dear Reader,

I'm going to be very vulnerable with you. When I sat down to write *The Rusted Scalpel*, I was in a real place of brokenness. I was going through some very tough things. Also, I was at a crossroads in my career as a writer and transitioning out of clinical medicine…a profession that I had spent years and years in training. It is where I was safe; I could make a living and provide for my family. Writing full-time felt like stepping off a cliff into the great unknown. So much was stripped away. Yes, the ego certainly does scream loudest when it is being escorted out. As I sat down to write the outline, I asked the Lord, why. Why hadn't He restored things, given me a break-through? The answer came fast and clear in my heart… **"Because I want you to write from this broken place. To be a beacon of hope for those that have lost hope. Timothy, you know what it feels like."**

I also want to address the topic of medication use head-on. As a Western-trained physician, I am so very thankful for the medications that we have in our toolbox. Our lives would be unrecognizable without the life-saving drugs such as antibiotics, heart and cancer medications, and so many others. With a tendency toward depression and anxiety in my own life, I am grateful to the research and development of medications that help us battle those. NO ONE should ever be afraid or ashamed when those medications are needed. As a surgeon, I am also thankful that I could give my patients relief of their pain, post-operatively with pain medications. But with all things there are dangers. Last year, over 60,000 people died from overdoses of narcotics of one kind or another. I, like you, get irate over pharmaceutical companies making billions of dollars on the backs of those they are supposed to help.

One thing I know for sure is: Life is tough—no one escapes without battle scars. In this crazy world, where does one find hope? Do you find it in the lesser comforts of life or a medicine bottle? The pharmaceutical industry offers us "Better Living Through Science", but there is always a cost. In *The Rusted Scalpel*, I explore this hard question: What if the drug manufacturers developed a drug that gave you the feeling of hope and happiness but came at the significant cost of losing your connection with God…would you take it?

But my dear friends, true hope can only be found in the Heavenly Father—that is the only place we find fulfillment, contentment, or even joy. When putting our hope in the promises of God, we must grab onto those promises with both hands and not let go. And if you're holding onto this hope with both hands you can't be holding onto anything else. I pray for you my friends that the glimpses of the Kingdom of God grow in your lives and like Paul prayed: *"…that He would grant you, according to the riches of His glory, to be strengthened with power through His Spirit in the inner man, so that Christ may dwell in your hearts through faith…"*

May your eyes be open to the truth… *Timothy*

Please visit www.TimothyBrowneAuthor.com
and sign up to receive updates
and information on upcoming books by Tim.

MINISTRIES

There are many wonderful organizations throughout the world helping the poor, the broken and the destitute. They can use your help in reaching the world. Here are some of my favorites that I have personal experience with:

Mercy Ships
https://www.mercyships.org

Hope Force International
http://hopeforce.org

YWAM Ships
https://ywamships.net

SIGN Fracture Care International
https://signfracturecare.org

Samaritan's Purse
https://www.samaritanspurse.org

Wounded Warrior Project
https://www.woundedwarriorproject.org

Dr. Tim sitting with the chief of a longhouse, Sarawak.

Meet the real "Daisy". Failed cleft palate surgery in the Philippines.

(right) Pigs that live under the longhouses.

(below) The kitchen of the longhouse.

(bottom) A typical longhouse with the clean-side and the dirty-side separated by the porch.

(top) An Iban Longhouse in Sarawak.

(above) The hand-sized spider was not fiction ... :)

The two oldest Browne boys with an Iban child.

Batang Ai river in Sarawak with longboats.